Hugh MacLennan

Hugh MacLennan was the winner of five Governor General's Awards for fiction. The New Press Canadian Classics series includes three of his other novels, *Each Man's Son, The Watch That Ends the Night,* and *Return of the Sphinx.*

Marian Mildred Dale Scott

The painter Marian Mildred Dale Scott was born in Montreal in 1906. Her work is in many public and private collections in Canada.

New Press Canadian Classics

Featuring the work of Canadian artists on its covers, New Press Canadian Classics is an innovative, much-needed series of high quality, reasonably priced editions of the very best Canadian fiction, nonfiction, and poetry.

New Press Canadian Classics

Hubert Aquin *The Antiphonary*, Alan Brown (trans.)

Margaret Atwood *Surfacing*

Sandra Birdsell *Night Travellers*

Constance Beresford-Howe *The Marriage Bed*

Marie-Claire Blais *Nights in the Underground*, Ray Ellenwood (trans.)

Clark Blaise *A North American Education, Tribal Justice*

George Bowering *Burning Water*

Matt Cohen *The Expatriate*

Jack David & Robert Lecker (eds.) *Canadian Poetry, Volumes One and Two*

Wayland Drew *Wabeno Feast*

George Elliott *The Kissing Man*

Mavis Gallant *My Heart Is Broken*

Anne Hébert *Héloïse* Sheila Fischman (trans.), *In the Shadow of the Wind* Sheila Fischman (trans.), *Kamouraska* Norman Shapiro (trans.)

David Helwig *The Glass Knight, Jennifer, It is Always Summer*

Hugh Hood *White Figure, White Ground, You Can't Get There from Here, The Swing in the Garden, A New Athens, Reservoir Ravine, Black and White Keys*

M.T. Kelly *I Do Remember the Fall*

Martin Kevan *Racing Tides*

Robert Kroetsch *Alibi, Badlands, The Studhorse Man, What the Crow Said*

Félix Leclerc *The Madman, the Kite & the Island* Philip Stratford (trans.)

Keith Maillard *Alex Driving South, Cutting Through, The Knife in My Hands, Two Strand River*

Antonine Maillet *Pélagie* Philip Stratford (trans.)

Gwendolyn MacEwen *Noman*

John Metcalf & Leon Rooke *The New Press Anthology #1: Best Canadian Short Fiction; #2: Best Stories*

Brian Moore *An Answer from Limbo*

Ken Norris (Ed.) *Canadian Poetry Now*

Michael Ondaatje *Coming through Slaughter, Running in the Family*

H.R. Percy *Painted Ladies*

Leon Rooke *Fat Woman, Shakespeare's Dog*

George Ryga *The Ecstasy of Rita Joe and Other Plays*

Carol Shields *Various Miracles*

Audrey Thomas *Intertidal Life*

Helen Weinzweig *Basic Black with Pearls*

new press CANADIAN CLASSICS

Hugh MacLennan

Two Solitudes

General
— PAPERBACKS —
Toronto, Canada

Published in 1991 by
General Paperbacks
30 Lesmill Road
Toronto, Canada
M3B 2T6

Canadian Cataloguing in Publication Data

MacLennan, Hugh, 1907-1990.
Two solitudes

(New Press Canadian classics)
ISBN 0-7736-7333-4

I. Title. II. Series.

PS8525.L45T8 1991   C813'.54   C91-094310-9
PR9199.3.M334T8 1991

Originally published in hardcover in 1945
by Macmillan of Canada
First Laurentian Library edition 1978
First Macmillan Paperbacks edition 1986

Published by arrangement with Macmillan of Canada
A division of Canada Publishing Corporation

Printed and bound in the United States of America

To Dorothy Duncan
with admiration and love

Love consists in this,
that two solitudes protect,
and touch, and greet each other.

RAINER MARIA RILKE

Foreword

Because this is a story, I dislike having to burden it with a foreword, but something of the kind is necessary, for it is a novel of Canada. This means that its scene is laid in a nation with two official languages, English and French. It means that some of the characters in the book are presumed to speak only English, others only French, while many are bilingual.

No single word exists, within Canada itself, to designate with satisfaction to both races a native of the country. When those of the French language use the word *Canadien*, they nearly always refer to themselves. They know their English-speaking compatriots as *les Anglais*. English-speaking citizens act on the same principle. They call themselves Canadians; those of the French language French-Canadians.

I should like to emphasize as emphatically as I can that this book is a story, and in no sense whatever documentary. All the characters are purely imaginary. If names of actual persons, living or dead, have been used it is a coincidence I have done my best to avoid. The parish known in the story as Saint-Marc-des-Érables is also imaginary. There may be other Saint-Marcs in the province of Quebec, but they are not mine.

Contents

Part one	1917-1918	Page 1
Part two	1919-1921	Page 202
Part three	1934	Page 254
Part four	1939	Page 328

Part One   1917-1918

1

Northwest of Montreal, through a valley always in sight of
the low mountains of the Laurentian Shield, the Ottawa
River flows out of Protestant Ontario into Catholic Quebec.
It comes down broad and ale-coloured and joins the Saint
Lawrence, the two streams embrace the pan of Montreal
Island, the Ottawa merges and loses itself, and the main-
stream moves northeastward a thousand miles to the sea.

Nowhere has nature wasted herself as she has here. There
is enough water in the Saint Lawrence alone to irrigate half
of Europe, but the river pours right out of the continent into
the sea. No amount of water can irrigate stones, and most of
Quebec is solid rock. It is as though millions of years back
in geologic time a sword had been plunged through the rock
from the Atlantic to the Great Lakes and savagely wrenched
out again, and the pure water of the continental reservoir,
unmuddied and almost useless to farmers, drains untouch-
ably away. In summer the cloud packs pass over it in soft,
cumulus, pacific towers, endlessly forming and dissolving to
make a welter of movement about the sun. In winter when
there is no storm the sky is generally empty, blue and glittering over the ice and snow, and the sun stares out of it like a
cyclops' eye.

All the narrow plain between the Saint Lawrence and the
hills is worked hard. From the Ontario border down to the
beginning of the estuary, the farmland runs in two delicate
bands along the shores, with roads like a pair of village main
streets a thousand miles long, each parallel to the river. All
the good land was broken long ago, occupied and divided

among seigneurs and their sons, and then among tenants and their sons. Bleak wooden fences separate each strip of farm from its neighbour, running straight as rulers set at right angles to the river to form long narrow rectangles pointing inland. The ploughed land looks like the course of a gigantic and empty steeplechase where all motion has been frozen. Every inch of it is measured, and brooded over by notaries, and blessed by priests.

You can look north across the plain from the river and see the farms between their fences tilting towards the forest, and beyond them the line of trees crawling shaggily up the slope of the hills. The forest crosses the watershed into an evergreen bush that spreads far to the north, lake-dotted and mostly unknown, until it reaches the tundra. The tundra goes to the lower straits of the Arctic Ocean. Nothing lives on it but a few prospectors and hard-rock miners and Mounted Policemen and animals and the flies that brood over the barrens in summer like haze. Winters make it a universe of snow with a terrible wind keening over it, and beyond its horizons the northern lights flare into walls of shifting electric colours that crack and roar like the gods of a dead planet talking to each other out of the dark.

But down in the angle at Montreal, on the island about which the two rivers join, there is little of this sense of new and endless space. Two old races and religions meet here and live their separate legends, side by side. If this sprawling half-continent has a heart, here it is. Its pulse throbs out along the rivers and railroads; slow, reluctant and rarely simple, a double beat, a self-moved reciprocation.

2

Father Emile Beaubien stepped onto the porch of his red brick presbytery and looked at the afternoon. It was the autumn of 1917. The October air was sharp enough to shrink his nostrils. The sky was a deep blue, a fathomless blue going up and up into heaven.

The priest drew in deep breaths of the still air. For his noon dinner he had just eaten roast duck. This good meal, and many other blessings, made him feel content and thankful. He decided he could relax a little from the constant strain under which he had worked since coming to this parish as a rather young priest seven years ago. Last Sunday the new church had been consecrated by the bishop: his church, the largest within many miles. This year also the harvest had been bountiful, and owing to the war farm prices had never been better.

He walked briskly back and forth, one hand on his pendant cross, the skirts of his black soutane swishing as he moved. There was great energy in his steps; energy also in the lines of his face. The cheekbones and nose were very large, the mouth wide and straight, the eyes seemingly magnified by the thick lenses of the glasses he wore. Two deep lines, like a pair of dividers, cut the firm flesh of his face above the flanges of the nose to the corners of the lips. His hair was black and closely cropped, somewhat like a monk's cap. His face was brown; his hands too were brown, and big-boned, and his posture gave the suggestion that under the soutane the bones were all big, the shoulders strong as a ploughman's.

The motionless air was suddenly cracked by two gunshots, and the priest paused in his walk to look up at the sky above the river. He saw three specks rise in it, and with eager interest he watched them. Two more shots cracked the air. One of the specks stopped, wavered and fell straight down. Frenette, the blacksmith, must be shooting ducks from his blind in the marsh near the river. It was years since the priest had done any duck-shooting himself, and he missed it because it had been the only recreation he had ever known. When he was a boy there had been little time from farm work even to shoot food; nor for that matter enough money to buy cartridges for his uncle's old gun.

He resumed his walking. By long habit his mind was vigilant to the parish about him. He carried the whole of Saint-Marc-des-Érables constantly in his thoughts. Quite literally he believed that God held him accountable for every soul in the place.

On this Saturday afternoon the village which was the core of the parish was deserted even by the dogs. Across the dirt road the brown houses, their steps edging shyly for-

3

ward into the road, were silent. There was no sign of life in their airless front parlours, concealed behind white lace curtains drawn as close and tight as blinds. The men were out in the fields for the fall ploughing, the women in the kitchens, the smaller children asleep, the older children at work. Farther down the road, the priest could see the sun glinting on the metal advertising posters that plastered the front of Polycarpe Drouin's general store with a strange mixture of French and English: *La Farine Robin Hood, Black Horse Ale, Magic Baking Powder, Fumez le Tabac Old Chum.* The store would be empty now except for Ovide Bissonette, who was getting more feeble-minded every year. Ovide would be asleep on a table piled with overalls, his eyes wide open and his legs dangling over the side. Polycarpe himself would be asleep in his rocking chair in the back kitchen.

Father Beaubien stepped down from the porch and walked slowly across a stretch of grass fronting the presbytery towards the new church. His feet rustled crisply in the newly fallen leaves. At one corner of his house was a large oak tree, its leaves yellow; at the other corner was a giant rock maple. The maple was a tower of silence, a miraculous upward rush of cool flame, every leaf scarlet and dry and so delicately poised that the first wind would tear the whole tower apart and scatter it on the lawn and over the road.

The priest passed over the rustling leaves onto the brown, packed-gravel area before the church. He stood still with his powerful hands folded under his pendant cross, his eyes lifted to the twin spires. He could not look at his church often enough. Sometimes at night during the past week he had wakened after a few hours' sleep and dressed himself and gone out of the presbytery, to cross to the new building. He entered it by his own door and stood in the darkness, watching the votive candles burning before the images; or wandered through the nave under the great canopy of the roof, with the stone cold as a grave-marker under his feet and the whole church shadow-haunted, and so still he could hear his own blood pulsing in his ears: the sound of God.

Now he stood staring at the solid grey stone mass. After

4

everything critics had said against the size of his church, it had been built. He felt both humble and proud that God had permitted a man like himself to build Him such a monument. It was the largest within forty miles. It was larger even than the largest Protestant church in Montreal where millionaires were among the parishioners. And Saint-Marc numbered less than a hundred and thirty families.

But Father Beaubien was not yet satisfied. The building itself was complete, yet it needed better heating equipment to make it comfortable in winter. The sheet-iron roof and the steeples were covered with bright aluminum paint, making the outside look finished and the whole glitter for miles in the sun. But he also required a new bell. The one he had was adequate when there was no wind, but when the wind blew against the sound the angelus was almost inaudible at the fringes of the parish. He also wanted more images for the chapel, and he wanted particularly an image for the gravelled area in front of the church. He saw clearly in his mind what it should be: a bronze figure of Christ with outstretched arms, about twenty-five feet high, with a halo of coloured lights above the head.

The priest breathed deeply and touched his cross again. Although the bishop had congratulated him on the church, he had also expressed concern about the size of the debt. At present, war prices were helping considerably, but the war could not last forever, and when it was over prices would fall and the debt would remain. The parishioners in Saint-Marc were nearly all farmers. They never had much ready money. And yet the priest had faith. The parish could rest indefinitely on the knees of God.

Thinking about the war, Father Beaubien's dark face set into a heavy frown. So far Saint-Marc had kept fairly clear of it. Only one member of the parish had volunteered, and he was on a spree in Trois Rivières when the recruiting sergeants got him. He was no good anyway, always missing masses. But this year the English provinces had imposed conscription on the whole country, trying to force their conquest on Quebec a second time. Conscription officers had been in the neighbouring parish of Sainte-Justine and had taken young French-Canadians out of their homes like

5

thieves to put them into the army.

The priest's solid jaw set hard. His superiors had ordered him not to preach against the war and he had obeyed them. He did not question their wisdom; they knew more than he did. But at least his parish knew how he stood. He thought of the war and the English with the same bitterness. How could French-Canadians – the only real Canadians – feel loyalty to a people who had conquered and humiliated them, and were Protestant anyway? France herself was no better; she had deserted her Canadians a century and a half ago, had left them in the snow and ice along the Saint Lawrence surrounded by their enemies, had later murdered her anointed king and then turned atheist. Father Beaubien had no fondness for the Germans and no wish for them to win the war; he knew nothing whatever about them. But he certainly knew that if a people deserted God they were punished for it, and France was being punished now.

He turned back towards his presbytery and paused on the lawn to pick up an acorn dropped from his great oak. As he did so the silence was cracked again by a pair of gunshots down in the marsh. The priest held the acorn in his palm, looking at it, then he polished it firmly between his thumb and forefinger. This nut was like his own parish of Saint-Marc-des-Érables. It was perfect: You could not change or improve it, you could not graft it to anything else. But you put it into the earth, and you left it to God, and through God's miracle it became another oak. His mind moving slowly, cautiously as always, the priest visioned the whole of French-Canada as a seed-bed for God, a seminary of French parishes speaking the plain old French of their Norman forefathers, continuing the battle of the Counter-Reformation. Everyone in the parish knew the name of every father and grandfather and uncle and cousin and sister and brother and aunt, remembered the few who had married into neighbouring parishes, and the many young men and women who had married the Church itself. Let the rest of the world murder itself through war, cheat itself in business, destroy its peace with new inventions and the frantic American rush after money. Quebec remembered God and her own soul, and these were all she needed.

6

Suddenly, as he went back to his porch, the priest heard the trotting hooves of a horse coming down the road into the village from the direction of Sainte-Justine. Shortly before dinner he had seen Athanase Tallard and Blanchard, Tallard's farm manager, drive past on their way out of the village. Now they were coming back, having met the afternoon train from the city at Sainte-Justine. Father Beaubien felt a twinge of uncertainty as the horse's hooves beat nearer.

Athanase Tallard was the only limit, under God and the law, to the priest's authority in Saint-Marc. Since the days of the early French colonization, the Tallards had been seigneurs. For more than two hundred years social opinion in Saint-Marc had depended not only on the parish priest, but also on whoever happened to be head of the Tallard family. Most of their seigniory had been broken up during the latter half of the nineteenth century and they collected no more rents. But the family still seemed enormously rich to the rest of the parishioners. Athanase owned by inheritance three times more land than anyone else in Saint-Marc, and he hired men to work it. He also owned a toll-bridge over a small tributary river at the lower end of the parish, and this brought him far more money than came from his crops. In many respects his surface authority was as great as that of the priest himself, and his manner of a great gentleman increased it.

The people of Saint-Marc had always been proud of the Tallards. They were of their own stock and neighbourhood, yet they had always amounted to something in the outside world. In the historic days of the eighteenth century they had been noblemen. A Tallard had been a seigneur and officer in the colonial army of France at the same time a kinsman of the same name, back in Europe, lost the battle of Blenheim to the Duke of Marlborough. Another Tallard had won a skirmish against the English redcoats in the Rising of 1837. But along with other institutions, they had gradually become more prosaic. Since the confederation of the provinces into the Dominion of Canada just after the American Civil War, a Tallard had always sat in parliament in Ottawa.

Unlike most French-Canadians, they had never been a

7

prolific family. Athanase himself was an only child, and after two marriages had only two sons. Although Catholics, they were traditionally anti-clerical, and apt to make trouble for their priests. Saint-Marc still talked about the grandfather of Athanase, who had once chased a priest through the village with a whip.

The horse came into Father Beaubien's view, trotting fast and pulling Tallard's best carriage. Four men were in the vehicle, two in front and two behind. It stopped before Drouin's store and Blanchard dropped off, touching his cap to Athanase before he turned to enter the store. Then the carriage drove on past the presbytery as Tallard looked and nodded to the priest, dipping his whip with a graceful flourish. The priest returned the nod and the carriage went on beyond the village along the river road.

Suddenly Father Beaubien's big hands flexed, open and shut. Recounting the scene in his mind, he realized now that the two men in the carriage with Athanase were English-Canadians. Their faces as well as their clothes showed it clearly. He dropped his hands to his sides and walked quietly down the path to the road and looked after the carriage. The road ran straight for a mile and he could see the carriage diminish to a small black speck before it turned at a tall maple tree and disappeared. The priest frowned. They had not entered the Tallard property. It was the Dansereau place they were visiting, and it was up for sale because Dansereau was a childless widower who had contributed heavily to the new church and now was in debt.

The priest stood for several minutes in the road, his hands folded under his cross now. When he heard steps approaching he turned around to see Tallard's farm manager coming from the store with a parcel under his arm. Blanchard touched his cap and the two men looked at each other, both with brown faces and large brown hands, black hair and black eyes, so thoroughly of the same Norman stock that they could understand each other without speaking.

'Good day, Joseph.'

Blanchard touched his cap again. 'Good day, Father.'

The priest spoke again and Blanchard came to a halt. 'Mr. Tallard well?'

8

'I would think so, Father. But he's sure a busy man these days, with the war.'

There was a pause during which they continued to sense each other. In Saint-Marc people were near to the priest or near to Athanase Tallard. Blanchard was near to Athanase, but this did not mean that he was hostile to the priest, or for that matter that anyone was hostile to anyone else. It was merely a subtle and accepted alignment of interests and personalities. Since the beginning of the war, some who had been near to Athanase had drawn imperceptibly away because Athanase had taken a strong stand with the English in favour of full mobilization.

The priest nodded down the road. 'Are Mr. Tallard's friends staying over the week-end?'

Blanchard thought a moment as he looked at the ground. 'I don't know for sure, Father. Mr. Tallard, he brought them over from the train.'

'Are they old friends of his?'

'I don't think so, Father. One of them he didn't know at all.'

'They've come to look at the Dansereau place?'

'I guess.' Each man knew exactly what was in the other's mind.

'They look like city men,' the priest said.

Blanchard twisted his cap in his free hand. 'They were English all right, Father.' He added after a moment's reflection, 'One of them got a wooden leg.'

The two men looked at each other, and then Father Beaubien nodded and returned to his porch. Blanchard walked off down the road with a plodding gait, one arm hanging, the other clutching his parcel.

The priest stood motionless for a long time. He could hardly believe that even Athanase Tallard would arrange for the sale of French land, land that belonged to his own people and once to his own family, to an English stranger. No English-Canadian had ever owned land in this parish.

Father Beaubien made a quick calculation. He had thought of taking an option on the Dansereau place in the name of the Church, but it had not seemed necessary. Saint-Marc was not like the parishes in the Eastern Townships

9

with English communities near at hand. In those places the Church always had to be quick with its option on available land, whether it happened to be French or English. But there was nothing to interest an Englishman in Saint-Marc. He thought the situation through carefully and was reassured after deciding there was no cause for alarm. It was in his nature to refuse to believe anything until it was proved.

After a last look down the road he went into his presbytery and closed the door behind him.

3

Two hours later Athanase Tallard showed his guests into the library of his old seigniory house. The men stood for a few minutes warming themselves before a fire of birch logs that burned on a huge, smoke-blackened stone hearth. As they talked they turned now and then to look out the windows to the alley of Lombardy poplars that ran straight as an avenue from the gallery to the river road, and beyond to the late afternoon sun glinting on the Saint Lawrence.

Although the three men were outwardly unconscious of the differences between them, they were so unlike in appearance as well as in manners that they might have come from three distinct countries and cultures. Athanase Tallard was tall and finely drawn. His aristocratic features were as brown as a walnut shell, the dark pigments of the skin heightened by a large white moustache. His movements were quick with an abundance of nervous vitality, and there was distinction in the way he gestured with his long hands.

Beside him stood Huntly McQueen, whose name was well known in the financial circles of Montreal. Beyond the fact that he had been born obscurely somewhere in Ontario, that he was a bachelor, that he was a great church-goer, and that he was rapidly becoming one of the richest men in Canada, little was known of his personal affairs. He was scarcely more than forty, but his manner and his habit of dress made him seem nearly as old as his host. Until today he had known Tallard only casually, though they had met fairly often in Ottawa.

John Yardley, the third man, was a retired sea captain

10

from Nova Scotia. He was about the same age as Tallard, nearly sixty, and he was equally tall. Behind rimless glasses his eyes were pale blue and they twinkled easily. He was lean and muscular, his face showed the marks of years of sunburn and windburn, his greying hair was cropped close to his skull, and his ears stuck out like fans on either side of his head. An artificial leg made him limp heavily, but otherwise his movements suggested the relaxed awareness of a man who has lived most of his life in the open, and some of it close to danger. It was Yardley who had wanted to inspect the Dansereau farm. Through his daughter, who had married into one of the old families in Montreal and had been living there many years, he had met McQueen, and McQueen had arranged this meeting with Tallard.

Seeing that his guests were at ease, Athanase excused himself. He explained that his wife was in bed with grippe and he must see how she was. It was a great pity, her illness, for visitors were rare in Saint-Marc and she would have enjoyed meeting them. He promised to return shortly.

When they were alone, Yardley let his eyes wander over the room. 'This must be one of the oldest houses in Canada,' he said. 'You know Quebec pretty well. How old would you say it was?'

'I can tell you precisely,' McQueen said. 'It was built by the first member of the family who came to Canada in 1672. When Tallard comes back you might compliment him on the place. The French are proud as Lucifer about houses like this.'

Yardley let a kind of smile play over his face and changed the subject. 'Too bad Mrs. Tallard's sick. I'd like to meet her, specially if I'm going to be her neighbour.'

'Surely you haven't made up your mind already!'

'Why not? I know what I want, and I think I've found it. I guess that's all there is to it.'

McQueen studied his friend with an expression of slow calculation. Although his face was as round as a full moon, there was a curious ruggedness about his features. His nose was dominant and his mouth firmly set, his eyes wide and intelligent. This expression of force did not extend to his ponderously soft body. As he crossed to the window he

11

walked with a padding movement, setting his feet down cautiously with each step.

'I wouldn't do anything hasty,' he said, looking out and peering from side to side. 'There's no doubt about it, haste never pays.'

'That's what everybody's been saying to me ever since I came to Montreal.' Yardley spoke with a twanging lilt that caught the ear. 'But I don't like waiting around. Never did.'

McQueen turned from the window. With a glance toward the open door, he spoke in an undertone from the corner of his mouth and his lips barely moved. 'You never can be sure where you stand with people like these. I know them. Our host, for instance. He married a girl young enough to be his daughter. Irish, and she can hardly speak a word of French. Strange business. Tallard has quite a reputation with women. I'd like to see what she's like myself. One hears things, you know.'

When Yardley made no reply he turned his attention to the books that lined the walls. 'Who'd have expected to find a library like this? Good books, too. Solid reading.' He shook his head. 'Nearly as many as I've got myself.'

Yardley limped over to the front window. His interest quickened as he caught sight of a ship, looking very small in the wide spaces of the river. It was a red and white lake boat, high in the bow with a low bridge forward and a single funnel set far aft over a squat stern. He watched it for a time, and then hearing the movement of a third person in the room, he turned. A small boy was watching from the door.

'Hullo!' Yardley said. 'Where did you come from?'

The boy continued to watch him with an odd mixture of shyness and curiosity. He was slim and dark-haired, and his eyes were shadowed by heavy lashes. He looked somewhat younger than his seven years.

'I was here,' he said at last. Two buck teeth appeared for a moment below a well-formed upper lip as he smiled back at Yardley. He seemed not to notice McQueen. Yardley limped across the room and put out his hand and the boy touched it diffidently.

12

'It's awfully big,' he said.

'It ought to be. When I was only a little older than you I had to use my hands like a monkey, and a monkey's got mighty big hands for the size of the rest of him.'

McQueen looked at them from his corner by the bookshelves with the expression of a busy man asked to admire his neighbour's baby. Yardley went on talking as the boy followed him back to the window.

'Why, when I was fourteen I was sent to sea, and in those days the boys were the ones they sent aloft. Man! We'd be up there on the r'y'l yards going with the swing of the mast, and the sea roaring white and green a hundred and fifty feet below, and we'd look down and get scared, and then we'd see a hard-case mate watching us on the deck and he'd make us scareder.'

The boy's mouth was open in wonder and Yardley smiled good-naturedly. He bent and touched his left leg. 'Feel that,' he said.

The boy poked it gingerly. 'It's hard.'

'Fella thet first went aloft with me, he had a timber leg just like thet,' Yardley said.

McQueen was still shaking his head when Athanase Tallard returned to the library. 'Tea will be here in a moment, gentlemen,' he said, his interest caught by McQueen's inspection of his books.

Yardley inquired about his wife and Tallard was beginning to say that she was better when he caught sight of the boy half-hidden by the folds of the draperies. 'What are you doing downstairs?' he said sharply. 'I've told you not to come in here when I have guests.'

'We've been getting acquainted,' Yardley said.

Tallard continued to hold the boy's eyes with his own. 'Remember your manners, Paul,' he said. 'This is Captain Yardley, and this is Mr. McQueen.'

The boy straightened his shoulders, his face drew itself into lines of seriousness, and he shook hands first with Yardley and then with McQueen, bobbing his head each time. He said, 'How do you do, sir,' twice and then left the room without a backward glance and disappeared down the

13

hall in the direction of the kitchen.

'Thet boy speaks better English than I do!' Yardley said. 'He your grandson?'

'Paul speaks both languages,' Athanase said, adding a little stiffly, 'He's my son, Captain.'

'Well, you're a lucky man, Mr. Tallard, having a boy like thet.'

Athanase gave him a sharp look, but his face rested almost immediately. He decided in the instant that he liked this sea captain. He pulled up chairs and the three men sat down before the hearth as the cook brought tea and cakes on a tray. Athanase poured and they made small talk while they ate. Then the cups were laid aside and Athanase and Yardley lit their pipes.

McQueen watched them. Sitting upright with his thighs round in his trouser-legs and his calves tucked in neatly under the chair, one plump hand fingering the pearl pin in his correct dark tie, he was as unobtrusive as he was observant. Being an Ontario Presbyterian, he had been reared with the notion that French-Canadians were an inferior people, first because they were Roman Catholic, second because they were French. Eighteen years of living in Montreal had modified this view, but only slightly. Now he observed the exquisite courtesy of his host as he talked with Yardley and he was impressed. Methodically, and without malice, he probed for a weak point. Tallard had authority, there was no doubt of that. His habit of gesturing could be discounted because he was French; otherwise it would have given him away as too emotional. McQueen nodded his head imperceptibly as he caught what he was looking for: there was a great deal of impatience in the face of his host, as well as in his manner. Tallard was probably a poor business man.

Athanase was unconscious of McQueen's scrutiny because he was leaning forward tensely as he listened to Yardley explain how he had lost his leg. The subject seemed to flow naturally out of his conversation with Paul.

'She came right up on us, Mr. Tallard, right out of the haze at about two thousand yards, and before the masthead let out his hail I knew for sure she was the *Dresden*. She was that ugly she couldn't be anything else, one of those stiff German craft with a bow like a cow-catcher. We hadn't sighted a thing all the way out of Australia, and then we ran slap into her. She swung broadside on and I saw her guns swivelling around on us, and man, it was a bad moment.' He stopped and no one spoke. After a second he went on, 'Well, thet's about all there was to it. It all happened too fast.'

McQueen's heavy face moved with sudden animation. 'But ... but Janet didn't tell me it was a German raider that ... that injured you, Captain. I thought you'd had some ordinary kind of accident.'

'My daughter didn't tell you for the damn good reason thet she don't know,' Yardley said. 'She's a nervous girl, just like her mother was before her. With her husband overseas she's got enough to worry about. No sense telling the women about the war anyhow.'

A log broke and fell apart, sending sparks onto the hearth. McQueen took a gold watch from his waistcoat pocket and glanced at it. Noticing the movement, Athanase looked at his own. 'The train for Montreal doesn't leave Sainte-Justine before an hour and a half,' he said. 'It takes only thirty-five minutes to drive there. You have plenty of time.'

But McQueen had something else on his mind. He had met Tallard in Ottawa the week before and had set this date for Yardley's visit. Athanase had said then that any English-Canadian would be taking a long chance buying land in a parish that had been French since the river was settled. However, if Yardley wanted to inspect the farm adjoining his own, he would be glad to make arrangements to show him over it, and he agreed to meet the stranger on the specified train from Montreal. McQueen had omitted to mention that he meant to accompany Yardley to Saint-Marc. He had long ago learned to save explanations whenever they could be avoided. The surprise on Tallard's face when he stepped off the train had given him a distinct sense of pleasure.

'I understand,' he said now, pronouncing each word carefully, 'that there's a good waterfall on the river that runs just below your parish.'

15

Again Athanase allowed his face to show some surprise. 'Yes, there is,' he said. 'When I was a young fellow, I used to fish in the pool just below the falls.'

'You can get a lot more out of a river than fish.'

'So you can.' Athanase grinned. 'Out of that particular river I get more than half my income. I've got a toll-bridge across it.'

McQueen shook his head from side to side. 'The feudal system may be profitable, Tallard. But a power dam would be a lot more so.'

'What do we want with a dam in Saint-Marc?'

McQueen's head was still now, and he stared out the window past Tallard's shoulder. 'It would all depend on the body of water in the stream,' he said. 'It would have to be checked by engineers. A factory would bring in a nice revenue in a place like this.' His heavy head rotated back and he looked straight at his host. 'You have a new church in the village, I see. The parish must be in debt.'

'But of course!' Athanase said.

Yardley watched the two men in silence, his eyes travelling from one to the other. McQueen gave the impression of an animal chewing a cud. The way Athanase emphasized his remarks with a flick of the wrist and a turn of his fine long fingers made him look like an actor intent on remembering his lines.

'You know, Tallard,' McQueen said, 'if French-Canada doesn't develop her own resources, someone else is bound to do it for her. Bound to.'

'Someone else does so already, Mr. McQueen. Your business friends in Montreal. They've grown fat on us.'

McQueen shook his head and raised a forefinger. 'I know that. I know it only too well. Some of our trusts have been irresponsible. What I want is to see French-Canada develop her own resources. I don't want to come in here and do it for you. I never go into anything without being assured first of good will on the part of all concerned.'

Athanase studied him with caution. 'Are you thinking Saint-Marc should be turned into a factory town? Is that your notion of improvement?'

'If there's sufficient power in that stream, it's my notion

16

of the inevitable.' He got to his feet and again pulled out his watch. 'We'll have time. I'd like to have a look at that waterfall. To be candid, I came down with the captain today for that purpose. Even though I didn't tell him so.'

Athanase looked from one of his guests to the other. He thought he detected surprise equal to his own on Yardley's countenance, but McQueen was already on his way to the door. He rose with a shrug of the shoulders. 'Certainly there's time enough,' he said, 'if that's what you've come for. And the view is good. I can promise you that much.' He led the way to the waiting carriage.

Driving home from Sainte-Justine after seeing McQueen and Yardley off on the train, Athanase was troubled. McQueen had appeared forcibly excited when they reached the falls and he saw their potential power. He was a peculiar man, hard to estimate. You could laugh at him because of his ponderous appearance and fumbling movements. But there was nothing fumbling in his manner when he had stood looking at the water tumbling over the rocks. He had said nothing for several minutes and the other two had stood watching him. Then he had given a precise calculation of the height of the drop and a careful guess at the number of cubic feet of water that poured over the precipice per hour. He had indicated the exact location where the turbines should be stationed. The other two men were tongue-tied in his presence. For the first time Athanase realized how it was that McQueen had made his way into the hierarchy of business families in Montreal, a group of men regarded by all French-Canadians with a mixture of envy and suspicion. Dollars grew on them like barnacles, and their instinct for money was a trait no French-Canadian seemed able to acquire.

He spoke softly to the mare and she responded by increasing her pace. He had many times wondered about the power in the falls himself, but his mind was not in the habit of running through technical and business channels. Now McQueen's possible plans held his interest more than he liked to admit. Some day the government would be certain to take away his right of toll on the bridge. They would

17

make some compensation, but it would not be much. Then his income would drop sharply. There was also another reason for his interest in McQueen's possible plans: his own growing restlessness. It was impossible to pretend that his political career was anything but a failure. Unless he attained cabinet rank, a member of parliament fooled himself if he fancied he wielded a tenth as much influence on the country as a man like McQueen. French-Canadians were always inclined to rely too heavily on politics as a means of exercising influence. They talked too much while the English kept their mouths shut and acted.

McQueen was right. Unless they developed their own resources they would soon have none left to develop. The English were taking them over one by one. If the process continued indefinitely the time would arrive when the French in Canada would become a race of employees. Perhaps because they were a minority, perhaps because their education was not technical, they had no real share in the country's industry.

Well, he was supposed to be one of the leaders of his people in Quebec. Why didn't he do something about it? He frowned and spoke to the mare again. It would be no simple matter to start a factory in Saint-Marc. McQueen might understand the machinations of Saint James Street in Montreal, but he knew little enough about the French. Quebec was tenacious. She had always hated and opposed the industrial revolution. Priests like Father Beaubien preached ceaselessly against the evils of factory towns. It was their intention to keep their people on the land as long as they could.

As though his thoughts about the priest had caused the man himself to materialize, Athanase looked up to see Father Beaubien standing in the village road a short distance ahead, obviously waiting for him. When he went into sharp action to rein in the mare, Father Beaubien came up to the side of the carriage and Athanase looked down into his serious face, clouded by the darkening twilight.

'Don't be alarmed, Father,' he said. 'Dansereau hasn't sold his land yet.'

The priest was offended by his abruptness. He preferred

18

conversations to move slowly, with hints and suggestions leading only by degrees to the main point.

'However,' Athanase went on, 'if the gentleman makes up his mind to buy, I shall certainly advise Dansereau to sell.'

The priest's fist tightened on the seat-rail of the carriage. 'But Mr. Tallard! The man is English. He is Protestant!'

Athanase smiled. 'I like the man very much, Father. If he buys he will probably pay cash. And cash' – he nodded toward the grey mass of the church – 'has been a rare commodity around here lately.'

Still dogged, the priest continued to grip the rail of the carriage. 'Something else must be arranged. An Englishman in the parish, owning land ... that would be a very bad thing, Mr. Tallard. Now you ... you could buy Dansereau's land maybe, if he must sell it.'

Again Athanase nodded toward the church. 'All wells, Father, have bottoms. I have invested heavily already.'

The priest did not take his eyes from Tallard's face and it was the older man's glance that shifted first. Part of his superior attitude toward the priest was caused by his greater age, but most of it was a development from the instinctive antagonism latent in their characters. Yet at bottom they had much in common; they were both Normans, and they were both notably stubborn.

'Listen, Father,' Athanase said. 'Suppose this Englishman buys the land. He'll be able to hire labour. Now I ask you something very serious. How much do we need someone to hire our able men and keep them in Saint-Marc? What will happen to Pit Gendron unless he gets a job? He'll go to the city, won't he? The same way Oliva Masson did. You warned us yourself only last Sunday that anyone who goes to the city is in imminent danger of losing his soul.'

The priest made no reply. His mind chewed slowly on Tallard's words and held on doggedly through the insult to the main point. If Pit Gendron, the youngest son of a large family, were forced off his native land, Father Beaubien would feel it as a personal failure. Yet there was no work for surplus young men in Saint-Marc. Something would have to be done to keep them from the city.

Suddenly more courteous, Athanase said, 'You worry yourself too much, Father. This Englishman is as old as I am. He has no sons and he won't keep the land forever. While he's here he won't hurt anyone. Maybe he won't want to stay. But if he does come, I don't want anyone to interfere with him, for I tell you something . . . he's a good man.'

The priest knew that the subject was finished. For a few seconds the two men were silent in the gathering twilight as they exchanged glances. Then Father Beaubien gravely said good-night and walked slowly back to his presbytery, his soutane swishing vigorously with each step.

4

It was a month later before Athanase Tallard came back to Saint-Marc to spend another weekend at home. Ottawa had become a depressing place to him and he was glad to be out of it. There he was at the focal-point of his unpopularity with the other members of parliament from his own province, who still refused to realize that the English-speaking provinces would have imposed conscription on the country even without what he had said to help them. So his stand in favour of a full war program had been completely useless to both sides of the controversy.

At the moment everyone in Ottawa was worried because the war was going badly again. Canadian troops under a British Commander-in-Chief were dying like flies in the mud before Passchendaele. Athanase felt a real resentment against the British, as though they had let him down personally. He had compromised his position with his own people in an effort to make French-Canada agree to conscription, and then the British made a mess like Passchendaele. No wonder the French-Canadian press roared against conscription when they saw thousands of casualties listed as the price of a few acres of mud.

As usual, he felt better now that he was back in Saint-Marc. The ground was dry and hard and the trees were bare, sharply silhouetted against a sky almost winter-blue. The whole country had a waiting aspect. The geese had gone

20

south weeks ago, the fields were manured, the fodder was all in. Any day now, the first snow would come.

After dinner he drove down to Polycarpe Drouin's general store to buy some tobacco and listen to the men talk. The store was always crowded on Saturday night, and this week it seemed to have even more than its usual quota of customers, for farm-work was at a standstill. Three checker games had been going on for two hours, and when Athanase arrived he noticed that a few of the men were already warmed by *whiskey blanc*.

Tonight the discussion was not about the war but all about Captain Yardley. Ten days ago he had bought the Dansereau place outright and had moved in immediately. Dansereau had gone to live with his sister's family down the river. Last Sunday, Yardley had gone to church and sat through the whole of High Mass, though he had not genuflected to the altar or tried to cross himself and had not known when to kneel or when to stand. Afterwards he had been seen entering the presbytery with Father Beaubien, and it was rumoured that he had given the priest twenty dollars for his poor box. The captain came into the store nearly every day and he paid cash for whatever he bought. He spoke French, but with terrible grammar and a queer accent mixed with many English words . . . worse than an Indian, Polycarpe Drouin said.

Athanase listened to the conversation without any comment. He never mingled with the villagers man to man, and it would have been resented had he tried to do so. Yet whenever he was with them on their own ground a special kind of friendliness established itself; it was as though they recognized each other and confirmed the fact that they were separate branches of the same tree.

Now Athanase realized that those who had met Yardley had not been able to help liking him. They admitted, almost defensively, that he was very different from their notion of an English-Canadian. He was friendly, there was nothing high and mighty about him, he was ready to ask them for advice. Apparently he knew a good deal about farming, and this seemed most peculiar in a sea captain. The priest had already arranged for Pit Gendron to work for him, and Pit

21

said he was a good man for a boss. But the priest had made no comment, and in speaking about the captain to Athanase the men were all cautious and indirect, not committing themselves.

Athanase spent nearly an hour in the store listening to the talk and asking about various members of the men's families, and then he drove home. As the mare's shoes clopped along in the dark he smiled to himself. Yardley certainly had a way with him. French-Canadians had salted down the Dansereau fields with their sweat for more than two hundred years; it was bound to seem to the collective instinct of the parish a kind of robbery for a foreigner to take over land like that. But apparently Yardley was going to get away with it. If he lived in Saint-Marc for the rest of his life he would always be regarded a foreigner, but there was no doubt that those who met him wanted to feel free to like him.

Athanase decided he was glad. It was peculiar for a man like Yardley to want to live in a place like Saint-Marc, but no doubt he had a good reason and in time it might be known. Tomorrow he would call upon him formally and make sure they were seen together. Since the priest had made no overt objection, his own acceptance of the captain would more or less settle his status in the parish.

Next morning he selected a heavy walking stick from the rack in the hall and started down the road to Yardley's place with Paul trotting by his side. Athanase walked vigorously, his long thin legs shooting out fast in nervous strides. It never occurred to him to walk more slowly for the sake of the boy. Paul sniffed the air like a puppy, smelling the smoke from burning brush that had drifted a mile down the wind from the place where Blanchard was clearing away the last debris before snow fell. When they turned off the road they could see their neighbour putting new weather-stripping about the sashes of a window. As they drew closer, Athanase noticed that he was very good with his hands and accustomed to working with them.

Yardley heard their steps and backed down from the step-ladder, turning about with a smile when he reached the ground. He was wearing a turtle-necked sweater and a pair of worn overalls. 'Hallo,' he said. 'I'd been wondering how

22

you were, Mr. Tallard. Things must be pretty hot in Ottawa these days, judging from the papers. I guess you're glad to be back.'

Athanase shrugged his shoulders. 'Not hot,' he said. 'Just stuffy.' He shook hands with the captain. 'I got back last night and we thought it was about time to welcome you.'

'Thet's mighty nice of you.' Yardley dropped his hand onto Paul's shoulder. 'I've been watching Paul go by and wishing he'd stop and see me sometimes.' He looked down at the boy's shy face. 'Come on in. I got something to show you.'

The place was bare inside. In what appeared to be the living room a fire of birch logs burned brightly on a large stone hearth. A Quebec heater stood black and gaunt in the middle of the room, with a black stove-pipe joining it to the chimney. Large wooden boxes lay on the floor with their tops pried off. There was no furniture except a table and two chairs.

'Not got the place fixed up yet,' Yardley said. He pointed to the boxes and added, 'Books. I got a lot of them. Been alone so much, if I didn't read I guess I'd go crazy. Pretty near learned Shakespeare by heart.'

From the shelf in one corner he picked up a large block of white pine, smooth and carefully planed. 'This is going to be yours one day, Paul.'

The boy stared at the wood, not understanding what the captain meant and too shy to say so. His hands opened and closed and then he took the block when Yardley held it out to him.

'When I finish, it's going to be a three-master. Know what thet is? A full-rigged ship, like we used to build down in Nova Scotia, but what they can't build there any more. She'll have a full suit of sails on every mast from the course right up to the skysails when I'm finished with her.' He took the block of wood and put it back on the shelf.

Athanase looked pleased. 'But that will take up too much of your time, Captain?'

'Give me something to do winter nights,' Yardley said. 'I guess they'll be long enough, out here.' He turned to the boy again and indicated the open boxes. 'How about you

23

taking those books out for me and stacking them on the floor? Me and your father want to talk. Leastways, I got the idea your father wants to talk to me.'

Yardley led the way to the porch and when they were seated on either side of the top step he said, 'I like thet boy of yours, Mr. Tallard. Missed having a son myself. You're fortunate. He's not the only one you got, is he?'

Athanase was silent for a moment. He got up and they strolled together around a corner of the house toward the barns. 'Why do you ask that, Captain?' he said at last. 'Some of the people in the village must have been gossiping about my family.'

'No,' Yardley said. 'Not to me anyway. I guess I thought I heard you had more than one child.'

'Don't make a mistake. If anything is really important – something with money in it, something deep inside a family – our people keep their mouths shut like clams.' Realizing that he was sounding mysterious and feeling a little foolish, he added, 'I have another son, older than Paul. By an earlier marriage. He's called Marius. The name was his mother's idea, not mine. He's in his first year at the university in Montreal.' Suddenly looking straight into Yardley's eyes he asked, 'Has Marius been out here while I was away?'

Yardley stood balancing on his stick, aware of a tension he did not understand. Behind his glasses his blue eyes were serious. 'I wouldn't even know, Mr. Tallard,' he said. 'I guess maybe I shouldn't have mentioned it.'

Athanase made a gesture of impatience. 'It's nothing. You see – this province, Captain – it's not an easy place to understand. You English, you say and do what you like and people forget easily. Here nobody ever forgets anything. Most of our people are quiet. They mind their own business and all they want is to be left in peace. But some have never forgotten their grievance against the English, and my elder son is one of them. He's a nationalist. With the war, and my stand on it . . .' He stopped abruptly, as though afraid of giving away too much.

They entered the barn together and smelled the sweet odour of stacked hay, the sour stink of manure and disinfectant. Athanase pointed to the loft and then to the stalls with

24

his stick. 'I see you bought the whole place, stock and all.

Yardley nodded. 'The stock he had was pretty good. I've been thinking I'd try to get together a herd of Jerseys, but I'll wait and see how things pan out with what I've got first.'

They looked through the barn and Yardley indicated the improvements he intended to make. When they emerged into the sunshine again Athanase surveyed him with obvious curiosity. 'One thing I'd like to ask, Captain. What brought you to Saint-Marc? Was it McQueen's idea, or your own?'

'Thet's a pretty long story, Mr. Tallard. When I sit down nights in front of my fire and start thinking how I got there, I feel mighty queer sometimes.'

Athanase said nothing, sensing the loneliness in the man and respecting it.

'I guess it's a lot easier,' Yardley went on, 'to remember things than to figure out why they happen. A sea-faring man keeps himself steady by thinking he's got a home some place ashore. But when he goes ashore for good, he generally finds the only home he's got is the friends he's made. And man, they're as like as not scattered all over the whole world.'

'McQueen mentioned your daughter. Is she living in Montreal?'

Yardley's face softened. 'Yes, and two granddaughters. I guess I couldn't ever get used to living in Montreal, though.'

They came back to the front of the house again, Yardley limping heavily. Paul appeared in the door, opened his mouth to speak, and then shut it again, waiting until the men had stopped talking. Yardley said, 'You finished with the books already?'

Paul shook his head. 'I left them 'cause the floor makes them dirty and there's no place to put them.'

'Guess thet's right.' Yardley turned to Athanase. 'Thet's a noticing boy you got.' Paul wandered off in the direction of the barn and Yardley took out his pouch, offered it to Athanase, then stuffed his own pipe with tobacco when Tallard refused, and slowly lit it, puffing steadily and completely hiding the flame of the match in his hand.

'I suppose you came out here,' Athanase said, 'because it was near your daughter?'

'It don't even make thet much sense.' Yardley took the

25

pipe from his mouth and held the bowl against the breeze. 'Listen, Mr. Tallard, you may think this sounds foolish, but for a long time I've wanted to live in Saint-Marc. It wasn't sensible, but I did.'

'Saint-Marc? How could you ever have heard of the place?'

'Well, it was like this. Thirty-five years ago I was at sea with a fellow from here. He talked about the place so much I . . . well, I got a picture of it in my mind that stuck. When things got so I couldn't stand it any more in Montreal, I thought maybe Luke had come back here and I'd be able to see him again.'

Athanase shook his head. 'But nobody from this parish has ever gone to sea.'

'You never heard of Luke Bergeron?'

'The graveyard is full of Bergerons. Luc, you said. There was a wild Bergeron once. A long time ago. He disappeared.' He stared at the captain. 'You mean you knew *him?*'

'Certainly did. French Luke, we called him. After a run of two hundred and eighty-seven days out of Halifax once, we found ourselves on the beach in Saigon, Luke and me and the blackest nigger thet ever came out of Barbados – and thet's an awful black man, Mr. Tallard. Back in 1877, thet was. I was quartermaster then, and Luke was the bosun, and the nigger, he was the cook. Man, were we glad to set foot off thet ship.'

Paul had returned and stood staring at Yardley with his dark eyes very round, his lips parted and his two buck teeth showing white.

'I been alone so much, I talk an awful lot. I noticed thet in Montreal. I'd get talking, and I'd keep on, and when I stopped nobody would say anything. They were smart people, I guess. But living in Montreal they never got to see very much, and they never believed very much either.'

Athanase smiled and looked at Paul. The boy leaned against the porch and kept his eyes on the captain.

'Well, anyhow,' Yardley went on, 'when Luke stepped onto the dock in Saigon he was a mighty surprised man, because outside the coolies all the white men talked French. He liked thet. And then one night ashore some of those

26

Frenchmen started riding Luke on the kind of French he talked. They said it was something awful to have to listen to – the same way Limeys used to make fun of the way I talk – and Luke got sorer and sorer, and then he lit into them. He was a mighty good man with his hands and he could use his feet like a lumberjack, but there was too many of those Frenchmen, and me and Luke and the nigger, we got beat up so bad we couldn't lift ourselves off the floor when the cops came in. So they put us in the jailhouse. The ship sailed without us, and when we got out of jail we were on the beach. So we signed on a French craft running the China Seas, and we stuck her for four years. This time Luke was the first mate and I was the second, and the nigger, this time he was the bosun. Thet was how I learned to speak French.'

Athanase's laugh rang out and even Paul laughed, but Yardley kept his face straight and watched them both. 'Those four years out East, Luke was a terrible lonesome man,' he said. 'He never got any word out of here.'

'If he came from those Bergerons up in the hills,' Athanase said, still smiling, 'it's easy enough to understand. None of them could ever read or write.'

'Luke couldn't either.' Yardley took out his handkerchief and blew his nose and the noise was so loud he apologized. 'Funny thing, me thinking there was a chance of finding him again. But Saint-Marc's all right anyhow. I wanted a farm some place. When McQueen said he knew you and said where you lived, and I remembered Luke, it all seemed to add up right.'

A silence fell between them and Yardley puffed steadily at his pipe, his eyes looking across the fields and the river road to the water. The Saint Lawrence was the colour of dull steel under a cloudy sky.

Athanase tapped the edge of the porch with his stick. 'I'd like to do anything I can for you, Captain. I wish I were here more often and in Ottawa less." He rose and looked about for Paul, but the boy had disappeared. Yardley got to his feet and they went back inside when Tallard said something about having left his hat.

'It's mighty kind of you,' Yardley said. 'Come to think of it, I guess I stuck my neck out, coming to a place like this. But it's up to me now. Trouble is, this leg of mine. The doctor told me it was the latest in artificial limbs. But man! Old Long John Silver on his wooden stump could do a better job behind a plough than I can. Lucky thing the priest fixed me up with a good man for the heavy work.'

'Doctors!' Athanase said. 'Mine tells me I have the high blood pressure. Life was peaceful before they invented that machine, and there was blood pressure.'

Yardley pulled the two chairs before the fire and they sat on in the bare room, Paul crouched silently in front of the hearth listening while he looked at the glowing embers. The lost hat was forgotten.

'One thing I'd like to ask you man to man, Mr. Tallard. I'm not a Roman Catholic. Does it make a hell of a lot of difference around here, not being a Catholic?'

'Well, Captain,' Athanase said slowly, 'this is just like any other parish in Quebec. The priest keeps a tight hold. Myself, I'm Catholic. But I still think the priests hold the people too tightly.' He raised his hand from the stick as it rested between his knees. 'Here the Church and the people are almost one and the same thing, and the Church is more than any individual priest's idea of it. You will never understand Quebec unless you know that. The Church, the people, and the land. Don't expect anything else in a rural parish.'

In the empty room the glow of the fire brought out the sharp lines of Tallard's features. His long aquiline nose cast a shadow across one side of his face. His delicately pointed ears were set close to a high and narrow skull. From stiff grey hair, brushed straight back from the upward thrust of the forehead, his face tapered to a long, pointed chin. Had he worn a Van Dyke beard he would have resembled Cardinal Richelieu. Tufted eyebrows slanted upward into his forehead. The eyes beneath them were large and brown. They twinkled easily, and when the face was in repose they were sensitive. The mouth was stubborn and ironic. In comparison, Yardley looked plain and workmanlike beside him.

'Your priest here helped me a lot,' Yardley said.

'Father Beaubien works too hard. He worries too much. He has an eye for the length of the girls' dresses. He sees the devil every time a boy puts his arm around a girl when the

28

moon is full. Right now his new church has put the parish in debt.' Again a quick gesture with his hands. 'Me, I like a little pleasure in life.'

Yardley grinned, and Athanase said, 'Are you thinking of being converted?'

'No. I wouldn't feel safe doing a thing like thet. My old father, he whaled the Presbyterian catechism into me when I was a kid, so I'd feel mighty peculiar if I went permanent to another church.'

Athanase laughed aloud and glanced at Paul. 'Well, Captain, it will be taken for granted that you're a heretic in Saint-Marc. You never saw the light. You can't help yourself.' His smile faded. 'But it is serious, this religion in Quebec. Me, I am allowed a little latitude. It is presumed I can think for myself, up to a point.'

The talk drifted on, the fire burned itself out, and no one thought of time. Yardley told Athanase about his daughter, and his voice was wistful as he explained how difficult it had been for him to pick up any threads of intimacy with her after all the years he had been at sea. His wife had wanted Janet to be a fine lady, and when Yardley was given his own ship and some money began to come in, Janet had been sent to a finishing school in Montreal. It had finished her so well Yardley found it hard to realize now that she was his daughter at all. His wife had been dead for a number of years and Janet and her two girls were living with her husband's family, the Methuens.

Yardley described the place where they lived. It was a huge stone house on the southern slope of Mount Royal. Harvey Methuen's family was decidedly rich, the money coming from government bonds and stocks in breweries, distilleries, lumber, mines, factories and God knew how big a block of the Canadian Pacific. It was a large family, and every branch of it lived in stone houses with dark rooms hung with wine-red draperies, and they all had great dark paintings on their walls framed in gilded plaster. Yardley said they were so polite he never knew what was in their minds, and Janet was always nervous when he was around, afraid of what he might say next. He insisted that she meant well and still loved him, but he knew it was better for him to live some place where he could be near enough to see her and the children, but not in Montreal. His face softened as he added that maybe Janet would bring his grand-daughters to Saint-Marc in the summer for a long visit. Away from the Methuens, he thought she might feel easier with him.

Athanase shook his head up and down as Yardley talked. After awhile he said, 'Those Methuens are a pretty old family in Canada. I suppose that makes them set in their ways.'

'Well, I don't know Montreal so well. But I notice this. If a man has anything to do with brewing beer or the C.P.R., it seems he's something like a duke is in England.'

'He is certainly the big fish in the little puddle. We French, we watch them and smile.' He rose abruptly, looked about, found his hat, and stood with it, gesturing as he went on. 'The trouble with this whole country is that it's divided up into little puddles with big fish in each one of them. I tell you something. Ten years ago I went across the whole of Canada. I saw a lot of things. This country is so new that when you see it for the first time, all of it, and particularly the west, you feel like Columbus and you say to yourself, "My God, is all this ours!" Then you make the trip back. You come across Ontario and you encounter the mind of the maiden aunt. You see the Methodists in Toronto and the Presbyterians in the best streets of Montreal and the Catholics all over Quebec, and nobody understands one damn thing except that he's better than everyone else. The French are Frencher than France and the English are more British than England ever dared to be. And then you go to Ottawa and you see the Prime Minister with his ear on the ground and his backside hoisted in the air. And, Captain Yardley, you say God damn it!'

Yardley blew his nose loudly and Paul got to his feet and edged around the chair beside him.

'I don't see why you don't get out of parliament, Mr. Tallard,' Yardley said. 'With your ideas, and with a place here like yours, I wouldn't think you'd ever want to leave it.'

Athanase shrugged his shoulders and moved to the door. 'I'm not important to the land. I just own it. Maybe I'd get bored if I were here all the time. My manager and his men do the real work. You've seen Blanchard. He's a good man.' He added thoughtfully, 'Our people feel about the land the way they do in Europe, I think. It would be sentimental to say they love it, but I tell you one true thing – they look after it better than they look after themselves. They hoard it. It was a bold thing, Captain, your moving into a place like Saint-Marc. I hope you won't regret it.'

Yardley scratched the bristly grey hair behind his right ear. 'I got the same kind of feeling myself. Man to man, Mr. Tallard, I put most of what I got into this land. I aimed to stay when I bought it. It's good land and it suits me.'

Athanase nodded and his lean face was charming as he smiled. 'It's going to turn out all right, Captain. No one is going to make it hard for you here. I give you my word for that. But you may find it lonely. I do myself sometimes. My wife, she finds it lonely all the time.'

They shook hands, each conscious of a real pleasure in the discovery of the other.

'Tell me, Captain. Do you play chess?'

'I certainly do. I even got a set of men I picked up in India with elephants in place of bishops.'

'I prefer bishops. After all, the movement of the piece is diagonal.' His grin was raffish. He followed Paul out the door and on to the porch and then he turned. For a moment he hesitated, and then he said, 'Would you have dinner with us tonight? Madame Tallard is eager to meet you. It would make us both a very great pleasure.'

With Yardley's acceptance of the invitation, the man and the boy went off together the way they had come.

That afternoon it blew cold from the northeast, the wind built itself up, towards evening the air was flecked with a scud of white specks, and then the full weight of the snow began to drive. It whipped the land, greyed it, then turned it white and continued to come down hissing invisibly after dark all night long until mid-morning of the next day. For a few days after that the river was like black ink pouring between the flat whiteness of the plains on either side. Then the frost cracked down harder, the river stilled and froze.

31

Another blizzard came and covered the ice, and then the whole world was so white you could hardly look at it with the naked eye against the glittering sun in the mornings. The farmhouses seemed marooned and silent, and after dark the trees cracked with frost, and there were muffled sounds of animals moving in their stalls. Manure heaps grew outside the barns and stained the snow like iodine on a bandage. For months it was the same.

5

Marius Tallard was alone in his father's library. It was early evening and early April. He stood at the window looking at the watery sunlight pale on the sugar snow that lay flat on the plain. The poplar trees lining the drive were leafless and bare as brooms, their shadows long and very dark on the snow. Beyond the road, the river was a white expanse of rotted ice, streaked here and there with pallid yellow stains where moisture had seeped upward to the wind-crusted snow on top. An ice-breaker with a clubbed bow was hammering its way upstream to Montreal. The ship looked squat and tiny in the flat distance, but its power crashed far ahead of it. As it piled itself up on the ice and broke it, shuddering cracks ran miles ahead through the ice. The smoke from its funnel lay in a long scarf behind, veiling the opened channel.

Marius looked over the white fields that spread around the house and drew a deep breath. All that he could see was part of himself, and it made him feel important in a way he believed was mystical. Earlier in the day he had examined again the old familiar objects in the house that made it unique: the fine metal work of the chandelier in the dining room, made a hundred years ago by a local craftsman; the carved pine armoires in the upper hall, the row of pewter drinking vessels, all nearly two centuries old, lining the plate-rail above his father's desk. Because his family had been rooted here since the settlement of the river, he fancied that the spirit of French-Canada breathed with a special purity and understanding through himself. Because ordinary people failed to sense this the moment they saw him, he held

32

a deep, subconscious grievance against them.

He turned from the window back into the library. In the shadows the room looked pleasantly shabby, but dignified and old; in a sense, it was noble. The dry smell of the book bindings was redolent of antiquity, like the books in the library of the seminary he had attended until three years ago in Montreal.

He moved to his father's desk, stood looking at it for a moment or two, then inserted his fingers under the cover and lifted. It yielded a little, but did not rise. He went to the door and opened it into the hall. Here everything was dusk. A moose head with fourteen points on the antlers loomed at him from the wall opposite the door, and above it a solid staircase with an oak banister mounted to the second floor. Marius listened for a moment without moving. There were faint noises from the kitchen at the back of the house, but upstairs no sound.

He went back into the library and closed the door behind him. Oil lamps set on heavy marble pedestals were on the table and the mantlepiece, and one swung in a cradle secured to a stand near his father's desk. The great hearth, its stones blackened by a century of wood smoke, looked in the half-light like a bottomless cave. The room was cold as well as dark, but he lit neither lamps nor fire.

Marius opened a drawer in the lower part of the desk and hunted until he found a small, bent key. He unlocked the desk and lifted the top. Sitting down in his father's swivel chair he began nervously to search through the papers in it. On top of everything there was a copy of the previous Saturday's *Gazette*. He picked it up and glanced at the leading story. The Germans had broken through the British in their drive from St. Quentin. The British were being beaten again. He threw the paper down. What did it matter to the British? They would never admit they were beaten. They would only blame the French again, or they would find some other excuse. But maybe this time it was not going to be so easy for them to talk their way out of it. He wouldn't be surprised if the Germans rolled the British right back into the Channel. He didn't want Germany to win the war, but it would be a pleasure to see the British forced to admit at

33

last that someone had beaten them.

He went on to search through a confusion of old bills and letters, careful to note exactly where each paper lay so he could leave them as he had found them. Underneath a pile of letters he picked up a large sheet of yellow paper covered with his father's script. He held the paper so the light from the window fell on it. The material on the page must be notes for the book he knew his father meant to write. He had been talking about it for years, but so far as Marius knew, he had never got past the talking stage. In an undertone he read to himself: 'Marx is only half right when he calls religion the opium of the people. It may turn a lot of people into sheep, but it turns far too many of them into tigers. Its whole history is violent. Look at the Aztecs, Mahomet and Torquemada!'

Marius frowned. This was not what he was looking for, but it interested him enormously. He tilted back in the swivel chair and again paused to listen. The house was still silent. He read on, passing his left hand through his long black hair. His face carried a strained, tense expression, and his hair kept falling over his narrow forehead every time he bent his head forward. His face was thin and pale, with high cheekbones underlined by shadows. His body was slender and still pliable with adolescence. His eyes were large, like his father's, but without any humour, and as he strained to read in the bad light a sharp line formed between his brows and shot up to his forehead where a single vein was visible under the skin.

He went on to read the next note. 'Certainly with the masses religion must rest on fear if it is to exist at all. The masses can be neither mystical nor intelligent. Therefore the Protestant Church is destroying itself by trying to explain everything. No magic, no religion. No hell, no church.'

Marius wondered if this was heresy. Probably not quite, though it certainly suggested that the Church might have worldly motives. He dropped his eyes to the paper again. 'The masses are ruled by their own sense of guilt. Therefore nationalism and sex are the two time-tested mediums through which they can be controlled by small groups. Hammer in absolute patriotism and absolute purity as ideals, and you have the masses where you want them. You can always keep them feeling guilty by proving that they are not patriotic and not pure enough.'

Marius frowned again, not sure that he understood the full meaning behind the words. He read on. 'If some of our priests don't mind their step, they will turn the whole Church here into a nationalist political party. The hierarchy is too intelligent and cultured to want anything as crude as this, but unless our traditional fear of the English is eradicated, that is just what we are likely to get. Some of the lower clergy want it without a doubt. From most of them you can't expect anything better.'

The paper fell from Marius' hand to the desk. This was certainly heresy, suggesting that the motives of a priest of God were no better than those of a politician. He had for some time suspected that his father was a free-thinker. His fondness for the English was a part of it. So were the convolutions of his private life. Now Marius felt he had absolute proof that his father was also a liar. He lacked the courage to say openly what he believed, escaping the consequences of his heresy by rendering lip-service and going to church occasionally and keeping a pew. His political actions proved him a traitor to his race. Now this book proved him a traitor to his religion as well.

In sudden impatience Marius put both hands to the pigeon-holes at the back of the desk and began to turn them out. He was absorbed in his search until he thought he heard a noise. He looked up with a start, heard nothing, and then began pushing the papers and letters back in a frantic hurry. With a swift movement he closed the desk and locked it, slipped the key back into the drawer where he had found it, and stood up, tense and with moist palms. He went to the library door, opened it and listened carefully. There was no sound. He swore under his breath and closed the door again, moving softly back into the room. Then he let out a deep breath and stood there with his hands in his pockets, not moving.

He felt decidedly annoyed because he had found no money. It was as though his father had deliberately fooled him. Nearly always there was money somewhere in that desk. He had seen it since he was a child whenever he had asked for spending-money; sometimes there was as much as a hundred dollars in various sized bills. His father held five hundred dollars in trust for him, a legacy from his own mother. Until his twenty-first birthday he could not legally claim it, but he needed money now, badly, and he saw no reason not to borrow against the five hundred.

Part of Marius' anger was caused by the knowledge that his father was naturally generous with money. By French standards, he was even reckless with it. Athanase would have given him any amount had he asked for it, but to ask his father for anything was something Marius could not bring himself to do.

His breathing quieted and he went again to the window. A feeling of excitement, mixed strangely with sadness and pleasure, passed through him like a knife as he thought of his discovery. His father was a heretic. It gave him a tremendous sense of vindication. His father had never given regard to anyone's feelings but his own. Now he would ultimately be found out, and then the world would know which of them was right, which one had suffered unjustly.

He turned his head to listen but there was still no sound in the house. With a quickening in his blood he dropped on his knees before the bookcase beside his father's desk. He let his hand move over a row of slim volumes on the bottom shelf. They were art books his father had brought from Paris years ago; he had first discovered their presence in the house when he was thirteen. His hand found the volume he wanted without searching, and he went back to the window with it. His fingers trembled as he opened the pages.

Nude women gleamed from the smooth paper. He turned the pages and there were more nude women in reproductions of paintings by Titian, Correggio, Botticelli, Rubens and Ingres. As he looked at the lovely bodies he was both troubled and fascinated by his thoughts. These were the nearest he had ever come to the sight of a woman naked. So the forms lost individuality as conceived by the painters and became what he made them. They signified only the female being he did not know, the being which was beautiful and

36

dangerous and at the core of sin. His fingers shook as he turned the pages.

Then, as always happened when he opened the book, he became afraid the pages would be marked by his fingers. He dreaded that his father would some day know how often he looked at these pictures. Not that his father would have cared. It was a matter of guarding his thoughts and essential self from others; this had become an obsession with Marius.

He replaced the book and dropped into an armchair before the cold hearth, resting his head on cold leather. His father was very proud of this library; in a way he was proud of it himself, for it belonged to the family.

Steps were audible on the stairs. Marius sat upright, listening, tense. He was facing the door, and as it opened he saw his stepmother before she caught sight of him. Kathleen Tallard stopped still, staring. 'Great heavens!' she said, speaking in English. 'What are you doing here?'

Marius leaned back in the chair with an elaborate show of indifference.

'What's the matter?' she said. 'Are you in trouble?' Her voice had a husky, pulsing quality, but it was friendly, warm and frank.

'Can't I come home when I feel like it without you thinking something's wrong? It's my home, isn't it? I was born here, wasn't I?'

'Why sure it's your home. But you ought to be in Montreal. You don't have a vacation for another month. What will your father say?'

'What business is that of yours?'

She was silent a moment. Then she said, 'I only wanted to be pleasant. I don't see why you always talk that way to me.'

'Don't you?'

She turned from him and picked up a long-sticked match from a bowl on the table, struck it, lifted the mantle of the lamp that stood there and touched the match to the wick. Then she struck another match and lit the lamps above the hearth. After that she turned back to him with a smile. 'There. That's better. A little light makes even this place cozy. You need a fire, too.'

37

She bent and sprinkled kerosene from a brass can over the logs which were already set on the andirons, then struck another match and dropped it on them. Flames leaped over the kindlings and the birch logs, and a pleasant smell of burning wood seeped into the room as the smoke made wreaths around the stones at the edge of the fireplace before the draft sucked them up the chimney. Marius lay back in the long chair with his hands in his pockets and his feet straight out, watching this woman he always thought of as 'my father's wife.'

Kathleen stood up from the fire and moved with an easy, indolent grace to the centre of the room. The boy followed her with his eyes. 'You're in trouble, Marius,' she said. 'Wouldn't you like to tell me what it is?'

'Why should I? Nobody ever pays any attention to me around here. What's the idea of you starting now?'

She picked up a book from the table and laid it down again, her mild eyes watching him. She was thirty-one and he was twenty. The fact that she was much closer to his age than to her husband's was always an unspoken knowledge between them. 'You haven't come out here for fun,' she said. 'I know men well enough to know how they feel when they look the way you do.'

'I'll bet you know how men feel!'

Her voice flared up in lazy anger. 'If you say things like that I'll have to tell your father.'

He continued to stare at her, his eyes mocking. 'You wouldn't dare.'

She made a slow movement with one foot, as if to stamp in anger, but the gesture died. 'How do you know I wouldn't?'

His teeth showed white. 'Because you're afraid of trouble.'

Kathleen shrugged her shoulders and picked up some magazines, putting them down again and making their edges straight. One dropped to the floor and she bent to retrieve it while Marius watched her, his lips opening slightly. God, she was beautiful!

Ever since she had come to Saint-Marc nine years before, the house had seemed mysteriously evil, warm with sin. It was more than her beauty, more than the outrage he felt

38

because his father had married a woman young enough to be his own daughter. It was her particular kind of beauty. The contrast between Kathleen's white Irish skin and the intense ebony blackness of her hair was startling. Her lips were generous and her breasts were full, but her hips below this opulence were slender. As she straightened his eyes dropped. It was the way she moved and sometimes the way she looked at him that gave her so much power over his senses.

He looked beyond her to the shadows in one corner of the room. She was his father's wife. She was the mother of his half-brother. Paul was eight, he was pure, he knew nothing of his own origin; but he was this woman's son. She must have been a girl hardly older than he was now when his father had first gone to her.

Turning from the table Kathleen said quietly, 'You're afraid they'll get you, aren't you, Marius? It's conscription.'

For a moment his eyes met hers and yielded. Then he flushed. 'I'm not afraid of anything. Understand? They won't get me, either.'

'Well, I'm glad you came back. Your father will fix everything up for you. Just wait and see.'

'You think I'd beg him for anything?'

'But it wouldn't be begging – not from your own father! I'll speak to him, if you like.'

'No, you won't. He thinks the war's wonderful. Why not? He's safe. He's too old to be killed. Anyway, he sold out to the English long ago.'

'Oh, don't talk that way. Your father's a very clever man.'

'How would you know if he was clever or not?'

'A boy like you can't know as much about things like the war as his father does. You ought to be proud of him. And him a member of parliament in Ottawa, too.'

'Proud! My God! I have to apologize to everyone I know every time I see his name in the papers! I have to say, "Sure, I know my father sells us down the river to the English, but I'm not like him. I'm not fooled by him." Me – having to say that to my friends about my own father!'

Kathleen made a gesture of impatience and her face showed the mounting of a slow anger. Marius suspected that she saw through him completely and knew his secret thoughts as well as he did himself. There was a dreadful instinct in her for seeing into every male she met.

'Your father's always got on well with the English,' she said. 'Why not, I'd like to know? They respect him. So does everyone else.'

'Listen to what the students say and you'll find out how much he's respected.'

'Students! The English are all right. They let us alone.'

'Us?' Again the harsh laugh. 'Since when did you become one of us? You can't even speak French.'

Kathleen shrugged her shoulders and turned away. 'I don't know what's the matter with you. Why can't you be nice and natural? You and the English! What did they ever do to you? Next thing, you'll be saying old Captain Yardley is selling somebody out.'

Marius was lashing himself into anger. He got up and began walking back and forth in the room. 'Never mind about him. He's a harmless old fool. But his friends aren't. Look at that McQueen! The biggest profiteer in the country fixes things so his friends buy French land cheap. And my own father helps him!' He threw his arms wide in a theatrical gesture. 'And why not? He buys things cheap too.'

'You're crazy. Your father's not a business man.'

'He doesn't have to be. He bought you, didn't he?'

They faced each other, tense and angry. For a second he thought she was going to slap him and he made a sudden movement and caught her lifted hand. She swung in against him and he felt her body soft against his own and saw her eyes looking straight into his and for a second he forgot all about his father. So he stood there holding her wrists. Then he dropped his eyes and pushed her away, feeling shame strike his face like a wave of fire as he groped toward the door.

Footsteps sounded outside on the gallery. 'Who's that?' he asked sharply, his hand on the knob.

She looked at him calmly. After the things he had said, her poise was intolerable to him. Even her voice was completely expressionless. 'It's probably Captain Yardley. He's coming to dinner.'

'Where does he live – here or in his own house?'

'He likes your father.' She moved toward the door. 'Your father will be back from Ottawa tonight. They're going to play chess after dinner, the way they always do.'

Marius opened the door and made for the stairs. He bumped into Julienne on her way from the kitchen to open the front door. She stared at him, not knowing he was home. He clutched her arm. 'Don't tell anyone I've been here. Understand? I'm going back to town.'

Julienne stood staring after him as he ran upstairs. Then she shook her head and pursed her lips. There had always been trouble between Marius and the master. Well, it was none of her business. She went on to open the door, where Yardley's lean figure was silhouetted against the snow.

Upstairs in his room Marius stood in the semi-darkness. He was trembling. The image of Kathleen's lush body still brimmed in his eyes and he felt sick from shame. He struck a match and crossed the room, shielding the flame in his cupped hands. In the far corner he lit a candle. Then he struck another match and lit five more candles and the yellow light fell on a makeshift altar he had set up three years before when he was still at the seminary and thought he was going to be a priest. Above the altar was a small crucifix.

Marius stood looking at it and then he turned slowly away, his eyes filled with tears. They came to rest on a picture on the side wall. He saw the slim face of a woman with neat black hair parted in the middle and drawn off her forehead. The woman's eyes were lowered as though in modesty before the camera. It was the virginal face, almost the nun's face, of his mother.

Tears for his own loneliness overflowed his eyes as he fell on his knees in front of the altar and clasped his hands. The points of light on the candles swam before his sight. His mind was like a swelling liquid pain as he contemplated his own misery. His hatred of his father collapsed in a longing for his father's approval, never attained because stubbornness of pride made him refuse consistently to do a single thing his father wished. The terrible thoughts his stepmother roused in him burned in the same way he was sure hell must

41

burn, except that the torture of hell would contain more physical pain.

For many minutes he stayed on his knees, his lips moving in prayer, and slowly he became calm. Still kneeling after finishing his prayers, he tried to think more clearly. The war had finally caught up with him. Thoughts of the army filled him with dread, mixed with bitterness against the English who were forcing the evil of war upon him. And the dread and the bitterness served to cancel out his shame.

The candlelight made his shoulders a black silhouette in the gathering dark of the airless room. He got to his feet and looked at his watch. The train from town had reached Sainte-Justine some time ago and his father would be home any minute now. After having come all the way from town to get money he would now have to go back without it. And he would have to hurry to catch the west-bound train back.

As he went down the stairs on tiptoe, and as he stood in the hall quietly putting on his coat and drawing a muffler about his throat, he listened to the voices that came through the half-open library door. There was the clink of a bottle against glass and a chuckling laugh from Kathleen, then Yardley's voice clear. 'Down home we used to drink Demerara and when I was a lot younger than I am now I'd always get embarrassed, not being able to take it neat like most of them. You need a bull's gullet for neat Demerara.'

Marius missed Kathleen's reply, but he could hear Yardley go on, 'Barbados is a gentleman's rum.' Then, after a moment's silence, 'Mr. Tallard late again?'

Kathleen must have moved closer to the door, for he could make out her reply now. 'I never worry about him. He'll be here soon.'

Marius stood in the dark hall balanced on his toes, listening intently. He might miss his train, but he could not bring himself to leave. The pleasant voices in the lighted room held him.

'He worries, though,' Kathleen went on. 'Too much. He's not the way he used to be when I first met him, I can tell you that. He was fun, then.'

'The way the war's going, Kathleen, it's enough to make anyone worry.'

So he calls her by her first name, Marius thought. Well,

42

why not? She was the kind men instinctively called by a personal name.

'Still wanting to get back to the city?' Yardley said.

'What's the use of wanting?'

'There could be a lot worse places to live than Saint-Marc.'

'Where?'

Marius shifted his feet in the hall. Then Kathleen's voice went on, 'With all the other places in the world to pick from, it still beats me why you came here.'

'I'm not sorry,' Yardley said. 'Must say, though, I never thought I'd have to work so hard in my sixtieth year. Lucky thing my health's still good.'

Kathleen's voice was warm and lazy as she answered. 'Well, it's nice for me, your being here. He never thinks about me any more, you know. So I just drift. I guess everybody does and I guess it's nothing but luck where you drift to.' She laughed quietly. 'Well, I've had my lucky days, too.'

Marius took a step nearer the front door and laid his hand on the knob, but he was arrested again by Yardley's voice. 'What about that factory McQueen's so set on building here? Mr. Tallard any more interested in the idea?'

'Oh, he talks a lot about it.'

Marius was exasperated by the silence that followed. How like Kathleen to be uninterested in the only important thing Yardley had said. Factory? What factory?

'Out here you can talk all the time and it still won't mean that anything's going to come of it,' Kathleen was saying.

'Mr. Tallard does a lot more than just talk when it comes to the war. It takes courage, what he's doing.'

Marius could imagine the supple lift to Kathleen's shoulders as she shrugged them. It was a slow sway, as though she were easing herself from under a weight.

'Maybe he knows a lot about the war,' she said. 'I don't. All I know is that on account of the war I never see him any more and I'm stuck here with nothing to do. Marius was here today. He's bad enough any time, the way he feels about me, but now he's going to be conscripted he talks as if it was all his father's fault. And that means my fault, too, in his language.'

The large clock in the hall, its face hidden in the darkness except for a single corner where a shaft of light from the library struck it, was suddenly ticking very loudly.

'I'll believe in that factory when I see it,' Kathleen was saying. 'But I hope it's built. Some new people would come. Nobody here could run it.'

'You know, Kathleen' – Yardley's voice was measured – 'I'd kind of hate to see a thing like that happen here. And yet – I've looked over that waterfall pretty carefully. It's made to order. It probably will get built, no matter what any of us thinks about it.'

Every muscle in Marius' body was tense, waiting and listening. A new wave of anger was mounting through him. Turn a perfect old parish like Saint-Marc into a factory town! His imagination began to construct a finished picture, the deed accomplished. He saw chimneys spilling black smoke over the fields, the village cluttered with new, raw, cheap houses and cheap people imported for labour. The row of freshly-painted cottages where the English managers lived like lords of creation would be set apart from the rest of the village. A second conquest! First the English took over the government of your own country. Then they used you for cheap labour in their factories.

Unconsciously his nostrils twitched to the odour of roast pork coming from the kitchen as Julienne took the roast from the oven. Suddenly he realized how hungry he was. And he couldn't even stay and eat in his own house! He opened the front door without a sound, closed it behind him and stepped into the evening. The last clouds had rolled away after sunset and the sky was clear, faintly saffron toward the west with some residual light over the frozen river. The stars looked bright and close and there was a promise in the air. Spring would begin any day now.

Marius had forgotten about the train back to Montreal. As he walked down the road his black brows were close together. He would have to talk to Father Beaubien. He could stop a factory. There would be plenty he could say before such a thing was allowed to happen.

Back in the library Kathleen was holding her glass against the light, studying the golden murkiness of its colour. 'I'm sure it's something more than just me being his stepmother,'

she was saying. 'It's something from away back he holds
against his father. I wish I knew for sure what it was. It's a
shame for him to be so unhappy.'

6

Marius Tallard was drunk with a new knowledge of himself. He stood in the big hall before the meeting with his
feet apart, swaying from the hips, his arms folded across
his chest. Now and then his right arm shot out and the long
fingers of his hand wove gestures in the air. His white teeth
flashed rare and bitter smiles in his white face. His black
hair was loose on his long, narrow skull. He pulled emotion
out of the crowd and threw it back at them.

Marius had no idea how he was doing this, nor even what
he was saying. His own unhappiness and frustration had
been filling up a well inside him for ten years and now he
felt he could go on speaking out of it forever. The listening
crowd leaned forward and gave him back a mysterious
elation in exchange for his words. They loved each other,
Marius and all these strange people.

Fragments of the crowd detached themselves from the
whole and he talked to them in turn. Down in the fifth row
Emilie's wide, innocent face shook loose and floated up
against his eyes. She was staring at him like a young girl at
her first communion looking at the priest. Every little while
he looked back at her, avoiding the students who were
sitting just behind her. At the back of the hall four policemen stood with their arms folded across a pair of white
bandoliers that met and crossed over their chests. They were
huge men; in their black greatcoats with the white bandoliers and their stiff fur caps they looked like Napoleon's
guards.

Marius switched his eyes from Emilie and talked over
the crowd to the policemen. He was their man and they
were his people. They had discovered each other and the
moment was enormous.

Behind him the chairman sat heavily in his seat and
looked at the profile of the boy who was speaking, with
amused interest. The chairman's name was A. Marchand;

45

he had a shining bald head, a big paunch, lead-coloured skin, and the narrow eyes and lips of a professional politician. He was the one who had invited the university debating society to send a speaker for this anti-conscription meeting. It was an improvisation; originally Marchand had hoped to get Henri Bourassa, the famous nationalist leader, but Bourassa had not been able to come. His chance idea about getting a student had turned out better than he expected. Marchand smiled. What a student! Who would have expected the son of Athanase Tallard to turn up here?

Marius was now launched on his peroration. 'Here in Quebec,' he was saying, 'beside our own great river, we French-Canadians are at home. We say it once. We say it twice. We will always say it. Perhaps if we say it enough the English will understand us. We are at home here with our families and our faith. We don't ask much. All we have ever asked is to be let alone. When we say "Down with Conscription" we do not say we fear to fight. We say "Down with foreign tyranny and interference!" We say . . .'

Marchand knew by heart what Marius would say. After all, he had previously said most of it himself earlier in the meeting. To him this was just a small gathering in a dirty hall in the east end of Montreal. There had been hundreds of other meetings like it all over the province through 1917 and 1918, all of them protesting the conscription act which the English-speaking provinces had forced on Quebec. If Bourassa had been able to speak tonight, the meeting would have been news, for he was a great orator and a symbol. Without him this hall was just one more place where oratory was being sprayed out like an anaesthetic to deaden the French-Canadians' bitterness because they were a minority in a country they considered their own; because the pressure of the eight English-speaking provinces east and west of them, and of the United States to the south, made them feel they were in a strait-jacket; because now, with the world gone crazy, they were almost powerless against an alien people who called themselves countrymen but did not understand the peculiar value of the French and did not want to understand it.

Marchand felt all this sincerely. He knew the meeting

46

would do little good. It was a safety valve, nothing more. But he was also a politician, and so he had identified himself with a whole series of such meetings because he knew it would not be forgotten after the war. He would be remembered as a man who had fought for his people during the bad times.

When Marius stopped talking the crowd rose and cheered him. He made his way slowly down from the platform, then down the aisle to the door while the crowd shouted and congratulated him. His face continued to flash quick, tight smiles. A few hours ago he had been nothing. Now, because he had discovered that he could speak, his future greatness leaped like a giant before his eyes.

At the door Marchand caught up with him. He took Marius by the arm and drew him aside into a small ante-room, then stopped and wiped his skull with his handkerchief. 'My God,' he muttered. 'Some of the bums they let in here stink when they sweat!' He grinned at Marius, his parted lips showing two gold teeth. 'Never mind, young fella. The crowd that sweats is the only one that counts for a damn.'

He turned to wave through the open door to someone he knew. Beside him, seeing no one else, Marius said, 'It's a crowd worth saving, anyway.'

An English voice, speaking English, sounded sharply behind him. 'Save them from what, brother?'

Marius jerked around and found himself staring into a raw-boned face under a soldier's cap. The soldier stood leaning against the open door, sneering at him. Marius opened his mouth to speak but the words clogged in his mind and stuck.

'Never mind,' the soldier said in a flat voice. 'You said plenty already.' He turned on his heel and went out the door.

Marius gave a forced laugh and looked at Marchand's back. He was talking to someone who had come in another door and had not heard the soldier. Anyway, what difference did it make what an Englishman said? He waited for Marchand to turn around, hoping for some word of praise from him, but the politician was taking his time. Through the

47

open door of the vestibule Marius could see street lights and hear the noise of a tram rounding the corner of Saint-Denis Street.

Beyond the door Emilie was standing with his coat over her arm. He smiled at her and she smiled back. Her face still held awe of him. Marius knew she was only a simple girl, but knowledge of the emotion he had aroused in her filled him with excitement.

Marchand finished his talk and turned around, his jacket open and his thumbs hooked into the lower pockets of his waistcoat. 'So you're Athanase Tallard's son, eh?'

Marius nodded, then added a reluctant, 'Yes.'

'How old are you?'

'Twenty-one this week.'

Marchand's thin lips parted to show the tops of his gold teeth. 'You finishing at the university this year?'

'Yes. Next fall I start my law course.'

'You mean, you *hope* you start your law.' The heavy paunch shook in a sort of laugh. 'Well, you made quite a speech, young fella. Too bad your father didn't hear it.'

As he went on talking, Marchand watched excitement dilate the pupils of Marius' eyes and tried to calculate just how much a face like that would be worth to him. Every year the classical colleges turned out hundreds of boys who seemed to be able to do nothing but talk. Yet every so often a boy was thrown up with the intensity of a militant priest, but without a vocation for the Church. If you could get a boy like that into line you could certainly use him.

'The trouble with your father,' Marchand was saying, 'is he can't touch an ignorant crowd. Not like you can.' Suddenly the man's mood changed and the paunch was still. 'Listen,' he said, 'what was the idea of all that stuff you said against the English capitalists? Bringing Huntly McQueen's name into it. Who told you he was profiteering in medical supplies?'

'But – but everyone knows he is!'

'Maybe they do. That isn't going to make him like reading what you said in the papers tomorrow.'

The fear of authority was endemic in Marius, and now it

gripped him like a clenching hand. 'I only said what's true,' he answered sullenly.

'You've got a lot to learn,' the politician said. 'You'll find yourself in jail for slander if you don't watch out.'

Marius looked at the man and then away again. 'You're the one that asked me to speak,' he said.

Marchand made an impatient gesture with one hand. 'Listen. I'll tell you something. You can curse politicians all you want in public. That's okay. You can talk about our rights. That's okay, too. But the English part of this country is run by big business, even if they don't know it. And their big boys don't like their names thrown around in public, understand? Except maybe when they're on hospital committees and charity boards.' His eyes swivelled away and caught sight of Emilie standing by the door, passed quickly over her and turned back to Marius. 'They'd a lot sooner have us curse their race than kick for higher wages. You remember that next time. And for Christ's sake remember that French-Canadian nationalism isn't Bolshevism – or anything like it.'

The elation was steadily being pumped out of Marius. Marchand shrugged his shoulders, and when Marius said nothing he went to the door and beckoned a taxi driver who was waiting for another fare. Then he turned to the boy again. 'How's it you're not in the army?'

'I got my notice last week,' Marius said sullenly.

'Reported yet?'

'No.'

Marchand laughed. 'They'll get you for sure now. You certainly asked for it tonight, young fella.'

Marius tasted bile as his rage mounted. He hated Marchand. The old men were all the same; they were all liars. None of them meant anything they said. But the inbred fear of authority choked his anger back to sullenness. 'I only did what you wanted,' he said.

'Sure,' Marchand said. 'Sure. You did all right, too. Come and see me if you keep out of jail and the army. You did fine.' Without waiting for an answer he went out the door, leaving Marius to stare after his back.

Suddenly the boy felt better. Maybe Marchand envied him because he had the courage to say what he thought? He turned to Emilie, took the coat from her arm and put it on. Her eyes were shining as she told him how wonderful he was, but Marius wasn't listening. He was wondering about the students who had come down to hear him speak. What had they thought? Were they jealous of his success? Or had they thought his speech was cheap? They might have waited to congratulate him.

He waited for Emilie to pass through the door to the street, and then before he could follow her he felt a hand on his elbow. 'That bastard you was talking to. I heard him,' someone said. A tired, ageless face was beside him. The man wore a cloth cap and a ragged overcoat and the unwashed smell of his body hit Marius' nostrils. 'Don't you give a damn for that son of a bitch.' The earnest face came close. 'You made the best speech I ever heard, and I haven't got much to do but listen. I heard Laurier. I heard Bourassa. And tonight I hear you.'

He held out a hand and Marius took it. Then the man was gone and Marius was out in the air, standing beside Emilie. He looked both ways up and down the street but he saw nothing. His eyes were incandescent. He had been compared to Laurier and Bourassa! It wasn't an educated man who had praised him. That would have meant nothing. What counted was to be able to reach the crowd made up of men like that. He passed a hand over his eyes. Holy Name, that was truly greatness!

He took Emilie's arm. 'Come on,' he said. 'It's nearly midnight. I'll take you home.'

As they went down the steps he noticed the English soldier who had interrupted his talk with Marchand still standing by the curb. Their stares met in the half-light and Marius felt the man's insolence in the pit of his stomach. The feeling passed when he and Emilie began walking east. He sucked in the spring air and looked up to the roofs opposite, his mind picturing hundreds of acres covered by similar buildings, all of them filled by helpless people who could not talk; empty people hungry for words; people waiting to be led. Marius was convinced that a man who could make a good political speech could have what he wanted of the world. Government and speeches seemed to him identical.

On the corner they passed three soldiers talking quietly together under an arc lamp. Marius looked them over with hostility. When he recognized the language they were speaking as French he was exasperated. One wore the ribbon of the Military Medal and the other two had wound stripes. They reminded him that all French-Canada was not against the war. One of the finest regiments in the British Empire was French-Canadian.

Beside him Emilie was saying, 'You feel good, Marius? You looked good up there. It made me shiver.'

He pressed her arm. 'I feel all right. But I'm frightened, too.'

'Silly! Up there on the platform with all those famous men!'

'They weren't so much.'

'No? Well, you're awful smart, anyway.'

He laughed, pleased. Though Emilie was unconscious of the processes of his mind, she had re-established herself as a symbol by the remark. She was an ignorant country girl, but she was one of his people.

They walked steadily east through air moist and mild with the first warmth of spring. A fugginess hung between the dirty old buildings and the beams of light from the blue arc lamps looked thick and almost opaque through it.

Emilie had been going out with Marius ever since her family had brought her to Montreal two months before. She knew he was far above her class. She understood only part of what he talked about, for he used bigger words even than her village priest had done. Yet sometimes she dreamed that the difference between them was not so great. Marius might be educated, but he lived alone in a room so untidy she thought his landlady disgraceful. He often seemed as unhappy as a lost dog, and she understood about things like that. He needed her.

'I hope your father won't mind your being out so late,' Marius said. 'I didn't think it would be as late as this.'

'That's all right. P'pa won't mind.'

Emilie did not add that what her father thought no longer

51

made any difference to anyone. She knew it, but she could never have explained the reasons. He had been a farmer all his life, working a strip of poor land on the lower Saint Lawrence and going up to the woods back of Lac Saint-Jean in the winters for the lumbering. He always got boils from the steady diet of pork and beans he lived on in the lumber camps and a few years ago his lungs had gone bad. His farm had to be sold for debt, and now he was a sweeper in a munitions factory in Montreal, a man with no status. Having lived all his life in a small place where he knew everyone, where his family might be poor but still counted as a family, he was now nothing. Every week he remarked that it was wonderful how much money they were making. But he was not happy about it. City prices ate it all up. They went to Mass every Sunday and put a tenth of all they earned on the plate, hoping God would bless them for it. Every week her father put a few coins in a box in the kitchen and counted up what they had saved. Then he would shake his head. At this rate he would have to live to be a hundred before they would have enough to buy land again. The knowledge was slowly crushing him.

Emilie found work in a small restaurant at the east end of Sainte Catherine Street, and it was there she happened to meet Marius. An order had been given to her in English. She understood nothing of what was said, and Marius had interpreted for her when he saw her confusion. When the man who had ordered in English had gone, Marius made a date to meet her when she was finished working that evening.

At first she had been careful and suspicious of him, but he had not even tried to kiss her. After that she had trusted him. She treasured her virginity with all the tenacity of a poor girl who knows it is her only asset and never forgets that it can be lost only once. Saying little when they were together, listening closely and trying to understand him, she had gradually learned to know him better than he dreamed. It was only when he talked about his father that he frightened her. It seemed a terrible thing for a man to hate his own parents, no matter what they were. Marius said his father was a member of parliament, but Emilie's ignorance of such matters kept her from seeing what difference that could make.

He was still talking about himself when they reached the building where she lived. It was a drab, three-story structure with a row of one-room shops on the ground floor. The windows at the back overlooked an ash-covered square lined with billboards. Lord Kitchener beckoned from one of them, saying in English: I WANT YOU. Beside him a man with a sad expression asked: AVEZ-VOUS AUSSI DE LA PEAU MORTE?

In the shadow of the dark doorway Marius was gesturing with impatience. '. . . and then they boast about how cheap we work for them.'

Emilie was sure he was wrong, and she wanted to shield him from his own mistakes, but she had no words to explain what she meant. 'But the factories give P'pa a job, don't they?' she tried. 'We'd have starved for sure. P'pa says his foreman is French, too, and . . .'

'Sure the foreman is French,' Marius interrupted. 'They use some of us for cheap labour and then they use some more of us for cushions to fall back on.'

'Well, I don't know. The English boss spoke to P'pa once last week. He said he was all right.'

'And how much did that cost him? He didn't ask where your father lives, did he? And your father doesn't ask where the boss lives, either.'

'I don't know what you're so excited about. We live all right. And pretty soon we'll live better. Maybe we'll buy another farm.'

Emilie's stupidity hurt Marius, but it also proved where his own future lay. There were so many of his people who couldn't understand what was obvious to him. Plenty of English and French-Canadians worked together in stores and in factories and got on with each other. He didn't like it; he would teach his people to hate the English the way he hated them. The fact that he knew no English-Canadians well except his stepmother didn't enter his thoughts.

Emilie was standing silently beside him in the dark doorway, so he drew her close and kissed her. She turned her

53

lips to his, and he passed his hands quickly down the curve of her hips, then around her waist as he strained her close. After a moment she put her arms about his neck. He felt her short, peasant's body press his own firmly. She was very strong. Suddenly he grew hungry for her, and feeling the surge pass through him he kissed her desperately, then abruptly let her go.

'Good-night, Emilie,' he said. 'I'll see you in a day or so.'

He turned and without looking back he went along the way he had come. Alone in the dingy street, a sense of relief and exhilaration came over him. He looked up at the sky. The moon was entering its last quarter, surging through a wrack of cirrus cloud high above the dark roofs. Even in the city the spring air was sweet. He found himself remembering Saint-Marc as it looked from the ridge behind the parish on such a night as this.

He stopped at the corner to wait for a tram. And then he saw the soldier who had been at the meeting. The man had followed him, and now he was waiting. Marius looked the other way, but the fellow came and stood close beside him. He took a quick glance up and down the street, but there was no one in sight within a couple of blocks. An arc lamp overhead made a bluish splash of light on the pavement, and across the street another lamp brought out the stripes on a barber's pole.

The soldier edged in against him. 'Listen, you goddam peasoup, you're too fast with your mouth. Sure, I followed you. Somebody's got to shut that trap of yours.'

Marius was trembling. He had no defense against physical violence. 'I don't know what you mean,' he said in English.

'No? Well, I'll tell you.' The soldier came closer, taking his time. The smell of stale whiskey was on his breath. 'I been over in France. See? There's a war on there. And a lot of French guys from right here was in my outfit. They're doing a job. And back home bastards like you kick them in the ass. Yellow sons of bitches like you stay here and shoot their mouths off.'

Marius turned and looked at the soldier's face. Everything he most hated about the English was in it. He saw hardness and coldness, a supreme ability to outrage others, a way

54

of forcing themselves on more sensitive people, but never letting themselves be touched in the process.

'Why don't you run?' the soldier said. 'You're so yellow you look green.'

Once Marius had seen a lumberjack just out of the woods handle a man in Saint-Marc who was drunk on *whiskey blanc*. He drove out with his foot now the way the lumberjack had done and caught the soldier on the shin. The man hopped back, lifting his leg to ease the pain. Before he could shout Marius hit him and the soldier went down. Marius fell on him, his knees taking the man in the face. He heard the soldier's front teeth crack and his skull snap on the sidewalk. He got up and stared at the limp body. A little splutter of blood started out of the soldier's mouth. Marius began to tremble violently, afraid he had killed the man. He looked quickly up and down the street, saw a figure moving toward them about two blocks away, then bent and placed his ear against the soldier's chest. The man stirred and tried to grip his neck with his arm, but Marius broke loose and got to his feet again.

He stood panting, his black hair over his eyes and his felt hat on the pavement a few yards away where it had fallen. The soldier was stirring like a knocked-out boxer trying to grope his way to his feet. Slowly he sat up, his mouth open and red with blood, bracing himself with his hands.

Marius watched him for a moment, then he picked up his hat and walked quickly away. The sight of the man's bleeding mouth, the sound of the cracking teeth, blazed and roared in his mind until he could see and hear nothing else. He looked back at the first intersection. The soldier was on his feet, swaying unsteadily, and a policeman was asking him questions.

Marius turned quickly to his left and began to run. He kept on running for three blocks, his hat in his hand, the echo of his pounding feet banging back at him from the housefronts. Suddenly he darted into an alley and then he stopped, doubled over and gasping until the wind returned to his lungs and he was able to walk again. He put on his hat, adjusted his coat, turned up his collar and pulled his hat down over his eyes. Under his coat his shirt was wet against his back. He put his hands in his pockets and began to walk west until he reached Saint-Denis Street. Here under the brighter lights he was no longer alone. A few drunks and loafers and late workers were still around, and a prostitute accosted him as he passed her. He boarded a tram and took a seat in the middle, alone in the long car with the wicker seats yellow as straw in the light.

He felt wonderful. He felt as if he had broken all the chains that had held him all his life. His chest swelled under his coat as he filled it with more and more air, and a smile appeared on his mouth, cutting deep wrinkles on either side of it as his thoughts rolled.

After tonight they would certainly try to get him. They might even print in the English papers that he was a wanted man. But no one would get him. Now or any other time. He would go to his lodgings and pack his bag and disappear. Montreal was a great city and there were many places to hide. It would have been better if he had found the money two weeks ago in Saint-Marc. But he would still be all right. There were plenty of people ready to help him, to help anyone who was determined to keep out of the army in order to defy the English and assert his rights as a French-Canadian. And he would be doing even more than that. He was saving himself før his career, a career that he knew now would be a crusade.

7

Paul had thought the winter would never end, but at last it was over and now the season of break-up called spring in Quebec was with them. Farmers were sitting in their kitchens under their holy pictures waiting anxiously for the land to dry out. Geese were flying north, and wind rushed fiercely over everything. Sometimes it woke him up in the middle of the night as it rattled the bare branches of the old maple tree against his window.

Spring was a bad time of the year. It was when they had chosen to crucify Christ. All the symbols of Holy Week were still fresh in his mind, the nails and the hammer, the ladder and the sponge, the images of the saints veiled in the church, the darkness that had covered the earth. He tried to remember autumn. That was the time he liked best. In the autumn pools of water turned sections of the sky upside down and held them fast in a mirror, while crimson maple leaves circled silently down from trees and struck the water and floated there, sending a quick shimmer of scarlet across the dust of silver bubbles thick on the bottom. Twice last autumn, on silent nights with a full moon, he had heard miles away the cough of a rutting moose.

But it wasn't autumn now. It was spring. Paul walked slowly along the road this Saturday morning on his way to get the mail. As he passed each field he looked at it carefully and saw how the land was emerging out of the snow like a living thing. The lower fields were brown and wet, and crows pecked and brooded in the old furrows. And above the wet flat land the whole sky was in turbulent motion. A north wind rushed through watery sunshine and made the shredded, driving clouds look like torn laundry blowing loose across the sky.

On the river side of the road he passed an old disused stone mill. It had a cone-shaped wooden roof and a wheel that no longer turned. Swallows built their nests in it, and on summer evenings they swooped in and out of the crevices. Once it had belonged to his family, long before he was born, and all the farmers of the neighbourhood had been compelled to grind their grain in it. Eighty years ago, up on the ridge behind the parish, his great-grandfather had marshalled his company of men among the maples. The English in their red coats had formed up in the village before the old church and tried to capture the ridge. Then his great-grandfather had stood up and waved his hat and ordered his men to fire. One by one the advancing English soldiers had begun to drop until the whole line had been forced to retire. There was a book in his father's library telling all about the battle.

Now there were magazines in the library telling about the present war, and there was Captain Yardley whose leg had been blown off at sea only three years ago. He was part of this war. In Saint-Marc there were no marching men, no recruiting posters, no bands. But the war was there just the same, or at least just over the horizon. Paul's father subscribed for lots of illustrated papers in both English and French, and Paul was allowed to read them and look at the pictures. He knew what Trafalgar Square and the Arc de Triomphe were like, but he was never sure how far they were from each other. Because of these papers France and England seemed much more important than his own country. Because of them, too, his mind was filled with war-images night and day: the *Invincible* blowing up at Jutland, and after the explosion only six sailors surviving on a single raft, cheering the other ships as they stormed past; the French army huddled behind barbed wire at Verdun under the rain; Canadians bayoneting Germans in bright moonlight in Sanctuary Wood.

Paul was still thinking about it when he reached Polycarpe Drouin's store. For some time the post-office had been here, too, and now it had the added interest of a single gasoline pump before the door. Cars had become fairly numerous on the road, and a number of English-speaking men stopped each day for gasoline or tobacco. Lately Drouin had put up signs which he felt would help the public to understand better what he sold. In raised white letters on one window were the words *Épiceries* and *Groceries*; on the other *Magasin Général* and *General Store*. Two letters of *Épiceries* had fallen off the week after Polycarpe put them up, and he had not yet got around to replacing them. The rest of the store-front looked like the backs of popular magazines. Every brand of tobacco and soft drink sold in the province was represented by coloured tin plates nailed on the wooden frame of the store window, each one designed in the hope of taking the eye away from all the others.

A year ago Drouin had introduced another decoration for the store-front, a small bracket over the door holding three faded flags. One was the Red Ensign of the British Mercantile Marine with a Canadian crest in the corner. Another was a square white cross on an azure field with a fleur-de-lis in each corner which had come to be accepted as the flag of Quebec. The third and middle one was the white and yellow ensign of the Pope.

Paul entered the store, and when his eyes had accustomed

themselves to the darkness inside, he saw Drouin doubled forward over the counter like a jack-knife, with his pointed chin on his hands. Frenette, the blacksmith, was sitting on the counter and Ovide Bissonette was chewing tobacco as he sat on a table piled with overalls, his feet dangling over the side. Without a word Drouin reached to a shelf behind his head for Mr. Tallard's mail. He passed over three letters and two bulky newspapers, and Paul put the letters in the pocket of his jacket and folded the papers under his arm. The other men recognized this regular morning event as a proof of Mr. Tallard's importance. None of them ever received mail unless an absent relative became sick or died.

'P'pa wants a pound of tobacco, too,' Paul said. 'You know the kind.'

Drouin took a red tin of Hudson's Bay Imperial Mixture from a confusion of other tobacco tins and pushed it across the counter. His thin face took on a look of shrewdness, drawing it even thinner His long hooked nose hung like a tap over his lips, and except when he smiled he looked like an undertaker. When he smiled his face broke into a maze of kindly wrinkles.

'That means your Pa must've got back from Ottawa last night,' he said.

'Yes.'

'I bet he must have a lot on his mind.'

Paul had nothing to say to this. Drouin shook his head again. 'Your Pa smokes too much. He wants to look out for the ulcers.'

Paul's eyes, dark brown and wide-set, were unusually earnest. 'What are they?'

'You get them from smoking too much. An uncle of mine, he smoked like a stove, all the time his pipe, and he got them. He died last year.' Drouin shook his head and leaned forward on his elbows again and became silent.

The other men in the store were also quiet. They knew each other too well to feel that talk was necessary. The principal news was the weather, but they had finished discussing that. Paul drifted away from the counter and tried to peer beyond some food advertisements in the window to see if Captain Yardley was coming. He had promised to meet him at the store this morning. There was no sign of the captain so he turned back. He always liked it here. He liked the smell of raw, useful merchandise mingled with the strong odour of tobacco burning in old pipes. He liked looking at the bags of feed and the farm tools and listening to the monosyllables as the men talked.

Frenette was built like a hogshead. He was wearing an old pair of overalls and heavy farm boots. He lurched away from the end of the counter and moved toward the boy. His huge hand, thick with bone and black with hair, tapped the papers under Paul's arm. A grin opened his wide face. 'What's the news today, Paul?'

He took the papers from under the boy's arm and spread them out on the counter. The English paper he pushed aside, but he followed the headlines of *La Presse* with his forefinger, pronouncing each word aloud. 'Bad, eh?' he said. 'You see this? The English, they put everyone in the army and still they lose the war.'

He handed the papers back to Paul and the boy folded them and replaced them under his arm. The door opened and two more men came in. One was a farmer from the upper end of the parish, the other a hired man from the farm beyond Yardley's. They were both lean, with earth-coloured faces and drooping moustaches and sun-squinted eyes. Nods were exchanged as they slumped into comfortable positions against the counter.

'The weather, she's a bastard for sure,' said one of them.

Drouin took two plugs of Master Mason and tossed them onto the counter. Each of the newcomers extracted a ten-cent coin from a pocket, dropped it on the counter, picked up a plug, bit off a chew and slipped the plug into another pocket. Their actions were automatic and almost in unison.

'Three pounds of sugar,' the farmer said.

Drouin set a pan on the scale and began scooping out sugar from a large white bag behind the counter while the farmer kept his eyes carefully on the scale, making sure that Drouin's finger did not lie on it while he calculated the weight. The sugar was poured into a paper bag and passed over the counter. The farmer paid for it and let it lie there.

'You hear the news from Sainte-Justine?' the hired man said.

Drouin shook his head slowly and Frenette lifted his chin to show he was listening. Bissonette gave no sign of interest.

'Some soldiers came in there last night. They walked around the town, trying to get people talking. Then they started throwing some liquor around. Then, round about midnight it was, they went up to Etienne Laflamme's place and took Napoléon – that's Etienne's oldest boy – right out of his bed.'

'The hell they did!' Frenette said.

'Yeh,' the hired man went on, 'and Etienne's old woman screeching like a wildcat and the soldiers, the bastards, talking about a warrant. They took Napoléon right out in his drawers.'

'Tabernacle!' shouted Frenette, waving his arms about.

'The old woman couldn't get over that. The kid dragged out in his drawers. She had Napoléon's other pair in the wàsh and he was dragged out in his old ones. That's what bothered her.'

Frenette banged his fist down on the counter and began to shout. In his lumber-camp days he had been a dangerous man on a Saturday night. He still liked to fight after he had a few *whiskey blanc* if he could find anyone to stand up to him. 'Just let the English come here!' he kept saying. 'Let them see what happens if they try to get me!'

'Well,' the farmer said, 'there's nothing Etienne can do now. They got Napoléon in uniform already, sure enough.'

'All you bastards,' Frenette said, 'you sit around here saying there's nothing to do now. We'll find something to do!'

Drouin leaned a little further over the counter. 'Mr. Tallard can do something, maybe?'

He looked around for Paul and when he found him he stopped. The boy had moved quietly away from the counter when the two strange men came in. In the middle of the floor was a model Percheron stallion. It stood there lifesize with a whole set of harness on its back. Drouin had got it cheap at a fire sale in Sainte-Justine. He was very proud of it and thought it more handsome than a statue in the church. Paul began to finger the harness while his ears listened. It was not the first time men in the store had begun to talk about his father and then stopped abruptly when they remembered he was there.

Frenette said, 'Listen, Paul – what about your brother? Is this true what I hear, that Marius goes into the army soon?'

Drouin coughed but Frenette paid no attention. Paul came shyly out from behind the horse. 'Marius is in college,' he said.

'Sure, sure,' Frenette said. 'But just the same . . .'

'Heh,' Drouin said. 'You think Mr. Tallard will stand for it if they put the conscription onto his own son?' He spread his hands as though he were measuring cloth. 'You can push Mr. Tallard just so far.' He showed how far with his hands. 'Then you better watch out!'

Suddenly Ovide Bissonette, on the overalls table, woke up. 'What's that you say?' he squeaked in a high, cracked voice. 'What about Mr. Tallard?'

Paul looked at him in fascination. Everyone knew that Ovide was crazy. Years ago he had been a trapper in the far north and the men said the loneliness had touched his head. Now he did nothing but loaf around the store, and on Monday mornings he was supposed to sweep the burnt matches off the steps of the church. Sometimes he took out his beads in the store to tell them, no matter what was going on, but generally he slept on the overalls table with his eyes wide open. Now he pointed a scrawny hand at the group of men in front of the counter. 'Mr. Tallard, he goes to hell maybe. But his wife, she goes for sure.'

'Shut up,' Drouin said. He grinned at Paul and revolved a finger at his temple. 'You don't mind him, Paul. He don't know what he says.'

But Paul did mind just the same. The priest had told him all about hell and how the fire was real except that it replenished the flesh the instant it burned it off so the burning went on forever. He wished Captain Yardley would come. Again he retreated behind the horse, hoping the men would forget about him. He occupied himself with an examination of the farm tools racked on that side of the store. There were rakes, axes, hatchets, hoes, spades, scythes, and even trowels. He picked up an adze. Captain Yardley was wonderful with an adze. He had watched him use one to shape the keel of the ship he had made.

In front of the counter the men were still talking. 'The war ought to stop,' one said.

'Sure.'

'Look at Mrs. Pitre of the back concession.'

'What about her?'

'Before the war she had seven children and they all lived. Since the war she's had three and they all died. The war ought to stop.'

'The trouble with the English is they got no moderation,' Drouin said. 'Now me, I'm behind the war all right, only not too much.'

Paul went to the window and looked out again. This time he saw Captain Yardley coming down the road, moving with his bobbing limp. He went to the door and waited for him. When John Yardley entered the store with the boy at his side he greeted the group of men amiably and asked for his mail. Drouin handed over a letter and a newspaper and said politely, 'The news looks not so good today, eh, Captain?'

Yardley passed his eyes over the headlines of the *Gazette* and his lips tightened as he read.

'Looks like we lose the war, eh, Captain?' Frenette said.

Yardley shook his head. 'That's one thing you're wrong about.'

'A lot of other people got different ideas maybe.'

Yardley looked at the blacksmith and then he grinned. He began to talk fast in his bad French. 'Now you listen, Alcide. You fellas around here are just trying to get me sore, talking thet way. You know goddam well we don't lost this war, and you know you don't want to lose it, either.'

Frenette grinned. From any other Englishman he would not have taken Yardley's words. But he knew the captain well by now and liked him and that made the difference. Yardley simply took it for granted that he was liked.

'I never said I wanted to lose the war, Captain. No. But you tell me what difference it makes if we do.'

'I'll tell you,' the farmer said. He did not know Yardley well and regarded him as a complete foreigner. 'You listen and I'll tell you.'

'All right,' Yardley said. 'Go ahead.'

'Right now in the winters,' the farmer said, choosing his words slowly, 'me and the kid, we go north to saw wood for the English lumber company. Him on one end of the cross-cut saw and me on the other, we saw wood for the English.'

'You mean, you saw it for a dollar-fifty a day,' Drouin said.

The farmer's sharp, chewing voice went right on, paying no attention to the interruption. 'Now suppose we win the war. What happens? Me and the kid, we go on sawing the wood, same as now.' He paused and then went on. 'But suppose we lose it? Maybe I keep on sawing, same as before. But goddam it, this time I got an Englishman on the other end of that saw, for sure.'

Yardley grinned and the other men guffawed. 'I don't blame you fellas for how you feel,' the captain said. 'Guess I'd feel the same way if I was you. Only I'm not, so I don't.'

He started for the door and Paul followed him outside, the store silent behind them. Yardley looked at the clouds blowing through the sky and smelled the earth and wished it were not earth he was smelling but salt water. He hungered for a smell of the sea. One thing he had never grown accustomed to in Quebec was the way the weather jumped about. Down in Nova Scotia you could tell a change of weather hours ahead. All you had to do was look at a pennant on a masthead or the drift of chimney smoke and gauge the wind, and then you knew. Up here even a barometer fooled you.

He said to Paul, 'Two months more and we'll all go fishing. You and me and Daphne and Heather. My grand-daughters. They're coming out to visit me.'

Paul's dark, grave face did not alter expression. 'P'pa says no.'

'He forgets how old you are. When I was your age I was bait-boy.'

'What's that?'

'We used to go out in big yellow dories, myself and some men in sweaters and oilskins and sou'westers, and we'd go after the cod off the ledges. I'd keep the lines baited while the men fished. Clams, I used. Why sure – you're old enough to row a boat all by yourself.'

Paul felt better. Anything was all right if the captain said so.

They had left the houses of the village behind and the wind was so strong Paul's cap nearly blew off. 'Captain Yardley . . .' he began, trying to hold the cap with one hand and his father's papers with the other. When he said nothing more the man looked down and saw that the boy was worried about something. He seemed to be sealing himself away into his worry, wanting to be coaxed, with a child's caution wanting to make sure he was safe before he said anything about his troubles.

'Go ahead, Paul. You know you can talk to me about anything's on your mind.'

They walked on in silence for awhile, and then Paul said, 'They were saying something in the store about Marius. About Papa and Marius.'

'Well. – I guess thet's nothing new.'

'Will Marius have to be a soldier?'

'Lots of men are, these days. It's not so bad, being a soldier.'

He quickened his pace, feeling something of the boy's nameless apprehension. There had been a small but noticeable rise in feeling against Athanase in the village lately. It would come into the open if Marius were conscripted. Even Yardley could see that Athanase's stand on the war was not understood here at all. If Marius were conscripted and his father did nothing to keep him out of the army, it would appear to the parish that Athanase was deserting his own family, and that was an unforgivable sin. Yardley preferred not to talk to Paul about Marius. He had met the elder Tallard son only once, but it was long enough to realize that he was one of the few people he knew who would not let himself be liked. Marius seemed to Yardley to be the mathematical product of the conflict within the country and also within his own family.

'Gosh, but Marius hates the English!' Paul said. 'That's why he hates Mother.'

'Go easy there, Paul. He don't hate your mother.'

'Oh, yes, he does. I know. I think he hates P'pa, too, only he's afraid of P'pa. Captain Yardley?'

65

'Yes?'

'Will Marius kill an Englishman if they try to put him in the army?'

'He wouldn't know how.'

'Is it hard to kill someone?'

'Well, you got to know how to go about it.'

'Did you ever kill anyone, Captain Yardley?'

'Never did. But thet nigger I shipped with out east – I saw him kill a fella once.'

Paul stopped in the middle of the road. 'How?'

Yardley felt better with the talk off the Tallard family. 'Well, this nigger had the biggest moustache I ever saw. It was so long thet when he went to sleep he used to pass the ends of it behind his ears and make them fast with a reef knot, end to end behind his head. Otherwise it was always ketching into things when he was sleeping in his hammock. Well, one night – '

Paul was suspicious. 'A negro with a moustache?'

'Thet's what I'm telling you.'

The boy's laughter bubbled. 'But negroes don't have moustaches, Captain Yardley. Not black negroes. I read that in a book. Was this a black negro?'

'Black? Say, thet fella down in the hold on a dark night was so black it's a fact not even the ship's cat could see him. Well, anyhow, one time a dirty little dago lad we had on board, he took out his knife and slit the nigger's moustache off on one end, and when the nigger woke up to stand his watch, feeling around to untie the knot, he found he had only half a moustache and he let out a yell. Man, did thet black man know how to holler! Seven years growing, thet hair was.' Yardley looked down at the boy, grinning. 'Well, when he saw this dago lad laughing at him, before anyone could stop him, he jumped the dago, and the skipper heard his neck crack clear above the hatches.'

Paul laughed because the story had no sense of disaster the way Captain Yardley told it. He started to test its veracity by asking more questions, and then he saw Father Beaubien coming down the road toward them. His black soutane was flapping in the wind and the pendant cross swayed across his lean stomach. As they passed, Yardley greeted him and Father Beaubien nodded briefly, holding back his smile.

When they were well out of earshot, Paul said, 'Last week in the store I heard somebody say that Father Beaubien doesn't like P'pa.'

Yardley laughed to hide a recurrent uneasiness. 'They meant it was me he don't like.'

'They said P'pa.'

'They meant me.'

'But why?' Paul was very serious. 'Everyone likes you.'

'Well, I guess Father Beaubien don't think he can afford to approve of me. You see, Paul, I'm a Presbyterian. It's a hard thing to get used to, being disapproved of for being a Presbyterian.'

'Would I like it, being a Presbyterian?'

'Well,' Yardley said, 'thet's hardly a thing people like. It's something a man hasn't got any choice of.'

They were now well out on the river road and the wind from the north rushed past them in raw gusts. The river was ruffled by waves blowing across the current.

'Captain Yardley,' Paul said, 'do you like Montreal?'

'No. I can't say I do. Why?'

'Mama does. She wants to go back to live there.'

Yardley made no reply.

'When I'm a man I'm going to see all the cities,' Paul said. 'I'm going to sea, like you did. I'm going to see the places where Ulysses was.'

Older people always make a mistake with children that age, Yardley thought. They consider them babies. Paul remembered everything he read or saw in books, and everything he heard. Yardley had decided that at Paul's age a human being generally knew at least nine-tenths of all he would ever know.

Paul was happy now as they walked along, thinking about the *Odyssey*. He wanted to see the place where the salt water was azure blue the way pictures showed it, and the men had straight noses and the women wore flowing robes. He thought of Ulysses tied to the mast, and the sailors with wax in their ears rowing him past the island where beautiful women, white-skinned and black-haired like his mother, sang over

67

a heap of bones. That was a very sensible thing Ulysses had done with the wax. And on the other side of that sea there was the Holy Land where Christ was born. Paul thought it must be very gloomy there. He looked up out of his thoughts and his lips moved in a smile. He was happy at that moment, without knowing or thinking why.

When they reached Yardley's gate, the captain said, 'You'd better run along home with those papers. Your father will be sore enough to whale us, the way we've kept him waiting. Soon as the weather turns and it gets warm – you and me, we'll have a summerful of fun.'

'That will be wonderful!' Paul said. He touched his cap gravely and went on home.

Yardley stood and watched the boy go off down the road, growing smaller in the flatness against the outline of bare trees tossing wildly in the wind. A sense of poignancy, of the beauty of things which derive their loveliness from their fragility, broke over him in a wave, surprising him with its contradiction of his own basic optimism. Yes, everything would be truly wonderful, even growing old till you were like a sun-bleached hulk would be good if you could be always among people who knew no fear. Among people who never groped at their neighbours like blind men in a cave. In a world where thoughts of war never stabbed into your personal peace like a needle.

Though Yardley had never had an academic education, he had slowly learned how to read books and how to think. As a sailor, and then as a ship's master, he had known solitude in strange places. He was persuaded that all knowledge is like a painted curtain hung across the door of the mind to conceal from it a mystery so darkly suggestive that no one can face it alone for long. Of ultimate solitude he had no fear, for he never let himself think about it. But he knew that if he once started, fear would be there.

Once in the tropics he had moored his ship in the lee of a promontory hundreds of miles from any charted habitation. Through a whole afternoon he had waited while some of the crew went ashore under the second mate to look for water. Leaning over the taffrail he had watched the fish gliding through ten fathoms of sunlit water below. Sharks and barracuda moved in their three-dimensional element, self-centred, beautiful, dangerous and completely aimless, coming out from a water-filled cavern hidden beneath the promontory and slipping under the ship's keel, fanning themselves for seconds under the rudder, then circling back into the cavern again. A moment he saw them in the golden water and then they were gone, and the water was as if they had never been there. The first mate had come to him for an order and broken his contemplation, but the memory of the hour had never left him. Self-centred, beautiful, dangerous and aimless: that was how they had been, and he could never forget it.

Here in Saint-Marc, where he had planted himself of his own volition, he had been lonely. He had come to love young Paul as though the boy were his own son. And he knew they would all fight over him yet. The obscure conflict within the Tallard family would certainly centre on this youngest member. Beyond that, the constant tug of war between the races and creeds in the country itself would hardly miss him, for people seemed so constructed that they were unable to use ideas as instruments to discover truth, but waved them instead like flags.

As Yardley limped up the path to his house his mind saw a vision of all the Tallards pulling Paul; Marius on one arm and his mother on the other, Athanase at the head, and the priest with his powerful hands on both feet. He smiled to himself, deciding that the image was nonsense. A windy day was always a bad time to start figuring things out, especially if a man had been too much alone.

He closed the door on the day and threw some logs on the fire. Then he went into his kitchen to heat a bowl of soup and cut a slice of bread for his lunch.

8

The two parlour cars on the early afternoon train from Ottawa to Montreal were filled with politicians and lobbyists on their way home for the weekend, and Athanase Tallard was among them. On his knees were two newspapers, one French, the other English. He had read each of them through

69

once. For awhile he sat quietly, occasionally looking out the windows, then he opened the French paper, turned to the editorial page and re-read what the editor had to say about the speech he had made in the House the previous afternoon.

'The career of M. Athanase Tallard is excellent proof that no man can run with the hare and hunt with the hounds,' it said. 'At least not in the province of Quebec. In the first half of his latest speech he tells us that the rest of the country does not understand Quebec. In the last half he talks about conscription like a Toronto jingo. As spokesman for French-Canada, he has completely discredited himself. Your protestations, M. Tallard, deceive no one but yourself. You can be with us, or you can be against us. You cannot stand in the middle, supporting the English Imperialists with one hand and trying to appease us with the other.'

Athanase put the paper down. The editorial hurt him; it also made him exceedingly angry. He picked up the English Toronto paper. In its editorial columns he read: 'This last speech of Mr. Tallard, who in the past has given the impression of being an enlightened French-Canadian, is a pitiful example of the kind of hedging which the eternal Quebec pressure forces even on its better members of parliament. Mr. Tallard's words of yesterday cannot fail to give comfort to those dissident elements . . .'

Athanase threw both papers on the floor. What place did reason or intelligence have in politics? The newspapers were like kids picking sides for a fight. The crisis of the war was only making them worse, not better.

He looked down the row of red plush chairs and saw nothing but the bald heads of politicians and business men. There was a single man in uniform in the car, a major with a desk job in the military district in Montreal, but in spite of his polished boots and buttons the man was no soldier. He was merely a contractor in uniform, looking perfectly at home as he talked to a politician in the next chair.

Athanase could hear snatches of their conversation.

'The trouble is, the war hasn't been sold to Quebec.'

'Can you sell a war?'

'You can sell anything.'

Athanase noted that the major's shoulders had a permanent stoop. Not even three years in the army had cured him of the habit of leaning forward in order to be confidential in all his conversations.

'The point about Quebec is,' the major went on, 'you need a man really sympathetic to the French-Canadians. But what does the government do? They send Toronto Orangemen to us in Montreal to help with recruiting. An Orangeman couldn't even sell a bonus in Quebec. Now what I'd like to see . . .'

What you'd like, Athanase thought, is a job with more rank and more money in it. He closed his eyes and tried to sleep. To rest his mind he thought about Saint-Marc. It was now the first week in May and the land should be nearly dry. Blanchard would probably be ready to start planting by Monday. Sitting there with his head resting on the antimacassar of the chair, Athanase looked old and very dignified. His face was like a tired eagle's. Against his walnut-coloured cheeks the spray of his moustache was blue-white.

Groping for sleep, all he found was a welter of thoughts swirling out of the dark of his mind. He tried to keep them back but it was useless. Ultimately all the various tides of a man's nature rose up together, he thought, and unless he managed to resolve them, they broke him apart. Well, at least one thing was clear: his political life was a failure. His stand on the war had done no one any good. It had merely destroyed all the old pleasure of his days and the work that filled them.

He remembered how he had once been able to enjoy himself easily, how he used to like food and occasionally to drink to excess in a highly witty and civilized way. Sometimes he and Kathleen had gone to horse-races and made special trips into town to see a play. And before Kathleen there had always been hockey. Once he had owned a share in one of the professional clubs, and for three seasons he had watched every game from the players' bench, knowing every man in the league to call by his first name.

Those had been good days before everything got complicated by the war. He liked the French style of hockey, a team with small, stick-handling forwards and defensemen

71

built like beer barrels. Every year a few new boys would come into the league from the smaller towns, and before the season began he and the other owners, with the manager and trainer, would sit in fur coats in the empty rink, windows open to let the water freeze, and size up the new boys. All those youngsters had retired as veterans long ago. He remembered the big times in the dressing room on the nights when the season ended. The brewery sent over a barrel of beer and they broached it together, the beer tasting exactly right in the fuggy room with the smell of sweat and liniment, and the boys horsing around, and then everyone relaxed on the benches and beginning to boast. It had seemed a good world when hockey was important in it.

'Hullo, Tallard!'

He opened his eyes and saw the heavy face of Huntly McQueen looking down at him. He took off his pince-nez and pressed his fingers into his eyes, gently stroking them open, then replaced the glasses on the bridge of his nose and sat up. McQueen dropped into the vacant chair next his own and sat with his knees apart, his jowls sunk in his high stiff collar.

'Well, how's everything in Saint-Marc these days? How's Captain Yardley getting along?'

'Quite well, I should think,' Athanase said.

McQueen looked out the window and studied the farms of the lower Ottawa Valley through which they were running. The sun was bright on the river and the Gatineau Hills climbed to their left. Then after a moment he turned from the window and said with a chilly smile, 'Your son made quite a speech the other night.'

Athanase stared at him. 'What speech?'

'Didn't you know? I assumed you had seen the press reports. About a fortnight ago, or maybe less. In Montreal.'

Athanase shook his head. 'I hadn't heard about it. At the university? I believe he's a member of the debating society.'

McQueen made a deprecating motion with his chubby hand. 'No. It was one of those anti-conscription rallies Marchand's been holding. As a matter of fact, he mentioned me – your son, I mean.'

'I knew nothing about it. Should I apologize for him?'

'No. . . . No. One has to expect that sort of thing. Though I must admit I have an aversion to seeing my name in the papers.'

Athanase set his teeth as he felt the blood-beat quicken in his forehead. Was it his fault that he had never been able to do anything for Marius except pay for his education? What was this thing that rose between a father and his son? Kathleen? Partly, but it was more than that.

'The boy's excitable,' he said. 'It's a bad time for boys of his age, days like these.'

'Of course. Of course.' McQueen's voice purred with sympathy. 'By the way, you knew he'd disappeared after the speech?'

An expression of suffering appeared on Athanase's face. 'No,' he said quietly. 'I hadn't heard. I'm sorry. I suppose he's trying to avoid conscription. I'd hoped he wouldn't do a thing like that.'

'This conscription policy of the government is a mistake anyway,' McQueen said. 'It's swimming against the current. That's always a mistake.'

Athanase made a movement with one hand and his features suddenly came together again in a dominant pattern. 'It's the idea of compulsion that's wrong. You English – why can't you have sense to see that Quebec will always resist the least suggestion of compulsion?'

McQueen raised his eyebrows. 'But, Tallard, you yourself – "

'I know what you're going to say. That I supported the bill. So I did. I knew the English provinces would break us if they could. If Quebec kicked back too hard she would only smash herself. I tried to cushion the shock, and of course it was useless. My own people didn't understand. Besides – there's France.'

Since the start of the war, a fear that France might be destroyed had haunted Athanase. Since the days when he had been a student in Paris he had retained a feeling that France stood behind him: French culture, French art, everything that made *la grande nation*. With France behind him he had been able to feel superior to any Englishman or American he met. When the war made England and France allies, he had hoped the alliance might be extended into Canada sufficiently to wipe out permanently the bad old memories between the two races. Something of the sort might have happened if the government had shown any sense of the situation. But the English provinces had preferred compulsion.

'Well,' McQueen said, aware of his thoughts, 'no war ever brings people together permanently. It only seems to do it for a time. Organization – that's the magic we want.' He waited to see if Athanase would take up his point, then went on. 'I've not forgotten that project we talked about in Saint-Marc last fall, Tallard.'

'Project?'

'The waterfall – a factory in Saint-Marc.'

'Oh, yes. That.'

'It's still a sound idea. I've made some investigations. Of course we mustn't be hasty, but – ' He leaned forward and his chubby hand tapped Athanase's knee. 'Listen, Tallard. I'm interested in more than money, you know. Millionaires – railway barons – I respect their ability, but they don't interest me. I want to see this country of ours properly developed. No one with sense should ever try to swim against the current. You see that, don't you? And the current is unmistakable. Wouldn't it be a lot better for your province to have its industry shared by French people than to have us run the whole thing? Believe me . . .'

His voice assumed an evangelical tone as he expounded his subject, and Athanase listened quietly. The train slowed before a station, echoes banged back from a row of cars standing on the next track. Athanase gestured in the direction of the window. The train beside them was crowded with troops. They were packed into old cars, the soldiers sitting three to a seat and standing in the aisles. They were sweating and their collars were open. So they would have to travel for another thirty hours down to Halifax. After that they would be crowded into the hold of a ship like fish in a can.

'An instructive picture of a country at war. No?' Athanase said. 'It's revolting.' He gestured toward the politicians and lobbyists in the comparative comfort around them. 'We ought to be ashamed of ourselves.'

'You take things too seriously,' McQueen said.

'Maybe. But if those men' – he nodded toward the troop train – 'if they also take things seriously . . . what happens then? Eh?'

McQueen's mouth turned up at the corners. 'Their seriousness would not last long. Men like those can be made to forget very easily.'

'Men like those are winning the war for us.'

'Of course. They always do.'

Their train started slowly, surged ahead with a jerk, then pulsed smoothly on its way. 'Now about that factory in Saint-Marc,' McQueen said.

It was half an hour before Athanase found himself alone again. He watched McQueen's back as he lurched off to his own car. The man had disturbed him again, excited him. He had wanted to rest and now his mind was filled with a flood of new ideas. If his political career was ruined, what else should he do? What else could he do? The war had made him too restless to be satisfied with doing nothing. Yet he had done very little in the fifty-eight years before the war.

Sometimes the situation in which he found himself gripped him with the force of a nightmare. He was a failure, there could be no doubt of that. Always he had dreamed of pressing his mark on Quebec, his own special mark, but the substance of his province was too hard. In reality he had never even tried; always it had been easier to release himself into some kind of private adventure, or let his imagination take the place of action. He closed his eyes and the ghosts rose. His vague ghosts were missed opportunities; the more tangible ones were women.

The memories of the women he had known he handled like a collector caressing old glass. In these day-dreams he always pictured himself as a young man, but possessing the knowledge and experience he had acquired by many years of a varied life. Women had always been necessary to him, and his imagination had never been complete without the colour they gave it. A faint smile moved over his dark face and vanished again as his thoughts moved, as they always did in these dreams, to his first wife.

It was a bitter piece of irony that in marrying Marie-Adèle he had chosen the one woman he then knew who could feel no sexual attraction for him whatever. Of course he had not been able to know it in time. French-Canada had always maintained a strict society, and marriage was the absolute basis of it. Marie-Adèle's delicacy and haunting innocence had fascinated the poetry in his nature. He had hoped to play Pygmalion in making her a woman of the world. She had been very beautiful. With a figure always that of a young girl, she had been fragile and tiny, with veins distinctly visible under the skin of her hands and inner arms.

Even before the birth of Marius she had estranged herself from him, and after Marius was born she acquired a peculiar absorption in prayers and visions. Gradually her religion had become her whole life. Even now, nine years after her death, her piety was remembered in Saint-Marc. She had gone to Mass every morning, and in the afternoons she could often be seen in church on her knees before the Virgin, with her hands clasped and her head thrown back in an ecstasy of adoration.

At first her revulsion from him had been an agony to Athanase. He had convinced himself that he was a gentle husband, and he had certainly respected her innocence. But as time passed he gradually admitted that there was nothing to be done. His stubbornness yielded to a spiritual stubbornness in her greater than his own. Life between them could be tolerable so long as it never again became intimate. Divorce was out of the question; his own form of loyalty to her would never have considered it anyway. But his nature remained imperious, and some years after Marius was born he discovered that he was still attractive to women, and that he needed them more than ever. For a time his life degenerated into a search for some woman who might give him what Marie-Adèle refused. He had found many and he remembered charming moments with them, but on the whole he bitterly regretted this period of his life as a time of waste. He found he could be neither one thing nor the other: a celibate nor a cynical boulevardier. He thought too much, and whenever he liked a woman he had known, he wanted to be loyal to her as well.

He often wondered how much Marius knew. The boy worshipped his mother's memory. Athanase sighed. There was a mystery too deeply rooted in his relations with Marius for him to comprehend its full meaning. He had loved the boy. He still did, but apparently love was inadequate where there was no understanding.

The fields, beautiful in the afternoon sun, slipped past the train. They were running through French parishes now, and on both sides of the train there were familiar figures with bowed shoulders going about their work, an essential part of the general landscape. French-Canadians in the farmland were bound to the soil more truly than to any human being; with God and their families, it was their immortality. The land chained them and held them down, it turned their walk into a plodding and their hands into gnarled tools. It made them innocent of almost everything that existed beyond their own horizon. But it also made them loyal to their race as to a family unit, and this conception of themselves as a unique brotherhood of the land was part of the legend at the core of Quebec. Even when it exasperated him, Athanase was still proud of it.

Across the aisle two men were talking in English. Out of carelessness or indifference their voices were plainly audible.

'This whole province is hopeless,' one of them was saying as he swept the scene through the windows with his hand. 'They can't think for themselves and never could and never will. Now in Toronto we . . .'

Athanase's lined face remained motionless as he listened to them. The satisfaction in their voices as they talked about Quebec spread like grease.

'Labour's cheap here. That's one good thing. But my God, trying to do any business here gets you so tangled up with priests and notaries you don't know where you are! Now in Toronto . . .'

Athanase swung his chair around and turned his back on them. If there had been the slightest suggestion of kindliness, the least indication of a willingness to believe the best of Quebec in such men as this from Ontario, Canada's trenchant problem would cease to exist. He let his brows fall into a frown now and he deliberately breathed deeply as though in search of fresh air to fill his lungs. Little by little he managed to pull his thoughts back to himself.

McQueen had left him with a decision to make, and he hated decisions. He thought about the peculiar compelling power in Huntly McQueen, an attribute surprising in anyone of his rotund appearance. The man also had an enormous array of facts and figures at his disposal. As soon as possible he was going to send surveyors out to Saint-Marc to look over the ground, because he wanted the river measured for its power potential. If the reports were satisfactory, he wanted to form a company and set up a textile factory, with Athanase Tallard as junior partner. There was no doubt that McQueen was serious about the proposition and completely confident that a factory in Saint-Marc would be profitable, providing his initial impression about the waterfall was confirmed.

Athanase sighed. It was certainly a challenge. McQueen was approaching the hard shell of Quebec from another angle, and probably from a more practical angle than politics could ever offer. In every generation there arose French-Canadians who tried to change the eternal pattern of Quebec by political action, and nearly all of them had been broken, one by one. Indeed, they broke themselves, for while they fought for change with their minds, they opposed it with their emotions. If they went far enough, they were bound to find themselves siding with the English against their own people, and if nothing else broke them, that inevitably did. It was a very old pattern.

He fingered his white moustache. But changes were certain to come, nevertheless. They would either come from the outside, from the English and Americans as they were coming now, or they would come from French-Canadians like himself. Science was too much for any static force to resist. Science was bound to crack the shell of Quebec sooner or later, and it was certain in doing so to assail the legend.

The train roared past another station without stopping, slowed down only slightly for a bridge, crossed an island and another bridge and then pulled into the station at Sainte-Anne-de-Bellevue at the tip of the island of Montreal.

During the latter years of his reading he had become increasingly fascinated by the various facets of modern science. Automatically it made him critical of Catholicism. Now this scheme of McQueen's appealed to him strongly because it would put him definitely on the side of science, on the side of the future instead of the past. He felt the power of scientific achievement, and even if he knew little enough about its technical aspects, he resented subconsciously being excluded from a share in its development. Science was sucking prestige from the old age of faith and the soil. And prestige was a matter of power. One by one other nations had surrendered to science. In time, Quebec must surrender, too, learn to master science or be crushed by others who understood how to manipulate the apparatus she neglected. But how could Quebec surrender to the future and still remain herself? How could she merge into the American world of machinery without also becoming American? How could she become scientific and yet save her legend?

Athanase felt the dilemma deeply within his own soul. Quebec wanted prestige but not change. By some profound instinct, French-Canadians distrusted and disliked the American pattern of constant change. They knew it was ruthless, blind and uncontrollable. Trying to think the matter through calmly, Athanase admitted that his arguments for science were little more than arguments against a religion he had rejected. And he had rejected it chiefly because of his resentment against the power of the priests.

When he was calm, he could admit that his failure to do anything positive in his life had been caused by this deep split within himself. Always, before the reasoned act, an unseen hand reached out of the instinct-ridden past and tapped his shoulder. It was the same with all his people. When they resisted change, they were resisting the English who were always trying to force it upon them. And he loved them for their stubbornness.

The train surged onward, the wheels clicking over the joints, and outside spring was growing out of the earth like a miracle. New grass and grain was in the fields, new leaves were beginning to show on the trees. Only his brain was old, Athanase decided. It was as stale as an empty committee-room when the politicians have gone out for lunch. And yet through the empty staleness his thoughts refused to be still. Paul's future must soon be decided. There was no doubt about it, the boy's future depended to an enormous extent on the kind of school he attended. Unless he took a firm hand in steering Paul's career, the boy would become involved in all the same old dilemmas. The simplest way to avoid that happening would be to send him to an English school. And again the legend would be challenged.

The train passed more slowly through suburbs of Montreal, skirting the base of the English section of the city. And then without excitement it pulled into Windsor Station. Athanase got out quickly, carrying his own bag and speaking to no one. A few tracks away his train for Saint-Marc was almost ready to leave, and he climbed aboard and sat in a day coach. It was after sunset when he got off at Sainte-Justine.

Beside the station a black horse stood in the shafts of a carriage, munching oats in a feed-bag, and a slumped figure was bending down the springs of the front seat of the carriage where he slept. For twenty years François-Xavier Latulippe had driven the livery in Sainte-Justine, and in all that time he had not been known to speak audibly to a soul. No one could remember now whether it was by choice or necessity.

Athanase laid his bag on the floor of the carriage and climbed in after it. He clapped the driver on the shoulder. 'François-Xavier! God, it's good to be back in the fresh air again. Drive me home!'

Latulippe got out and removed the feed-bag from the nose of the horse, got in again and made a clicking sound with his tongue. The old horse broke into a slow trot and headed for Saint-Marc.

Athanase leaned back in the carriage and drank in the evening air. The sun had set and the shadows were fading from the fields. Out on the river an empty collier was churning downstream with its propeller breaking water.

Another ship was visible in the distance and Athanase saw that its decks were outlined by lights. It must be one of the first liners of the year on her way to Montreal from England. Only a few days ago she must have been blacked out, and the people aboard her had been freezing as she picked her way through the straits of Belle Isle.

The odours of spring were multiple in the evening: ploughed earth drying and cooling after sunset, gummy buds swelling to bursting point on bare trees, the flat smell of the river washing its banks high. The horse's hooves clopped steadily, and Latulippe sat motionless, the only indication that he was alive being the horsy smell which seeped off his clothes. In the fresh air it was rather pleasant. As they passed through the village of Saint-Marc, Athanase saw lights in Father Beaubien's presbytery and in Drouin's store. They passed the old stone mill, then the Tallard land came into sight and the row of poplar trees running straight as an avenue in France from the road to his own door. A great crow swooped overhead, coming down in a long loop from the top of a poplar to settle on a fence post, where it crouched black and reverent in the gloaming like a priest in prayer. Westward the last saffron light of the day lay over the Laurentians: sunset in Ontario, late afternoon in the Rockies, mid-afternoon in British Columbia.

Athanase looked toward the maple grove on the ridge behind the parish, stark against the residual light, and again he breathed deeply. Why should anything have to change here? Why? It was perfect as it was. Tonight it was better than at most times. He was very glad to be home.

He paid Latulippe at the doorstep when the man held out his flat palm for the money, and then he went into his own house as the carriage drove off. Kathleen was not in the living room or the library. Julienne came out of the kitchen when she heard him and said that Madame had not expected him until tomorrow and had gone over to Captain Yardley's.

'Is Paul asleep?' Athanase said.

'Well, I don't know. But he's undressed as he should be and in bed. Maybe he's reading. I looked after him all right. Don't you worry, Mr. Tallard.'

Julienne had been part of the house for a very long time.

She was so familiar Athanase scarcely noticed her. 'Everything else all right?' he said.

She broke into a torrent of talk about the weather and how Blanchard expected to begin seeding tomorrow and how Paul had spent the last three afternoons at Captain Yardley's. Athanase cut her short. 'Is supper ready?'

'There's ham and tongue and cold roast beef. I can hot up potatoes in a few minutes, sir.'

'All right, Julienne. I'll be down shortly.'

He went to his own room and undressed, deciding to change from his city clothes into something more comfortable. His nerves still felt tight and he wondered if sleep would come hard tonight. In the mirror he saw his naked body. The chest was thin and the calves hairless, the flesh looked both loose and thin over his bones. Not much of a prize now. He thought of Kathleen and was lonely; not so much for her, because he would be seeing her in less than an hour, but for the man he had been when the muscles were still on his body and he was proud of them. He pursed his lips. Was that another of his many mistakes, to have married a girl as young as Kathleen? It had not seemed a bad thing to do at the time. He remembered a phrase he had heard in college, Sophocles saying how thankful he was in his old age no longer to need a woman – 'I feel as if I had escaped from a savage master!' Well, he was no Sophocles and he wished he were younger. Kathleen's vitality by its mere existence mocked him now.

He glanced back at the mirror. All that counted in what he saw imaged there was the head. With a sensation of incredulity he realized for the first time that his head was beautiful. But it was an old man's beauty. What use was his head to Kathleen?

When he was dressed again he went into Paul's room, carrying a small lamp in his hand. The boy was asleep, his dark hair tousled on the pillow and his lips parted as he breathed. He had a child's secret look as he lay there, and suddenly Athanase was aware that tears were growing behind his eyelids. This son of his was so withdrawn it was hard to realize that he and Kathleen had anything to do with his existence. As he laid his hand softly on his son's

82

forehead the boy's eyes opened and he was awake.

'P'pa?'

'Yes?'

Paul smiled. 'I'm glad you're back.'

The remark touched him. 'I didn't mean to wake you. Now you must go back to sleep.'

'I've been asleep.'

'But only for a little while.'

'It feels like a long time.'

Athanase smiled. Paul looked as he did when he woke in the early morning, ready for a new day. Often when Athanase went to wake him he would find the boy on his knees on the bed peering out his window at the river. Paul would turn around and his eyes would look far away, as though he had been outside the world.

'P'pa? How long is a dream?'

'Oh, about half a second.'

'No!' Laughter bubbled. 'It couldn't be, could it? I've been dreaming so many things. It must have taken a long time.'

'What were you dreaming about, Paul?'

'Oh, I don't know exactly. It's sort of hard to remember now. But I was there and then you came.'

'You must go back to sleep now.'

'Yes.'

Athanase bent down and kissed his son's forehead and found it cool. Then he turned away and left the room with the lamp in his hand. The big house seemed empty as he went downstairs for his supper.

When he had finished he put on his hat and coat and called to Julienne, 'Go to bed whenever you please. I'm going over to the captain's.'

He took his favorite stick and opened the door. He could hear Julienne moving in the kitchen as he closed it behind him, and he wondered if she were lonely, too.

9

On Saturday morning, Athanase felt so fine after a good night's sleep, he decided to begin the actual writing of the book on religion which he had been planning for the last six years. He opened his pine desk, sat down in his swivel chair, selected a pen carefully, and took a long look at the clean sheet of paper he had placed squarely in the middle of the desk.

The first sentences had been in his mind so long they wrote themselves: 'The basis of all religious belief is the child's fear of the dark. When the child grows into a man, this fear appears to lie dormant, but it is still in him. He invents a system of beliefs to render it less terrible to him. Among primitive tribes we call these beliefs superstitions, but among civilized nations they are masked by the honoured name of religion. God, therefore, is mankind's most original invention, greater even than the wheel. The purpose of this book is to trace and explain . . .'

He stopped and looked out the window. As a matter of fact, the purpose of the book was not to trace and explain anything. It was mainly to state certain aphorisms like the one he had just written. You saw their truth or you didn't. To write more pages in proof of the obvious was a waste of time.

Athanase surveyed his sentences, smiling as he read. They seemed to him great thoughts clearly expressed. He glanced up at the print of Voltaire hanging above the desk and kissed his fingers gaily in its direction. Yes, these were great thoughts. He wondered if they were also his own.

He leaned back in his swivel chair, stuffed his pipe full of Hudson's Bay, lit it and breathed in the smoke. He looked out the window and saw a fine spring morning. Then he swung his chair inward and surveyed the library, saw again the old chairs and the splendid stone hearth blackened by decades of smoke. He looked at the print of Rousseau hanging beside Voltaire. Rousseau was wearing a fur cap, and it made him look like an early French-Canadian colonist, almost a *coureur de bois*. It was a good room, good and familiar. But was it excellent in his eyes merely because it was old? Perhaps the basis of all conservatism was the tendency to identify the familiar with the excellent? Was this also a great thought? Also his own? He realized that his mind was wandering and again bent over the white paper on his desk. Then Paul came in with the papers.

Athanase took them and laid them on the corner of his desk. 'How would you like to go away to school, Paul?' he said as the boy was about to leave the room.

Paul stopped and looked at his shoes. 'I don't know,' he said.

'Next year you'll have to go somewhere to school. You can't stay here forever.'

Paul's face showed such alarm that Athanase noticed it. Every now and then he observed that his son seemed frightened of things. 'My dear boy, you'll like it at school. We'll choose an English school. You'll learn science. You'll find out what makes the world go around.'

'But doesn't it go by itself?'

Athanase laughed, not realizing that his laughter blighted the boy's instinctive response. 'Yes,' he said. 'But you'll learn why.'

'Isn't it because God wants it to?'

'Yes, yes, I know.' He picked up one of the papers from the desk and spread it out. 'Next year you will go to a fine English school. You'll still be a Canadian, mind you. Don't forget that.'

For a few moments Paul watched his father reading, then left the room silently and went outside. Athanase turned back to his work, but the words no longer marched. A book on religion was a tremendous job. Any book was. He frowned over the page of manuscript, and then Kathleen appeared in the door and paused on the threshold.

'Come in,' he said. He was glad of an excuse to stop working. He watched her cross the room, watched her pass one hand absent-mindedly over the window ledge and then lift her fingers to inspect them for dust. She rubbed them clean against her skirt. The untidiness of her dress and her hair this morning made her look older than her thirty-one years. He waited for her to speak, but she said nothing as she gave her attention to the scene beyond the window. A breeze from the river ruffled the sticky young buds on the double row of poplars, and it billowed the starched white curtains at her side. Athanase felt her boredom like a visible presence in the room.

'I must go out in a few minutes to talk to Blanchard,' he said. 'Want to come with me?'

She turned from the window and moved back into the room quietly, like a lazy cat. 'No,' she said.

'It would do you a lot of good. The air's soft today. You ought to get outdoors more often.'

'I don't like it outside.' The tone of her voice was neither bitter nor sarcastic. Rather, it carried a trace of an Irish lilt that made it sweet and carelessly gentle. She wandered about the room, looking at the books on the shelves without allowing her attention to rest on any of them. Then she opened a drawer in the end of a book-littered table and took out a package of cigarettes.

'Those are stale,' he said. 'Here. Have one of these.'

She did not bother answering, but pulled a cigarette from the package in her hand and set it between her lips. Then she moved to the mantlepiece to look for matches. A litter of cards and papers and old envelopes lay there among the bric-à-brac. Kathleen was always looking for things, but never in a hurry; sooner or later she found them. Now she picked a loose match from a small bowl and struck it with a crack on the stone front of the hearth. When the cigarette was burning she turned slowly around with the smoke inhaled, then she let it pour from her nostrils slowly, easily, as though there were no end to it.

'Where's the dog?' she asked.

'He has fleas. I put him out. I wish you wouldn't bring him into the house. He's a farm dog.'

'I've never seen any fleas on him.'

He began to tap the edge of his desk with a pencil. There it was between them. It had grown steadily during the past few years, and now there seemed to be nothing he could do about it. He was too old for her. His ideas of developing her mind had been an absurd failure. Her instinct held it against him as a grievance, even though her nature was easy-going and accepting, for he had not married her because of her mind and they both knew it. Now whenever they were too long alone together they bored each other. Yet she was still beautiful. Watching her shrug her shoulders, pick up a magazine and lay it down again, smile at her own thoughts, he felt again within himself the stir produced by the astonishing contrasts in this woman, her white magnolia skin against the blackness of her hair, her full breasts with the slender, independently moving hips beneath them.

'What about the factory?' she said. 'You saw McQueen on the train.'

Athanase pursed his lips and frowned. 'He's serious about it. Queer people, some of these English business men. They make up their minds too quickly about things. He insists there's going to be a great future for textiles in this country after the war. Maybe . . .'

'Maybe what?'

'I don't know. I might go in with him. After all, it's not as if the idea were new to me. I've often considered something of the kind myself. A successful factory would mean a lot of money. But it would mean a lot of changes here, too.'

'And that would be terrible, wouldn't it?' She shrugged her shoulders indolently. 'Well – I suppose you could be lucky.'

'With McQueen, it wouldn't be a matter of luck. He's a man of scientific knowledge. He knows what he's doing.'

'Perhaps.'

'Of course,' he said reflectively, 'so many arrangements would have to be made . . . I can't believe anything will come of it. I'd have to put up all the capital I can raise to get a real share in it. It would mean a mortgage.' He shook his head. 'And I've never liked mortgages.'

'Sure,' she said. 'Of course there's a catch in it. If it means a chance of getting out of here – there's bound to be a catch in it somewhere.'

He dropped his eyes to the pencil still tapping on his desk. Kathleen always made him feel guilty for leaving her alone in Saint-Marc when he went to Ottawa. But it was impossible to take her with him. Paul could not be left alone indefinitely, though a few days would not matter with Julienne to look after him. At least, that is what he tried to tell himself. The fundamental reason why he no longer took

Kathleen with him to Ottawa was the fact that she could never fit the life she had to lead there.

Irrelevantly, he said, 'I've only wanted you to be happy.'

She watched the white line of hair against his wrinkled neck. 'What kind of happy?' Her voice was good-natured in spite of her words. 'Your kind?'

'We've gone over it so many times.' His voice was sharp with exasperation as he kept his eyes on the tapping pencil. 'I know what you're going to say. You've never felt alive out here. But what about Paul? It's good for him.' He swung around and looked at her. 'Come here.'

She made no move. 'You're sending Paul away to school. You told him, but you didn't tell me. Just like that – you decide to send him away.'

'Listen,' he said, 'you always knew this was coming. Paul's eight years old now. You always knew he'd have to go away to school. I told him this morning because I'd just made up my mind. That's all there was to it.' Again he motioned her to his side. 'This does us no good. Come here.'

'What's the use, Athanase? You never want to talk to me about anything any more. I might as well be Julienne.'

A faint sparkle appeared in his eyes as he shook his head. 'You ought to look at yourself in the glass before you say things like that.'

She moved toward him half-grudgingly and sat on the edge of the desk, one leg stretched down so that the toe of her slipper touched the floor. He looked at the line from hip to thigh and then down to the slim ankle. When he laid his hand on her thigh she gave no response.

'You've been drinking,' he said.

'I was cold.'

'You were never cold in your life.' He waited for her to take the challenge as she once would have done. A remark like that in the old days might have led to anything, for she had a childlike frankness, a complete readiness to admit desire whenever she felt it, even to talk about it and build it up with words. Now she made no response. Why? Had his own neglect killed the magic that had once been between them? Or had it simply grown old, like himself?

'You shouldn't drink before lunch,' he said. 'You know better than that.'

She shrugged her graceful shoulders. 'Listen Athanase – at school Paul will be unhappy. A boy his age away at school!'

'I don't want him spoiled. Besides, you know perfectly well he can't continue as he's going. The school here – Good God, do you think he can grow up in that?'

'Around here he won't get spoiled. Nothing spoils if it's kept on ice all the time.'

He gave her a sharp look. There were tears in her eyes.

'Take me away from here, Athanase!'

He patted her knee. 'Is it as bad as all that?'

'I'm dead here. If I spoke French I'd still be Irish and that would make Saint-Marc still treat me like a foreigner. Anyway, I'd always be alone because I'm your wife. None of them have ever forgiven me for marrying you, after your . . .' She stopped, slipped from the desk and moved back to the window with the lazy, rhythmical movement that was as much a product of an earthy gentleness, almost of a strangely individual innocence, as the deliberately sexual movement it appeared to be. She pressed her forehead against the glass and watched an ox-cart move sluggishly down the road.

'No one in Saint-Marc would dare interfere with us, and you know it,' he said.

'Aren't you forgetting Marius?'

'Oh! So it's him again!'

'He doesn't ever forget things.' She waited a moment, then went on. 'He was here a fortnight ago.'

Athanase's head rose and he stared at her back. 'You've waited a long time to tell me.'

Kathleen turned from the window and looked at him, her voice still languid. 'He didn't want you to know. I don't know why. He didn't say anything much. Julienne told me he spent the night at the presbytery with Father Beaubien after he left here.'

'What did he want with him?' Athanase snapped, clearly exasperated. 'Did he imagine Father Beaubien could help him dodge the draft?'

'Maybe I ought to tell you the rest of it. Father Beaubien came here too, last week. He asked a lot of questions.'

'What about?'

'I don't know exactly. But I think he knows about the factory. I guess Marius must have told him, but I don't know how Marius knew about it. Do you?'

'My God!' he shouted. 'Every time a dog breaks wind in this place the whole parish knows it!'

She moved easily back to the centre of the room as he opened drawers in his desk and shut them again to vent his anger. 'Don't get yourself so excited,' she said. 'It's bad for your blood pressure.'

'My pressure's all right. I could still do a ten-mile walk if I felt like it. Listen . . .' He gestured as though to draw her attention back. 'What did Father Beaubien say about the factory?'

'Say?' She laughed. 'Do any of them ever say anything straight out to me? He just hinted around. I don't even know for sure if he meant the factory. I didn't tell him anything.'

'Are you sure?'

She shrugged and turned her back. 'How could I? What do I know about it? Or anything else? You certainly haven't told me much. But he doesn't like us, all the same. It gives me the creeps, the way he doesn't.'

'Never mind that. If he makes trouble, by God, he'll be sorry. Who does he think he is? My grandfather' – he jerked upright, his moustache bristling – 'horsewhipped a priest once.'

She looked at him reflectively. 'You'll get into trouble talking that way. It's bad luck, saying things like that about your own priest.'

He wondered if he had ever felt more exasperated. All his discussions with Kathleen roamed about irrelevantly inside a full circle and ended exactly where they started. 'You talk about luck as if it were a human being,' he said. 'You're just superstitious. That's the only hold your religion has on you.'

She made no reply, her mind distracted by the sight of Paul in the yard playing with one of the puppies from the barn. She returned to the window to watch him with a sudden, alive interest. Athanase kept his eyes on her profile. It was a strange situation in which he found himself. He saw the pride in her face as she watched Paul's movements. They seldom talked much to each other in his presence, she and the boy, but apparently they had no need of words for their communication. Anything Paul did was all right with her. She let him leave his clothes and toys all over the place and willingly picked up after him. She let him bring the barn cats and dogs into the house and only laughed when their fleas were transferred to him. She was certainly spoiling the boy. Paul was a compartment in her life which she took for granted the way she took everything for granted, except her presence in Saint-Marc.

'You know,' she said, turning back from the window, 'maybe you're right.'

He had forgotten what they had last been talking about. Maybe he was right about what? The small clock on the desk ticked loudly, its sound mingled with the deeper clacking of the grandfather's clock in the hall. Outside in the yard the puppy barked with excitement. Suddenly a smile appeared at the corners of Athanase's lips and twitched wider into his face. Their eyes met and held. The bond between them was illusive, but at that instant each was aware of its strength beyond the outline of definitions.

Kathleen dropped her eyes to her skirt as though recognizing for the first time that it was untidy. She began to press its folds into pleats, slowly, evenly. As he watched her his long fingers stroked his chin. To be able to stir this woman again, to excite the sparkle that had once intoxicated him, to see her take pleasure in being alive – could he do it? Probably not. His mistakes with her had been too many. That undying passion of his for trying to change people and make them over was an incredible weakness. He couldn't even make it work on himself.

As if playing for time, he said, 'You really are lonely here, aren't you, my dear?'

She broke from the look in his eyes and turned to watch Paul again as he raced with the dog around the corner of the house.

There was no real need, he reflected, for them to continue to live out here the year around. It had merely been his habit to do so. All his ancestors had grown up on this land,

and he was accustomed to it. It had seemed unthinkable that Paul should not do the same. But now that he had made up his mind to send Paul away to school, it was stupid to pretend that Kathleen had to remain here. They could always spend their summers together on the land. She probably wouldn't mind that so much. Of course, there were expenses to consider. Two establishments would run to a great deal of money. But he could afford two houses. And if he went in with McQueen on the factory proposition . . .

'Kathleen,' he said, 'I think we'll take a house in town next winter.'

She shook her head without turning around. 'No. I've heard you talk before.'

'This time I mean it.' He got up and stood beside her at the window, one arm around her waist. Her body was soft and pliable under his fingers, yet supple with latent strength. Then he took his arm away. 'If you can bear to stay here through the summer,' he said, 'we can move into Montreal in the fall – when Paul goes away to school.'

Still she did not believe him, but stood quite still trying to calculate his expression.

'Next Monday when I go back to Ottawa you're to come along with me as far as Montreal,' he said. 'You can spend the whole week in town and I'll meet you there on my way back. After all, why not? It's spring. You need a holiday. But see to it' – he pointed his long index finger at her nose, smiling – 'that you have a house for us by the end of the week. I'll leave that up to you.'

Her face expressed a mixture of incredulity, hope and caution. The total effect was of a child afraid of being disappointed. Athanase had never permitted her a decision of her own since they were married. She had no idea how much he might be worth, for all she ever saw in the way of money was the allowance he gave her regularly.

'After all,' he said, as though reading her thoughts, 'you can't depend upon me forever. You're grown up now.'

He waited for her smile but it did not come. He was disappointed. 'What's the matter with you today?' he said, remembering the mobile face of the girl he had married. 'Aren't you pleased?'

'I just can't believe it, that's all.' But belief was slowly beginning to dawn in her eyes. She touched his hand. 'You're doing this for me, Athanase?'

'Maybe. But I should have done it long ago.'

'You really want to live in Montreal?'

He was embarrassed. 'I love you, Kathleen.'

She flung both arms about his neck and he felt them firmly straining, and his body frail in their grasp, as she yielded herself against him in a way that once had maddened him with excitement. Her lips were soft on his cheeks as she kissed him. Then she released him and left the room, almost running in her eagerness.

'I'll tell Julienne I'm going away next week,' her voice came back. 'Even if I still can't believe it.'

Athanase went back to his desk and then remembered that Blanchard had wanted to talk to him today about the planting. It would not be a real discussion; Blanchard would tell him what he had decided to do, grumble about the weather, gossip a little, and that would be all. Blanchard had been working for twenty-five years on the Tallard land. Some day he would let him have one of the upper fields as a reward for his loyalty. The price would be very small; just enough to keep everyone from thinking that Blanchard had got it for nothing.

He felt bold today, bold and decisive, and he enjoyed the sensation of power it gave him. As he went out to the hall to get his hat and coat he reflected on what seemed to him the supreme irony of human life. A man had to come near the end of it before he acquired enough experience and wisdom to qualify him to begin the process of living. He grinned to himself. Father Beaubien had a point there. If life was not a long preparation for dying, what sense could be made of it?

10

In the scullery at the back of the house Athanase came upon Paul. 'What are you doing here?' he said. 'I thought you were outside.'

'I was just looking for Napoléon's ball.'

93

'Oh, you were.' Athanase bent over and peered behind a flour barrel. 'I'm looking for my walking stick. The Irish one with the knobs on it.'

'It's not here, P'pa.'

'How do you know it isn't? Look around for it.'

Paul did so, but he knew the stick was not there. He knew everything about this scullery, for he liked the place better than any other part of the house. It was a huge storeroom, running the full length of the back section of the ell. In the fall after harvest it was filled with barrels of apples and flour, with beets, carrots, potatoes in sacks and dozens of jars of newly made jellies. It smelled drily of a mixture of earth, vegetables, fruit, smoke and kerosene. Hams and sides of cured bacon hung from the rafters, and sometimes in the winter the whole split carcass of a beef was there. The place made Paul feel comfortable. If there was ever a famine like the one they had in Egypt that Father Beaubien had told them about, he could be as safe as a squirrel in the scullery.

'It's not here. It really isn't, P'pa,' Paul said as he emerged from behind an apple barrel.

Athanase grunted. 'Well, if the old captain can walk all over the country on one leg, I guess I can walk up to the sugar house on two without any help. Want to come along? Blanchard's up there now, isn't he?'

Paul followed his father out the door and immediately Napoléon leaped at him, barking. They set off toward the ridge behind the farm buildings where the sugar cabin was hidden in the trees of the maple grove. Napoléon ran ahead of them, smelling the ground and then the air alternately.

'Last year after the sugaring, that cabin was left in a bad mess,' Athanase said. 'The men shouldn't be so careless. Have you been up there this year?'

'It's all right now, P'pa.'

'Hmm. Well, we'll see.'

Paul was accustomed to the way his father never listened to what he said and never took his word for anything. Captain Yardley always listened to him, and then talked about what he'd said as though it mattered.

They walked through the quadrangle of barns and sheds, past the chicken run and on through a hedge of thorn trees to a path that ran upward beside one of the fields to the ridge where the maple grove stood in magnificent silhouette against the sky. New leaves had not yet clouded its outline and every branch and twig was as sharply drawn as though with a mapping pen. They walked for a quarter of a mile to the upper field and then Paul stopped and pointed to a bowed figure that had detached itself from the farther fence and now was moving across the field toward them. 'Look!' he said. 'There's Mr. Blanchard.'

Athanase stopped to wait for his manager. The bowed figure grew steadily larger as he came across the ribbed furrows with a lurching, heel-hitting walk. As he drew near he touched his cap. 'There ain't any need of you going up to that sugar cabin, Mr. Tallard. I already looked after it.'

'There's not much you leave for me to do around here.'

Blanchard nodded and the expression on his creased face remained the same. He was wearing battered overalls above a pair of old corduroy trousers and a faded red shirt. His clothes seemed to have grown on his squat body. They were not as close to him as his skin, but they were as much a part of him as the hair was part of a bird dog. He waited immobile while Athanase looked over the field. Then after a moment he said, 'Everything all right, Mr. Tallard?'

'Looks fine. How are your men this year?'

Blanchard lifted his hands and hooked the thumbs over the belt where it appeared clear of his overalls at the hips. His drooping black moustache was flecked with grey, and his hands and face were the same shade of earth-brown, as though the land might have been his mother. In a way it was, for his ancestors in Normandy had been peasants before William the Bastard conquered England. An impression of well-being, almost of goodness, emanated from Blanchard along with the smell of stable and sweat. He was probably the best farmer in the country; certainly he was almost a satisfied man.

'That Louis Bergeron,' he said slowly, reflectively, 'I told you he was no good.'

95

'I'm afraid you're right.'

'It was you hired him last year, Mr. Tallard.'

'I know.'

'He's the one made the mess out of the sugar house. Stole about four gallons of syrup too, the bastard.'

'Well, we won't hire him again.'

'Better not,' Blanchard said.

They stood silently looking over the land. 'What do you think of this upper field?' Athanase said finally.

Blanchard's boot, gummy with moist soil, kicked the side out of a furrow and his eyes dropped automatically to estimate how this section of the field was drying out. 'It's good land,' he said.

The field ran along the beginning of the slope for about a quarter of a mile to the top of Yardley's property. At the far end of it stood the cottage where Blanchard lived with his wife and seven children.

'You always liked this upper field. No?'

'Here all the land is good.' There was feeling in Blanchard's simple statement. He had been born in a back concession among the hills, where farmers broke their backs trying to make potatoes thrive among rocks.

'You've been with me quite a long time,' Athanase went on. 'I've been thinking some about it lately.'

Blanchard looked straight ahead and his eyes stayed level, but Athanase could sense the covetous excitement rising in him. Blanchard looked down and kicked another hole in the furrow and deliberately changed the subject. 'This new bank in Sainte-Justine, Mr. Tallard. You hear about it?'

'Of course. What about it?'

'Can you trust it, Mr. Tallard?'

Athanase smiled. 'It's a branch of the Royal Bank of Canada, Joseph.'

'Yeah.' A pause. 'That's what they say.' Another pause while he scratched his head. 'Well, I guess I do all right the way things are.'

For the past twenty years Athanase had owed Blanchard nearly half his wages. It was the farmer's way of saving money: to be owed by someone he trusted. Nothing could persuade him to go near the notary. He had heard about a notary absconding from a parish on the other side of the river nearly twenty years before. And a bank seemed even less safe. He couldn't believe that clever men would go to the trouble of building a bank and hiring clerks to run it unless they made a profit. And where was the profit to come from, except from the depositors? Blanchard preferred to be owed by Athanase, and he knew what was due him to the last cent.

'Well,' Athanase said, 'when do you start the seeding?'

'Maybe Monday, I guess. Father Beaubien blessed the seeds last Sunday.' He looked up at the sky. 'It could rain.'

They started walking back toward the house, the two men side by side and Paul and the dog slipping and stumbling through the furrows at the field's edge.

'Do oats go up this year, Mr. Tallard?'

It was an important question and Athanase was supposed to know the answer better than the papers because he was a member of parliament. Every year he was asked such questions, and every year he told the questioners gravely what he and they had read in the newspapers or been told by someone else. 'They'll go up all right,' he said. 'God help the country, though. It can't stand these war prices!' The last statement he knew was unnecessary. Blanchard would dismiss it as a peculiarity a rich man could afford to have. Had a foreigner like Captain Yardley said it, he would have been considered contemptible. It was all right for Athanase; he was one of themselves.

'How would you like it, Joseph, if you had a piece of land of your own?' Athanase brought the words out casually. 'Your oldest boy is about ripe to help you now. A man ought to have some land of his own.'

Blanchard shot a stream of tobacco juice from the corner of his mouth and it hit a stone with a loud smack. 'Yeah, I guess he's old enough, Mr. Tallard.'

'You've always liked that upper field. Your own house is on it. Maybe we can fix it up.'

Blanchard rubbed the back of one hand across his eyes.

Athanase affected not to notice the gesture and its cause. 'There are going to be some changes in Saint-Marc, but you'd better not repeat what I say.' With the field in prospect,

97

Athanase knew Blanchard would not even repeat the words to his wife. 'I might as well see the notary and have him draw up a deed. We'll get it fixed up within the next month.'

Blanchard made no reply and his lined, brown face continued to brood over the land. Athanase felt the communion close between his man and himself. It made the world seem worth while on a fine morning like this. Paul sensed that his elders had ceased talking their business. 'Can I plant some seeds this year, Mr. Blanchard?' he said.

'Sure. Sure. If your P'pa says you can.'

'You promised I could have a garden of my own.'

'Sure, Paul. Radishes and lettuce. I guess you can't go far wrong on them.'

Paul was disappointed. 'I want to grow something hard.'

Blanchard turned to Athanase and gave a heavy wink. 'Well, you come along to the barn. Maybe we got something else. Maybe carrots. They'll be longer to grow.'

'Can I see the seeds now?'

'Take him along with you, Joseph,' Athanase said. 'You're the one to turn him into a farmer. I can't.'

He watched the boy follow the lumbering gait of Blanchard across the barnyard and into the barn, the puppy frisking behind them. Then he took a deep breath of the fresh air, savouring the smell of manure mixed with the dry, balsamy odour of ten cords of spruce billets piled in the open woodshed. He decided he felt very well indeed today. Kathleen and the doctor exaggerated his blood pressure. The only thing that ever bothered his pressure was the mess in Ottawa and his incurable folly in expecting anything sensible ever to result from politics. Definitely there was no point in an able man wasting his time in parliament unless he was in the cabinet, and he felt he should have been considered for a ministry long ago. The party said he lacked administrative ability. Damn them, Athanase thought. Those men in Ottawa, particularly the English, thought you were impractical unless you were as dull and pompous as a village notary. What did they know about his ability? He could understand men's characters; he knew how to handle them. All they knew was a succession of facts.

He went into the house and took a stick from the rack,

then walked down the river road away from the village, swinging the stick as his long legs moved under him like a pair of animated dividers. When he finally reached the tributary, the toll-bridge attendant, one of the many Bergerons, came out to speak to him. Collecting thirty cents from each vehicle that crossed the bridge was about all the work he was capable of doing.

Athanase left the bridge and began to walk up a bridle path that followed the stream toward the gully. The river was in spate now, swirling high along its banks. It drove so hard it would have rolled a horse under within ten feet of the shore. He plodded upwards, stopping occasionally to rest, until he reached the place where the gully became precipitous. The falls thundered down before him, a permanent cloud of spray hanging over the cauldron where the water boiled below. The slopes were at least a hundred feet on either side at that point. They formed a deep basin where cattle pastured, and the upper slopes were farmed by the Tremblay family. Athanase tried to estimate just where the Tremblay land began. If a dam were built here, Tremblay would have to sell some of his property.

Suddenly the full force of the idea exploded in his mind. All his life he had lived here without so much as dreaming of the possibilities that lay under his own nose, while McQueen had taken a single look at the falls and had seen everything at once. Why could people like himself never see such things unless they were pointed out first by someone else?

Now he could even imagine the factory standing in clean lines before him, the water backed up by a neat rampart of cement, the dynamos suave with power in the belly of the engine house. The falls continued to thunder in his ears. Power! His own land would be transformed to suit a new age, giving sense to the last ten or so years of his life!

Because his mind was always tuned to the general pattern and never could escape it, the logic of the project added its appeal. His earliest Canadian ancestor had come up the Saint Lawrence with Frontenac, not so long after Cartier himself. That Tallard had found nothing but a forest here, but his Norman instinct had smelled out the good land underneath the trees, and his military imagination had been gripped by the invulnerability of this whole river area. With Quebec City like a stopper in the bottle, the English fleet could never touch him here. And fanning out behind the river and the shield of the Appalachians, he and his brother officers had planned the vastest encircling movement in recorded history: a thin chain of forts through Montreal, Detroit, Pittsburgh, Saint Louis, all the way to the Gulf of Mexico, penning the English into the narrow strip of the continent by the Atlantic. That was imagination on the grand scale. If there had been the same imagination at the court of Versailles to back them up, this whole continent could have become French for good.

But the English, working sporadically and generally for money, never planning anything, had inherited the continent by default when the politicians around the French king had decided to write off the Saint Lawrence area as so many acres of snow and ice. After that, the French who were left in Canada had seemed unable to discover any common purpose except to maintain their identity. How they had done it was a miracle. But the purpose had also been like a chain around their necks, making them cautious, conservative, static. Now once again the English, working sporadically for profit, were appropriating what they wanted in the Saint Lawrence Valley. His own people put toll-bridges across rivers and floated timber down them, but by instinct the English harnessed them to the future. Beyond that the English in Canada never went a step. The production, acquisition and distribution of wealth was about the only purpose they ever seemed able to find.

This was going to be one time, Athanase decided grimly as he stood watching the water pour itself away through the gorge, when industry was going to be made to mean something more. He knew what he wanted here: the factory would become the foundation of the parish, lifting the living standards, wiping out debts, keeping the people in their homes where they had been born, giving everyone a chance. It would enable them to have a model school that could provide modern scientific training. Then they would have a hospital, a public library, a playground, finally a theatre as

100

the parish grew into a town. It would be a revolution, and he would be the one to plan and control it. With McQueen to select the technicians and manage the finances, there was no reason why it should not be a success.

He turned and began to retrace his steps, thinking of nothing else all the way home. On the following Monday, he decided, he would tell McQueen of his decision when he went into town with Kathleen.

By the time he reached the house he realized that he was tired. He left his hat and coat in the hall and called to Kathleen. She answered from upstairs, then came running down, looking happier than he had seen her in months. 'I'll tell Julienne you're back,' she said. 'Your dinner will be ready in five minutes.'

He went into the library and sat down, and the moment he relaxed in his chair, fatigue and reaction set in like a wave. He began to see the difficulties ahead. The factory would be a gamble, maybe McQueen would cheat him, maybe he was a fool to risk his money in a venture he knew nothing about technically. And there was Father Beaubien; the priest would be desperate when he learned that a factory was to be established in his parish. He had once served his time as curate in an industrial town, one of the worst of many bad ones. What would he do if he saw the possibility of Saint-Marc developing into a factory town, with English managers living on its outskirts, Protestants independent of his authority?

Athanase set his jaw. Even Father Beaubien could be handled. The bishop would certainly see advantages in the money a factory would bring to the parish; percentages of all pay envelopes could be channelled to the Church; English managers were glad to make such arrangements since it cost them nothing and helped to establish good will where they needed it most.

He passed his hands over his forehead, easing the tensed muscles between his eyes. If only he had done something as positive as building this factory long ago, while he still had the energy of his youth! It had been so much easier to enjoy life in those days than to dominate it, so much easier to spend long months in Paris than to worry about conditions in Saint-Marc and Ottawa. He could still see the sidewalk café near the Place Saint Michel where he had eaten his first Paris breakfast. The butter pats were pale yellow and the globes of water clinging to them glittered in the morning sun, the same sun that shone full on the front of Notre Dame a few minutes' walk away. He could still feel the creaking painted chair as he gave it his weight, leaning back to sniff Paris in the morning, looking at the midinette at the next table who had so willingly returned his smile. After all these years he could still remember the thrill of being at home in the motherland of his own language, noting the differences in pronunciation between more archaic Quebecois French and that of the Parisians, enjoying the quizzical expression on their faces as they tried helplessly to estimate the department of France from which he had come. No English-Canadian or American could ever know a comparable thrill at finding himself in London. You had to be a French-Canadian, one who had kept faith with the language for two centuries in the face of a hostile continent, to savour the pride and vindication of such a homecoming.

Athanase's lined, walnut-coloured face was still soft with recollections when the dinner bell rang. On his way to the dining room he remembered how he had once dreamed in a vague way of bringing back something of the spirit of revolutionary France to the older, wintry, clerical Norman France of Quebec. But he had not done it. Probably nobody could do it. On the other hand, if the spirit of France could not grow here, surely the spirit of the new world could. After all, the French in Canada were also North Americans.

He felt tired with all this remembering and sipped his soup gladly. Looking across the table at Kathleen, he winked at her gravely.

11

At precisely two minutes to nine-thirty on Monday morning, Huntly McQueen stepped out of his Cadillac town-car and entered the Bank Building in Saint James Street. He was dressed in a dark suit, a black coat, a black hat, a dark blue tie very large in a winged collar. In the tie he wore a pearl pin.

He passed through a pair of bronze doors, was saluted by the ex-sergeant of Coldstream Guards who stood there in livery, and entered a marble atrium as impersonal as a mausoleum. He joined a group of middle-aged and elderly men waiting for an elevator at the far end of the atrium. They were all dressed exactly like himself. Nods passed between them, they stepped into the elevator, shot each other a few more discreet glances as though to make certain that nothing important had happened in their lives over the weekend, then stared straight ahead as the cage moved upward.

On the second floor Sir Rupert Irons got out. He had a heavily hard body, was square in the head, face, jaws and shoulders; his hair was parted in the middle and squared off to either side of his perpendicular temples. His face was familiar to most Canadians, for it stared at them from small, plain portraits hanging on the walls of banks all the way from Halifax to Vancouver. Even in the pictures his neck was ridged with muscles acquired from a life-long habit of stiffening his jaw and pushing it forward during all business conversations.

On the fourth floor MacIntosh got out. He shuffled off toward his office, a round-shouldered, worrying man who carried in his head the essential statistics on three metal mines, two chemical factories, complicated relationships involving several international companies controlled in London and New York, and one corset factory.

On the seventh floor Masterman got out, to enter the offices of Minto Power. Although Minto harnessed the waters of one of the deepest and wildest rivers in the world, there was nothing about Masterman to suggest the elemental. He was a thin, punctilious man with a clipped moustache, a knife-edge press in his dark trousers, and a great reputation for culture among his associates in Saint James Street. He was one of the orginal members of the Committee of Art. He also belonged to a literary society which encouraged its members to read to each other their own compositions at meetings; he was considered its most brilliant member because he had published a book called *Gentlemen, the King!* The work was an historical record of all the royal tours conducted through Canada since Confederation.

One floor higher, Chislett got out: nickel, copper and coal, a reputation for dominating every board he sat on, and so great a talent for keeping his mouth shut that even McQueen envied it.

The elevator continued with McQueen to the top floor. The thought crossed his mind that if an accident had occurred between the first and second floors, half a million men would at that instant have lost their masters. It was an alarming thought. It was also ironic, for these individuals were so remote from the beings they governed, they operated with such cantilevered indirections, that they could all die at once without even ruffling the sleep of the remote employees on the distant end of the chain of cause and effect. The structure of interlocking directorates which governed the nation's finances, subject always to an exceptionally discreet parliament, seemed to McQueen so delicate that a puff of breath could make the whole edifice quiver. But no, McQueen smiled at his own thoughts, the structure was quite strong enough. The men who had ridden together in the elevator this morning were so sound they seldom told even their wives what they thought or did or hoped to do. Indeed, Sir Rupert Irons was so careful he had no wife at all. They were Presbyterians to a man, they went to church regularly, and Irons was known to believe quite literally in predestination.

The elevator stopped to let McQueen out. His own preserves occupied half the top floor of the Bank Building. Beyond a sizable reception room there were half a dozen small offices in which carefully selected executives did their work. McQueen's private office was in the far corner, reached through the room of his private secretary.

His round face smiled abstractedly at the switchboard girl and the typists as he went through the large room. It was his practice to enter his office by this route rather than through the private door from the outside hall to which he alone had a key, but he never lingered on his way. As he opened the door to his secretary's room she looked up brightly. 'Good morning, Mr. McQueen.'

'Good morning, Miss Drew.'

'It's a fine day.'

'Yes,' he said. 'It may well turn out a fine day.' He let a cool smile fall in her direction before he went into his own office, where he took off his hat and coat, hung them methodically in a cupboard, straightened his tie, pulled his coat down in the rear, and stood looking out the window as he did every morning before he settled down to work.

McQueen's office overlooked one of the panoramas of the world. Its windows opened directly on the port of Montreal, and from them he could look across the plain to the distant mountains across the American border. The Saint Lawrence, a mile wide, swept in a splendid curve along the southern bend of the island on which the city stood. Everything below the window seemed to lead to the docks, but there were few ships in them now. Since the war most of the ocean-going craft sailed under convoy from Halifax. The few vessels that were visible were all painted North Atlantic grey, with guns under tarpaulins pointing astern.

McQueen's satisfaction constantly renewed itself through his ability to overlook all this. He felt himself at the exact centre of the country's heart, at the meeting place of ships, railroads and people, at the precise point where the interlocking directorates of Canada found their balance. Saint James Street was by no means as powerful as Wall Street or The City, but considering the small population of the country behind it, McQueen felt it ranked uniquely high. There was tenacity in Saint James Street. They knew how to keep their mouths shut and take the cash and let the credit go. They were bothered by no doubts. They had definite advantages over the British and Americans, for they could always play the other two off one against the other. Americans talked too much and the British made the mistake of underrating them. McQueen smiled. That gave the Canadians an advantage both ways. More than one powerful American of international reputation had lost his shirt to Sir Rupert Irons.

McQueen turned from the window, letting his glance rest casually on the furnishings of the room before he became immersed in work. By the window was an oversized globe on a heavy wooden stand. Behind his desk was a relief map of Canada, ceiling-high, dotted with coloured pins at various points to indicate where his enterprises and interests were located. An oriental rug covered the floor. Opposite his desk was an oil painting of his mother, with fresh flowers in a bowl beneath it.

Because of the manner of its furnishing, this office had acquired something of a romantic reputation in Saint James Street. Some men considered it eccentric. Few were permitted to enter it, and those who did exaggerated the luxury of its furnishings afterwards. It did nothing to lessen the respect in which McQueen was held as a man who kept his mouth shut about all important matters, talked freely of trivialities, and was uncannily successful.

A change of expression appeared on his face as he crossed to his mother's portrait. Every morning Miss Drew put a dozen fresh flowers in the cut glass bowl on the small table beneath it. The flowers were never arranged quite to suit him, and now he spent some time moving the stem of each daffodil until the effect met his approval. He looked up at the picture. His mother's was a small, sad face, lips tight, hair in a frizz over her forehead, neck enclosed by the sort of dog-collar made fashionable by Queen Alexandra. Her face as a whole distilled a Scottish kind of sternness, a Scottish melancholy that finds pleasure only in sad ideas. Except when he was alone in the room McQueen never even glanced at the portrait, but whenever he had a decision to make he shut everyone out and communed with the picture, and after he had looked at it long enough he was usually able to feel that his mother was silently advising him what to do. It was the most closely guarded of all his secrets.

Now he turned to his desk and his expression changed again. His eyes, widely set and intelligent in his moon-face, became opaque in their blueness. His lips compressed themselves. Deliberately he read through his mail and the letters crackled as he thumbed them through. When he reached the bottom of the pile he buzzed for his secretary.

Miss Drew opened the door soundlessly and stood waiting. She was fifty, she wore nothing but tweeds winter and summer, her hair was dull grey and she had been with him since the beginning of his career in Ontario twenty years before. He suspected that she knew the details of his enterprises as well as he did himself. But not the sense of balance, the delicate grip of the whole; not the logical feel for cause and effect that pulled the future out of mystery and sometimes caused McQueen to wonder if he were a genius.

Gaunt and angular, spectacles on her long nose and notebook in hand, she waited until McQueen indicated that he was ready to give her dictation. She pulled a chair to the side of his desk, opened her book and held her pencil poised. Nothing could have been less personal than Miss Drew at this hour of the morning.

'Any calls?' he said at last.

'Mr. Masterman's secretary phoned to remind you of the meeting on Friday. Mr. Buchanan called. I put the memorandum with your letters. Mr. Tallard called. He wants to come in today before lunch.'

'Ah!' said McQueen.

'I told him to come at eleven-fifteen unless he heard to the contrary. He left a room number at his hotel.'

'Good. Don't call him. Show him in at once when he comes.'

The letters took three-quarters of an hour in dictation. McQueen spoke in a rotund voice unleavened by any expression and he used every worn-out phrase known to business. He was so wordy that all his correspondence was half as long again as necessary. When the last letter was finished, Miss Drew picked up the papers he had handed her one by one and rose to leave.

'What time did the cable go to Lloyd's?' he said, leaning back with his thumbs hooked in his waistcoat.

'Just after you left last night.'

He nodded. He knew that if any further news had arrived from London she would have told him, but the matter was on his mind and it relieved him a little to refer to it. In 1913, anticipating the war, he had purchased three tramp steamers at bargain rates from a foreign firm. A fortnight ago one of them had been torpedoed in the Irish Sea with eleven fatalities. McQueen had not been able to sleep the night the news arrived. The war had suddenly been removed from headlines and statistics where he could calculate and understand it, to a level sharply personal.

107

'Anything I've overlooked?' he asked.

'Well, perhaps I should remind you that this is the day Mrs. Methuen comes in for the check on her investments.'

'Yes, I know. When you bring me her list, bring the file on the Hamilton Works, too.'

Miss Drew went out as soundlessly as she had come and in a few moments she was back with the two files. Taking them from her, McQueen glanced briefly at the list of investments and thrust it to one side of his desk. 'When does Mrs. Methuen come in?' he said.

'At ten forty-five.'

'Very good. That's all. I don't want to be disturbed.'

He concentrated on the papers in the file relating to his factory in Hamilton. Alone with the figures, at peace with them, seeing in his mind every detail in the factory they tried to define, the outlets, the sources of raw materials, he tried to weigh the profit and risk involved in maintaining the independence of the machine-tool industry he had built out of practically nothing. It was his oldest enterprise and he was proud of it. But now Irons had indicated a desire to have him merge in a combine with him, and Irons' conception of a merger was about the same as a shark's when it encounters a herring. McQueen tried to calculate how Irons could be made to lose interest.

He pushed the file away, still thinking. Facts and figures were no help to him in this problem. He had a distinct idea that Irons was not so much interested in acquiring the machine-tool factory as he was in guaranteeing that McQueen himself should come under his domination. This was Irons' method. He seldom built up any enterprise himself, but he had a genius for absorbing control from others. He dealt with men, not facts. He was notoriously uneasy if he saw a rising man who seemed both formidable and capable of retaining his independence.

Stubbornly, McQueen continued to weigh the incalculables. A victory over Irons would not be unpleasant. He might go in with him, avail himself of the superior financial strength Irons would bring to the company, and then fight him for control. But no, that would be stupid. He was not strong enough for that yet. Nor could he risk an open outwitting of Irons. He might manage it, but the time would come when Irons would ruin him for his temerity. It must be his own special kind of victory, that for a time appeared a defeat.

After a time McQueen reached a decision. Irons was an impatient man, and he was arrogant. When he met a man across his desk and felt in a position to despise him, he was satisfied. The sensible course for McQueen was to do nothing. When he met Irons across his desk, and he had never dealt with him yet, he would see to it that Irons formed the right opinion of him. And the right opinion in this case must be that McQueen would be a nuisance to associate with; also that he was too small-minded ever to become a rival. McQueen chuckled. He would make himself appear fussy and indecisive. He could already see Irons staring at him with those biting little eyes of his, deciding that he was a second-rater, that he could be scorned and overlooked with safety.

McQueen permitted himself another smile, almost sheepish. After all, an appearance like his own was sometimes an advantage. He liked to compare himself to a cushion. He was always ready to yield to pressure, but it was in his nature to resume his natural shape, very slowly, once the pressure was removed.

He was still smiling to himself when Janet Methuen arrived at eleven o'clock. McQueen had not expected her to be on time. No Montreal woman ever was. He had spoken to her about the habit several times because it upset his sense of precision. Now as she came in, some of his annoyance showed on his face and this flustered Janet. In turn, her embarrassment produced an answering embarrassment in McQueen. However blank a face he managed to show to men, with women he felt the shyness of a boy at his first party. He covered it now with a clumsy brusqueness.

'Sit down, Janet,' he said. 'Sit down.'

Janet Methuen glanced nervously from side to side, then crossed the oriental rug to his desk, looking more as if she were entering a strange drawing-room than a business office. She dropped into the chair he had pulled up for her.

'It's too bad to have to bother you like this, Huntly. But

109

you know what a fool I am about business. You know I have to . . .'

He sat down carefully, settled himself in his chair and raised a hand in a gesture designed to make her hold her tongue. It was a firmly plump hand and carefully manicured. There was a black signet on the little finger and a dust of dark hairs showed near the wrist. 'That's what I'm here for,' he said.

Janet laid her bag on the desk and flattened it with a gloved hand. She watched with habitual nervousness as McQueen adjusted his pince-nez and picked up the list of her securities. Because she had made a successful marriage into Montreal society, she was acutely conscious of those who belonged to that society and those who did not. McQueen did not. But the time was not far distant when he would. It was only a matter of patience and care to make no false moves on his part. Janet's father-in-law, General Methuen, had indicated his liking for the man; he never seemed to be aware of the true cause of McQueen's interest in him.

As she looked about the room Janet's eyes were inclined to dart from one thing to another; they were large eyes, almost beautiful in her small neat face. Intense restlessness was her most marked characteristic, and as a result she was much too thin. She was barely thirty. There was no trace on her figure to indicate that she was the mother of two children. Except for her excessive leanness, she bore no resemblance to Yardley. Today she wore a black broadcloth suit, a black straw hat, and a white georgette blouse was visible under her jacket where it opened over her chest; and it was a chest, not a bosom. She had no idea that McQueen greatly admired this flat neatness, for no woman with a bosom could be quite a lady in his eyes.

A room that contained two people and no conversation got on Janet's nerves. 'I feel terribly grateful to you for all this trouble, Huntly,' she said. 'Really I do. I was saying to General Methuen only last night . . .'

McQueen's hand rose again to silence her. Without raising his eyes from the papers before him, he muttered, 'A promise is a promise. When Harvey went overseas I said I would look after his affairs.' Then he closed his lips tightly.

110

Looking for something to do to quiet her uneasiness, Janet stretched out a gloved hand and picked up a copy of the *Gazette* from the corner of the desk. After a quick glance at McQueen, she began to read. Her eyes darted from column to column. They came to rest on the report of a speech against conscription made by a politician with a name she couldn't pronounce.

'Isn't it terrible about the French-Canadians, Huntly?' she said.

'Eh?'

She displayed the paper, holding it by the corner so that it hung down diagonally. 'At least where Harvey is he doesn't have to read this sort of thing. It makes me quite ill.'

'Please, Janet. Just a minute!'

'I'm terribly sorry.' Her voice trailed off and she picked up the paper again. She read a few lines and then looked up to see if he was angry. He appeared to have forgotten her presence entirely. After a few minutes he shuffled the papers, matched their edges, then pushed them from him and took off his glasses.

'I think some of those mining shares ought to be converted into war bonds. They're sound enough as they are, but these days . . .'

'Whatever you say, Huntly. I told you I don't know.'

He tried to be patient. 'But Janet, you must attempt to understand what you're doing. Harvey would want you to understand.'

Step by step he explained to her what happens to money when it is transferred from one security to another, and the results on her income from this particular transfer. 'It's a matter of judgment, in the final analysis. There will be a slight decrease in your income, but not an appreciable one. Not appreciable at all. On the other hand, after the war, if the mining shares . . . well, let's look at it purely from the standpoint of patriotism. You understand – '

'Oh, yes. It's clear now. Do it by all means,' she said hurriedly.

He nodded, drew a deep breath and swung his pince-nez gently on the end of a black cord. 'Otherwise everything is in fine shape,' he said. 'A fine, conservative list. It should last forever.' He allowed himself to smile at her. 'Now tell me about yourself. About the children. Everything all right? I haven't seen you in a month.'

'Oh, yes. They're all right.' She lifted the newspaper again, her forefinger pointing to the conscription speech on the front page. 'Huntly, why don't they put these people in jail?'

'Now then, Janet, now then! Wouldn't that be an unconsidered thing to do? After all, that's how the French are.'

'But General Methuen says they've let us down. And he always used to stand up for them against Toronto people. Before the war, of course.' She laid the paper down on the desk and folded it firmly. 'He's terribly disappointed in them now.'

'You mustn't get yourself worked up,' he said.

'I can't help it. I *am* worked up.'

Yes, McQueen thought, there was no doubt about it, Janet was tired. She worked on every war committee in Montreal. She spent two hours a day in a canteen in one of the railway stations, and this was the worst job of all. She had told him last winter that some of the soldiers used horrifyingly vulgar language when they talked among themselves, and she had asked him if they were good troops.

Janet also rationed herself strictly in the matter of food. She studied the reports of the British Food Controller every week, and was careful to allot herself the same rations allowed people in Britain. To make herself feel worthy of the British she was prepared to go hungry.

'Tell me what you hear from Harvey,' McQueen said.

'There's nothing to tell.'

'You mean you haven't heard from him lately?'

'No. Not since I saw you last. I just don't know.'

There was fear in her eyes. He saw it, and then he looked at the clean lines of her nose and cheekbones, so clean they would soon be gaunt. She was such a nice little woman. She was passing so bravely through a difficult time. Indeed, she had never found life easy. He felt soft with sentiment as he thought about her. As she began to talk about her two daughters and some of the trouble they were causing her, he thought about the night he had first met her four years before.

He and General Methuen both served as trustees in the Presbyterian Church, and the general had been greatly impressed by the dexterity with which McQueen had bargained off two contractors against each other. As a result, one of the contractors had agreed to build the minister a new manse at little better than cost. The general decided that McQueen might well be a man worth cultivating, and on an impulse invited him to dinner at his home on the slope of the mountain. It meant that McQueen at last had something more behind him than a bank account and a reputation on Saint James Street.

The Methuen family had been leaders in the Square Mile of Montreal society from the days of the old garrison, when Sir Rupert Irons' grandfather was still in his shirt-sleeves. The general himself had served in the militia, been a lieutenant-colonel in the Boer War, and now was a brigadier with the home guard. His daughter-in-law was a stranger to Montreal society, but marriage had opened the door for her. The wife of a Methuen was acceptable without question.

That night at dinner McQueen first became acquainted with Janet and her husband, Harvey Methuen. Afterwards he had cultivated the acquaintance carefully. Harvey was the kind of young man McQueen had always envied. He was an athlete, he was physically powerful; but he was also charming, with British manners and mannerisms. He played golf and tennis, some polo on his own ponies, he rode well, was a member of a hunt club, and had been an officer of the militia since his days at the Royal Military College. His suits came from Savile Row, his shoes from Daks, his pipes from Dunhill, his values directly from his immediate background. He was big, curly-haired, and frank. It was McQueen's private opinion that he had no real ability, but this was no handicap. A man like Harvey Methuen had no need of it.

'How long is it going to last, Huntly?'

Her question brought him back to the moment. There was warmth behind her words; warmth, dread, and the haunting fatigue produced by anxiety that had never left her since Harvey's regiment first reached England in December, 1914.

'About three years,' he said.

She bent her head and for a moment covered her face

with her hands. McQueen sat looking at her, annoyed with himself for such a blunder.

'Listen, Janet,' he said quickly. 'That was a slip of the tongue. It won't last much longer. By Christmas it will be over, probably.'

A pathetic hope appeared for a moment in her eyes, then faded into defiance. 'You don't have to be kind to me. *I* haven't suffered. *I* haven't really given anything to help win the war.'

His mind performed a rapid calculation. It was a miracle that Harvey was alive after all this time. He had beaten the law of averages by nearly two and a half years. But he had been wounded a year ago, recovered, and was back in France again.

'I haven't heard from him for nearly five weeks,' she said. 'That's too long, you know.' Even in her anxiety her voice was a clipped imitation of the British. The Englishwomen who had run the finishing school to which her mother had sent her had done all they could to prevent her from talking or thinking like a Canadian, and they had done their work well.

'Don't worry,' McQueen said. 'The Canadians haven't been in the line lately. I know that for a positive fact.'

'He's not with the Canadians any more. He was transferred to the British last January.' Her voice was filled with pride. 'He loved it.'

'I see.'

'Is it true they don't know what happened to the Fifth Army?'

No, McQueen thought, they know only too well what happened to it. He rose and went around to her chair, leaned over and shyly laid a hand on her shoulder. He felt the bone hard under his fingers. She wriggled out from under his touch and he flushed slightly as he withdrew his hand. It was no use; women always despised him when he touched them. He went back to his chair and sat down heavily.

'Don't worry,' he said again, calling on all resources until his voice sounded almost resonant. He watched her respond to his unsuspected force as he had seen so many others respond. It was a quality he could tap at will, though it fatigued him to do it. A very valuable asset. 'Let's be logical,' he said. 'If anything had happened to him you'd have heard by now. He probably wrote all right, and the letter was lost at sea.'

She dabbed at her eyes and her nose with a white handkerchief and then got quickly to her feet, standing very straight. 'Thank you, Huntly. I've been extremely silly.'

'Not at all. Not at all. Just human, Janet.' He waved her back to her chair. 'You were telling me about Daphne and Heather. How are they getting along?'

Some of the strain left Janet's face, but she continued to stand, leaning on the back of the chair for support. McQueen rose and stood on his own side of the desk.

'They're quite a responsibility,' she said. 'If they were only more alike. Heather's a positive hoyden. Exactly like my father.'

'But Captain Yardley is a fine man!' McQueen's voice almost purred. 'After all, for a man of his age to buy a farm and run it himself – and at a time when farmers are so necessary for the country!' Janet's face continued to brighten. 'And I understand he's going to make an excellent thing of it, too.'

'But he simply won't ever change,' she said. 'He's so stubborn. I didn't realize he was doing this as a duty. I thought he was just being willful. Why didn't he tell me? Out there with all those French-Canadians! General Methuen hardly knew what to make of it.'

'How's Daphne?' he said.

'I'm afraid she may become a very vain girl.' Janet frowned. The smallest thought in her mind immediately exaggerated itself on her face. 'Candidly, do you think Brock Hall is the right school for her?'

McQueen tried to look solemn. He was about to accept an appointment to the board of governors of Brock, a step which gave him great satisfaction. It was worth a lot socially to be on the board of a private school patronized by the Square Mile. 'Brock has an excellent reputation,' he said. 'And I don't know about Daphne becoming vain. I think you probably overstate the case. She'll certainly be very beautiful. A most natural development, considering her mother.'

'Oh, Huntly!' Janet seemed annoyed by the compliment

and McQueen flushed. 'But Heather has no discrimination at all. She's just like Father – likes everybody and everything. Why, only yesterday . . .'

McQueen stroked his chin and smiled as he listened to a long story. Before it was ended the buzzer sounded on his desk and Janet became confused. She made apologies for keeping him so long, as he led her to the door that opened directly into the hall. She had no idea that the signal on the buzzer had been a pre-arranged convenience for putting an end to her call.

When he was alone again, McQueen looked at his watch. It was nearly eleven-thirty. Athanase Tallard was fifteen minutes late. So the French were unpunctual, too? Or was it just Tallard, probably from long association with the English? Anyway, it was a fact to remember.

He glanced up at his mother's portrait, looked at it for a long time. They had gone through a lot together. Now he was reaping the fruits. He felt her pride in him like a mantle on his shoulders; she would be still more proud in twenty years' time, and she would find a way to convey the sense of it to him if he never lost touch with her. Always it had been like that, before she died as well as since her death. Whatever he did, wherever he went, she was beside him.

His father, a Presbyterian minister in a small Ontario town, had died when Huntly was a child. After that his mother had taken him to Toronto, wishing to be near her brother, who owned a small tool factory there. The brother's help was limited to inviting them to Christmas dinner every year. He believed that giving financial aid only weakened the recipients' characters. So Mrs. McQueen had supported herself and her son by tutoring backward schoolchildren and composing Sunday School quarterlies for a religious publishing house. She was paid very badly, the publishers having persuaded her that their work was profitless, done only for the greater glory of God.

Huntly had grown up in a four-room flat, in an atmosphere saturated with education, prayers and golden texts. Some of his mother's texts still overflowed into his business correspondence. At the public school he had been the fat boy, and bullied for it. The experience tended to make him believe that the Shorter Catechism's view of humanity was optimistic. But he had done well in his school work, better at high school, and he had gone through the University of Toronto on scholarships.

The year he graduated from college his uncle died. The fact that he happened to die in this particular year, and left to his nephew his nearly bankrupt tool factory, seemed to McQueen a divine accident. It had saved him from becoming a professor. Within five years he had made enough money out of the factory to sell it at a decent profit. Proceeding logically, and already enormously learned in production techniques, he established the machine-tool industry in Hamilton. That was the year he acquired Miss Drew as a secretary.

When he transferred his offices to Saint James Street, a reputation had preceded him. For one thing, he had been one of the first men in the country to settle a strike by the simple expedient of offering the workers a joint labour-management committee. As he had foreseen, the strike-leaders were elected to the board by their men. After that he either divided them against each other, or used them as a colonel uses his N.C.O.'s. Before long they were more conservative than he was himself, and the suggestions they made for improved production paid many times over the small increase he had granted in the men's wages.

After that his advance had been rapid. He seemed incapable of making a bad investment. When Max Aitken made a fortune from cement, he tagged along into a nice profit for himself. He did well with railways and better with ships, and he anticipated the war precisely. By 1917 it had made him a multi-millionaire. He was called a profiteer, but he stood it equably because he knew it was unjust. When peace came everyone would see that there was no sounder man in the country than he. All he had done was to draw logical conclusions and act accordingly. He was well read, devout, and he knew a good deal about history. Because he had made use of that knowledge, they called him names. Well, let them. In time they would change their minds.

It was only lately that he had become dissatisfied with the

117

pattern of his career. He wanted to produce. He wanted to make himself an integral part of what he considered a world trend. He was no longer interested solely in profit. Organization was the new order of the day.

To organize Canada seemed a colossal task; impossible, most of his contemporaries would say. Economic lines ran north and south across the American border, not east and west through the country. But it could be done. If a man owned and controlled sufficient means of production, twenty years from now he might impose his will to an extent undreamed of as yet. McQueen wanted some metal mines, lumber mills, textile factories, a packing house, construction companies, engineering works . . . there was no limit to what he wanted to complete his picture. Further, he wanted his enterprises so well spaced over the country that his influence would touch every part of it. Sir Rupert, with his bank behind him, with his many companies, had such influence now. But Irons was interested in profit, not in organization.

In McQueen's mind, this driving ambition was cloudy in its outlines, precise in some of its parts. Essentially he was cautious, and he would build his house brick by brick. If his plan turned out to be unworkable, and it well might, he would have enough sense to stop long before he had made a fool of himself. In his private files rested detailed schemes for projects all over the country. One of them was for a textile factory in Saint-Marc. So far, he owned nothing in Quebec. To work in French-Canada was a gamble, even though labour was cheap. The French were peculiar people and he did not know them well. There was also their Church to consider. What he needed was a liaison, and the man to fill the gap was Athanase Tallard.

When the buzzer sounded again on his desk he smiled. 'Cast your bread upon the waters,' he murmured to himself, 'and it will return after many days.'

12

By Wednesday of that week Kathleen had found a house. It was a narrow, three-storied Georgian adaptation with low

118

steps, grey stucco over brick walls, a fanlight above the door, and a diminutive garden in the back. It stood in one of those streets of Montreal which remind Englishmen vaguely of London, caused more by the smell and the greyness than the planning of the district itself. Most of the inhabitants of this block were English-speaking, but the house stood only a little west of Bleury, a street which runs through Montreal like a frontier, dividing the English from the French.

Kathleen had taken no chances in making her choice. It was not her idea of a nice house to live in; she would have preferred something more modern. But she knew Athanase liked old places and she was sure he would be satisfied with this one. He had been definite about the rent, setting a maximum figure that turned out to be low. This house was going to cost more than he wanted to pay, but she was sure she could persuade him to take it.

Now as she walked back to the hotel from a matinee at His Majesty's, she relished the sense of the crowds around her. It was late afternoon, the air was soft with spring, clouds drifting across Mount Royal on a light west wind trailed shadows over the roofs. At the hotel newsstand she bought a *Star*, then passed slowly across the lobby to a chair and sat down, the paper in her hand. She opened it at the theatre page and glanced for a few minutes at the advertisements, then folded the large sheets and sat still with the paper in her lap, looking around.

The lobby was fairly crowded. There were many officers in a variety of uniforms, and an importantly dressed Englishman with white hair and a wooden face was sitting opposite. On a leather-covered sofa beside him three elderly Americans were smoking strong cigars while they talked business in Brooklyn accents. There was a discreet and aimless coming and going of men all over the lobby, and Kathleen was pleased by it; merely the movement pleased her, the strange faces, the sense of suppressed excitement rising in herself.

After a time she got up and walked down a long corridor of small shops to the elevator. When she got there an officer with a major's crown in the box of his sleeve was waiting.

119

He glanced at her quickly before fixing his eyes on the floor. When the doors opened he stood aside to let her enter and she noticed that his eyes had found her again. She looked away, but as they rode up together she was acutely conscious of his presence, and her suppressed excitement stirred with more liveliness. Giving another quick sideways glance she saw that he was still watching her. He wore a wound patch on his upper sleeve and on his chest was the purple and white ribbon of the Military Cross. Kathleen was not a small woman, but she felt tiny in the elevator beside this man. He had the chest and shoulders of a lumberjack, wiry red hair, and huge veined hands that hung straight down by his sides. She noticed through the mirror in the elevator that the top of her head came only to his shoulder.

The elevator clicked to a stop on the third floor and let her out. The corridor was dark and airless as the crypt of a church, and the heavy red carpet on the stone floor so silenced her footsteps that her own movement gave her an eerie sensation. Before she had reached the door of her room she realized that the major was following at a discreet distance. He passed while she was unlocking the door, and he did not turn around to look at her again. After she had closed the door she removed her hat and coat, then her dress and her shoes. She put on slippers and a flowered silk kimono and sat in an armchair by the open window, looking at the city.

Her old sense of the city's wholeness returned to her; it gripped her feelings and imagination the way she remembered it from girlhood. She heard the street cars banging across the nearest intersection, the intermittent sound of motor horns, the faint shuffling of thousands of moving feet. The crowds passing under the window seemed all about her. She stretched out her long legs as far as they would go. The stretched toes touched, and her arms went up behind her head as her eyes closed. She smiled. It was good to be peaceful again, to be one's self; it was wonderful to be unknown in the crowd.

She thought of Saint-Marc with loathing, as she told herself that if it had not been for Paul she would have left Athanase rather than go on living there any longer. In

Saint-Marc she had never been permitted to be herself. She was the wife of Athanase Tallard, an institution, and the people despised her because she was a foreigner. She knew they gossiped about her, saying that any woman with a figure like hers ought to be ashamed of herself for not having a child a year. What the young men said was worse, even if their thoughts were secret. The faces of one or two of them showed how often they wondered what she was like naked, never boldly or purposely, as if they considered themselves candidates for her body, but with a sort of sly shame. She knew that expression far too well ever to miss it. Besides thinking her sinful, they also assumed that she was not naturally a lady. Ultimately they found out everything in Saint-Marc. Father Beaubien had once criticized her for wearing a dress she particularly liked, saying it was too bold. After that she had deliberately worn ugly, unquestionably decent dresses in Saint-Marc, but she was afraid to tell Athanase why she did so, for fear he would quarrel with the priest and make matters still worse. Could it be possible she would be finished with Saint-Marc after another summer?

Outside in the spring air the evening had not yet begun, but it was late enough for her to feel hungry. She rose and shed the kimono, letting it drop to the floor and stay there. She crossed to the long mirror in the door of the wardrobe and wriggled out of her underclothes. Finally she peeled off her stockings and stood looking at her reflection. After a time she picked up a brush and began to stroke her hair, not thinking of the arc her arm made in its rhythmical movement, nor of the dutiful reflection in the glass.

She knew what she wanted. She wanted men; not to sleep with, not necessarily to touch or even to hold, but men who would look at her in a way suggesting that these things could be if she wished. She wanted men who would laugh with her at the kind of jokes she liked and not be forever serious about the Quebec problem and the Ontario problem and the religious problem. As far as she could see there was only one problem in the whole country that mattered, and that was everyone minding other people's business and never letting anyone have any fun.

Except in the city. The way she remembered her old life

in Montreal, she had at least been free. Maybe the respectable ones were not free, but for people like her there had been liberty of a kind. In the Rue de l'Assomption where Kathleen had grown up, the street counted, not the people. They were in work or were out of work, occasionally the neighbours would help when somebody was sick, but beyond this anything could happen and nobody would really care. In that street you were born knowing there was no sense in caring. There was luck in the street, good and bad, but nobody could plan his own future. You could only take luck when it came and use it while it lasted.

An old whorehouse had stood on one corner of the Rue de l'Assomption and nobody worried about it. Night and day it stood there with blinds drawn, and in the twenty years she lived next door to it, no light had ever showed from any of its windows. It was quieter than any church. As long as anyone remembered, it had been like that and she guessed it was probably like that still. The men who visited it used to walk quickly up the high front steps with their hats pulled down over their foreheads and their coat collars turned up, and they looked straight at the door while they waited for it to open. Later they walked quickly away without glancing right or left. Every Sunday the Madam walked down her front steps dressed in black, her figure a neat right-angled triangle from her projecting bosom to her tiny ankles. A black prayer-book was always clasped in her gloved hands. Leo Ryan, the youngest son of the family next door, told Kathleen when she was fourteen that the Madam was very strict and permitted no swearing or drinking in the house.

But the whorehouse had little part in the life on the Rue de l'Assomption. It was not for the neighbours. Most of them were working people, not even bound together by class since they did not have common schools or a common language. The French children went to French-language schools where they were taught by French-speaking nuns, and the Irish and the Poles went to other church-controlled schools where English was spoken. The English and the Jews on the street went to a Protestant school where teachers who were paid the same wages as unskilled mechanics taught in a system no one had examined for defects in the last thirty years.

Kathleen was the youngest in a family of four. In a three-storey house, they lived in the right half of the second floor. Below them was a family of Jews from Galicia and above them was a crazy Englishman who said he was the younger son of a bleeding earl and that it was a bleeding shaime, him having to live in a place like this.

Her mother died when she was ten. After that her elder sister kept the house until she got married and moved to Worcester in Massachusetts. Then Kathleen kept house for her father and two brothers, working after school to clean and cook and mend for them. She left school when she was fifteen. Her elder brother had a job for a time in a carriage factory, but when he got married he moved with his wife to Hull to work in a match factory there. The younger brother wanted to be a professional hockey player and Kathleen was very proud of him. When he was twenty-five he broke his thigh and tore the cartilage of his right knee and had to hang up his skates for good. He stayed around Montreal for a time shifting from one unskilled job to another, and finally drifted away. When Kathleen last heard of him he was married and living in Oakland, California.

Then she was alone with her father who was a barkeeper in a saloon in the financial district. Connors got Wednesdays off, and of course he never worked on Sunday. When the weather was good on his free days he would sit motionless on his balcony overhanging the narrow sidewalk and stare at the front of the house across the street. Every house in the block was exactly the same as every other house, and on fine days in summer all the balconies were crowded with families rocking back and forth, watching each other.

As Kathleen grew into a young woman Connors took a baffled and uncomprehending pride in her. Often he cocked his eye under heavy brows and said, as though seeing her for the first time, 'Holy Jesus, child! If you ain't like a little blue flower!' And then he would add, 'With looks like yours, you can marry the brewer himself.'

Every day of the week except Saturday Connors drank four bottles of Molson's ale and stayed sober, but on Saturdays he got drunk regularly on Irish whiskey. He took an obscure pride in the fact that he would touch no ale but Molson's, and he boasted that he had once shaken hands with Mr. Molson himself. No one could be found who had seen him do it, but he stuck to his claim.

Just before Kathleen's eighteenth birthday Connors died of cirrhosis of the liver, leaving no debts and no assets but the furniture in their flat. For Kathleen, his death was the beginning of a freedom she enjoyed for three years. She had no fear of the city because it was the only place she knew; it was her real home. Having no status in it, she received the subtle compensation of being able to imagine she owned a share in all of it. She could look at Lord Strathcona's mansion on Dorchester Street and think how wonderful it was that her city had a building exactly like a medieval castle; and not only that one, but many. They were just like pictures she had seen in a magazine.

Although Kathleen had little education and no special training, she was never worried about how to earn a living. More than anything else she wanted to go on the stage, but there was no native theatre in Montreal or anywhere else in Canada, and she had no money to go down to the States and take her chances there. So she got a job selling tickets in a theatre where repertory companies from England and New York played regularly. After six months of standing in a booth so small she could hardly turn around in it, she gave up the theatre and took a job selling stationery and greeting cards in a department store. It was little better than selling tickets. For a time she worked as salesgirl and part-time mannikin in a wholesale dress firm, but the pay was poor and her employer expected her to go out with every cigar-chewing buyer who took a fancy to her.

And then she found a job she really liked. For nearly two years she was a hat-check girl in one of the fashionable hotels. Besides looking after men's hats, coats and sticks, she listened to their jokes, asked about their families, smiled at them indiscriminately, liked them all, and occasionally went to dine with one or another of them in places where their friends were unlikely to see them. She loved the compliments she received, the small presents they gave her, often with no strings attached, and the knowledge that she was something of a character in the hotel. Her one talent was in full use, and so she was completely satisfied, for Kathleen's talent was merely to be herself: easy, natural, giving and

124

accepting without question, never thinking beyond the moment.

It was in the hotel that she met Athanase. He was handsome and vigorous, his hair was just beginning to turn grey, his wit was quick, and they responded to each other at once. She liked older men, especially the ones with no pretences, for they were more likely to be gentle, and they were always grateful to her for being what she was. It had never occurred to her that Athanase would ask her to marry him. Had he been an English-Canadian she would have refused him. She had seen enough of the English in the hotel to guess that their friends would give anyone like herself a very thin time if she married into their society. But she knew little of the French, and nothing whatever of the French in the country outside Montreal. It was only after she reached Saint-Marc that she learned how much tighter a French family unit can be than an English one, and how much stricter and more traditional French standards are than English ones.

It was not so bad at first. There was the novelty of being mistress of a large house, of having servants, of being idle. Then Paul was born and he absorbed her. It was only after Paul became more independent that Saint-Marc began to bore her. And then the war broke out and things went wrong for Athanase in Ottawa and he aged overnight. Against his Norman stubbornness her Irish good nature had no chance.

She put the brush down and stood still again, looking herself over with eyes that paid little attention to what they saw reflected in the long glass. When the telephone beside the bed began to ring she was startled. It was a moment before she moved to answer it, and then she sat naked on the edge of the bed and lifted the receiver. A man's voice, low-pitched and quietly confident, came over the wire in response to her 'Yes?'

'Would you be gracious and have dinner with me tonight? We haven't met, but we came up in the elevator together half an hour ago. I don't enjoy eating alone. I hope you don't either.'

She smiled as she listened to his carefully chosen words, and glanced down at her naked thighs. 'Just a minute,' she said.

She set the receiver down and reached for her kimono

and slippers. Then she picked up the instrument again and listened as the idle wire buzzed quietly between them. 'Do you know who I am?' she said. 'I'm not in the habit of – '

'My dear lady,' he interrupted, 'in this country people repeat formulas too often, don't you think?'

She recoiled from the receiver and looked at it. He must be one of the educated ones. The confident bass voice went on explaining why he was calling her and she listened to its tones rather than its words. It held a suggestion of enormous vigour, but at the same time it was controlled and surprisingly gentle. She remembered him as a man just under forty. 'Your silence disappoints me,' he was saying.

A slight frown lined her forehead as she tried to think what to do. 'But I'd planned to go to the theatre tonight,' she said.

'Definitely?' It was evident he was trying to repress the eagerness from his voice. It was a good sign; if he was eager and nervous he was certainly not the kind of man who hunted a girl with calculation and then despised her once he got what he wanted. She heard him laugh.

'I'll introduce myself,' he said. 'I'm Dennis Morey My home is Winnipeg and that's where I happen to be going now. I'm just back from France.' The voice stopped, then added irrelevantly, 'It was awfully cold at sea.'

'I wouldn't want to be unfriendly to anyone just back from the war.'

'That's grand!' The deep voice made a big thing out of 'grand,' then lilted slightly as he said more softly, 'What's your name?'

'Kathleen.'

'And the rest?'

'Why not let it go at that?'

His voice became almost business-like. 'Shall I call for you at your room, or in the lobby?'

'I'll be downstairs at seven-thirty.'

She hung up the phone without waiting to hear him say anything more, and then she laughed quietly to herself. For nearly a minute she sat on the side of the bed. She was still smiling as she dressed and began to make up her face as she hadn't dared in Saint-Marc. Excitement grew warm in her veins like alcohol. It was very sweet. It was life returning. It was water after a long thirst. Even though she was hungry,

126

she took her time, and it was nearly a quarter to eight before she stepped out of the elevator on the ground floor. She could see Dennis Morey standing alone waiting at the end of the passage. As he walked quickly toward her he seemed a huge man, but she noticed that he was light on his feet.

An hour and a half later they were finishing a large and very good dinner. They had eaten hors d'oeuvres, vichyssoise, broiled mackerel that came whole on a platter with the skin crackling crisp, then roast duck and after that French pastries. They had drunk sherry with the soup, and a light chablis with the fish, and a champagne with the fowl. Coffee sharp with chicory came in small aluminum drippots with straight wooden handles. When the waiter brought it, Dennis Morey ordered port to follow.

He leaned back in his chair, easing out his Sam Browne belt another notch, and glanced at his watch. 'Now,' he said, smiling across the table at Kathleen, 'let's talk.'

She laughed at him. 'What have you been doing for the past two hours, I'd like to know?' She lowered her head and the candlelight made the whiteness of her neck unbelievably soft.

'You may not believe me,' he said, 'but I've been totally silent for the last three years.'

She raised her head and idly stretched out her hand to pick up her wine glass. Kathleen knew instinctively when no words were better than any she could think to say.

'God! The way you move! I could sit here all night and watch you. There's music in your body.'

She knew what he meant. There was music in the way she felt as she listened to the sound of his voice defining the evening's magic. When he stopped talking and just sat and watched her, she said, 'What do you mean – silent for three years? Where have you been?'

'In an army mess. Also in various trenches, holes, dugouts and cellars in the vicinity of Lens, Monchy and various other places I'd rather forget.'

'Don't officers talk in the mess?'

'They do. They also play gramophones. When I get to hell there will be gramophones, and they will all be playing *The Long, Long Trail*.'

'I thought you liked music?'

'Your kind of music. I'd go a long way for that.' Then his face hardened. 'I was too old for it. I've outgrown the dirty joke stage. And God, those puritans when they talked about women! No matter what they pretend, that's what they are. I was too old for it.'

'You don't look very old.'

He paid no attention to her words. 'Then some of them who'd been with the British would get technical and talk like staff officers. We all got technical, but you could smell the way the staff did it a mile off.' He stopped. 'Does this bore you? It certainly bores me.'

'You're a funny man. You're not a bit like – '

'Like what?'

'Nothing. Go on.'

'I'd rather look at you. God, you're lovely!'

Warm and easy in his presence, she held his eyes across the table and they both smiled. He towered over the table even when he hunched his shoulders and leaned forward on his elbows, and his vitality seemed to fill the room. It made her realize how starved she had been for just such vital strength, but more than anything else she liked the way he was completely unconscious of everything else that passed in the restaurant. They were the last diners in the place and the waiters were impatient to be rid of them. From the corner of her eyes she could see the head-waiter standing motionless by the door. He looked as austere as a cardinal in the flickering shadows cast by the candlelight. But Morey was still talking.

When he paused she looked into his intense eyes. Her husky voice was warm with friendliness as she said, 'When are you going to tell me about your wife?'

'How do you know I'm married?'

'The same way you know I'm not a widow.'

The wine waiter filled their glasses with more port. The glasses gleamed in the candlelight against the shadowed white cloth. Rubies, she thought. She was fascinated by the way they caught and held and transformed the light.

'She's a good woman,' he said. 'She's a good mother to three children. I've got two girls and a boy. In my own way – in my own way, I said – I'm loyal to her. In this country

128

we may be stupid, but our Goddamned puritanism makes us loyal. Even me.'

She saw his fingers tighten on the stem of his empty glass, and then the glass fell apart and lay in two pieces on the cloth. He went on as though nothing had happened. 'When I joined up I thought the war might help. Or maybe I'd be killed. That's what makes wars so popular, you know. The failures, the drunks, the washouts, the fellows running away from themselves, the ones that are plain bored . . . they're the ones that mob the recruiting offices the first day of any war. The sober citizens come along later. It's always been the same, and I tell you, it always will be. It's a lot easier to die than to live.' He looked up with a twisted grin. 'Though of course when the time comes to die you discover even that's all balls.'

He snubbed out the cigarette in his fingers and lit another one. 'Well, the war's over for me. Tonight's my last breath of freedom. And you're the one I found for it.'

She made no sound or movement.

'Ever been in Winnipeg?' he said.

She shook her head.

'Winnipeg could have been one of the cities of the world. Some of the world's best people live there. But of course, we're puritans. So the place is just Winnipeg. God help us . . . why do people hate beauty in this country the way they do? As if I didn't know the answer!'

The waiter ghosted up to the table and silently removed the wreckage of the wine glass, knocked the ashes from the tray onto a plate, then replaced the emptied tray and ghosted back to the door again. Morey froze until the waiter was gone, then he hunched forward over the table again and spread the cloth smooth, his huge hands moving like a sculptor's on clay.

'Imagine a flat plain,' he said. 'Not a narrow strip like you have here by the Saint Lawrence, but hundreds of miles of prairie stretching in every direction as far as the eye can see. Imagine it green. Imagine above it a sky so blue your eyes can hardly bear to look at it, and cumulus clouds pure white. Imagine the whole sky seeming to move.' He lifted his hands from the table and fixed his eyes on hers to hold them. 'Like a great majestic bowl with the earth flat beneath it. Sky the giver, earth the accepter. Male and female . . .'

She watched him as if mesmerized.

'Now,' he said, 'imagine a building made of grey granite, reinforced with steel smelted out of the best Lake Superior ore. Imagine the building slim and light as a sword in front, and long and light in profile. Imagine it six hundred feet high, towering off that flat plain, with set-backs like decks for gods to walk on and survey the earth. Imagine the sky blue and the white clouds moving past, so close to its pinnacle that you could stare up from the ground and see the slender profile of that building and think it was moving, too. Imagine it' – he jerked the words out one by one – 'clean-angled, balanced, slender, light – mercilessly right. And new, by God . . . like the country that made it!'

He stopped suddenly and silence fell between them until he broke it with a wan smile and a tired voice. 'Maybe it's just as well not to imagine it. Canadians would never permit such a building to exist.'

'Why not? It sounds wonderful.'

His large hand seemed to sweep her words aside. 'Why not? My God! Just look at this town of yours! An imitation of every example of bad taste in the universe, and as dull and almost as dirty as Liverpool. And if I ever made a statement like that in one of your fashionable clubs here – God, they'd be pleased! After all, if Montreal looks even a little like Liverpool it must be British, and that's exactly how they want it – the ones who build their monstrous buildings.'

The ideas were coming too fast for Kathleen. She couldn't keep them connected, but somehow it didn't seem to matter, for she understood perfectly how he felt. 'You don't like the British much, do you?'

'I didn't say I didn't like them. I do. But Canada isn't England, and too many Canadians try to pretend it is. Generally they're the rich ones, and they pay the money and make the choices. Does our western prairie look like anything in England, for God's sake? Then why try to cover it with English architecture?' He shrugged his shoulders. 'After awhile they'll get another idea. They'll pretend we're exactly the same as the States. And they'll start to imitate ideas from down there. But is there anything in the States like the Saint Lawrence valley? For that matter, is there anything in the States like us – the collective us?'

Kathleen was bewildered and she fell back on her smile. 'I don't know,' she said. 'Has this anything to do with your wife?'

'Not at all.' His voice dropped to a monotone. 'And everything. She's a good woman. Sorry. I've already said that, haven't I? She likes roast beef and potatoes five times a week. She goes to church twice every Sunday. She belongs to the Imperial Order of the Daughters of the Empire and does good works. She sends our three children to good schools on my army pay and sacrifices all her own comforts to do it. I've never once heard her complain about a thing. She thinks art and architecture are refined hobbies for me, but she doesn't feel we can afford to buy paintings. She's right. We never could. She bought a moose-head at an auction just before the war and hung it in the hall. She's always hoped I'd settle down. She's never done a single mean thing in her life or said an unkind word about anyone – even about me. She's thirty-five and quite pretty. She hasn't a grain of imagination, and no humour whatever, but she's a good woman, and I'm not sneering when I say it.'

He got to his feet abruptly and pulled out the table with a violent heave. 'Come on,' he said. 'Let's get back to the hotel.'

Kathleen sat still, taking her time. The magic that had been with them a while ago had almost melted away, and she wanted it back.

'I forgot to tell you,' he went on in a matter-of-fact voice, standing with the table held out, 'that in civil life I was never an architect. I merely wanted to be one. I've farmed, sold insurance, worked for the Canadian Pacific and the Hudson's Bay Company, and gambled on the grain exchange. Now I haven't the slightest notion what I'll do when I'm demobbed, but whatever it is, I don't expect to like it. I'm going home tomorrow. Come on, Kitty – the life history's over.'

He picked up the check, glanced at it and threw some bills onto the table, nodded to the waiter and followed her to the door. When he had retrieved his cap, he guided her down the steps with his hand gentle under her arm, and they stood for a moment in the empty street under the trees looking up at the sky. It was deep with night-purple, star-filled. He bent and kissed her ear. 'You're wonderful, Kitty. I won't talk any more. You know what I am now.'

She said nothing and they walked to the corner in step, his hand still under her arm. In the taxi neither of them spoke. When they entered the hotel lobby he took his room-key out of his pocket. 'You go first,' he said. 'My room?'

Her eyes were wide. 'But I don't . . . I . . .'

'You don't have to say anything.'

Her eyes swung around, trying to escape him, to escape herself and the wild excitement rising within her. 'Let's have coffee and talk some more,' she said.

'Let's say we'll sit in my room and talk, then.' He smiled down at her. 'It's just as you want it, Kitty.'

'I don't . . . not to your room. I won't go there.'

He put the key back in his pocket and grinned at her. 'All right. I've not forgotten your number. I'll get some cigarettes.'

She went off toward the elevators and he crossed the lobby to the newsstand. With a fresh package of cigarettes in his pocket, he picked up a copy of the *Gazette* from a stack on the counter, tossed a nickel in its place and began to read. The Allies were continuing to retreat, the British falling back through places so familiar they would still be part of him if he lived to be a hundred. As he saw the old names he could almost smell the places they represented. 'To hell with it,' he said.

An hour later Kathleen was lost in contemplation of his head, outlined like a monolith against the lamp on the bed-side table. His lips moved without a sound, and then his deep voice came out softly. 'You're miraculous! Are you always like that?'

'Are you?'

'No.'

'I'm not, either.'

'It's the music in you. I knew it the moment I saw you. You don't even guess how wonderful you are.'

'More than the others?'

'More than anyone. It's a great art – like dancing.'

'You mean – as if we were made for each other?'

He turned his head and looked at her, then put one finger on her lips. 'Don't say things like that. You don't have to talk. Nobody's made for anyone else.'

'I think they are.'

'People like you and me . . . maybe it happens for a minute and the minute makes everything else worth while. Not so hard to go on. But that's all.' His great weight stirred beside her, the shoulders hunched against the light, then he relaxed.

Calm spread throughout her limbs; her mind was like a lake with ideas drifting harmlessly over its surface like clouds, memory already busily storing away the moment filled with the imperious power of the man, his fingers like iron on her yielding shoulders, on the inward-bending small of her back. Then her thoughts began to rebuke her, telling her that this was a sin, for her perhaps the worst of all. Yet more thoughts drifting cloud-like in the wake of the rebuke advised her that this had happened in accordance with some deep necessity, and that even though for others it might be a sin, for her at this particular time it had been good, and that if nobody else knew of it no harm had been done.

He seemed to be asleep and she was content to lie quietly at his side. Then with a feeling of total and accepting helplessness, and of amazement at herself, she thought for the first time that night of Paul.

13

The train left Montreal Island and entered the bridge, and a deep hoarse rumble filled the car. The day-coach was half-empty, throbbing with the iron rumble, and dust motes stirred in the reddish light shot through the windows from the setting sun. Kathleen kept her eyes fixed on the sunset. In the seat opposite, Athanase was hidden behind the spread pages of *La Presse*.

A dreamy peace was in all her limbs, a physical ease mingled with a vivid sense of relief because Athanase had

133

noticed no difference in her when they had met. He was so filled with his plans for the factory that he could think of nothing else. Since before lunch, after his arrival from Ottawa, he had been with McQueen. He had spared himself only half an hour to examine the new house and the lease had been signed without argument.

Abruptly the iron rumble ceased, the river disappeared, and they were out on the plain with farmhouses and barns and fences casting long shadows that pointed toward the east. The river was flushed with the sunset and the trees lining its banks looked frail and small, almost like stalks of grain in the distance. Athanase folded his paper and laid it on the seat beside him. He leaned over and patted her knees, she returned his smile, and for a second they seemed more like old friends. Some of his old gaiety had returned, some of his self-confidence, and he looked younger. He tapped his bulging brief-case. 'I've got to go back to school,' he said. 'McQueen gave me so much stuff to go through. . . .' He rubbed his hands. 'It's fine to have facts to solve for a change, not people.'

Kathleen let him talk. A few days more and her night with Dennis Morey would have slipped away from her, warm and rich in the memory; a few weeks more and it would be almost as remote as though it had happened to someone else. Illogically, she would have been troubled by thoughts of her own disloyalty had she been forced to take part in the conversation, but merely sitting and listening eased her mind. With Athanase so excited and eager, it seemed obvious that her night with Morey had taken nothing from him.

When Athanase first told her about the factory she had been afraid it would mean they could never get away from Saint-Marc. But when she was made to understand that the financial control would be from Montreal, and the market managed from there, she was relieved. Only technical managers would be forced to live in Saint-Marc itself.

'Of course,' Athanase was explaining now for the third time, 'I shall have to spend a lot of time on the spot. For me, this is going to be more than just another factory.' He went on to explain that he would arrange for a mortgage on the Tallard property. Already he had taken steps to convert his bonds into company stock. When the company was incorporated he would be the second largest shareholder.

Kathleen appeared to listen, but from the whole monologue she derived little except the conviction that at last her luck was changing. Living in Montreal, she would be free to be herself. After awhile she would persuade Athanase to travel. Through her mind passed a vision of fine hotels in New York, herself dancing to a fine band in Palm Beach by moonlight. Perhaps they might even take a trip to California.

When they drove up the poplar-lined avenue to the house Kathleen was almost glad to be back, to find everything the same; it convinced her that nothing had happened during the past week except a matter-of-fact trip to Montreal on business. Paul was still up and eager to tell her all the things he had done while she was away. She went upstairs with him and sat in his room while he prepared for bed, telling him about the musical comedy she had seen in town. After he had washed and brushed his teeth he crawled between the sheets and lay on his back listening to her, wondering what it would be like next year in the city he had never seen, in a new school. Now that his mother was back the world was once again gay and full of wonder.

14

Spring leaped quickly into full summer that year. One day people woke and saw that the buds had become leaves and the mud dried into friable earth. There was great activity over all the parish as the planting was completed. Before it was finished the first blackflies appeared in the spruce of the distant forest; then they were in the maple grove on the ridge behind the Tallard land. By the Queen's birthday on May twenty-fourth it was almost as hot as midsummer. The heat simmered in delicate gossamers along the surface of the plain, cloud formations built themselves up through the mornings, and by afternoon they were majestic above the river. The first green shoots of the seeds that had been consecrated on Saint Marc's Day appeared above the soil in the sunshine.

One afternoon Paul came in with his ears swollen by

blackfly bites, asking Julienne to do something for him. She washed them with bay rum, talking all the time, and very grumpy about it. The first hot days were her headache season, and she kept a steady brew of camomile tea on the stove to fill cup after cup. As she washed Paul's bites she asked him if he had an earache also and appeared to be somewhat disappointed when he said no. For years Julienne had an earache every December as soon as the thermometer went below zero, and she treated it by sticking a piece of fried onion in the canal, plugging it with a wad of cotton-wool. Every time Athanase caught her doing it he argued with her and finally threatened to get her to a doctor in order to save her hearing. By the time the argument was over the earache had disappeared.

Through June the heat increased. An altar for the Fête Dieu was set up in the open air just off the river road beyond the village, in a bower of green branches and garden flowers. The whole parish made a procession to it with holy banners. Children and choir-boys went first, then the women, the unmarried ones in the lead. After the married women Father Beaubien walked alone, and behind him the Host was borne by the church-wardens. Polycarpe Drouin and Frenette were scarcely recognizable in their best suits and freshly cut hair. Older boys and the men followed the Host, and as the column moved out of the village along the road the choir-boys began to lead the singing of hymns. On the wide surface of the plain, with towering clouds above it, the untrained procession looked very small as it moved along the road. When the altar was finally reached, everyone kneeled on the ground and the Host was uplifted. At the end of the service they all returned to the church by the way they had come. That night a soft rain fell and the parish relaxed, for now the crops were in the hands of God.

June passed into July. The peas and beans and carrots and onions that Blanchard had allowed Paul to plant were growing well in his little garden back of the barn. In the large fields the oats, barley and hay were growing to a head. Blanchard was satisfied. Beside the fields on the Tallard land, he had a crop of his own at last. As he walked over the ten acres Athanase had given him, he would pick up a clod of earth and crumble it in his fingers, and if he happened to be in his own field when the angelus rang, he would bow his head reverently, for he felt that the bell now rang especially for him.

This was also the first year John Yardley had seen crops growing on his farm. They gave him a deep satisfaction. He calculated that within another year he would be able to make the farm pay for itself. His small herd of jerseys would be enlarged as soon as it seemed feasible, and next year he would add to the flock of chickens. It might even be wise to get a few pigs. Every evening when the milking was done he stood on his porch with his old spyglass and swept the river for ships. There were a good many this year. He examined their decks and tried to estimate how well they were being kept, what their cargoes were and what their destinations. Sometimes he felt an acute loneliness as he watched the moving ships, but in spite of it he was fairly content. Janet had given her word to spend the summer with him, and she and the children would soon be here. During the winter he had remodelled one of the upper bedrooms for her, installed a bathroom adjoining it, and fixed up the room beyond as a nursery. Before the planting season he had made a special trip to town to buy a new bed for her, and while he was there he had asked a salesgirl in Morgan's to select the kind of curtains and bedspreads she thought a dainty woman would like. For the two girls he had bought dolls of a size to match the dolls' house he had built for them.

Parliament went into recess early that summer and Athanase returned to Saint-Marc for a long rest. Soon McQueen surveyors would begin to go over the ground for the factory; they would have finished long ago were it not so difficult to get competent men to do the job with the war still on. While he waited, Athanase decided to enjoy himself. He brought rocking chairs out to the front gallery and spent many hours reading there. For a few days he tried to chew gum to break the habit of smoking, but he disliked it so much he went back to his pipe, determined to ration himself to three pipes a day. Now that his future was so full of promise, he felt he must take more care of his health.

But he still fretted about the war. It got into every corner of his mind like sand in one's shoes on a beach. He also worried about Marius, for nothing had been heard of him since the spring. The conscription board of their military district had written to ask where he was, but he would not have told them had he known. He guessed Marius was being kept under cover by friends in Montreal. It made him wonder constantly if the boy had enough to eat and a decent place to sleep. Feeling an illogical mixture of shame at his attitude and pride in his stubbornness, Athanase was certain only that wherever Marius was he was unhappy, that his hatreds were growing, and his future already turning sour. Once he might have prayed about a situation like this, but he had given up praying a long time ago.

Father Beaubien was also worried. He prayed to God each day for guidance to deal with a problem which had been growing ever since he had come to Saint-Marc. The problem was Athanase Tallard. The priest was further above his people than a ship's captain is ever above his crew. Lately he had felt lonely even with God. In the recesses of his heart he believed he was failing his vocation because he never seemed able to perform a miracle beyond the sacrifice of the Mass. Three years ago he had failed to stop a flood when the river rose through the marsh into neighbouring farms and ruined the crop on two farms that year. After God, in His greater wisdom, had permitted the water to keep on rising, Athanase Tallard had mocked him. Of late he had begun to think of Athanase as the embodiment of all the forces of materialism which threatened French-Canada, and his own parish in particular.

If only he could collect enough facts on which to administer a reprimand he would be less worried. During the night when Marius had slept at the presbytery more than two months ago, the boy had told him many things, and Father Beaubien had reason to believe most of what he said. But Marius was excitable and in no state of grace, for he refused to relinquish this passionate hatred of his father. The Tallard family were his parishioners and he felt he should be able to think for all of them. It was his duty to exercise over them the authority of an infallible church. But Athanase made the task as difficult as he could.

Father Beaubien knew he had not been trained to meet a

man like the head of the Tallard family in such a situation. He had been born in one of the poorest parishes on the lower river below Quebec City. All the families had been equal there. The father of each one of them had obeyed the curé, and all without question had partaken of the life of the parish as the soil and the priest ordained it. There had been no rich men in that vicinity able to hire labour for their farms instead of working themselves and having a large family of sons to help. But here, after two marriages, Tallard had only two children. Of all the charges which he was harbouring against him, this seemed the most impious to Father Beaubien.

When the situation had been turned over with a faithful admixture of prayers to the point of action, Father Beaubien set out for the Tallard house. He walked quickly up the drive and lifted the iron knocker shaped like a wolf's head that was set squarely in the middle of the wide maple door. With determination he let it fall, and then he stood there waiting, black as a raven in his soutane against the whitewashed stone of the house. Only his face and the backs of his hands were not black; their tan was flushed over by the heat of the day.

When the door opened and Julienne recognized the caller, she bobbed and took his black straw hat with a great show of respect. He passed his hand over the close-cropped cap of his hair and followed her to the library after he had been announced. He found Athanase with his books and papers in confusion about him. It was the first time he had been in this room of the house and he had never seen so many books before in his life, except in the library of the seminary.

'Well, Father – this is a pleasure.' They shook hands and Athanase gravely waited until Father Beaubien had chosen a chair facing the desk. With a quick movement the priest swept his soutane under him and folded his powerful brown hands in his lap. He was clearly not at ease.

Athanase returned to his swivel chair and swung around to face his visitor, his long legs crossed. The priest glanced up at the prints of Voltaire and Rousseau. With an attempt to meet the polished courtesy of his host, he said, 'Those pictures look old. Are they family portraits?'

'No, Father.'

139

The priest's eyes, large behind his thick glasses, looked around the library, noting what seemed to him the wealth of it. As his eyes found the many English titles on the shelves he could hardly conceal his distrust. 'I have little time to read books,' he said. He swung his eyes back to Athanase. 'Marius tells me you are writing a book on religion, Mr. Tallard. I'm surprised you find the time yourself.'

The tufts of Athanase's eyebrows rose. 'How Marius knows anything about what I'm writing I can't imagine. I've never discussed it with him.'

Father Beaubien leaned forward, his knees parted and his hands folded in the hammock-spread of his soutane. 'Be that as it may,' he said, 'I don't want to take up too much of your time. I've come to speak to you of several matters. About Marius first of all.'

Athanase frowned. 'I understand he spent a night with you not so long ago.'

The two men looked at each other like strange dogs. Athanase had dropped any attempt to be gracious, and Father Beaubien was taken aback by his attitude. Even though he had expected something like it, he found it difficult to accept. Athanase Tallard was unlike any other man he had known. Once, when he had been curate in an industrial town, he had known men who had been corrupted by the life of the place, had become entangled in labour disputes and had lost their faith. But those men had been ignorant. They could only express their opposition to the priest by sullenness, and in a way he had been able to pity them. Now, looking at the ironic expression on the face of Athanase, the priest felt the beginnings of anger. All the other men in the parish knew that he loved and watched over them. All the others knew that the cloth he wore had raised him above ordinary mortals.

'He's a good, religious boy, your elder son.'

'Good? Yes, I hope so. But hardly religious.'

'Perhaps I am a better judge of that.'

'Perhaps. But I certainly know that many attitudes manage to mask themselves under the name of religion.'

The priest's hands clenched and unclenched on his lap. 'At one time your son had a vocation. He was called by God to the priesthood.'

'No,' Athanase said reflectively, 'I don't believe that such a vague feeling in an immature person can be called the voice of God. True, Marius thought he wanted to be a Jesuit.' He shrugged his shoulders. 'You know yourself what came of that.'

'I know God's work was interfered with in this house.'

A quick flush touched Athanase's cheekbones. 'Father Beaubien – I don't appreciate this examination you are giving me. However, let me tell you a few things. When Father Arnaud at the seminary refused to allow Marius to continue, he did so because he did not believe Marius would make a good priest. Neither did the bishop, who was my old friend before he died.' Each of the words was weighted. 'The bishop had no use for political priests who act as village czars, and are never happy unless they're pulling strings while some politician brays nationalism from their church steps. With Quebec flags all over the place. The bishop was afraid Marius would make that kind of priest. So did his rector. That is why he was advised to leave the seminary when he did. Of course,' Athanase added, 'both the bishop and the rector studied in France.'

Not a muscle in the priest's face moved as Athanase subtly insulted him. He had taken plenty of snubs in his life. He knew that Athanase affected to admire the higher clergy and despise the lower. He knew that in countries like France, where millions of the people were atheists, the power of the clergy was strictly limited. But he also knew that if Quebec was more deeply Catholic than any other part of the world, the Church could thank village priests like himself for it. They were plain men who obeyed God and understood the people; they were not mystics.

Looking straight at Athanase, he said, 'I know my duty to the bishop, Mr. Tallard, and I also know my responsibility to God.' He lifted his chin. 'For nearly three hundred years your family has lived in this parish as good Catholics. But what about you? Why don't you attend Mass and confess?'

The flush deepened on Athanase's cheeks. 'That, I should say, was my own responsibility. I don't choose to discuss it with you, Father.'

'I don't intend to discuss it with you. You are a proud man, Mr. Tallard. But even if you were Prime Minister, you'd still be a member of a disciplined church, and I'd still be your priest.' He realized that he had made a dent and went on to force his advantage. 'I am responsible to God for the souls in this parish. I have come to ask you what you intend to do about Marius?'

Athanase looked away. 'What can I do?' he said. 'I've done my best.'

'Think carefully, Mr. Tallard. He is your eldest son, your heir. Have you ever shown a father's natural feeling toward him? Have you ever really gone out of your way to help him?'

Athanase looked back sharply into the dark eyes of the priest, enlarged behind the thick glasses. This man might be plain, but he had power. Some secret knowledge in his mind was exerting a subtle force upon him. What it was he couldn't guess.

'I've done the best I could, Father. Marius is a difficult boy.'

'If Marius goes into the army' – Father Beaubien kept his eyes and his voice steady – 'a horrible life will take hold of him, and it will be your fault. Think of the conditions under which he will have to live! Unbelievers in the next cot, debauched young girls in the garrison towns, too many soldiers without – '

'Father Beaubien,' Athanase interrupted him, 'because I supported a war program in parliament, there is no reason for you to suppose that I believe war is good. I can do nothing to keep Marius out of the army. I'm not the law of the country.'

Silence fell between them. The priest was not convinced, but he was calculating his next move. 'Your family,' he said slowly, 'has always been looked up to here in Saint-Marc. What has happened to your family is a bad thing, bad for the whole parish. They see enough bad examples as it is these days. But to see a father and son at enmity – '

'There is no enmity in my heart. What Marius feels I can't help.'

'I must question that statement, Mr. Tallard.' Again the intimation of hidden knowledge. 'You are no longer seen in church. You never do anything for God that the people of the parish can see. They talk about that. What are they going to think of me if I do nothing while a man like you shows no respect for the Church?'

Athanase shrugged his shoulders.

'Ever since I was called here,' the priest went on, 'you have opposed me. When young Jules Tremblay wanted to leave his father's farm to work in the States, you advised him to go even though his father needed him. At the time of the flood, when I called for novenas to the Blessed Saint Marc, you mocked me. You completely forget that in this parish I am the representative of God.'

Athanase made a gesture of impatience. 'I have never mocked anyone. At the time of the flood I did suggest that Saint Marc would be a lot more pleased with us if we helped him out by digging proper drains down in the marsh. Floods have been a pest there for years. Long before your time in this parish.'

The priest made no answer and Athanase ruffled some papers on his desk, then rose and walked to the window. With a flick of his hands he spread the curtains and looked out. He wanted to be on the porch in the sunshine, resting. He wanted to think about something else. All his life he had been intolerant of authority unless it was the authority of the mind, of the logical idea. Merely because this man was a priest . . . In the hall the grandfather's clock began to toll the hour solemnly. When it had finished and the last stroke had ceased to reverberate, he turned back.

'I had no wish for this discussion with you, Father. Me, I am always ready to let sleeping dogs lie. But I tell you this again, I do not wish to discuss souls with you. My soul is my own responsibility, not yours or anybody else's, and it will have to take its chances without your help.'

The priest raised his hand as if to stop the words, as if to avoid hearing them. With a mighty effort he kept calm. 'Your family, Mr. Tallard – whether you like it or not' – his hand fell – 'is part of my parish.'

Athanase returned to his chair and sat down heavily. 'Listen, Father – we are making unnecessary difficulties. If I've been rude I apologize. Let this discussion terminate itself. I don't interfere with your work in the parish. Don't you interfere with mine.'

The priest made a brushing gesture with his large hand.

'By being the sort of man you are, you interfere with God's work. It is already known that you intend to send Paul to an English school. What do the people think of that?'

Athanase relit his pipe and puffed savagely. 'That won't change him from being French.'

'An English Protestant school?'

'He'll still be a Catholic.'

'Then why not a French Catholic school?' The priest's eyes were insistent and steady. 'It's no use trying to pretend with me, Mr. Tallard. Facts like those – they speak for themselves. Paul is a baptized Catholic. What do you want to do – destroy his soul?'

'I want him to learn to mix naturally with English boys. I've never believed in this artificial separation. I want our people to feel that the whole of Canada is their land – not to grow up with the impression that the Province of Quebec is a reservation for them. Besides, I want Paul to get a scientific education.'

'And aren't the schools of his own race and faith good enough?'

'Under certain circumstances' – in spite of his anger, Athanase smiled – 'yes, quite good enough.' The smile faded. 'Listen, Father – you will not dictate to me in the matter of my son's school. That is beyond your authority. It is beyond even your own conception of it.'

Father Beaubien slipped a hand under his soutane and took out a handkerchief. He mopped his forehead and cheeks to remove the beads of perspiration that stood on them. In the silence the grandfather's clock could be heard clacking steadily. When he had replaced his handkerchief the priest rose. 'This is a good parish,' he said quietly. 'It's blessed by everything a Christian farmer could hope to have. Beyond us here, everywhere, there is the Devil's work. Look at it, Mr. Tallard, and in the name of God, don't be so proud and stubborn that you refuse to see it. Look at what this war has done to people's souls. Look at the trivial, futile kind of life materialism has produced in the States. How can an ignorant, simple farmer keep his faith in God when he sees how the wicked thrive? He is lured into the towns and what sort of infidelity awaits him there? Every year the Devil's work grows stronger.' A deep, resonant earnestness entered

Father Beaubien's voice. 'To me, it is wicked to see a Canadian who does not resist these things wherever he finds them.'

Irony showed itself in the lines of Athanase's face, in the set of his eyebrows and the turn of his mouth. 'Your world is very simple, Father. I respect your simplicity. In spite of our disagreements, I presume you will still accept my parish dues, just as you accepted the extremely large check I gave for your church.'

Sadness touched the priest's face as he looked away. Antagonism, of nature and of idea, stood between the two men like a living presence. It was heightened by the fact that each knew the inner core of the other so well, for stubborn, tenacious Norman blood was in both of them. Yet both, admitting a grudging respect for the other which grew out of pride in race, would have preferred to like rather than hold this enmity as a bar to friendship.

'I warn you, Mr. Tallard,' the priest said formally, 'I intend to protect my parish. God is not mocked.'

Athanase moved past the priest and opened the library door. The two men looked into each other's eyes, and then Father Beaubien strode through the hall to the outer door, opened it and went down the drive to the road, his soutane swishing. Athanase followed him to the gallery and watched him go. He wished he had reminded the priest that the Church was more than any single parish, more than the spiritual leader of any parish. He wished he had said there were many ecclesiastics he greatly admired; at least said it more clearly. He wished he had left Father Beaubien in no doubt whatever that if he had approached his mind, as the old bishop had done, he would have been delighted to talk with him for hours. And yet . . .

He returned to the library. Although he professed to respect little but logic and mental brilliance, Athanase sensed a peculiar power in the priest. In spite of himself, he could not despise Father Beaubien. He dropped into a chair and placed the glasses firmly on his nose. Suddenly he realized that he was tired. The blood was pounding out a headache behind the bones of his forehead, and his shirt was moist with sweat.

It was a day in early July when Janet Methuen stood in Poly-carpe Drouin's store with a letter in her hand from His Majesty the King, via the Canadian Ministry of Defence. She read it through, and when she had finished she lifted her head and looked around the store, seeing nothing. She began to walk forward and bumped into the side of the Percheron model, her arms hanging at her sides, the letter in one hand and the envelope in the other.

Drouin came from behind the counter. His voice was soft and kind, his face wrinkled, his eyes friendly. 'You are all right, Madame?'

Janet turned her head rigidly and saw his tap-like nose and the wrinkles about his eyes blur and then waver into focus. She saw him look at the letter in her hand and immediately she lifted her chin. She was as pale as unbleached muslin.

'I get you a drink, maybe?' Drouin said.

She heard her own voice, like a scratchy phonograph in another room, 'I'm quite all right, thank you.' But she continued to stand without moving.

Drouin went to the kitchen behind the store and returned with a glass of water, spilling some of it in his hurry. When he offered it she gave him a frozen smile. 'I'm quite all right, thank you,' she repeated tonelessly.

Her mind kept repeating a phrase she had read months ago in a magazine story: 'I mustn't let people see it. . . . I mustn't let people see. . . . I mustn't let . . .' The words jabbered in her mind like the speech of an idiot.

Drouin looked sideways at the only other person in the store, a farmer who had come in to buy some tar-paper. Their eyes met and both men nodded. The farmer had also seen the long envelope with O.H.M.S. in one corner.

'Get a chair, Jacques,' Drouin said in French. 'The lady wants to sit down.' But before the man could get one to her, Janet went to the door and walked out. The silence in her wake was broken as the chair hit the floor. Drouin shook his head and went around behind the counter. 'That's a terrible thing,' he said.

'Her husband, maybe?'

'The old captain says her husband is overseas.'

The farmer scratched his head. 'When I saw that letter this morning,' Drouin went on, 'I said to my wife, that's a bad thing, a letter like that. You never hear anything good from the government in Ottawa, I said.'

The farmer was still scratching his head. 'And she didn't cry,' he said. 'Well, maybe she don't know how.'

Drouin bent forward over the counter in his usual jack-knife position, his chin on the heels of his hands. After a time he said, 'You can't tell about the English. But maybe the old captain will be hurt bad,' he added, as though he had just thought of it.

Out on the plain the sun was overcast by smoke from distant forest-fires to the north. On the river the hull of a lake boat was lifted chunkily by the mirage. An iron-wheeled cart clanked slowly past Janet, but she was unaware of the farmer standing in the front of it, holding the reins. The tobacco stains in his heavy moustache were orange in the eerie light. His cart held a load of steaming manure. After it had gone by, Janet stopped and drew several deep, panting breaths of hot air. She looked about and saw that she was no longer hemmed in by the sides of houses and the faces of strange people. She touched her eyes with the back of her hand and took the hand away dry. Then she began to walk very fast down the road to her father's house. All the stories she had ever read in which one of the characters received bad news of a bereavement began to chase each other through her mind. Idiotically, they got out of control, they became herself. She was each of the characters in turn, bravely keeping her personal grief from intruding on others, she was nothing but memories and the things which had made her what she was.

At school, years ago in Montreal, she had been a shy girl without money among girls whose families were rich. She knew none of them, but they had all grown up together. When they looked pointedly at her clothes and asked where she came from, she had not been able to answer because they made her feel that she came from nowhere. Her father was at sea nearly all the time, sailing around the world, and her mother moved from one port to another to be near him while he was ashore. Before Janet had been in the Montreal school a fortnight she realized that proper people go to sea as passengers on a liner, not as sailors. From then on her father's profession was never mentioned; it was better to speak of her mother, who had been born in England.

Ursula Yardley's values were those of her class, and her class had always been the colonial civil service. Her father had upheld the white man's burden in the minor colonies and did everything so correctly he was incapable of doing anything really well, looking forward always to the day when he could retire to Sussex. She never lost the conviction that she had married beneath her, nor that she must somehow inform everyone she met in Canada of her social status in England. But John Yardley's salary had never been ample enough to permit her to take Janet back to the old country to live in the manner to which her mother had been accustomed. So she had moved restlessly about the Empire, finding it better to be poor in the colonies than at home. She died in Montreal while Janet was still in school, proud because her daughter was finally being accepted by the right families, but regretting to her last breath the fact that she had never been able to return to England.

Janet's sense of inferiority remained long after her marriage to Harvey Methuen. She found she had married more than the boy with whom she had fallen in love at a dance; she had joined a tribe. The Methuens felt themselves as much an integral part of Montreal as the mountain around which the city was built. They had been wealthy for a sufficient number of generations to pride themselves on never making a display. Instead, they incubated their money, increasing it by compound interest and the growth of the Canadian Pacific Railway. They were all Scotch-Canadians who went to a Presbyterian church every Sunday and contributed regularly to charities and hospitals. They served as governors of schools and universities, sat as trustees on societies founded to promote the arts, joined militia regiments when they left the Royal Military College, and had the haggis piped in to them at the Saint Andrew's Day dinner every winter.

Methuen women never ran to beauty because too much in

the way of looks in a woman was distrusted by the family. They were expected to be irreproachable wives and solid mothers of future Methuens, not females who might stimulate those pleasures the men of the family believed had caused the ruination of the Babylonians, Greeks, Romans, French, Italians, Spanish, Portuguese, Austrians, Russians and various other minor races of the world.

No Methuen found it possible to feel inferior to the English in any respect whatever; rather they considered themselves an extension of the British Isles, more vigorous than the English because their blood was Scotch, more moral because they were Presbyterians. Every branch of the family enjoyed a quiet satisfaction whenever visiting Englishmen entered their homes and remarked in surprise that no one could possibly mistake them for Americans.

The tribe accepted Janet and considered her a good woman, but she had never been able to feel at ease with them. At Harvey's side she had felt secure, for Harvey was greatly respected by the tribe and none of them believed he could ever do anything wrong. But since the war Janet had felt more than ever unsure of herself. Harvey was so filled with self-confidence; he had such an easy way of laughing; he was the only one who was able to joke with her and make her smile in spite of herself. After he left for overseas she missed the positive direction he gave her, and she was sure she could never uphold the standards her position in the family required.

Again and again she had a recurrent dream in which she entered General Methuen's library in the big house on the side of Mount Royal and saw her father-in-law sitting very straight in his leather armchair next to the red draperies under the gilt-framed landscape in which a French-Canadian farmer drove a white horse and a black horse through the snow. He was reading the *Strand Magazine*, and in her dream her skirt dropped to her ankles and exposed her thighs in tights like those of a chorus girl. General Methuen never spoke in her dream. He sighed heavily as he went on with his reading and pretended not to notice.

Janet had always known Harvey would be taken from her and she would be left alone again. As she walked fast along the river road this thought beat repeatedly at her mind, confused with scenes from the magazine story, with her mother's tight, lined face, with her own voice like a phonograph record repeating endlessly, 'I mustn't let people see it. . . . I mustn't let them see. . . . I mustn't . . .'

Suddenly Daphne and Heather were there on the road before her. She stopped when she saw them, her hand at her lips. They must have come from the clump of maples at the corner of her father's land. 'I mustn't let them see,' the voice in her mind repeated. Then another figure darted from behind the trees and she saw it was young Paul Tallard. His dog was at his heels and he was carrying something in his hands that looked like a dead bird. Janet let her hands drop to her sides. Paul was a nice boy even if he was a French-Canadian and had an impossible woman for a mother.

'Look, Mummy!' Heather called. 'Look what we've got!'

The dog began to bark as he ran down the road to Janet. He frisked about her legs and she nearly tripped over him. Then she found herself standing in the middle of the road with the three children around her. Daphne was an ash-blonde, very straight and neat, taller than the other two. Her clean middy blouse made a sharp contrast with Heather's dirty smock, streaked where brown mud had been carelessly wiped from the palms of small hands. Paul's hands were also dirty. He stood with large liquid eyes looking up at her, offering the dead bird for her to see.

'Napoléon found it in the bog,' he said.

'But he didn't kill it,' Heather interrupted, her voice rising with excitement. 'He just found it. Look, Mummy, at his leg. He's a heron, isn't he?'

Paul thrust the bird forward and she saw that one of its feet was missing.

'He stands on one leg anyway, so he didn't need his other foot,' Paul said.

'Or is it a crane?' Heather said. 'Which is it, Mummy?'

'It's a blue heron,' Daphne said, standing apart from the tight group made by Paul, Heather and the dog. 'We had it in school.'

Janet scarcely heard what they said. She looked over their heads and saw nothing. Then Heather said, 'What's the matter, Mummy?'

'Nothing. Why should anything be the matter?'

'Oh, I don't know exactly.'

'Is there a letter from Daddy?' Daphne said. 'If there isn't, there ought to be.'

Janet felt she was swaying, the earth lurching under her, and her knees were numb. 'Run along now,' she said. 'Don't go into the bog again.'

'But Mummy, why not?' Heather said. 'It's fun in the bog.'

'It's dirty, Heather. And you always get so filthy. Why can't you be like Daphne?'

'But, Mummy!'

She was walking down the road again, the children following.

'Why isn't there a letter from Daddy?' Daphne said. They were near Yardley's gate now. 'Daddy's a major,' she heard Daphne explain to Paul. 'He's in France.'

'I know it,' Paul said. 'It must be wonderful to be a major.'

When Janet turned into the gate she saw that her father had visitors on the porch. Yardley was sitting on a chair with his wooden leg crossed over his good knee, and Athanase Tallard and Mrs. Tallard were on either side of him. Janet turned to the children. 'Run along now and play.'

'But can't we really go into the bog any more?' Heather said.

'Oh, go anywhere. But run along.'

Napoléon began to bark shrilly as he went chasing a red squirrel down the road, his tail high and his ears back and flapping. The squirrel shot up a tree and Napoléon stood underneath barking steadily. Paul dropped the bird and went after him, Heather gave a shout and followed, and Daphne turned to her mother. 'Heather's awfully noisy, don't you think so, Mummy?'

Janet passed her hand over her forehead. 'Do run along and play with them like a good girl,' she said. As she went up the drive everything blurred before her eyes. Vaguely, his image staggering in a haze, she saw Athanase lift himself from his chair as she reached the steps, and she heard her own voice asking him not to bother. No, there was no mail this morning, none at all. No, don't bother, please don't anybody bother, she was going upstairs to her room to write letters.

As she opened the house door the coolness of the interior bathed her hot skin. She walked carefully upstairs, thinking about placing her foot on each tread, and by the time she reached her bed she was panting. She dropped onto the bed with relief, and as an easing of her tension set in she could hear the conversation from below as it floated up in the still air. Kathleen laughed heartily once or twice, and there was a chuckle from Mr. Tallard as her father's twangy voice went through one of his innumerable stories.

'Well, this horse I was telling you about was called Okay, and I never saw a stallion with a better name. He could stud like a rabbit and never lose a second off his pace, and the fella thet owned him made a nice sum of money, considering it was in Nova Scotia. Calvin Slipp, his name was, and he was the hardest-shell Baptist I ever saw come out of the Annapolis Valley. And thet's a Baptist to end all other Baptists forever. Calvin was a horse-doctor by trade, and a mighty smart one, and man, if you played poker with him on Saturday night you lost your shirt. He used to take Okay all around the Maritime Provinces to the fairs and exhibitions, year after year, till he got the piles so bad he couldn't sit his sulky and had to hire another driver....'

Upstairs Janet listened in spite of herself with a feeling of horror. How often he had embarrassed her in Montreal with his stories! She hated herself for disapproving of him, for she loved him and he had always been gentle and kind to her. But there he was telling a story like that, with the Tallard woman listening and she upstairs with her whole world collapsed and the future breaking over her with wave after wave of horror. She turned on the bed and murmured, 'God give me strength! Oh, God help me!' with her teeth clenched. How could she tell her children that their father was dead? Her beautiful children, her beautiful, beautiful children!

Through the open window floated the inexorable monologue of her father's voice. 'Now right there in thet same town was another Baptist named Luther Spry, and I guess maybe he was even harder-shelled than Calvin ever got around to being, for he was a deacon in the church. Luther was a racing man himself, owned a livery stable in the back part of town, and he had a mare name of Mademoiselle. In her own way she was just about as good as Okay, so the boys naturally were thinking what a great thing it would be if Okay could be put to the mare. Thet way they'd have a world-beater. But the trouble was, Calvin hated Luther's guts ever since the time Luther beat him out for being deacon in the church, and Calvin said he'd see Mademoiselle covered by a cart-horse before he'd let Okay get so much as a sniff of her. So the boys figured . . .'

Janet pulled herself off the bed and went into the bathroom to look at herself in the mirror. Her face was still the same. She closed her eyes and pressed her fingers over them until they hurt so much she couldn't stand the pain. Then she washed her face in cold water. Still her senses remained paralysed. This moment, the most terrible in her life, stayed with her, it wouldn't go away, it didn't get larger or smaller, but it remained unreal. She continued to stare at herself in the glass, wondering if this was insanity, this paralysis of feeling. She dried her face and returned to the bedroom.

'So just after moonrise,' came her father's voice, 'Luther and the boys came into Calvin's backyard with Mademoiselle on the end of a halter. It was a real nice October night, the way you get them down home in a good fall, with most of the leaves off the trees, and their feet were rustling in the leaves and the moon was making shadows through the bare branches. Mademoiselle began to whinny and Okay was inside the stable stamping around and kicking his stall the minute he got wind of her, and next door in the Baptist church the organ was going full blast and the whole prayer-meeting was singing *Rescue the Perishing* as loud as they could. The boys had to laugh, knowing Calvin was in there singing thet hymn. So they unlocked the stable door . . .'

Janet leaned from the window but she was unable to see the figures on the porch because of its shingled roof. It was easy to imagine them down there, her father's wooden leg cocked over his good one, Kathleen leaning toward him in that intimate way Janet always detested, Mr. Tallard with the ironic smile that baffled her completely.

'Man, but Okay gave thet mare a beautiful cover! The sweetest ever seen in thet town. And next morning when Calvin went out to the stable . . .'

Suddenly Janet screamed. The sound pierced the heavy

atmosphere and rested in the spine of everyone within ear-shot. She screamed again, and then she began to cry, 'Stop! For heaven's sake have pity and be quiet!'

She jerked herself away from the window and fell onto her bed, her whole body wracked by dry, shaking sobs. Through it all her eyes remained dry. She heard her father's wooden leg tapping as he hurried upstairs, but she kept her head on her outstretched arms when he entered the room. She felt his hand on the back of her head and heard him uncrumple the letter on the bed beside her, while the sobs kept shaking her whole body.

'Janet,' he said softly. 'Janet child!' The bed sagged as her father sat down beside her. He lifted her easily and held her in his arms and she tried to turn her face away from him. After a moment he tried to make her look at him, and for a second she did, but her eyes closed as soon as they met his own. Her lips kept opening and closing, and behind them her teeth remained tightly clenched.

'Go on and cry, Janet,' he whispered softly. 'You must.'

For a long time they remained like that, but Janet did not cry. A breeze sprang up from across the river and the smoke in the air moved out of the valley. A hay-wagon rumbled down the road, dropping fragments of its load in a trail behind.

16

Looking at the crops and the river and the line of forest behind the parish that summer, it was hard to believe the country had now been four years at war. But the war was there, over the horizon, threatening Quebec the way so many things over the horizon had always done: not only the fighting, not the killing and the cruelty, but the enormous-ness of it, the way it had grown into a world industry, the new machinery and the growing madness and the altars to national gods.

In the rest of Canada no horizon held it off. In all the little towns along the double tracks that held the country together from one end to the other the war ate into everyone's mind. People went to bed with it, and during the days it worked beside them like a shadow of themselves. They could never do enough for it. Names like Ypres, Courcelette, Lens, Vimy, Cambrai, Arras, the Somme, had become as familiar and as much a part of Canada as Fredericton, Moose Jaw, Sudbury or Prince Rupert.

Perhaps in Quebec the serene permanence of the river itself helped confirm the people in their sureness that their instinct was right; that the war was the product of the cities which constantly threatened their tradition, of English-American big business, factories, power dams, banks, trusts, heavy industry and the incessant jabbering noise of the outside world which bombarded their own idea of themselves, roaring that they were weak, unimportant, unprogressive, too backward to understand the magnificence of the war. And beside, there was the faith. All through the Laurentian country thousands of Sulpicians, Jesuits, Dominicans, Benedictines, Franciscans, Trappists, Servites, Carmelites, Ursulines, Little Sisters of the Assumption, Grey Nuns, lay-brothers and lay-sisters, bishops, parish priests, vicars and seminary students worked on in the unbroken tradition out of the Middle Ages and contemplated the Catholic God. Against the light of Eternity, the war seemed only a brutish interlude.

So the country brooded on through midsummer, each part bound to the others like a destiny, even in opposition forming a unity none could dissolve, the point and counterpoint of a harmony so subtle they never guessed its existence.

17

McQueen's surveyors appeared in Saint-Marc at the end of the first week in August and stayed six days in the parish. They were put up at the Tallard house and went out to the gorge every day with their levels and transits and notebooks. They pegged lines across the stream at various points from the falls toward the road, and worked in a flat-bottomed boat secured to the lines, while they lowered an aluminum propeller on the end of a wired shaft to measure the velocity of the current at various points along the channel. Then they plotted a course for the railroad spur which would have to be built to serve the factory. Their course took them across several farms, and Athanase went ahead of them to explain to the farmers that what the surveyors were doing was an important secret which would turn into a lucky development for them. To Tremblay he explained that if certain projects went through he might want to buy one of his fields; there would be a lot of money in it for him if no one else was told about it.

At the end of the week the surveyors went back to town and a few days later McQueen wrote to Athanase asking him to come to Montreal at once to get the organization of the firm under way. Before Father Beaubien or anyone else in Saint-Marc had quite made up their minds to question him, Athanase was gone.

In Montreal, McQueen told him the layout was perfect, there was plenty of power in the river and no difficulties about the terrain. Plans had already been drawn up by an architect for the building. Athanase studied them with keen interest and gave his approval. All arrangements for incorporation he left entirely to McQueen. He took out a first and second mortgage on his property in Saint-Marc, held in McQueen's name, and converted the loan, together with the proceeds of the sale of his bonds, into stock in the company. All his eggs were in one basket now and the realization of what he was doing sometimes frightened him when he was alone at night. But during the day, when typewriters clacked, telephones rang, drawers were opened and closed, conferences were held, enthusiastic opinions ran high, letters and documents accumulated in files, and architects, engineers, business managers, experts on textiles, and stenographers all beamed confidence, Athanase was quite happy in the swim of so much excitement.

His own important part in the proceedings came to a head when he received word from Ottawa that the government would build the railway spur as soon as the foundation of the factory was laid. Athanase beamed when he read the letter from the minister. He had calculated the political side of this project perfectly, as McQueen had expected him to do. The government had no wish to see him lose his seat, and the railway spur would be put down to his credit in the next election.

156

Meanwhile the spread of rumours in Saint-Marc found their focus in Polycarpe Drouin's store. Polycarpe himself looked wise and said it meant an election for sure. Anyone using a level and transit was bound to be employed by the government, and the government never did anything except before an election. Frenette said the parish was going to be divided into two parts and a new church was to be built near the falls. Onésime Bergeron said Mr. Tallard was fixing it so the whole parish would be handed over to the English. Ovide Bissonette made no prediction, but he was sure that whatever happened, it would be something bad. Tremblay and all the farmers whose land had been touched by the surveyors kept their mouths shut. For a fortnight all conversations with the priest were shifted by monosyllables to the subject of the surveyors, but Father Beaubien, looking as stern as the general of an encircled army, merely thought hard and also kept his mouth shut.

18

Marius Tallard sat on a bench in the corner of the station waiting room in Montreal and ate the sandwich Emilie had just given him. He took large bites and swallowed before he had chewed properly. The movement of his jaws showed how thin he had become, with the sharp cheek-bones making deep shadows on his white skin. Emilie waited until the sandwich was half consumed, and then she said, 'You better be sure it's a safe thing, you going back home now.'

Her timidity irritated him. 'What's safe anywhere?' he said, his mouth full of bread and ham. 'I'm tired. I'm going home.'

Emilie accepted his explanation without question, as she did everything he said.

'But don't get the idea I'm going back to my father,' he went on. 'I'm through with him. But that land out there – it's mine as well as his. I hate Montreal anyhow.'

'Sure, sure. Sometimes I think about the country too. Sometimes.' She smiled at him with a sort of vacant tenderness.

The waiting room smelled of stale cigar smoke, spittoons, disinfectant, orange peels, unwashed clothes and sweating flesh. All the assorted bits of humanity that sat stiffly or lolled on the benches were ill at ease and unwilling to be there. They were devoid of background, without status in this interim between leaving one place and arriving at another. There were farm women with their best clothes wilted and bundles tied with cord hugged close at their sides. There were sailors and soldiers showing the effects of a weekend leave in the city. There were couples, and single men with cheap suitcases at their feet who might be anything from lunch-counter clerks to steamfitters in the normal course of their day. Now they were nothing, nobodies waiting for trains to take them some place else. For a fraction of time the big room became alive and everyone in it was united by a common interest. A girl in magenta silk, holding the arm of a man in a black suit and a bowler hat, broke away from a splash of shouting and laughter in the concourse, ducked through a shower of rice and confetti, into the waiting room, through it, and on to their train.

Marius finished the sandwich and wiped his mouth with a rumpled handkerchief. He looked up at the clock on the wall at one end of the room. The instrument might have been put there especially to annoy him. 'Wait – wait – wait! That's the best thing I do nowadays.'

Emilie touched his forearm with her fingers. She wanted to take the strain from him, to make him quiet, but he refused to let her. Now he jerked his arm away. She wanted to ask him where he had been and what he had been doing during all the weeks she had not seen him, but she said nothing. It was something to be thankful for that he had called her at the restaurant just before she was ready to leave.

'I guess you got no money, maybe?' she said after a while. 'Maybe that's why you go home?'

'Well, what if it is?'

'You should of come to me. I'd see you weren't hungry.'

He laughed harshly. 'I've been getting my education.'

'You been back at the college?'

'Don't be so simple. Do you think you get an education in college?'

'Mon Dieu, you got no need to bite me.'

158

'I've been learning things that count. How the poor feel, for instance.'

'I could have told you.'

He appraised her with a sarcastic smile. 'I found out the poor have no brains. They believe whatever they're told so long as it's easy to remember. But the main thing is, they're all lazy.'

He got up from the bench and thrust his hands in his pockets. All the luggage he possessed was on his back. A passing soldier glanced at him and Marius made a point of staring until the man looked the other way.

'In this town,' he said, looking over Emilie's head, 'all the poor I met were French. We're the ones that get splashed with the motor cars of the English.' He looked down at the girl beside him. 'Did you ever stop to think how comparatively few English live in Montreal?'

Emilie shook her head. She had no interest in what he was saying, but the way he said it gave her a sick feeling inside. He stooped down and picked up a grain of rice that had been thrown at the honeymoon couple. Eyeing it as he turned it over in his fingers, he went on. 'In Montreal the French outnumber the English three to one. In the province we outnumber them more than seven to one. And yet, the English own everything!' He held the grain of rice under the nail of his thumb and stared at the floor. 'The English in Montreal, they own nearly the whole of Canada. And yet once upon a time the whole of Canada belonged to the French.'

Emilie tried to smile. She tugged at his coat in an effort to get him to sit down again, but Marius knew he talked better on his feet. 'In the factories all the bosses are English. One English boss, five hundred French workers. Funny, no?' He cracked the grain of rice solemnly between two nails at though it were a flea. 'But on the whole,' he went on, 'it is the laziness of the poor one should first observe. The rich are equally stupid, but I think maybe the rich are frightened, and frightened men are not generally lazy.'

Emilie got up from the bench and stood close beside him. In contrast to his drawn and bitter leanness, she looked plump and healthy. Her commonsense wanted to make him

159

stop all this talk. It was probably clever, but clever people only got into trouble. Only priests should use clever talk like Marius.

Again she tugged at his sleeve. 'What are you going to do now?'

'How do I know?'

'Will they get you? You think maybe they know where you're going?'

Marius looked at her sharply and then he walked rapidly out of the waiting room toward the tracks. Emilie had to move her short legs unnaturally fast to keep up with him and her heavy hips wobbled in time with her trot. She knew Marius was frightened. When a man talked like that he was always scared of something. Whoever was after him had found out where he'd been hiding, and now he had to get out of town.

When they reached the gate Marius showed his ticket to the conductor. The man glanced at it and let them pass through to the platform. They walked down a line of standing coaches and Marius finally selected one that was nearly full. He stopped at the steps and looked down at Emilie. The set expression on his face melted and he looked irresolute, almost pitiful. 'If I only had some money . . .'

He bent and kissed her fiercely, then released her and went up the steps without looking around. She stood where he had left her and her hand rose and then fell again. He had kissed her so hard his teeth had bruised her lips. Nothing had passed from him to her but the pain. Even in kissing her he had locked her out. She turned after a few moments and walked slowly back to the station concourse. What ought she to do? She had saved seven dollars. Maybe if she went to church and put the money in the box and prayed to the Virgin, the Holy Mother of God would intercede and make Marius kinder and happy, so everything between them could be good. If she wanted to be blessed she must first deserve the blessing.

19

For Paul, it was a momentous day. He got up just before dawn and dressed quietly, then went downstairs in the dark in his stocking feet so as not to wake the others in the house. He put on his shoes in the kitchen and went out to the scullery. He took his fishing rod from the corner where he had left it the night before, walked down the drive in the dark and turned into the river road toward Captain Yardley's with the rod over his shoulder. He felt very important being up before anyone else in the parish.

As he walked along the road the first suggestion of light began. It touched the horizon and spread out soft and grey as it crept up the sky. The world quickly grew larger. A rooster crowed, his voice musical in the distance. By the time Paul reached the captain's back door there was just light enough to see the trees down by the river's edge a quarter of a mile away.

He looked in the window and saw the captain sitting at the table drinking hot cocoa and eating biscuits. The oilcloth on the table gleamed yellow in the light of a lamp. Daphne and Heather were on either side of him. Paul tapped the glass and saw the captain look around and Heather get up and leave the table. A moment later she opened the door for him. Her eyes were large and wide awake.

'Fun, Paul!' she said.

He rested his rod against the side of the house, put his arm about her waist and they went into the kitchen together. Daphne looked sleepy and the captain was telling her she ought to eat more. Paul noticed that her eyes were red and wondered if she had been crying on account of her father. Heather had cried a lot a few weeks ago, but now she never spoke of her father any more.

'Drink your cocoa, Paul,' the captain said. 'Should have had porridge ready, but these two ladies here, they're too fine to eat porridge.'

'But Grampa,' Heather said, 'you told us it would put hair on our chests. That would be horrid.'

Yardley let the remark pass. He was unusually quiet. Paul drank two cups of cocoa and ate two pilot biscuits spread with butter. They all broke the pilot biscuits into sharp-edged pieces and dipped them into a bowl of molasses.

Daphne looked at her sister. 'Molasses on your chin again,' she said.

Heather wiped her face absently and looked out the

window. Light was spreading over the fields. 'Will the fish all swim to the bottom when the sun comes up?'

'Most of them,' Yardley said. He rose and stumped out to the porch, picked up three rods and added Paul's. 'We'd better be going. Did you leave the bait can in the boat last night?'

'Yes, Grampa,' Heather said. She turned to Paul. 'The loveliest worms. They liked it in the can. They wriggled so I could see they liked it.' Seeing that her grandfather was moving off, she bent over Paul and whispered gravely, her breath tickling his ear, 'Grampa's been awful sad lately.'

'I bet your Mummy's sadder,' he said in a hoarse attempt to whisper in turn.

'Mummy's heart's broken,' Heather said. She followed Daphne onto the porch, Paul beside her. 'I should be sad too. It's no fun being an orphan.' But almost immediately she forgot what she had been talking about and ran ahead of the others down the path to the road.

They walked in Indian file down to the river through a path in a field planted for oats, and the dew-bent stalks brushed their legs. At the river's edge Yardley unlocked a flat-bottomed boat from its stake among the reeds and shoved it into the water. The timbers of the boat scraped hoarsely on the shingle, the water took its weight and the stern slid out into the river so smoothly it seemed to kiss it. Paul stood by the bow while the girls got in. The boat was wet with dew, the moisture making a veil of tiny beads over the paint, and when Paul put his hand on it he felt the coldness wash his skin and saw the beads dissolve into a film of water the same grey colour as the paint. Heather upset the bait can and the rolling tin tinkled sharply. She went down on her knees and pushed the escaping worms back again.

'Are you ready?' Yardley called.

They said they were.

In the small backwater where they were the river had no current. It looked as broad as a lake, and because there was a mist over it they couldn't see the other shore. It seemed very mysterious to Paul as he thought of all the water in the river sliding through the country under the mist.

Yardley stepped in and balanced himself, then went past

162

the girls on the centre thwarts to the stern. 'Shove off, Paul!' His shout cracked the wet stillness. It was loud enough to reach a masthead. Paul gave a heave and the boat went clear. He followed it and rested his knee on the stem, then slid inside and sat in the bow. Yardley brought the boat around and sent it forward into the river and the mist, standing with his wooden stump braced against the side and sculling over the stern with a long, flat oar.

'Is that the way the fishermen scull the dories in Nova Scotia?' Heather asked.

'That's how.'

They moved into deep water with no sound but the creaking of the oar and an occasional splash as it broke water. The bow nodded gently back and forth as the sculling oar propelled them onward. When they came to a shoal where a stake was driven into the river-bed Paul moored the boat and they cast their lines. By sunrise Paul and Heather had caught two fish apiece and the captain had four. Daphne had not taken any, though she had lost two.

While they fished, the sun rose. It rolled like a ball out of the river and its rays shot through the mist like red arrows. The ball mounted and paled to gold, shredding the clouds apart. Paul thought it was like the candles blazing over the altar, gleaming on the cloth-of-gold chasuble of the priest at Mass, the cry going up to the roof and the suggestion that this golden light was the colour of glory. The mist stirred and lifted in veils. Flashes of light struck out from the church steeple in the village. Farther upstream there was a similar gleam from the steeple of Sainte-Justine, and across the river another. Then the aluminum paint on the church roofs began to shine; the world was bright and it was day. In all the parishes up and down the river the angelus rang. The notes had a muted, rolling sound as they came over the water. Paul bowed his head and Daphne looked at him oddly. He kept his head bowed as he murmured a prayer to himself, and Daphne finally glanced at Heather with a smile that was half embarrassed and half amused. The captain frowned at her.

When the angelus ceased ringing Daphne said, 'Do you always do that?'

'Yes. When I'm awake. It's for the angelus.'

'It's a funny thing to do.'

'Thet's rude,' Yardley said. 'Talking about other people's religions.'

'But I just think it's funny Paul being a Catholic, that's all.'

'Catholics think it's a hell of a lot worse, us being Protestants.'

'Mummy says you shouldn't say hell,' Daphne said.

Yardley eyed her reflectively. 'Listen, young lady – some day I'm going to tan you.'

Heather said, 'Don't mind Daffie, Paul. She's nasty. She's a horrid little girl.' She picked a worm from the bait can and dangled it before her sister's face. It was an earthy red, smooth and shiny, and as it dangled its corrugated tail curled up. Daphne made a face and shivered.

'Scared to put a worm on your own hook,' Heather said. 'Paul has to do it for you.'

'Grampa,' Daphne said with dignity, 'make Heather stop.'

'Thet's not nice, Heather,' Yardley said.

'Look at her hands,' Daphne said. 'They're filthy.'

Paul shouted and stood up in the boat. 'I've got a fish!'

They forgot everything else as they watched him play it in. He stood very serious with his lips parted and his two buck teeth showing, his brown eyes large as he drew the fish through the water, the line darting in quick circling jerks from side to side as it cut disappearing ellipses on the surface. Yardley manoeuvred the boat away from the fish until Paul had it alongside, then bent over the gunwale and dipped it in.

'Not bad!' he said. He picked the fish up in both hands, one on the head and the other on the body, and broke its back behind the gills. Daphne winced at the crunching sound made by the snapping backbone.

'I wish you wouldn't do that, Grampa,' she said. 'You know I hate it.'

Yardley looked at her for the space of several breaths, as if trying to figure her out. 'Can't let him gasp out his life on the bottom of the boat. Thet's cruel, thet is. Besides, it spoils the meat. Some fish got such strong juices in their stomachs they go right on working if you leave them lie. A dying fish pretty near digests some of himself.' He pulled out his watch and looked up at the sky. 'Well, I guess we better go back now. Your mother will be up for breakfast soon.'

20

Father Beaubien had not slept all night. Marius had come to him after dark and he had given the boy supper in his presbytery and a bed in his spare room. They had talked together for several hours. Marius was still asleep and he would have sanctuary for the rest of the day, then he would leave.

In the early morning while it was still dark Father Beaubien had left his bed, dressed and entered the church to pray. He had prayed for the soul of Athanase Tallard and he prayed for Marius. The boy was too bitter, too unforgiving; if he continued to develop this bitter cynicism the priest did not know what would become of him. Finally Father Beaubien had prayed for himself, asking God to give him grace and wisdom to protect his parish.

Shortly after ten he presented himself at the door of the Tallard house and was shown into the library. In a few minutes Athanase joined him there. Without preliminaries this time the priest said, 'I've been talking to your son again, Mr. Tallard.'

'Marius? Where?'

'That's unimportant. He is well, so far as his health is concerned. But he doesn't want to see you now, and I don't think he should. Later, perhaps, I hope he will see things differently.'

'Is he still in the village?'

The priest looked about the room and Athanase offered him a chair. 'I didn't come here to speak of Marius, Mr. Tallard. I came to speak of you.'

Athanase knocked the dead ashes from his pipe. 'Well?'

'I've been talking to Tremblay. And some of the other farmers whose land you propose to take away.'

'Well?'

'You can't do this to Saint-Marc, Mr. Tallard. You know that as well as I do.'

'What can't I do?'

The priest made a gesture of impatience but immediately his hand returned to the lap of his soutane. Spreading his legs under the black cloth he leaned forward in his chair. 'I know all about it,' he said. 'The details make no difference. You're trying to build a factory here.'

'Is that against the law?'

'Lawyer's arguments are useless with me. Are you, or are you not, planning to buy the Tremblay land for a factory?'

'And if I am?'

'I will tell Tremblay not to sell. I will tell every farmer you have already talked to not to sell.'

Athanase flushed and rose from his chair. A sharp wind pushed in the curtains at the window, ruffling the papers on the desk. As he closed the window Athanase saw that a sudden storm had arisen. A black thunder cloud was rolling across the sky, its shadow rushing like an eclipse over the land and swallowing up the sunshine on the river. A splatter of rain struck the window, there was a sharp flash, followed a second later by the roar of thunder. The room was dark now and the books brooded on their shelves. Athanase returned to his chair. The flush had left his face.

'You exceed your authority, Father. What am I to think of these visits you make to me? You have no cause to hate me.'

'Hate you? I prayed for you last night. Always, I have done the best in my power to understand you. You won't let me.'

The storm roared closer and the wind for a moment reached hurricane force. In a moment it had obliterated the quietness of the day. It screamed over the plain and bent the crops. It lashed cattle in the field and tore branches from trees. Grey driving rain washed the windows.

'Father Beaubien,' Athanase said, 'no matter what you think, we're living in the twentieth century. A factory here is inevitable. Either we French develop our own resources or the English will do it for us. The population of this parish is larger than the farms will support. Unless our people are to be forced over the border into the United States, work must be provided for them here.'

'The war is also a part of the twentieth century.' Thunder roared and the priest had to stop until the sound died away. 'Is that also good?'

The storm was now directly overhead and Athanase's answer was drowned in the next thunder-clap. Rain struck the windows a solid blow. Then for a moment the air seemed breathless, as though they were in the hollow core of the storm.

'Let me tell you something,' Father Beaubien said. 'In the place where I was first curate no one owned anything but the English bosses. There were factories there, but the people owned nothing. They were out of work a quarter of a year around. Good people became miserable and then they became cheap. They forgot about God. Some of them even tried to leave the Church. There were many illegitimate children because of the poverty and wretched examples the people had to see.' He looked straight at Athanase. 'And all the time simple Catholics who served God as they should were never rewarded. They saw English managers throwing money about while prices rose and they grew poorer. They blamed the priest for not being able to do more for them.' His voice rose. 'Always that's the story! You accuse me of disliking the English. As a people I have nothing against them. But they are not Catholics and they do our people harm. They use us for cheap labour and they throw us aside when they're finished. I won't let you do that here, Mr. Tallard. I won't let a man like you spoil this parish. And I don't think the bishop will either. Marius has told me things about you. Some of them I knew anyway, some I had not dreamed possible. Now I tell you in plain language. You are a good Catholic or you are not. You cannot defy the Church and God's own priest and feel no effects. If it comes to a fight between me and a man like yourself . . .'

The storm was rolling its way down the river valley but the rain continued to wash the windows. Imperceptibly the light was growing in the room. Athanase kept his eyes on the priest, no irony in them, but defiant with anger.

'Just what do you imagine you can do to stop this development?'

Father Beaubien's eyes had never left Athanase's face. 'Do

you think the people here will follow your lead when they know what sort of man you are? When they know you are a heretic?' Suddenly his words snapped at Athanase's brain. 'Do you think they've so easily forgotten your first wife?'

Athananse stared at him. For a moment his lips hung open, then closed.

'She was a saintly woman. She suffered unspeakably because of you, because of your sins and wicked thoughts and your sneers at religion.'

A deep flush spread over Athanase's face, pushing into his white hair. 'Did Marius . . .?'

'You remember when your first wife lay dying?' The priest's relentless voice went on.

The flush faded from Athanase's cheeks as quickly as it had come. His hands were shaking, whether in anger or in fear it was impossible to say. He got to his feet. 'This is enough,' he said in a choked voice.

Father Beaubien also rose, still holding his eyes.

'Do you hear me? This is enough. I ask you to leave.'

For a long moment the priest stood and watched him. Then he said, quietly and almost sadly. 'Mr. Tallard . . . please come back.'

When Athanase made no movement and gave no sign that he understood the import of the words, the priest turned and walked out of the room. When he had gone Athanase dropped limply into a chair, closed his eyes and let his arms hang loosely. Until this moment he had always felt utterly confident in his own brain. Because of it, he had been convinced of his superiority to the priest. And then Father Beaubien had reached out and touched the most secret and private memory of his life. With that touch, his strength was gone.

Inexorably his thoughts returned to the priest's final words. He felt his mind floundering to escape his childhood training, the sense of guilt aroused in him. He felt now that if Father Beaubien had remained a minute longer he would have collapsed before him. How explain to an ascetic what had happened the night Marie-Adèle died? How explain to anyone? How tell even himself that there is any logic in human life after such a night?

168

Her little nun's face lay on the pillows as white as the linen, pinched in against the upper jaw with two hectic red spots on the cheekbones. He stood there gripping the bedrail and behind him Marius was on his knees, sobbing and praying alternately. On the other side of the bed were Marie-Adèle's mother, and her sister, who was in the Ursuline Order. The confessor was there, the doctor was standing near the door, holy water and flowers stood with candles on the table. The priest had administered the last rites. He saw her girl's figure frail under the sheets and her eyes appearing to blaze out of her head, yet obviously blind, seeing nothing. He stood at the bedrail remembering the futility of their life together, the pity of it, and then the whole fragile aspect of human existence rose before his eyes and dissolved as his mind was dissolving, and he thought he could smell death. Then he could stand it no longer. He groped like a blind man to the door, and the doctor took his arm and led him out. 'It's all over now,' he heard the doctor say. Then he left, went down the corridor alone, out of the hospital into the street.

As he walked the streets of Montreal that night he did not feel the cold, even though it was fifteen below zero and trees were cracking in the frost. He walked for hours. The lobe of his left ear froze and he did not notice it. Finally he remembered Kathleen and went to find her. She came away with him and they walked together back to the hospital.

He had engaged two extra rooms in the hospital on the same floor with Marie-Adèle, one for himself, the other for Marius. Now, with Kathleen beside him, he entered the room where Marius was sleeping. The boy lay utterly still. He turned and went out, closing the door softly behind him. Then he entered his own room and Kathleen sat down on the bed beside him. He looked at her and she held his eyes, and with an understanding as simple as a child she gave herself to him that night. He cried himself to sleep in her arms and she lay awake holding him. When he woke the next morning he was alone in the room, the sun was coming up over the roofs of the city for another day, he saw it glittering on the snow crystals, and as he looked out the window he knew that he could now go on living. In the night just passed he had swum upward out of death. And he thought: Marie-

Adèle never lived for life, but in order to die, in order to enter the Kingdom of Heaven. And he thought: God rest her soul there, for her purpose is now fulfilled and her purpose never had anything to do with me anyway. She was at peace now, or she was nothing. But he was alive and had to go on living. And that morning he felt so grateful to Kathleen that he knew he would always be her debtor for what she had done.

He breathed heavily. His breath came in quick gasps as he looked at the bookshelves beside him. So Marius had known! So this was the thing that had lain between them all these years! And now Father Beaubien knew also.

Athanase forced himself to his feet. That night had made a profound difference in his life, more than he had ever been willing to admit even to himself. He had done something which almost any man, regardless of his religion, would consider heinous. But in his own instincts he could not condemn himself for it, nor could he admit the authority of anyone, priest or ordinary man, to condemn him.

Looking out the window he saw that the storm had passed and that brilliant sunshine was pouring down on the wet earth through a hole in the clouds. Then he knew that his head was screaming with pain. He put his hand against his forehead and sat down. He lay still in the chair for a long time, his head pounding, his eyes closed. When he next opened his eyes he saw Kathleen standing in the doorway. How long she had been there he had no idea.

'You look awful,' she said. 'What is it? You look sick.'

'It's my head again. Another headache, that's all.'

'What did Father Beaubien say to you?'

'He – he spoke about Marius, that's all.'

'Oh!' She looked at him, and knew it was not all. 'Have they put him in the army yet?'

'Not yet.'

Raising his eyes, he saw Kathleen's face bending over his, then closing in. The warm softness of her lips touched his own.

'Athanase . . . what happened?'

'Don't be frightened.' From somewhere out of his subconscious a new set of words came. They were quite unpremeditated. 'No one should be frightened of God.'

She drew away from him with a puzzled look. 'You're sure you're all right?'

He rose, passed his hand over his eyes, and walked out to the hall. 'I'm all right,' he said. 'Don't bother about me.'

He went upstairs at a normal pace, and she followed. He undressed slowly, calmly, and she stood by and picked up his clothes, one piece after another. Undressed, he relaxed in the coolness of the sheets and kept his eyes closed. He felt her hand on his forehead, then heard her steps receding and the sound of her door quietly closing.

It was good to be alone again. His blood pressure had given him quite a scare for a moment. But no, he was not ready to die yet. He would sleep, and by morning he would be fine. Too many problems were unsolved for him to die now. If he put his mind to them he would manage all right. A stubborn smile wavered across his grey lips and away again. No, he was not beaten yet, changes would come and he would guide them, he would hang on and no childish thoughts of guilt would stop him, he was not beaten and never would be.

21

That afternoon as the earth dried out Paul worked with Blanchard hoeing up potatoes. He kept at it for three hours and had blistered hands before Blanchard ordered him to stop. He went into the kitchen with Blanchard, and Julienne brought beer for the man and barley water for Paul. The bottle and the pitcher had been cooling under the well-cover and now they sweated in the heat of the kitchen. She gave them apple fritters, and Paul ate so many he had no appetite left at supper time and all he took was a glass of milk.

He went to bed immediately after supper very tired, and lay on his back with his sore hands clasped behind his head. He was happy about nothing in particular. Only last week he had moved into his brother's room because it was larger than his old one, and he liked it. Marius' room had shiny white wallpaper with a fringe of bluebirds around the cor-

171

nice, and it made Paul feel older, being in the room with all his brother's things still there. In one corner there was a shotgun and on the side wall a pair of snowshoes hanging crossed over a nail. In the cupboard Marius had left some suits and sweaters, a suitcase, and a sleeping bag he sometimes used in the fall when he went hunting. Above the bed was a bronze crucifix, and facing it the altar with the candles and the cross. Near the photograph of Marie-Adèle was a picture of Jesus with blood dripping down His forehead from the crown of thorns. It was the only sacred picture in the house except for the ones Julienne kept in the kitchen.

Paul had taken two books to bed with him. One was *The Three Musketeers* in French, the other *Treasure Island* in English. Captain Yardley had given him *Treasure Island* only a few days ago. and he wanted very much to read it because it was about the sea. He spoke English as easily as French, but he found it very difficult to make any sense out of the words when he read them, for he could not spell English yet. And anyway, he was too tired tonight to read anything. He lay awake in bed until the light began to fade and the swallows were swooping around the window. There was a nest of them under the eaves, and this was the main reason why he had wanted the room; also, it gave a better view of the river.

It was after twilight when he heard the door click open and looked up to see his mother come in. She was carrying a cat in her arms. She entered with a soft rustle of skirts and smiled when she saw he was awake. She sat on the edge of the bed and as it gave with her weight he slipped over against her. She dropped the cat on the bed beside him.

'I brought you Minou,' she said. 'Don't tell your father, now.'

He sat upright, grinning, and made a catch at the cat with his hands. Minou leaped away and sat on the end of the bed, her back to Paul and Kathleen. Paul lay back against the pillows and she put her hand on his forehead. There was a faint odour of perfume as she bent over him, and he lay back and thought her beautiful and smelled the faint odour of her perfume and felt safe.

'Where have you been, M'ma?'

'With your father. He's very tired and worried today.'

'Is everyone tired and worried when they grow up?'

'Oh, no – but your father's a very important man and has specially big things to worry about.'

Paul thought about this for a moment. 'M'ma – will Marius be sore about me being in his room?'

'Of course he won't! What an idea!'

'He gets awful sore.' A pause. 'M'ma – is Marius in trouble?'

'He's all right. He's a big man now.'

'But he won't come home to P'pa. Why does he hate P'pa?'

'He doesn't. Now don't you think about things like that. Promise? Little boys shouldn't think about things.'

'But – '

Marius is a big man, and he's clever, and big, clever men never get into trouble.'

He thought about this, his brown eyes grave. 'Do you only get into trouble when you're small?'

She smiled, picked up the cat and held its fur against her cheek, the cat settling comfortably on her shoulder. Then she lowered the animal gently to the bed, pressed her into the hollow made by Paul's knees and stroked her into quietness. 'There now,' she said. 'There now. You and Minou can put each other to sleep.'

Her hand was still on his forehead when Paul closed his eyes. She remained until his breathing became regular, then bent and brushed his forehead with her lips, and left the room on tiptoe.

Everyone in the house was asleep when Paul began to dream that Christ hung from a cross in the sky and that light poured down from Him holy to the earth. But underneath the holy light there was darkness, and terror moved through it with a droning sound. The drone ceased, the darkness rolled up like a curtain, and soldiers staggered out of an underbrush that covered the ground, lurching forward with weapons to kill each other. There were soundless explosions that remained motionless in the scene as they did in pictures. Paul saw himself crouching behind a rock witnessing what was happening, both hands gripping the top of the rock and his mouth opening and closing as he begged them to stop it, but no sound issuing from his lips. Then he saw two soldiers stabbing each other and they were his father and Marius. He looked up and the eyes of Christ on the cross rolled, and then he was awake with a cry in his throat feeling a hand clamped down over his mouth and his brother's voice sudden out of the darkness.

'Shut up!'

Paul sat up terrified. He saw the window pane a deep purple with stars behind it. The moon had already set. He saw a shadow move and then a match strike, light flare out from it and Marius' hair hanging down over his forehead as he lit the lamp. Light welled out into the room.

'What's the matter?' Paul whispered, trembling.

'What are you doing here?'

'They said it was my room now.'

'Oh, they did, did they!'

Marius crossed to the cupboard and then jumped suddenly, nearly knocking the lamp over. 'What's that?'

Paul saw a dark shadow on the floor fading out of the circle of light. 'It's only Minou.'

'What do you want a cat in your bed for?' Marius opened the cupboard door. 'Those cats are all lousy.'

'Have you come home?'

'I want some things, that's all. Don't ask so many questions.'

Marius undressed quickly, taking off all his clothes until he was naked. The lamp sent long shadows and lights up his body; he was so thin that every rib stood out and cast a shadow on the skin above it. He hung his old clothes in the closet and Paul caught their stale smell. Then Marius took out a suit and two sweaters and walked naked to the dresser, opened the drawer and took out some shirts. He dressed quickly while Paul watched him, thinking how fine-looking he was. Then he went to the cupboard again and came back with a suitcase and put the spare shirts and sweaters in it. He put on a pair of heavy boots, lifted the sleeping bag from its hook and rolled it up. He seemed to have forgotten Paul's existence.

When he had everything he wanted he put on his hat and

174

pulled it down over his forehead, then turned abruptly to Paul. 'You keep your mouth shut about this – understand!'

Paul nodded. Marius crossed the room and took the shotgun from the corner. He broke it open and squinted down the barrels, pointing it at the lamp. Then he snapped it shut again and replaced it in the corner. 'No good to me,' he grunted. 'No shells for it.'

Paul was now sitting on the edge of the bed with his legs dangling. 'You can't go hunting anyway – not till fall.'

Marius came over and stood looking down at his half-brother with his eyes hidden by the brim of his hat. 'Listen – what did you eat tonight?'

'Only a glass of milk.'

'I mean, what did the rest of them eat?'

'Roast lamb, I guess.'

Marius gave a short laugh. 'Well, I hope there's some left.'

'What's the matter, Marius? Where are you going?'

'Never mind where. And you didn't see me here – remember that. You keep your mouth shut.'

He picked up his suitcase and the sleeping bag and went on tiptoe to the door. A loose board creaked and he swore under his breath. He set the suitcase down while he gently opened the door and put the sleeping bag outside. As he did so the cat jumped through the opened door and he swore softly again. Then, carrying the suitcase, he went out and closed the door behind him.

It was the next morning about eleven o'clock when Athanase called Paul into the library. His face was stern as he told him to sit down. 'What happened in your room last night?' he said.

Paul hung his head.

'Marius was there, wasn't he?'

When Paul refused to answer, Athanase became angry. 'What do you mean not answering your father? What did Marius tell you?'

'He – he just took some things and left.'

Athanase grunted. This was too much. He had slept fairly well last night, but the moment he woke up the previous day's scene with the priest had hit his mind like a physical blow. And now, on top of everything else, there was Marius. The boy had left his traces all over the place. The ice-box was almost empty and Julienne's daughter, who cleaned the upstairs, had found his smelly clothes in the cupboard.

'Did he tell you where he was going?'

Paul shook his head. Without raising it, he said shyly, 'What's the matter, P'pa?'

'Nothing – nothing. But you should have told me when he came home, that's all. Run along now and play.'

Paul did as he was told.

Athanase sat thinking for several minutes, snapping his fingers spasmodically. After a bit he went out to the hall and called Kathleen in from the gallery. With a quick look around to make sure Paul was out of hearing, he drew her close. 'Paul doesn't know anything, but Marius took the sleeping bag. Do you think he's in the sugar cabin?'

She nodded. 'Probably.'

'The poor fool! The poor young fool!'

He took his hat from one of the prongs of the moose's antlers and put it on his head, selected a stick from the rack and went out to the gallery, Kathleen following.

'You'd better not walk all the way up there yourself,' she said anxiously. 'You shouldn't walk at all on a day like this.'

'I can't drive the horse up, can I?'

'Let me go too.'

'You'd be a great help,' he said, 'with Marius!'

He walked slowly past the barns through the fields up to the ridge, stopping for breath every fifty yards. It took him half an hour to reach the sugar cabin, and when he entered it Marius was not there. The sleeping bag was rolled out on the floor and the suitcase was in one corner. There were tins of food and a small sterno set and the remains of a leg of cooked lamb, all spread out on a plank resting over the grills where the sap was boiled in March. Athanase grunted and sat down on the only bench in the place. He took a notebook from his pocket, tore out a sheet and pencilled a short note telling Marius not to be a fool and to come down to the house. Then he went out and closed the door behind him.

On the walk back he encountered Daphne and Heather

coming through the grove with Paul between them. Heather spoke up at once.

'We just saw him, Mr. Tallard. We saw him and he wouldn't even speak to us.'

Athanase swore under his breath. These English children – he had forgotten at the moment that they were Yardley's granddaughters. He was humiliated that they should have seen a son of his in hiding; also concerned lest they tell their mother. He wanted to warn them not to mention to a soul that they had seen Marius, but his pride choked him. He walked slowly home, angry that English children should be here at all under such circumstances. What business was this of theirs?

By the time he reached his gallery he was very tired, and for nearly ten minutes he sat quite still in his rocking chair without even reaching for the newspaper Kathleen had laid on a nearby table for him. Finally he picked it up and for nearly half an hour read it carefully.

At last, after four years, the news was good. The Canadians had actually been the ones to send the German Army on its way back to the Rhine. The Royal Twenty-Second was right up in the front, where it belonged. Why couldn't a fool like Marius see that the Twenty-Second was as representative of Quebec as all the long-haired, big-mouthed, thin-shouldered friends he had made in college? He read the news with real satisfaction, but by the time he had finished the paper a sense of depression had returned again. The war had lasted too long. Too many men like Marius had become embittered. God knew how long it would be before these wounds healed.

A little before noon he heard footsteps crunching on the drive and immediately his nerves tightened again. Two men were approaching, one a sergeant of military police, the other a short, square man in business suit. Both had solid faces and the kind of eyes that stray around, concentrating on the details their superiors have told them to look for. Seeing them coming up to his gallery, Athanase became so angry he did not bother to rise from his chair when they introduced themselves as Rogers and Labelle. The sergeant was English, the other man French. Labelle did the talking, and his voice had all the mechanical solicitude for unimportant facts common to a hack policeman anywhere in the world.

Athanase listened, then said quietly, 'You're wasting your time. My son isn't here.'

Labelle glanced at the sergeant, then back to Athanase. It was obvious that he did not believe the answer, or expect to be told the truth. But he had to go through with his routine.

'We think he's here, Mr. Tallard,' he said, shrugging his shoulders.

Athanase exploded in voluble French. Where did Labelle come from? Who was his boss in the police force? What did he think he was doing here anyway? And finally, did he want to keep his job or lose it? Labelle listened, shrugged his shoulders a few times, and looked stubbornly at the ground.

'Listen, Mr. Tallard,' the sergeant interrupted in English. 'We got a job to do. We don't want any trouble. Your son's got to go sooner or later. All we want is a look around.'

'You won't look around my house.'

'He's been seen around here,' Labelle said.

'You're a liar,' Athanase said. 'Even if he were seen, no one in this parish would tell you, and you know it.'

'Now look here . . .'

Athanase pointed his long forefinger. 'Both of you,' he said coldly, 'get off my property! If you try to set foot inside my house – by God, I'll break the pair of you! Finish! Understand?' He picked up his newspaper and began to read.

The men looked at each other and again Labelle shrugged his shoulders. The sergeant's mouth lifted at one corner. 'All right,' he said, 'if that's how you want it. Don't blame us if there's trouble, that's all. We got a job to do.'

They went off down the drive together, and Athanase kept watching them around the edge of his paper until they were out of sight. They were moving back toward the village. He laughed shortly. They wouldn't get any news there.

22

Marius sat on a log outside the sugar cabin and smoked his pipe in the dark. The air was warm, and the night throbbed with sound like the inside of a sea-shell. The hoarse noise of the falls underlay all other sounds, but he could hear crickets in the fields, and even the ringing of frogs floating up in slow waves from the marsh near the river. Somewhere in the village a dog's barks came in quick, broken volleys softened by distance as the animal barked at the moon. Marius looked down through the boles of the trees and saw the fields pale in the light of a first-quarter moon, the glimmer reflected from the church roof, and the wide path of light on the river beyond. The maple grove was a huge net of shadows suspended from the treetops with the open patches of ground whitened by the moon. As he looked down the ridge he saw the whole parish spread below him like a map. A little spit of land jutting out into the river was black with shadow on one side and white with moon-colour on the other. A thin spire of smoke rose from a single chimney in the Tallard house. He checked the chimneys off one by one and estimated that the fire was in the kitchen.

He did not move. His mind was tired from three months of worrying and scheming and dreaming of the things he would have to do if he were ever to appease the soreness within him. But tonight the peace and familiarity of the scene almost made him feel well again. He told himself that he was home. He would never go away from here if he could possibly stay. He had never wished to have this hatred in his life, this battle he was doomed to wage. He repeated that all he and his people had ever wished was to be let alone. And thinking this, he asked himself in sudden incredulity why he must wage a battle at all, why he had always been so wretched that a life's work would be too little to make up for it?

His right hand was in his pocket, and his moving fingers were crumpling the note his father had left in the cabin that morning. Words entered his mind: 'I will arise and go unto my father . . .' God knew he wanted to go home. His father had written in the note: 'This attitude you have, blaming everything you don't like on the English, is senseless. No one is harming you but yourself. If an Englishman heard you talking he'd think you were crazy. Come home and talk to me. You are only twenty-one and many things seem more important at that age than . . .'

In the darkness Marius' lips tightened. It was easy to say he was young; as easy as to say that the English had done him no harm. They had hounded him like a criminal for the past three months because he wished no part of their imperialism, that was all.

Normally, Marius would have let it go at that. But tonight he was not normal. The summer night and the sounds in the throbbing air had made him quiet. He asked himself if he really did hate the English, and why. By nature suspicious, he was suddenly suspicious even of himself. The face of Kathleen rose before his mind. But his hatred was caused by more than one woman alone. He had always hated them.

He got up and began slowly to walk among the maple trunks in the moonlight, his hands in his pockets and his head down. He felt he would become as empty as a broken bottle if he did not get an answer; that the sense would run out of everything unless he knew. His father's words returned: 'You are only twenty-one . . .' But perhaps that was just why he did see the truth, because he was too young to have sold out any part of himself? The English lessened him . . . that was it. Merely by their existence, they lessened a man. You could become great and powerful only if your own people were also great and powerful. But what could his people do when the English constantly choked them? What could the French do, alone against an entire continent, except breed children and hope?

He came back and sat on the log again, tapped out his pipe and refilled it. His father was fond of saying that the average Quebec farmer was not a nationalist; that he was the plainest, most decent land-worker in the world. But he, Marius, he was no average man. He could see the truth even if ignorant people couldn't. And the truth was that under the English a French-Canadian could not become great. You had to imitate the English or they refused to look at you. You had to do things their way. If you were different, they automatically regarded you as second-rate. If you wanted different ends they called you backward. The Americans were just as bad. And all the time the English took what they wanted. They had the big business. They had the army, the railroads, the banks, they had everything. What was left to a man like himself but the Church, medicine, or the law? Father Arnaud at the seminary had said he was too personally ambitious to make a good priest. He set his teeth. Some day Father Arnaud . . . But now nothing was left but the law, for he knew he could never have the patience necessary to become a doctor. And in Quebec you could pick up lawyers at a dime a dozen.

He knocked out his pipe and rose, took a long look down the ridge and went back to the cabin. His nostrils caught the smell of dried-out lumber and the remaining reek of stale wood smoke. Inside the cabin the moonlight lay in a rectangle on the floor, preserving the cross made by the joints in the single window. He lit the candle, took off his boots and jacket and crawled into the sleeping bag with a sigh. He puffed out his cheeks and blew. The candle flickered; he blew again and it went out.

Marius was asleep when the English sergeant and the French plainclothesman flashed their electric torches on him. He tried to jump clear of the light. One light winked out, but the other followed him like a staring eye and his feet were caught in the sleeping bag and he knew he was helpless. He pulled himself half out of the bag and leaned back on his elbows.

A voice said in English, 'It's him, all right.'

Marius took a deep gulp of air and tried again to get his head free of the light; it was all he could see. The light followed him and he put his hand over his eyes.

The hidden voice spoke again, 'Get up!'

There was nothing else to do. He crawled out of the bag and rose without a word, sat on the bench and put on his shoes. A hand holding his jacket stretched out into the beam of the torch. 'You need this too. You're going places.'

He took the jacket. Then the light partially swung away

181

from him, his pupils dilated in the semi-darkness and he was able to see the shadows of the men's forms. The one in uniform looked big and tough. He was the one with the light. He was leaning with his back to the closed door and the light revolved slowly as he played it from his wrist.

Marius straightened and put on his hat. 'What time is it?' he said.

He got no answer. He looked around and saw Labelle standing in the patch of moonlight thrown through the window.

'Don't make trouble and you won't be hurt,' Labelle said in French.

Marius stared at him. This was the last humiliation; one of his captors was French. When he reached the door the sergeant made a grap at his wrist, and before Marius knew what was happening, a handcuff was locked on it.

'God damn bastard!' Marius said.

He jerked his hand up to hit the sergeant, and the man's arm lifted with it. Then slowly, easily, the sergeant pressed his arm down again. Labelle came up on the other side and took his other arm and with his free hand pulled the door open. They jerked him outside, and the moonlight flowed over the three of them. They stood there in a clear patch in the maple grove, Marius panting softly as he strained with both arms locked by the men on either side of him, his chest expanded with air. Then, as the men jerked him forward, he stumbled and nearly fell.

'Come on,' Labelle said. 'You show some sense, eh?'

His eyes bright and angry in the moon, Marius scrambled to his feet. They walked through the shadows of the grove to the brink of the ridge, then down the path along the edge of the field. They were three tiny black smudges moving down the wide, moon-washed cloth of the hillside.

23

The next morning the whole parish knew that Marius had been arrested. Mme. Drouin had been wakened shortly after midnight by a Ford backfiring outside the store and had got out of bed and gone to the window to see what was happening. The sergeant and Labelle were driving away with another man between them, and she had recognized Marius by the set of his hat. One of the Bergerons also knew about it. He had been in the store playing checkers and had left when Drouin closed up. He had then got a lift into Sainte-Justine from François-Xavier Latulippe. In Sainte-Justine he knew a girl who worked in the station hotel, and when he was leaving the hotel by the back door he had seen the sergeant and Labelle drive up in the Ford and drag Marius out. Marius was handcuffed, and the police had kept him in a room in the hotel all night.

All morning people kept coming into Drouin's with more stories. A woman claimed she had heard a shot in the night and that Marius had been killed. When told he was not dead, she said he had certainly been wounded, because there was a bloodstain on the road near her house. Drouin said he didn't know for sure, but he wouldn't be surprised but what the surveyors had something to do about it. The surveyors were from the government, and nothing good ever happened when the government had anything to do with it. Then Frenette came in and said he had been speaking with Father Beaubien. The priest had told him only one thing: that he knew who had reported Marius' hiding place to the police.

When Athanase entered the store for his mail, just before noon, the men all glanced at each other and only Drouin spoke to him. He immediately guessed what had happened, and his face was sharp with anger as he took his letters and walked out. He climbed into his carriage and started the mare on her way home. Then he saw Father Beaubien coming down the road from the porch of his presbytery to speak to him.

Athanase reined in the mare and glanced over his shoulder. He saw that the men had all come out of the store and were now standing around the gasoline pump watching.

The priest's face was stern. 'You'd better come inside with me, Mr. Tallard.'

Athanase continued to hold the reins. 'I don't think that is necessary, Father.'

The priest walked to the side of the carriage and stood

183

very erect, one hand on his pendant cross, the other at his side. 'I take it you know the police have arrested Marius? He was taken off your own land like a criminal.' A quiet intensity entered Father Beaubien's voice. 'That is what comes of your friendship with foreigners, Mr. Tallard. It was Mrs. Methuen who told the police where to find your son.'

Athanase flushed with anger. It seemed incredible. Then he remembered that the children had seen Marius up in the maple grove. They had probably seen him leave the sugar cabin.

'Do you need any more proof that I was right? You let Paul play with those English children, you make friends with them yourself. Now are you satisfied?'

Again Athanase glanced over his shoulders. There were nearly twenty people in front of the store now, all watching.

'I intend to protect my parish, Mr. Tallard,' the priest said slowly. 'The sort of things that happened last night – it is only one of many such examples we can look forward to if you have your way. Now then, I insist that you drop all your plans for this factory. I insist that you come back to the Church and live like a Christian.'

Anger choked Athanase. 'I won't stand for this. Who do you think you are – giving orders to me?'

The priest's large knuckles whitened as he clenched his hand on the seat-rail of the carriage. 'All right, Mr. Tallard . . . I've done the best I could.' Without taking his eyes from Athanase's face, he nodded sideways. 'Those people there – my parishioners – they're watching us. They aren't fools. They know a lot more than you think they do. They're waiting to see what will happen.'

His lips a straight line, Athanase continued to stare at Father Beaubien's set face.

'On Sunday, without naming names,' the priest said steadily, 'I shall tell the people the truth about you. I shall tell them that you are no longer a good Catholic. I shall tell them that you are a bad man and a bad example. I shall warn them against having any further dealings with you. It will be known to every voter in your constituency that you no longer consent to receive the sacraments of their Church. They will know that God will not bless them if they elect a man like you to represent them. I think you know as well as I what this will mean to you, Mr. Tallard?' He stopped. 'Do you still want to take your choice?'

Athanase felt the blood rush to his head and his hand clenched on the whip-handle. 'I will not be talked to in this way!' he shouted. 'Not by anyone!'

He raised the whip and the watching men, seeing his shoulder rise with it, were appalled by the thought that he was going to strike the priest. Father Beaubien stood absolutely still, watching him. Then, still with the whip above his head, Athanase said between his teeth, 'No one has ever dared talk to a member of my family like this in our own parish . . . not in more than two hundred years. You keep away from me! You keep out of my affairs, or by God . . .'

With a quick turning movement he swung around and brought the whip down with a crack on the mare's flank. The animal reared in the shafts and plunged wildly, then went down the road in a gallop, and Athanase bent forward holding the reins. By the time his gate was reached the mare had slowed to a trot. The welt made by the whip lay in a long, ugly line along her chestnut flank.

As Athanase took the harness off the mare he made up his mind. He would not remain in the position where anyone could presume to talk to him as Father Beaubien had talked to him this summer. Ever since the death of his first wife this moment had been coming. But he was finished with being between two stools now; he was finished with it for the rest of his life, and he would show the whole world that he was to be left alone.

24

Late that afternoon, John Yardley came back from the village walking slowly and seeing no one. He turned into the path leading up to his house, and when he limped up the steps he nearly stumbled over Daphne and Heather, who were playing with a child's cart on the veranda. Daphne was sitting in it and Heather was pushing from behind, and the wheels made a steady rumbling back and forth across the porch. The children stopped playing and said something to him. He mumbled an answer and went inside, then upstairs to Janet's room.

He found her by the window reading a story in *The Saturday Evening Post*. He hated mourning on any woman, and Janet seemed to him withered by the black dress and black stockings she wore. She looked at least a dozen years older than she had a month ago. Her lips were pressed thin and the lines on either side of her mouth had become severe, making her nose appear long, sad and disdainful.

Yardley sat on the edge of the bed and looked at the floor. 'Janet . . . there's something I've got to ask you.'

She folded the magazine and tensed herself. During the past month her silence had been constant. If she cried at all, it was when she was alone during the nights. When they had gone into town together to attend the memorial service for her husband, she had maintained the same frozen calm that had horrified Yardley when the news of Harvey's death had first arrived.

'I've got something to ask you, Janet,' he repeated. 'Maybe there's not a damn thing in it. But I've got to make sure.' His foot tapped the floor; then, lifting his lantern jaw, he faced her squarely. 'Did you tell those policemen where the Tallard boy was?'

Her eyes snapped open in defiance. 'So they did find him there!'

Yardley kept on looking at his daughter, and his pale eyes slowly filled with tears.

'Why shouldn't I have told them? They were police, and they asked me.' Her voice was high and strained. 'Why should these people be allowed to get out of it? Harvey didn't.'

The bitter, uncomprehending anger in her voice made Yardley feel sick. 'What's come over you, daughter?' he asked quietly.

'He was a cheat,' she said. 'That's all he was – a cheat.'

'You don't understand these people here. You never tried to.'

'I understand this much – something you forget about. If we let people like them have their own way we'll lose the war. It would serve them right if they did. If the Germans came here they'd soon see!'

Yardley held her eyes. 'They're our neighbours, Janet.'

'They're not my neighbours.'

'They're good people – all of them.'

'After what the war did to you, I'd think . . .' She bit her lip. 'Decent men give their lives, while they . . .' Her face began to flush as she worked herself up. 'It makes me furious, all this pampering of them. It's time they were brought to heel.'

Yardley shook his head wretchedly from side to side. 'Daughter . . . daughter! What kind of talk is this? Where did you ever hear people say things like this?'

Her flush mounted as she pressed her lips together.

'It's not natural for you to talk thet way. You're only repeating some stuff some damned fools thought up to make themselves feel important. Janet, a few more words like thet and . . .'

'If you've got no patriotism . . .' She stopped and again bit her lip.

Yardley removed his glasses and wiped his eyes. Then he rubbed the glasses slowly on the end of his necktie. His voice was soft and sad. 'It wasn't right, Janet, what you did. It wasn't a natural thing to do. Not all the wars in the world could make a thing like thet right.'

He put on his glasses again, slowly hooking them behind his big ears. Janet continued to look at her father severely, her face not so much angry as stubbornly uncomprehending and righteous. Realizing that there was no sense in talking to her any more, he got up and limped to the door, closed it behind him and went downstairs. The tears were still in his eyes, and as he went out into the hot air of the afternoon he felt more empty than he could ever remember having felt before. He had lost something. He was unable to describe its nature, but it was something he had always assumed to be his.

25

Paul was frightened. Something had happened in the household which he couldn't understand but felt was a disaster. Julienne had been crying, his mother had been crying, his father had been shouting at everyone. Now, without explanation, he and his father were going to Montreal on the train.

He sat on the edge of a seat in the day coach with his legs dangling. He was wearing his best suit and was making a constant effort to keep his hands from getting dirtied by the sooty covering of the seat. Opposite him, his father was hidden by his newspaper. He had been reading it for the past half hour, and Paul, sitting very straight with legs hanging and head turning occasionally to look out the window, felt cut off from him.

His father crinkled up the paper and laid it down, and Paul sensed that a moment of some importance had come. Athanase cleared his throat and surveyed him, and his old face gave a smile that was meant to be reassuring, but was not. 'Paul – there are some things you're old enough to know. Do you understand about Marius?'

Paul knew what had happened, but not from his father. The deliberate refusal to mention Marius' name in the house had made everything seem ominous and unnatural.

'Marius is quite all right,' his father said, still trying to be reassuring. He regretted never having been able to talk to children as Yardley did. He supposed there must be some special trick necessary in speaking to a child. 'Marius hasn't done anything bad. You're not to worry about him at all. He's all right.'

Paul looked down at his feet as they dangled above the floor and vibrated with the throb of the train. Feeling guilty, supposing he was expected to understand something which he did not, he asked his father in a low voice what had happened to his brother.

Athanase gave a forced laugh. 'He's going to be a soldier. We can all be proud of him.'

'But P'pa – he didn't want to be a soldier.'

'It will be different now. When he gets into uniform he'll like it.'

Athanase wanted to get the subject away from Marius, but when he tried, he found himself floundering. As he looked at Paul, the boy's eyes baffled him. 'I suppose you've been wondering why we're going into town, suddenly like this?' he said smiling.

'Yes, P'pa.'

'I'd better tell you. We're going to join another Church.'

He saw that Paul had no comprehension of the meaning of his words. The gap between himself and the boy seemed to grow much larger.

'You see, Paul – there are many Churches in the world. All sorts. Everyone has to belong to one. You and I are going to change our Church, and that's why we're going into town.' A new thought striking him, he added eagerly, 'You see, next year we're going to live in town anyway. We'll have to pick a Montreal church, won't we? We can't come out to Saint-Marc every Sunday for Mass.'

Paul continued to look at the floor. It was dirty and stained with tobacco juice which had slopped over from a spittoon.

Athanase went on. 'Let me explain. You see, you're going to an English school this fall. Mind you, that doesn't mean you're going to be English. You'll still be French and you're not to forget that. But . . . but you're not going to be a Roman Catholic any more.'

Paul continued to look at his dangling feet. 'What will Father Beaubien say?'

Athanase forced another smile. 'He won't have anything to say once we're Protestants.' He continued rapidly. 'In your new school you'll study science. You will become' – he waved his arm toward the window as if to include the entire panorama without – 'entirely different from all these people here.'

'Won't everyone know we're not . . . not . . .'

'Not what?' Athanase leaned forward and touched the boy's knee.

'Not Catholics?'

Athanase shrugged his shoulders. 'Well – yes, they'll know that. They know everything like that in Saint-Marc. But it won't make any difference. I'll write to the bishop – perhaps even to Father Beaubien – and tell him we're resigning from the Church.' He saw tears in Paul's eyes. 'Don't worry. We're not ordinary people, you and I.'

'Won't – won't I go to hell, P'pa?'

Athanase forced another laugh. 'No – of course not!'

'But I thought . . .'

189

'That was different. Listen, Paul. You don't imagine God would send a fine man like Captain Yardley to hell, do you? He's not a Catholic.'

The train clicked over the joints and Athanase leaned back in his seat and looked at his son. He tried to feel confident, but now that the rush of his anger at the priest had subsided he was so worried he was barely able to sit still. He repeated to himself that things had always been bound to come to this, that he had no choice in the matter. But what would now happen to the factory? He nodded to reassure himself. He mustn't forget McQueen. He would put it through. The English went into many towns and built factories without being opposed by the Church. But if McQueen knew that he had quarrelled with his parish priest would he still desire him as a partner? He sighed heavily, with some relief. McQueen had little real choice in the matter. The contracts were signed, and if McQueen wanted to build the factory he would have to include his partner in his plans. Besides, Athanase realized that if he worked quickly enough he could probably get the written contract from the government to ensure that the railway spur would be built.

More difficulties rose in his mind, and suddenly he was faced with the fact that he was acting like a complete fool. What was he taking Paul into town for now? They could hardly walk up to the minister of St. David's Church and announce themselves as Presbyterian converts. St. David's would accept them finally, but no Protestant minister would take a former Roman Catholic without much thought in the matter and a good deal of investigation. He beat his hand against his forehead. He was losing his grip, he was acting like a child. He would have to take Paul back to Saint-Marc tomorrow having accomplished nothing. Then he would have to return immediately to the city himself, and spend nearly a fortnight between Montreal and Ottawa making his arrangements about the factory, the railway spur and the change to St. David's.

He became aware of the boy's round eyes looking at him, and guessed that Paul wanted to ask a question.

'Is M'ma coming too?' Paul asked.

Athanase picked up his paper to hide his face. 'Your mother understands,' he said. But he knew he had failed Paul with that answer. To cover his embarrassment he lowered the paper and began talking rapidly. He explained how greatly their lives would be changed, how much money they were likely to make in the new enterprise. He outlined his plans for the boy. He would get a scientific education. He would go to college and travel, he might even go to Oxford and the Sorbonne, or perhaps to both places for further study when he had taken his degree in Canada.

'Not many boys will have the opportunities you'll have,' he finished. 'But you'll have to work hard from now on. Harder than you've ever dreamed of working. It's going to be up to you.'

The train clicked onward. Paul's eyes watched the dust dancing over the floor-boards, the dust motionless in the spillings from the spittoon, the grains of soot drifting over the dirty green plush of the seat. Oxford . . . the Sorbonne . . . New names!

26

During the following week the pattern of life led by the Tallard family in Saint-Marc for more than two centuries was abruptly fractured. As Athanase was away in town, Kathleen and Paul took the first weight of the shock, and for a fortnight events continued to pile up on them.

First Kathleen noticed that Julienne did her work unwillingly, almost without speaking to her; next, that Blanchard and the farm-hands worked in the fields but avoided the house. One morning Paul went into the village as usual to get the mail. Near the store some children were playing. When they saw him coming they stopped and stared, then crossed themselves and went to the other side of the road. He entered the store and Polycarpe Drouin handed him the mail without a word. On his way home through the village he heard his name called from a house and stopped to see what it meant. He saw an open window but there was no one visible. Then a woman's voice cried shrilly again, and he knew she was crying something at him, but she did not ap-

191

pear and when he looked down the road he saw it was also empty. The playing children had disappeared. He stood for a moment in fright, then began to run, and he kept on running until he was nearly home.

After this Paul kept out of the village. Each day, without comment, John Yardley brought the mail to them. He was alone now, for Janet and the children had returned to the city. He would have been ostracized by the parish as a result of Janet's betrayal had it not been for his extraordinary personality. The parish knew he was hurt and ashamed. He had gone into the store and apologized to Drouin and several of the other men there, making no excuses, simply saying he was sorry. He had gone to the presbytery and said the same to Father Beaubien. Almost against his principles, the priest had shaken hands with him.

One night there was a heavy wind with clouds in the sky. The darkness was intense and the wind rushed through it, hot and dry, and the poplars in the Tallard drive sighed like pouring water. Kathleen was startled by a loud crash in the library and went in to see what it was. When the lamp was lit she saw a stone lying on the carpet and felt the wind coming in through the broken pane. She did not mention this to Paul, but next morning he saw the broken glass and guessed what had happened. The window remained unrepaired, for Kathleen did not think it worth while to ask anyone to come up from the village to fix it. She did not even mention it to Blanchard.

On the second Sunday, Kathleen went as usual to Mass. When she entered the church she noticed that the Tallard pew was occupied by another family. She made no attempt to sit in it, but remained through the service in an empty pew at the back. After Mass she was the first to leave the church, and she went home without trying to speak to anyone.

Against Athanase's stubbornness Kathleen's will had broken long ago. Now she was coldly angry with him, not so much because he had turned himself and Paul into Protestants as because of the unnecessary trouble he had made for everyone connected with him. The idea that he might go to hell for his action did not seriously concern her. She believed in hell the way most people believe in Tibet; it existed, but as she had never met anyone who had been there, it had no reality for her. She had only twice in her life been frightened of hell, once when she had been very sick and once when she had been troubled by bad dreams the week her father died.

So now, while Athanase was away arranging his affairs, Kathleen stayed on in Saint-Marc with Paul and counted the days to the time when they would all leave the parish for good. It was now close to the end of August. All her personal belongings were packed and the whole household was ready to be moved. Nothing more remained to be done except to box Athanase's books and arrange for the movers to come out from the city.

At the end of the month Athanase returned to face the parish. His absence had made him feel somewhat more confident of his immunity than when he had left. In Ottawa and Montreal everything had seemed quite normal. The skies had not fallen there because he had left his Church. In fact, none of his friends in the cities knew anything about it yet. His affairs had gone reasonably well. In Ottawa he had received in writing the final word that the government would build the railway spur as soon as it would be required. In Montreal he had completed arrangements for joining St. David's Presbyterian Church. This process had been more annoying than he had expected, for the minister had insisted on several long and penetrating conversations before he consented to his formal admission. His trip would have been entirely satisfactory had he not been disappointed in his talks with McQueen. After his usual beating about the bush, McQueen announced that he would not begin work on the factory until after the new year. He had decided that the war was soon going to end, prices were going to fluctuate wildly for a period, and he wanted things to settle down before asking for tenders and placing his contracts.

In spite of his anxiety about the factory, Athanase's trip had given him back some of his old jauntiness. Kathleen noticed the change at once; she also noticed that some of it was forced. Underneath he was as nervous as a cat, and she waited quietly to see what he would do when he learned what the parish thought about him now. She did not have long to wait.

The first morning after his return, Athanase went into the village to get his mail and papers. He met Yardley as he was stepping out of his carriage and the two went into the store together. Athanase was talking so rapidly he failed to notice the expression of warning on Yardley's face, so the reception he received hit him squarely in the face.

Drouin laid his mail on the counter and immediately turned his back. Athanase spoke pleasantly and got no answer. He picked up the mail and glanced about. All the other men in the store had turned their backs too. When he spoke to Frenette the result was the same. He might have been talking to an empty room.

He leaned over the counter and tapped Drouin's shoulder. 'What's the matter today, Polycarpe?'

Drouin muttered something unintelligible as his eyes dropped, and he shifted clear of Athanase's hand. There was a long moment of silence. Yardley quietly picked up his own papers and stuffed them into his pocket. Athanase kept looking at Drouin, his face drawn and formidable. 'Have you lost your tongue?' he said sharply.

There was still no answer. Athanase knew he should have let it go at that, but his stubbornness kept him there. He turned and tapped Frenette on the shoulder. 'What about you, old friend? Are you dumb too?'

Frenette faced him a moment, his beer-barrel body solid on his short legs, then shifted his eyes and backed away. The old habit of respect was in his face. So was a kind of affection and a great desire to be friendly in his own way. But he stepped back just the same.

Then something exploded in Athanase's brain. 'God damn you – haven't I been here long enough for you to know who I am? Frenette – there's a window broken in my house. I want you up there this afternoon to fix it.'

Frenette mumbled something incoherent.

'What's that you say?'

'I said I was sorry, Mr. Tallard.'

'You damn fools!' Athanase lifted his stick and banged it

down on the counter. 'You poor . . .'

Then he felt Yardley's hand on his elbow, and throwing an angry glance over his shoulder he caught the expression on his friend's face. Yardley looked both sad and embarrassed at the same time. He stepped quietly between Athanase and Drouin.

'How about you cutting me a sheet of glass, Polycarpe?' he said quietly. 'I guess you know what the measurements are. I told you last week. I'll be back in the afternoon to get it.'

Drouin answered eagerly, in grateful relief. 'Don't bother, Captain. Me, I'll look after it myself. This afternoon, for sure.'

Yardley kept his hand on Athanase's elbow and moved with him to the door. They climbed into the carriage and Athanase cracked the whip so loudly it sounded like a rifle-shot. His cheeks were flushed and he began to talk in loud excitement. Almost at once Yardley interrupted him.

'Don't try to say anything now. Later on maybe, you and me can talk it over, but right now there's no sense in it.'

That afternoon, just after lunch when Athanase was alone in the library, Julienne knocked and entered. She was not wearing her apron but her Sunday clothes: a black dress and a black hat with a feather on it. She stood just inside the door, stocky, sullen and a little bewildered. 'I'm giving my notice,' she said.

Athanase could hardly believe the words. Julienne had been in the house since she was a young girl. The whole meaning of her life was a part of this family. He took off his glasses and forced a smile. 'Sit down, Julienne, sit down and tell me what's the matter.'

'This isn't a Christian house. I can't work here any more.'

She said these words as if she had memorized them. He put on his glasses and again looked at her. 'Don't be a fool!' he said.

She continued to stand there, stocky and as stubborn as he was himself. 'You got no right calling me that, Mr. Tallard.' Then her stubbornness collapsed and she began to blink. 'Oh, Mr. Tallard . . .' The tears flowed over and came down her plump cheeks, and with a choking sound in her throat she rushed out the door and closed it behind her. Athanase jumped from his chair and followed, but by the time he had reached the front door she was already down the drive on her way to the road. She was trying to run, moving her heavy body with a waddling motion that would have been comical had it not been so pathetic.

Athanase stood on the steps. 'Julienne!' he shouted.

She did not stop or turn around. He saw her reach the road and take the turn toward the village, pulling her black hat squarely down over her forehead on the way. She had a married sister living in one of the newer houses beyond the church, and now her sister's place would have to be her home.

For several minutes Athanase stood staring after her. When he turned around he saw Kathleen behind him in the doorway. 'What did you expect?' she said, and with a slow and indolent movement went back into the house.

An hour later there was another knock on the library door, and this time it was Blanchard. He stood with his feet apart, and even while standing motionless he gave an impression of plodding forward. Both hands clutched his cap, and as he looked at the floor he kept turning the cap between his thumbs and forefingers, slowly around and around. Athanase waited for him to speak. He leaned back in his chair with his finger-tips pressed together under his chin in an inverted V and looked at his man.

Finally Blanchard's Adam's apple moved up and down as he cleared his throat. 'I'll be staying till the crops are in, Mr. Tallard.' He made a short movement with his head. 'The other men – I'll keep them around too.'

Athanase said sharply, 'And after that?'

Blanchard continued to revolve his cap. 'I been thinking . . . with my own field, maybe with that piece of land . . .' Then he blurted out, 'Next year I won't be working for you any more, Mr. Tallard.'

'Good!' Athanase snapped at him. 'That's fine. Now I suppose you want your money?'

With a swift movement he swung around in his chair and

wrenched open a drawer in his desk. He pulled it out so
violently that some of the papers fell on the floor. Immediately Blanchard lurched forward and bent to pick them up.
Athanase bent at the same time and the two men looked at
each other, blood rushing to their lowered faces, each
checking the movement of his hand. 'Never mind, Joseph!'
Athanase said coldly.

Blanchard straightened and took a step back, stood with
his feet apart, his eyes lowered, revolving his cap. Athanase
reached for a black account book and thumbed it through.
Then he pressed down a page and studied it, frowning. He
picked up a pencil and noted down a set of figures, closed
the book and said to Blanchard with a bitter, almost academic irony, 'I owe you for nearly half of twenty years'
work. Taking into account the compound interest, and sub-
tracting what you paid for the field this spring, it makes
seven thousand, six hundred and forty-two dollars. Is that
right?'

Blanchard shook his head. 'And thirty-nine dollars, Mr.
Tallard.'

'You've been the thriftiest man I've ever seen in our parish. Now you're almost rich. I suppose you have plans for
this money?'

Blanchard nodded.

'Very well. I'll write you a cheque. It's been in a separate
account in my bank for you all along.' He took his cheque
book from the drawer, tore out a cheque, and with quick,
flourishing strokes above and below the lines, filled in the
names and figures. After doing this he bent the cheque
crisply lengthwise through the middle and handed it to
Blanchard, who took it with both hands, looked at it cautiously, then slipped it in his right pants' pocket and held it
there with his hand.

'Don't worry,' Athanase snapped. 'If you lose it, I'll give
you another. Put it in the bank at Sainte-Justine. If you can't
take my word for it, ask the priest.'

And then he was ashamed of himself, and a wave of sadness broke over him with intolerable force as he saw that
Blanchard was weeping. The man stood in front of him
sobbing from his chest, and a film of moisture spread down

his browned cheeks to his jaw. Athanase got to his feet. 'Pull yourself together, man!'

But when he grasped Blanchard's hand and felt the answering pressure he knew his words had been stupid. He stepped back and in a partial daze saw the library door close behind Blanchard's back. He dropped into his armchair and sat quite still for nearly five minutes, then he reached blindly to the nearest bookshelf. His hands turned the pages of the book he had found and finally held a place almost automatically. He removed his glasses and wiped his eyes, then rubbed the glasses on his handkerchief and set them on his nose again.

It was a book of Greek lyric poetry, old and dog-eared. His grandfather had bought it, his father had studied it, he had used it himself during one term at the classical college. He had forgotten most of his Greek, but the Jesuits had pounded the paradigms into him and he still remembered many of the words. The book had fallen open at a fragment of Simonides, and he tried to puzzle it out.

He read, groping at the words, losing their exact meaning but slowly feeling his way through to a forgotten intimacy. He remembered that he had read these lines many times before, that once he had considered them remarkable, for there was a note beside the poem in his own handwriting. He noticed with curiosity that his writing had been much smaller in his student days. Then he suddenly recalled the whole fragment, remembering the rector sitting behind the desk going over the translation, his lean face alive with the pleasure of the poetry. 'Being a man, do not say what happiness is, nor seeing a happy man, how much time he will have ... for it is swift, like the turn of a dragonfly, the change!' Athanase let the book fall shut over his fingers and closed his eyes, and for several minutes lay back inertly in his chair.

Then he got up and went to the door. 'Kathleen!' he shouted.

He heard her moving upstairs, then her feet as she came slowly down, and he went back to his chair again. She entered with her familiar languid motion, and he wondered in amazement if the expression he saw on her face was pity.

No one had ever pitied him; it was awful if pity should become necessary. More than ever as he watched her, the latent vitality in her body gave him a deep feeling of shame.

'Sit down, my dear,' he said quietly. 'I want to talk to you.'

She opened the drawer of the table and took out cigarettes, and she did not sit down until she had lighted one. He drummed on the arm of his chair with his fingers. 'Well,' he said, 'it looks as if we leave here for good. You must feel happy about it.'

She shrugged her shoulders.

After a moment, he said, 'I wonder if I know how you feel about anything any more?'

'You never ask me. You just go ahead and do things your own way. What difference does it make how I feel? Or what Paul or anyone else feels any more?'

'There are some things I must explain to you.' And then he did not know how to continue. He wanted to tell her that he would have been satisfied to continue living in Saint-Marc if he had known that she was also satisfied, but he knew she would not believe him. He wanted to tell her that because he was no longer any use to her as a man, the least he could do was to make money so that she could live the sort of life she had always desired. But he knew that if he said this it would account for so little of the reason why he was turning his life upside down that it would be hypocritical, and that she would merely look at his face as though it were a curtain and not even bother answering.

'Every man . . .' He fumbled with the words. 'Every man has to act according to some principles. He – he must make his life aim at something. He must live in accordance with the times. That's going to be the tragedy of so many people we know – they'll have to pass through a long period of transition from their present way of life to the way science compels us to live. Maybe Marius is a reflection of the tragedy of that transition. He doesn't understand, of course, but – but I do, Kathleen. I've understood it for years. That's why I . . .' He stopped with the feeling that his words were like drops of water falling into an empty bucket. There had never been any sense in talking to Kathleen about ideas.

'So that's why you had to quarrel with Father Beaubien!' she said. 'That's why you had to drive Blanchard and Julienne out of the house! That's why you're making a Protestant out of Paul!'

Her voice was perfectly level, without obvious anger or hurt; she merely recorded the facts. But if her words meant anything, he thought they meant that she despised him.

In sudden anger he spurted out at her. 'Don't be deliberately stupid, Kathleen! You may not know it, but ideas are the things that change the whole world. Let me explain . . .'

She got up and tossed her cigarette into the hearth, where it lay smouldering among ashes and waste paper. 'You don't have to explain anything. You've been explaining things all your life and look where it's got you! You're over sixty, Athanase – and you're just as stubborn and headstrong as you ever were. Let's not talk about it any more. Let's get out of here and forget all about it.'

She left the room, and when he was alone again Athanase wondered how it was that an ignorant woman who had known a man with her body could understand him better than an intelligent man who could speak to his mind. He felt crushed. He had wanted to explain that every man must act in accordance with his own inner compulsion. Now he knew that she had guessed what this compulsion was, that it had often been no more than the product of his physical condition at various times of his life. His nature had always demanded a new idea of itself, and when he had his vigour, women had provided it. Now no woman could satisfy him, nor he a woman. Nothing was left him but principles and ideas. 'God,' he thought, 'is that all there is to it?' And then it occurred to him that perhaps all wars and revolutions and movements of history started from sources just as trivial and undignified. He saw the people in their churches and nationalisms huddling together under flags and banners in desperate attempts to escape the knowledge of their own predicament. They were all silhouettes moving almost accidentally for seventy years or so over the ridge of the world between darkness and darkness. Among them he saw himself. Then he laughed harshly, mocking himself, Kathleen, everyone he could think of. 'When I make money she'll think I'm right! They all will!' And the thought that he had never known a person who sincerely despised money gave him a faintly bitter feeling of vengeance for his own inadequacy.

That night Athanase tried to play chess with Yardley, but the game went so badly that he lost his queen in the first five minutes and surrendered. They went out to the porch and sat in silence together. It was a warm night and the last crickets of the season were loud in the fields. A full harvest moon washed the plain, and far out in the river a ship which had left Montreal before sunset cut the moon's path blackly.

Suddenly he heard singing. It came from the road where the singer was hidden by trees and darkness. But the voice reached them clearly, for it was a rich baritone with a familiar lyric quality. Athanase lifted his chin, glanced at Yardley's profile and then away. *Rossignolet sauvage* . . . it was only Frenette feeling good after a few drinks of *whiskey blanc*, on his way home from a game of checkers. He was merely letting his voice pour out in the first song that had entered his head. But the music and the words were more than Frenette, for both were racial memories. No wild nightingales had ever sung along the Saint Lawrence, but there had been many of them in copses by the Orne and the Seine, now and centuries ago. In Quebec they had not been forgotten.

Part Two   1919-1921

27

The war had been over for six months, and now the first battalions were coming home.

Some of them had lived through half a week of the first gas attack, breathing through rags saturated with their own urine while they fought the Germans before Ypres. Some had existed in the cellars of Lens for weeks, gnawing their way underground through the town like rats, wall by wall; and each new cellar had meant grenades and the L-shaped rip of bayonets. Some had seen the top of Messines Ridge blossom like a fire-shot black flower into the sky, carrying with it the shredded limbs of a whole division of Germans mixed with thousands of tons of dirt. Some had gone up the slope of Vimy and fought all day with the Prussian Guard they had been told would be dead when they got there, and at the next dawn they had seen each others' helmets encased with sheet-ice from rain that froze as it fell. Some had stood up to their necks in cold water stained with blood and human excrement while they waited for hours to crawl a few yards closer to Passchendaele. Some had been drunk on sacramental wine found when they had dived into a hole in the ground to escape bombardment, and so had discovered that they were in the crypt of a church, that the occupied ground was a village, that the village was the objective of a three months' offensive. Some had crawled like snakes through the standing grain east of Amiens after the break-through of August 8, 1918. Some had seen friends loosen and fall around the coal piles of Mons on the last morning of the war, then had gone in past them to gut the last snipers of the war with their bayonets. Some had marched at attention across the Rhine bridges into the clean, untouched German towns. Some had won medals. Some had acquired trench feet, scars, clap, gas-burns, syphilis and hallucinations that came in the night. Some had learned a peculiar peace through an ultimate knowledge of themselves. And now, having done the whole duty of a soldier, they were coming back to the middle classes, to the farms and forests and the wooden railroad towns, to the gaunt stone cities like Toronto and the sprawling wind-swept ones like Winnipeg. They were coming home to a land still so near the frontier that in most of it everything was black or white, uncomplicated, where wickedness was barely intelligible unless it were sexual.

They were returning to what they thought was good because it had been familiar. When their ships drew in to Halifax, they smelled their country before it rose to them over the horizon, and their nostrils dilated to the odour of balsam blown out to sea from the evergreen forests that cover most of Nova Scotia like a shaggy hide. On the train through the Maritime Provinces they smelled the orange peel, lysol, spittoon and coal smoke staleness of the day coaches, and they looked through the windows with their rough khaki collars open, sweating into the stale air the sharp, animal smell of massed soldiers. They saw, as if for the first time, how empty the country looked, how silent it was. They noticed the towns like collections of grey and brown wooden boxes scattered as if by a hand's gesture in the clearings, dirt streets running through them and perhaps a short stretch of asphalt near the brick or sandstone post-office. They noticed the red brick or board railroad stations, nearly every one the same; in Truro, Springhill, Amherst, Sackville, Moncton, Newcastle, Campbellton and Matapedia. They saw the little Nova Scotia trout streams, each one shallow and freshly splashing over amber-coloured stones. They saw the Miramichi, wide and steel-grey, curving flat calm out of the spruce forests. When they woke up the next day they saw the Saint Lawrence, smooth and opaque like a strait of the sea. Then the train rumbled over the bridge and ran through the factories into Bonaventure Station in Montreal.

That afternoon they paraded through the city, and on the reviewing stand on Sherbrooke Street generals with red tabs and red officer-faces and politicians with grey faces and silk hats saluted them under the Union Jack, the country having no flag of its own. And the soldiers marched at attention through the crowds, only their eyes preserving the traces of what they had done and where they had been. For most of the battle-tension had relaxed now; nearly all of it was gone. They were returning to the human race, floating upward into the illusion of the middle classes again. Now that they were home the last realities were fading. The war was becoming what their minds made it; not the broken instants, the clawing into the earth, the stepping out into ultimate loneliness when the earth jogs up through the feet and legs into the brain and makes each step forward a new thing; not the feel in the arms and shoulders as the bayonet slips into the belly without resistance, or stupidly sticks on bone with a trivial sound, the action so different from what it ought to be: the enemy's face not what was expected, the instant so mind-destroying that the felt knowledge comes that the mind is nothing, the man nothing, only the fear and the outrage real, the moment so private no one can communicate it – only afterwards to look into the eyes of another and understand that he knows it too, and knows that any words about it will be stupid, for words are human and have a history, and this has none. But now the war was slipping back into pictures again, almost into the same pictures the civilians and the advertisers had made of it, whole pictures fabricated by the mind, not broken moments; place-names and dates and what the corporal said to the sergeant-major, the mind going back to its builder's work, curing itself by making war what it never was.

So today they marched through Montreal, and the pipers played them along with *The Blue Bonnets* and *The Hundred Pipers*, and before the French-Canadian regiment the band played the *Sambre et Meuse*. In the English section of town the crowd had always been behind the army, had worshipped the idea of it. In a war it had never made, the country had given everything, doubling and raising and redoubling the ante again and again until all it was and ever hoped to be was forgotten, as the stakes were piled up on the table for the great powers to manipulate into a victory. The country had suffered a quarter more action-deaths than the United States out of a population a fourteenth as large. Now it was over, and thank God. Now the whole duty of colonials was done, the surviving troops were home, now the future could rest with the great powers till the next time.

And so, because this was the accepted military procedure, even the drill-books they used being imported, the troops marched at attention past the generals and politicians. The crowd cheered them. When the French passed, the English cheered them wildly. Sometimes French and English in the crowd caught each others' glances and admitted a respect. The parade passed, a local celebration, not noticed elsewhere because the grief and pride of small nations is unimportant to others, strictly a family gathering, everyone knowing that if they spoke of what they had done in a voice loud enough to carry across the frontier they would only seem like a small-salaried man talking big money to the president of the company.

The women were the ones you noticed in the crowd, for the day was more theirs than the troops. You could see the tight, grey faces of the ones whose men were not there, and you could also see an unusually naked expression in the others. These strained for the sight of a single man, eyes leaping to the familiar face when it marched into view while in a private agony each woman hoped to find it the same, still lovable, able to be magnetized back to the cage again from what it had seen and where it had been, from the horror and the hunting and the Champs Elysées and Regent Street, to the suburban house and the tenement, the groceries, doctor's bills, insurance premiums, pay cheques, slippers before the fire and three square meals a day. Women's bodies, unenjoyed for several years, stirred in involuntary anticipation.

Janet Methuen waited for the parade, standing with her father in the bay window of a friend's house near the McGill campus. Yardley had come into town today because Harvey's old regiment was returning, and he had thought Janet might be unstrung by the celebration.

He found her surprisingly calm. Much of the rigid nervousness had left her during the past few months. Her thin face was pale, but her movements were quieter than they had ever been. Yardley could not tell if she had died inside and did not care any more, or if she had gained real confidence for the first time in her life.

They had said little to each other, for Yardley had reached town only an hour ago, and Janet was on the point of leaving her house when he had arrived. Now they stood in the window together looking across the street to the elms of the campus, the college buildings slate-grey behind them, the bluff of Mount Royal above. In the room at their back was a discreet murmur of voices. Yardley knew none of the others. The house belonged to a Mrs. Stanstead, a widow whose son had been Harvey Methuen's best friend before both were killed.

Yardley continued to stare out the window. Most of the flags across the street were Union Jacks, but there were also a few Tricolours and Old Glories. He noticed that the crowd here was entirely English. Farther east it would be French. It was the sort of thing you always watched for in Montreal.

Suddenly Janet said, 'General Methuen has been simply wonderful. Yesterday he told me he wants us to take over the whole second floor of the family house.'

Yardley smiled sadly. 'Thet sounds like you've settled on living in Montreal for good.'

'They've made me a part of the family. It's the only place I've ever belonged.'

He looked over the heads of the crowd through the elms to the mountain, and his chin lifted as he heard the faint strains of the coming pipes. He thought that if sound were an element, this would be singing water. As he swung his eyes back to her face he noticed how young she still looked. It saddened him to see her so ready to sink into middle age.

'I don't have to think of anything any more,' she said quietly. 'The children are in school. General Methuen says he's perfectly satisfied with them. When they finish here they'll go to Lausanne for a year. Now the war's over things will soon be the same again.' She added, 'Harvey's mother went to Lausanne.'

'You talk like you'd come into harbour, Janet.'

'I know how Harvey wanted the girls brought up.'

His pale eyes were steady behind his glasses as he looked at her long, severe face. 'Child – I wish you'd marry again!'

She was more astonished than shocked. 'What a time to say such a thing!'

'Most times I never get a chance to say anything.'

'At least you might . . .' The lips came together in a line and she said nothing more.

He put a heavy, blue-veined hand on her shoulder and felt the bone sharp under it. 'Listen, Janet – maybe I never learned to say the right thing around here, but not even the Methuens are much different from anyone else, and anyhow there's no future in saying nothing at all, the way they do. Memories may be sacred, but they don't keep a man warm nights – no, nor a woman, neither.'

She gave a quick glance over her shoulder, thankful that no one else in the room was close enough to hear him. 'Father – will you please stop! It's – it's horrible!'

But Yardley had been solitary for seven months, without any more chess games with Athanase or talks with Paul and Kathleen, with nothing but the animals and the farm work and his books; these, and his astonishing health that still permitted him to do a young man's work. For months he had been trying to figure out how to put this to Janet and had not succeeded in writing. So he said what he thought now.

'Thet's fine, what you say about the Methuens. I'm right glad to hear it. But by God, Janet – you're a fine figure of a woman and you're still young. Most of them, they're old people. And they don't own Daphne and Heather. Nobody owns anyone in this world. People make a hell of a lot of mischief pretending they do.'

The forbidding line showed between her eyes. 'Father, will you ever get it into your head that everyone isn't like the seamen and farmhands you've lived with all your life?'

'They're not so different,' he said stubbornly. 'For thet matter, the way I see it, people aren't so different even from animals. Even the wildest ones can get mighty lonely. I think sometimes we imitate the animals in most we do. It's a sure thing we imitate them when we go hunting, and . . .'

She gave a nervous laugh. 'If you were anybody else I think I'd . . . Father, you're rambling!'

He had the impression that she was not listening to a word he said. He stood for a time looking out the window, dreading the approach of the troops. If Harvey were alive he would have been a major; perhaps even a lieutenant-colonel. He would have marched home at the head of a battalion. Montreal was his town. His home-coming would have been a local event, for the papers were always affectionate to the old families.

'Where are Daphne and Heather watching from?'

'Up the street – with the rest of the school.'

She made no movement to show him where they would be. He did not even expect to see them before he went home to the country again. The pipe-music was louder now, and down the street he saw a rustle of movement in the waiting crowd.

Paul was standing with more than a hundred and fifty boys of his school in a special place reserved for them along the curb of Sherbrooke Street near the reviewing stand. The older boys were in cadet uniforms, carrying Lee-Enfields. They were standing easy, and shifted restlessly, and there were sporadic noises of oiled metal clicking as they shot the bolts of their rifles and looked down them. All the boys felt very important to be there in the best place in front of the crowd. Paul was at the end of a line of younger boys, next the cadets. He was wearing a small peaked skull-cap with the Frobisher crest in gold on its front. He had a navy blue jacket piped in the school's colours, a school tie and bare knees, and he looked exactly the same as every other boy his age in the line.

They had all come in from the country that morning to see the parade, and the day before the headmaster had assembled the school and given the boys a lecture about how the homecoming of troops had been celebrated since the days of the Romans. Frobisher had lost ninety-two old boys killed in the war. During the three months of the past autumn the school had suffered a casualty a week, and every time news was received of a death, the boys were assembled and the headmaster read the name of the one killed in a solemn voice, and told of his record at school and in the army, remembering some particular thing he had done or said when he was at school, or how he had scored a goal in a hockey match against Bishop's, or how he had made a long run in football, or perhaps how he had won a prize for his work. Once the headmaster read a personal letter addressed to him by General Sir Arthur Currie about an old boy. Each time after a name was read, the school bowed heads for a short prayer and then stood at attention and sang *God Save the King*, looking up to the picture of King George, draped with the Union Jack, their eyes lighting at the same time on the large group-photograph that also hung behind the platform, containing the picture of Sir Rupert Irons, surrounded by Chislett, Masterman and MacIntosh, the men who formed the guiding committee of the board of governors.

Next to Paul in the line, a freckle-faced boy called Fraser was arguing with a blonde boy called Andrews about their elder brothers.

'My brother killed three Germans with a bayonet,' Fraser said. 'That takes a hell of a lot more than to kill them with an aeroplane.'

'He was only in the infantry!' Andrews said. 'Infantry's old-fashioned.'

'The hell it is! My brother said if the war'd gone on a bit longer the infantry'd be using stuff like you never heard tell of. They'd of sat in the trenches and squirted liquid fire at the Germans for miles. You can't squirt fire out of any aeroplane.'

'That's nothing, my brother said aeroplanes were all ready to use rays and stuff. They were going to fly over cities and press buttons and the Germans down there, they were just going to fall apart, he said.'

'The infantry could have rays too!'

'I bet they don't give any rays to the infantry!'

'Anyhow,' Fraser said, 'it takes more to kill a German with a bayonet than with an aeroplane. Sergeant-Major Croucher said so.'

'How do you know your brother killed anyone with a bayonet? Good soldiers don't say if they kill anyone. They just kill them and they don't say anything afterwards.'

'My brother didn't say anything,' Fraser said. 'Sergeant-Major Croucher told me about it, see.'

'Good soldiers don't talk,' Andrews said. He turned to Paul. 'Isn't that a fact, good soldiers don't talk?'

'How does he know? He hasn't got a brother in the army.'

'I have so!' Paul said.

The pipes sounded far down the street, and a rustle went through the waiting crowd like wind through leaves. Paul heard Sergeant-Major Croucher's voice bellowing at the cadets to stand at ease, then at attention, then at ease again, then easy. Rifle butts banged the asphalt, followed by silence. Croucher stood in front of his cadets, very straight with a swagger-stick under the clamp of his arm. He was a two-hundred pounder with a face like Old Bill, and had fought through the retreat from Mons with the Grenadier Guards. He had been twice wounded, won the Military Medal, been invalided out of the army in 1917, and since then had been gym and cadet instructor at Frobisher.

'Now watch carefully,' he said to the cadets, 'And don't forget what I told you.' He made no effort to raise his voice, but it was so naturally loud it carried the length of a block. 'Mark how the troops salute when they pass the stand and remember next inspection day how they done it.'

Croucher always told his cadets that troops that were too lazy to salute with a bang were troops he wouldn't trust to hold a brewery cellar in an election riot. On inspection day you could hear the Guards salute half a mile away.

Paul looked across the street. Farther down were boys from a city school who looked different from the boys in Frobisher because they did not wear caps and jackets like a uniform. Directly opposite Paul were the girls from Brock Hall. The younger ones wore their hair in pig-tails down their backs and all of them were dressed in navy-blue smocks and black ribbed stockings. They had been marched in a crocodile under a pair of long-striding Englishwomen down to Sherbrooke Street to take their appointed places. Beyond them were groups from the public schools as far as you could see for two blocks.

Paul looked at the bristly back of Croucher's neck and again at the wiggling figures across the street. The girls stood more quietly than the boys, turning their heads until the pig-tails bobbed but keeping their feet still. Suddenly in the blurred rows of faces Paul saw someone familiar. It was Daphne, stiff in her school uniform. If Daphne was there, perhaps Heather was too. He saw a sailor hat move in the second row and under it Heather's face with the nose turned pertly up and the chin wagging as she talked. He hoped she would not see him, for she might wave if she did and then the fellows would jeer at him for knowing a girl. You had to be as old as a cadet to know a girl without being jeered at. He pulled the peak of his cap farther down, hoping he would look so tough she would not recognize him. He wished the school wore ordinary caps so you could break the brim and pull the loose part down over one ear and look really tough, spitting out of the corner of your mouth the way the hard fellows did. No one could spit and look tough as if he meant it wearing a pea-bouncer English cap and old school tie.

The pipes drew nearer, and leaning out of the line, Paul saw the swaying kilts of the band and then the flash of sunlight on fixed bayonets. He wondered if these were the actual bayonets that had fleshed Germans in France.

Huntly McQueen sat behind the walnut desk in his office, and his face was blandly expressionless as he looked at Athanase. 'I'm sorry, Tallard, I'm afraid there's nothing to do – nothing at all. It's most unfortunate.'

Athanase tried to keep the hopelessness from showing in his face. All winter he had been trying to persuade himself that things would turn out well, while he waited for McQueen to make up his mind to begin construction. McQueen knew he had changed his religion; indeed, he had congratulated him on that, although Athanase had suspected a peculiar look in his eyes when he had done so. While living in Montreal, Athanase had found it easier to pretend that his quarrel with the priest was unimportant. He had lost nearly all his old French friends, and this hurt; but in Saint James Street nobody seemed to care about matters like that. At any rate, arrangements for the factory had proceeded so far that Athanase had felt sure McQueen would not allow himself to be blocked. Prices could be offered to Tremblay and the other farmers that they could not bring themselves to refuse. A contribution could be made to help clear the parish debt. The bishop could not fail to see the advantage in that. In time, Athanase had pretended, the quarrel would be forgotten. He gave McQueen a calculating look. It was apparently not forgotten yet.

'You mean . . .' Athanase swallowed. 'You mean you want me to get out?'

McQueen took his time answering. a deliberately measured pause, to break the natural flow of feeling between himself and Athanase. 'I certainly don't *want* that,' he said finally.

'Then . . .' Athanase looked down, pressing his hands so tightly together that the knuckles showed white. During the past seven months his face had become as gaunt as an eagle's beak; and yellowish. He looked a sick man. Glancing across the desk at McQueen's heavy face, he suddenly hated him. McQueen was weighing and discarding him. It was a devastating experience to be weighed and discarded at his age by a younger man.

'After all, Tallard,' McQueen said slowly, as if chewing a cud, 'I told you in the beginning I would never try to force my way into a place unless assured in advance of good will.'

'And my usefulness to you was to provide good will – and a cheap price – was that it?'

McQueen regarded him placidly, his expression showing a resigned melancholy. But at the same time his pale blue eyes seemed to be looking right through Athanase and through the wall to some distant point in the future.

'You mean,' Athanase said in sudden bitter astonishment, 'you mean that *without me* you'll build this factory? They'll make no objection so long as *I* have nothing to do with it?' His cheek twitched in fury. These damned English! 'Me – I've been hurt. I admit it. I've finished myself in Saint-Marc thanks to this factory of yours. I've finished myself with parliament, with everything. And now . . .'

'Come, Tallard, be reasonable. You French-Canadians make too much trouble for yourselves – far too much.'

Flushing angrily, his shoulders leaning aggressively forward, Athanase snapped back at him. 'You English – you talk of making trouble! You upset our lives. You get into wars and conscript us. You throw us over the minute you can't use us any more. But you – you never make trouble. No! You're far too busy making money instead.'

McQueen made a soothing motion with his hand, but his eyes still had the hard, distant look. For a second Athanase had the feeling that McQueen was angry with him for having permitted personal affairs to interfere with his business plans, and that this was his peculiar method of inflicting punishment. But if so, McQueen gave no indication of it. He remained impassive, objective, even meek and inoffensive in a hard and distant way.

'You're getting angry,' McQueen said finally. 'You simply mustn't do that. It's quite useless to get angry over anything.' Not moving, his eyes unchanged, his ponderous voice as uninflected as a Presbyterian minister's at prayer, he continued, 'After all, your problem is rather unique, don't you see? After all – what are you to be loyal to: what every French-Canadian thinks or what you think yourself? There's no doubt about it, that's the whole trouble with this province. A business man hardly knows where he is, working here.'

Athanase snapped at him, 'What's this lecture to do with the point?'

McQueen smiled blandly. 'Now Tallard, be reasonable. We English have our faults, but these things one finds in this province – after all, we have to take them into account when we do business with you. After all, this case of yours proves the point perfectly.'

Athanase felt himself choking. Gripping McQueen was like trying to close your hand over a rubber balloon. And all the time the pale blue eyes never wavered from his face, and he felt like a fly under a microscope. He gestured fiercely. 'Listen, I'm not interested in your theories. What has this to do with our business? Theories – at a time like this! What do you try to say? What am I going to do? That's the question,' he said, his voice rising. 'What am I going to do?'

Athanase was too excited to realize that his words were naive, that they would be registered by McQueen as just one more proof of his business incompetence. He dropped his eyes. Indignantly he told himself that he was not incompetent, it was just that he had never been trained for this smileless poker game the English and Americans lived for. What if he had been childish during the past winter in his obstinate clinging to his dream? A man had to cling to something. He had to make a start sometime. He had to show before he died that his life was not a total waste.

'After all,' McQueen said, 'this is not a catastrophe. Your affairs will be left just as they were before. You can liquidate the mortgage if you want to. Naturally, I intend to take over your interests in the company. I may tell you, Tallard . . . I might easily have manipulated things so that you would have lost all you had. As it is, you don't lose anything.'

'Lose anything?' Athanase stared. 'My God!' He had already lost every single thing that counted. At best he would be a pensioner for the rest of his life. Only a fortnight ago he had learned that the provincial government was shortly going to end his rights of toll on the bridge.

Suddenly McQueen said, 'Why didn't you tell me about your quarrel with your priest? It would have saved time – as well as a lot of unpleasant friction.' The blue eyes were now very hard. 'You surely must have known the meaning of a development like that.'

Athanase was angrily silent. He struggled to think. 'You're going to build without me. You have fixed it so that the land will be sold and your plans can go ahead so long as I have nothing to do with it – is that what you're trying to tell me?'

'I wouldn't make any definite statement yet. We certainly don't intend to start immediately.'

Athanase rose abruptly and crossed the room. From the window he could see the Saint Lawrence steel blue under a bright sky, and he pulled the window up, feeling choked for fresh air. The window rose with a smooth surge letting a rush of air into the room. The papers on the desk rustled and McQueen's hand shot out to bang them down. Athanase lowered the window to a slit and returned to his chair.

'After all,' McQueen said, 'you've still got plenty to do.'

'How long do you expect me to keep my seat in parliament now?'

'Well . . .'

In the silence they could hear the faint, high singing of bagpipes. McQueen's ear seemed to cock to the sound, a frown touched his face and he shook his head. 'You know, Tallard, those returned soldiers are going to present quite a problem. The war has accustomed them to all sorts of hasty action. We may well be in for a bad time here. I don't see how the country can ever be the same again, after what they've been through. Let's hope the government takes a firm line with no nonsense. After all, they must be protected from themselves.'

Athanase stared at him, indignant at the irrelevancy and shocked by the astonishing realization that McQueen was not being hypocritical. He had really meant every word he had said. Then his own anger blew everything else out of his mind. 'You started me in all this. You came to *me*, McQueen – I didn't come to you. Now you want to throw me into the discard. All right! I was a fool to expect loyalty from a business man. I can see they've been getting at you. But just how do you think you can put this business through in Saint-Marc by yourself if you couldn't do it with me?'

'The parish is in debt.'

'You mean you've approached the bishop about it?'

McQueen's face gave nothing definite away. 'I certainly showed the bishop what a fine thing it would be for the community. I pointed out that unless work was provided many of the young men would have to leave.'

Athanase nearly choked. This was his own great argument.

'It seems,' McQueen continued, 'that the bishop has somewhat different views on industry in general from those held by your Father Beaubien.'

'Are you telling me that the bishop will take *you* – but that he won't have the factory so long as I have any connection with the company?'

McQueen shook his head. 'You mustn't be so personal about everything, my dear Tallard. The bishop didn't even mention your name.'

'But that was the impression you got?'

215

'There are many factors to consider.' Again McQueen shook his head. 'After all, Tallard – after all! You know yourself that this situation is unique. You made an open issue of your quarrel with your Church.'

Athanase froze into a calm. His face became grave, reserved, aristocratic. 'All right!' He got up and pointed his long finger in McQueen's face. McQueen blinked at him stolidly. 'It's the old story. You play us off, one against the other. You do it so naturally you don't even know you do it at all.' His voice broke in its effort to hold in the spilling anger. 'Someday the whole country will pay for this sort of thing.'

He turned, straight and dignified, toward the door. McQueen bustled around his desk and laid his hand on his shoulder. 'My dear Tallard – what can I do? No one can swim against the current. You don't know what you're talking about. I played nobody off against anyone else. This was a business proposition, that was all. I wanted to build a factory. The bishop agreed with me that a factory would be desirable. That's all.'

'I was under the impression that we were partners,' Athanase said coldly.

He slipped out from under McQueen's hand and took a step nearer the door. McQueen paused to touch a flower into place beneath his mother's picture.

'I wish you wouldn't go away angry,' McQueen said. 'You seem to have some personal – some fixed idea in your mind and you're fitting this affair into it. My dear Tallard, we must keep personalities out of business. I'm sorry, there's nothing I can do.'

Athanase opened the door, McQueen remained with him. 'Now please,' McQueen said, 'don't do anything rash. Come in any time and we'll talk things over again. I'll speak to Miss Drew and she'll settle our financial arrangements.' He smiled and held up his finger. 'And here's a tip. Avoid the stock market, for it's not going to keep up much longer. There's going to be a depression very soon.'

Athanase strode out without taking McQueen's hand. He reached the hall and rang for the elevator. So that was that! A fool, his mind told itself, a fool, a fool, a fool! His whole life had been an insane groping around in a circle to discover reality, and everything he touched kept turning to smoke. Round and round in a circle of explanations, nothing real anywhere but always the reasons for why there was no reality, round and round the mulberry bush, round and round and round.

He found himself alone in Saint James Street looking for a taxi. The street was empty. It was a gaunt, scarred cavern hideously cold and ugly, this street where the English made their money. How could a man like himself have hoped to be successful here? He did not even know the rules. A fool, a fool, I met a fool in the street, a fool alone in the street not even able to find a taxi to take himself home! Why was he alone with nobody else here? The parade, of course. All the office workers were uptown in their patriotism to see the parade. Except McQueen. He was working as usual. A fool, a fool in the street! He walked west to Victoria Square and boarded a tram which rumbled emptily up Beaver Hall Hill. When it reached Dorchester Street he rang the bell and got out.

He found himself in a square partially shaded by tall trees that looked small against the buildings, two sides of it lined with slate-grey houses, an island between slums on the east, and business and financial areas on the other three sides. It was like a relic of Georgian London.

Athanase looked up at the green leaves overhead. Another spring; and in Saint-Marc the consecrated seeds were in the earth and the blackflies would be swarming in the maple grove after sundown. A fresh spring for a world free of war forever!

Holy Mother of God, what could he do now? He turned a full circle on the pavement, spinning slowly on his leather heels, but saw nothing except the staring fronts of the buildings and the four streets branching emptily away from him. What could he do? What could he even think of doing now?

Somewhere out of his boyhood at the classical college floated a line his mind had stored for years. He could remember the black-gowned rector, that Jesuit with the wonderful voice and the ascetic face, translating it to the top

217

form: 'And of those trees you cultivate, not a single one will follow you, their brief master, save only the loathed cypresses . . .' And the rector had spoken of the terror of the pagan's death who had written those lines. His own death! But when he died he would not even own his maple trees any more. Even the deeds to the old land would be gone from the bank vault then. There would be no point in keeping land on which he could no longer live. Everything would go, as so much had gone already: status, family, friends, livelihood. But why worry about friends at this late date? They were gone already.

Nearby was a club which he had recently joined but had seldom visited. It was one of the old English clubs, filled with men successful after the English fashion, rich, dignified and incredibly ignorant. He thought of the long chairs in smooth black leather, the mahogany panelling of the walls, the pictures so dark you couldn't see what the frames contained, the cold drinks that never made any of them drunk because not even a quart of alcohol could make any of them forgetful of his neighbour's opinion. He could not go there any more now. They would talk about him if he did; but discreetly, in a patronizing tone, and never to his face. 'Too bad.' 'Yes, but what can you expect?' 'What I've always said, they just aren't practical.' 'After all, look at the education they get.' 'They ought to stick to the law and the church.' 'Damned good lawyers though, I have one for a partner, clever little devil. Don't know what I'd do without him.' 'It's the old story, what I've always said, east is east and west is west and never the twain . . .'

'This has got to stop!' Athanase said aloud.

He looked quickly around, but there was no one near enough to have heard him.

Farther east was a French club to which he had belonged for years. But he could not enter there now, for they had demanded his resignation. Where could he go? He could not go home because the parade was crossing Sherbrooke Street and it would be at least another hour before there would be gangway across the street. Where could he go? There were so many people to avoid now. He thought again of McQueen and the anger welled in his stomach like bile.

218

As he stood on the sidewalk, wind swirled his coat about his knees. Then he lifted his chin defiantly. Why was he ashamed? Was a man a traitor to his race just because he had done his best and failed? And who said he had failed? There was still time to show them. McQueen had said that business was going into a depression. Yes, but twelve months ago he had said the war would last another three years, then had changed his mind a few months later and so postponed the factory. If he had not changed his mind the factory would be half finished now. Would it? Anyway, suppose there was a depression? There was a depression after every war, but first there was always a brief boom, too. Did McQueen know history as he did? What did McQueen know of anything except that cold wiliness the English and Americans always had when it came to money? He would show them yet, he would make a million. And when he had his money he would not sit on it like an incubating hen the way the English did, so frightened of doing anything their neighbours hadn't thought of first that they never did anything at all. He would endow a public library and set it up in the heart of the French section on Saint Denis Street. The Athanase Tallard Memorial Library! If he made enough money he would endow libraries all over the province; there were less than a dozen now, and none of them were first class. His libraries would be big, big as churches. He would show them all, French as well as English. He would prove that a man could leave the Church and still be faithful to the people. Did the priests think they had a monopoly on public service?

Then his chin sank and he thrust his hands into his pockets and walked slowly westward. Slowly, but still sour with bitterness; thoughts about McQueen continued to crawl around in his mind. He remembered a sentence of McQueen's and gave it a different twist: 'The tragedy of French-Canada is that you can't make up your minds whether you want to be free-choosing individuals or French-Canadians choosing only what you think your entire race will approve ...' Like all the English, free with advice! But do they ever help a man? Do they ever stretch out a hand? Do they ever really want us to have a chance?

Kathleen would be out watching the parade now, and of

course enjoying it. She was spending a lot of money since they had moved into town, but she was certainly happier. She had a flair for dress, and already she looked years younger. What was she doing with herself all the hours she was out of the house alone? Did she know other men? He did not think so, though perhaps she did. At least he was not like a selfish old man, keeping his young wife under lock and key away from all pleasure. But now the thought of Kathleen seemed strangely distant, like the memory of someone he had known long ago when he was young. What did it matter now that she was beautiful, that the rich body was so warm and skilled? Incredible, that for most of a lifetime a man could imagine that beauty was enough, or that women could satisfy the ultimate solitude.

Then a door in his brain seemed to swing wide open on hinges to disclose what looked like the atrium of an enormous museum. With dreamlike speed the corridor filled with men and women he once had known. God, had he known all those women? Where were they now? What were their names? But it is unreasonable, it is highly fantastic, that I could have known this woman so well and not be able to tell you her name. . . . The people moved silently about in the atrium: children, teachers, priests, farmers, lawyers, politicians, judges, soldiers, and among them the women. But it is not correct, they are all dressed the same way, their clothes are all of the same fashion and some of these women are surely dead, they must be, for it is not reasonable they should all have lived as long as I have, that is not reasonable at all. . . .

Passing his hand over his forehead, he felt moisture on it. The bones of his skull seemed to be vibrating, then pumping in and out. He heard his voice, like a stranger's, mutter in his ear, 'I'm not well, it's nothing, but just now I certainly need to sit down.' Then he looked and saw the same street, the same buildings, the same trees.

He walked slowly westward until he reached Saint James' Basilica. He had done well to come this far alone. He still had his will power, the Tallard tenacity never let a man down. He stopped and looked calmly up to the row of greened-bronze saints that lined the pediment brooding down over the street. A good street to bless, considering the number of financiers who passed to work on it, the number of prostitutes who accosted you on it, the hundreds of people, each with his own secret little sins, who walked it every day. It needed the blessings of all the saints and of Bishop Bourget besides, who stood there near the pavement, also in bronze. An iron-willed man, an ecclesiastical prince – they said he had confronted even the Papal Legate with his unbreakable will. His own father had known Bishop Bourget, he himself had once been blessed by him, but now the man was a statue and the bronze had oxidized and he was as green and permanent as the saints above him, and somewhere his soul, his indissoluble essence. . . .

Athanase walked up the steps and passed through the vestibule into the nave of the cathedral. The incense-charged silence within was so cool he could taste it, the holy Catholic taste, the air breathed so many times by the anonymous little people of the city who thronged the cathedral Sunday after Sunday. Automatically, out of his childhood training, he genuflected to the altar.

Then he glanced quickly around. No one had noticed him. A few old women were on their knees with eyes glazed with reverence as they stared at the candles above the high altar. A tram driver and a workman were kneeling in the last pew, and as he passed them his nostrils twitched to an odour of stale sweat. They were praying, finding God after a hard day's work.

'What am I doing here?' he murmured, 'me, of all people – how can I be here at a time like this?' But his legs felt so weak he could not have gone out had he wished. He moved slowly to a pew a few rows up from the workman and the tram driver, and sat down with his hat beside him. His knees went forward and found the kneeler, and his eyes blurred as he folded his hands and looked steadily at the candles flickering in the half-darkness.

That evening Marius ate dinner in a cheap restaurant downtown and tried to talk about himself above the noise to Emilie. He had not seen her since he had been conscripted nine months ago, for this was his first leave from the army.

He was still in uniform, and had no idea when he would be demobilized.

The restaurant was overcrowded and smelled of unclean floor-corners, ice-cream spills on glass-top tables and sour dishwater. Since Marius and Emilie had arrived, the place had filled up with soldiers. Now the soda fountain was lined with men in khaki sitting on stools eating the things they had not seen for three or four years. One soldier had five sodas in front of him all in different colours. Another was eating a banana royal. One had a marshmallow sundae with chocolate sauce and another had a pineapple sundae with nuts. They were all talking loudly except the man with the sodas, who kept a straw in his mouth all the time. They were discussing food. One man was going to have a big breakfast tomorrow with corn flakes and cream and powdered sugar, and on top of that he was going to have bacon and eggs. Crisp bacon, not the white, fatty stuff he'd been eating the past three years. One wished it were August so he could have corn on the cob. A big corporal didn't want to eat anything for weeks except T-bones smothered in onions, thick and medium done.

Then they began talking about women. All the time he had been overseas the corporal hadn't been able to find the kind of woman he liked. They were like schoolteachers or, by Christ, they were like whores. He talked in a factual explaining voice. 'I want my women like my steaks. I want them medium.'

The man with the marshmallow sundae looked around. 'Brother, so far as I can remember, you've sure come back to the right country.' He pushed aside his empty dish and turned to the man with the banana royal. 'The guy was never satisfied. Last month him and me were in Piccadilly and a couple of women picked us up must have been countesses or something. Real class. And right in front of the Ritz the guy starts telling them about a skirt he knew in Birdville, Ontario.'

'Why not?' the corporal said. 'I like a comfortable woman.'

The man with the sodas took the straw out of his mouth. 'What kind of a place is this Birdville, anyhow?'

'They got a railroad station there.' The soldier licked some syrup off his spoon and laid it down on the counter. 'They got a general store and a church, and they got a hotel for the drummer that comes around in the spring.'

'Hell!' The man went back to his sodas. 'It sounds like Toronto!'

The voices faded out again and Marius leaned over the table to Emilie. 'In the army I made a bet with myself. If ever I heard them talk about anything else but women and what they ate or drank I'd give a dollar to the Red Cross.'

'But they treated you all right?' Emilie said.

Marius showed her two stripes on his left sleeve. 'I'm a corporal now. Five months after the war ends, the army gets around to making me a corporal.'

He bent to his food again, and while he ate, Emilie kept her eyes on him. He looked healthy and almost tough, he had gained weight and the whites of his eyes were clear. But he still ate as though he expected someone to jerk the plate away from him the moment he stopped. When he had finished his dessert he wiped his mouth fastidiously with his napkin. He noticed for the first time that Emilie was much better dressed than she had been a year ago. She looked almost like a city girl now. He noticed also that her hands were smoother, and that she spoke more carefully, with better grammar.

His eyebrows rose and he asked suspiciously, 'Did you get a raise?'

'I don't work in the restaurant any more.'

'Did they fire you?'

'I left. That job – it was no good for me.'

'What are you doing now, then?' His voice was sharp with suspicion.

'I got a new job.' Her eyes showed she was proud of herself and hoped he would be pleased. 'In a dress factory.'

'What dress factory?'

'Greenberg – you know, up on Bleury?'

He cracked his hand down over her wrist and held it. 'You mean you're working for the Jews?'

'They pay me good money. I get twelve a week. If I do better I get a raise maybe. Lots of girls . . .'

223

'So you work for the Jews!' He kept holding her wrist and staring at her as she wondered what she had said wrong this time. 'I thought you called yourself a Catholic!'

She pulled her wrist away. 'You stop that. You're hurting me. Maybe I do work at Greenberg. Who do you think you are – a priest? Father Gervais knows I work there. Maybe you'd like it better if I starve? Who said a Catholic can't work for a Jew?'

The noise at the fountain was rising again. A tall soldier with an angular face had stopped eating to make himself heard. 'When I get home to the Missus I'm finished batting around see. I'm going to show her right off I'm through with all that stuff. If you guys are smart you'll do the same.'

'What's the use? They can always tell.'

'My Old Lady's a very religious woman,' the angular man said, 'and she can't tell on account of she never thinks about stuff like that.' He was very serious. 'I'm not kidding. It was all right before the war but now it's going to be different.'

'Like hell!'

'I'm telling you, the women are all set to get their hands on us again and tame us down. You take a look at their faces. I'm telling you, they're after us.'

The man with the sodas shoved another glass across the counter and called to the Italian for more straws. He pushed a jarful across.

'You fellas better get wised up to yourselves,' the angular man went on. 'I'm telling you, they're ganged up to get hold of us, for sure.'

Marius sipped his coffee and leaned back, watching Emilie. His hand was lying on the table beside hers, long and sensitive. He touched the sleeve of her dress. 'You got that in the factory?'

She smiled proudly. 'I worked late a whole week for that dress.'

'Nice man, this Greenberg!'

The restaurant door opened with a bang and a soldier with three valour ribbons on his chest came in with a rush. He was short enough for a bantam battalion, and as he cocked up to the big men at the bar he bent his hands backwards on his hips and flapped his elbows like a rooster's wings. He crowed. 'For Chrissake!' he shouted, flapping his bent arms. 'The stuff you guys are drinking! Where's your morals?'

The man with the five sodas was now on his fourth; it was chocolate and full of brown bubbles. He kept on sucking and said out of the corner of his mouth, 'I bet Pete's canned so he stinks.'

Marius set down his coffee cup again and looked at Emilie. 'What are Jews like when they're drunk? Funny thing – I never saw a drunk Jew!'

'Mr. Greenberg treats me good enough. He never gets drunk.'

'He just runs his hands over you while he fits the dress – eh?'

'Him!' She wished Marius would not be so unpleasant. 'He's a little old man all bent over.' She giggled self-consciously. 'Seventy years old, maybe.'

Marius' face twisted. 'I know an old man that doesn't let a little thing like that stop him.'

Emilie blushed.

A roar of noise exploded from the soda fountain. 'Who started it?' the drunk was shouting. 'You mean you don't know? Bloody Limey M.P. crimed me and put me under a black sergeant for fatigue. Did that nigger jump when my bayonet started travelling up his ass!'

The man who had been eating the banana royal now had a cherry sundae with a dust of nuts over the top. He turned lazily to the drunk. 'You mean a little runt like you started that riot?'

'I'm the guy that got all you bastards back home,' the drunk shouted. 'If it hadn't been for me you'd still be over there now.'

The Italian behind the fountain was smiling and wringing his hands and saying 'Gentlemen, gentlemen!' The man with the sodas said to him with a straight face, the straw still in his lips, nodding toward Pete, 'See – he's quite a guy!'

'How do you mean you got us home?' the man with the cherry sundae said.

'We burned down the camp in the riot, didn't we? After

225

that – hell, the Limeys couldn't get rid of us quick enough.'

The angular, serious man put his arm about the bantam's shoulder. 'Now listen, Pete – you got to sober up. Last time you got so sick you couldn't eat for days. I got to look after you, Pete. I'm not forgetting what you did for me that time.'

'For Chrissake, who's talking about the war?'

'Discipline, Pete!' the angular man kept saying. 'Remember that time we were sitting half a week on top of a mine? Remember that?'

'This guy a pal of yours?' the man with the sodas said.

The angular man almost shaped up to him. 'Is he a pal!'

'Can the war!' Pete shouted. 'Stuff it up! After what I did the whole bloody merchant marine wasn't good enough for us guys. They had to give us the *Olympic*.' He belched and staggered. 'You ought to give me a statue.' He flapped his arms again and crowed like a rooster.

'Gentlemen,' the Italian smiled and showed white teeth as he leaned forward. 'Gentlemen – I got customers.'

The noise quieted down and Marius rose. 'Look at that oily Italian sucking up!' He lifted his voice and shouted, and the man came running, one hand holding his apron. 'How much do I owe for this rotten meal?'

The Italian smiled another mouthful of white teeth. He seemed to think Marius drunk too, but he was very respectful to the uniform. 'One dollar feefty,' he said.

Marius threw down a bill and a fifty-cent piece, and the coin rang on the glass top of the table. 'Next time a lady eats here,' he said, 'you wipe off your tables first.'

When they were outside on the street, Emilie took his arm. 'The table was clean enough,' she said.

'Listen,' Marius said, 'I learned one thing in the army. You shout at a man and he always gets the idea he's to blame for something. Before he has time to figure it out, you've got him where you want him.'

She did not answer, for she was not quite sure what he was talking about.

'I wonder how many sergeants are going to be out of jobs?' he said. 'A sergeant without anyone to shout at – yes,' he went on, nodding, 'that's going to be a useful thing to remember. The next few years whenever I see a discon-

226

tented man I'll remember he used to be a sergeant.'

They walked slowly eastward along Sainte-Catherine Street. The city was alive tonight. It pulsed with the vitality of the new men who had entered it.

'What are you going to do now?' Emilie said.

'Do? What does anybody ever do in the army?'

'Sure, sure. I mean, when they let you out?'

'That's the big question,' he said, mysteriously.

'I guess maybe you go back to college, no?'

'That's another question.'

As they walked along the street together the crowds surged about them under the light, the sidewalk was packed with men and girls strolling in the warm spring evening because they had no other place to go. There was an expectant happiness in the air, and not many of the soldiers they passed were drunk. Some stood alone on street corners with quiet expressions on their faces as though it were so good to be home that just standing still was all they needed to make them happy. They passed a sergeant-major on the corner of Saint-Lawrence Main talking in French to a tram driver. He wore five medal ribbons and the badge of the Regiment Maisonneuve. He had a great chest and shoulders, jet black hair and an eagle face, a wide moustache showing solid black against tan skin. He could have doubled for Frontenac. Marius looked at him, then jerked his eyes away.

They walked on, drifting eastward into the French part of the city.

'Let's go where you live,' Marius said suddenly. 'I want to meet your father.'

'Oh, no!' she said.

His fingers squeezed her wrist sharply. 'I want to meet him. I've never even seen him.'

'I told him about you. It's all right me going out with you.'

Marius stopped under an arc light and stood off, watching her face. It was pale in the flickering light. God, he thought, what an ordinary face! So ordinary he sometimes found it difficult to remember what she looked like. Why was he here with a girl like this? Out of all the women in the world, why spend his time with her?

But he knew the answer. He could not go with beautiful

227

girls because he hated them all on sight. They traded on their looks and that made them as false as hell. And as he watched Emilie, something of her instinctive goodness softened him. What if she did not come from his own class? French girls of his own class were so strictly brought up he was afraid of them.

His searching eyes made her embarrassed, and he saw her glance away. And at that instant she touched him deeply without knowing it, and as his eyes dropped to her square figure set on its stocky legs he suddenly knew that he could not do without her. Instantly a flash of joy passed through him. The feeling was so rare and strange it brought tears to his eyes.

'Come on,' he said gruffly, taking her arm, 'let's go to your place.'

Emilie walked quietly beside him. Tomorrow she would go alone to the church and say her prayers, asking God to take away his bitterness and to make him kind.

28

Paul had been at Frobisher School for nearly three years. He was now twelve. He had become so much a part of the place that he spoke English all the time and thought and even dreamed in English. He liked it here, for he had learned how to play games. He played football in the fall and hockey from December to March. In the early spring there was boxing, and Sergeant-Major Croucher said he was a natural at it. He had a very quick straight left, the punch the English boxers like better than any other, and he was fast. In early summer, in the long days before term ended, the boys put on white flannels and played cricket very badly on the square green field in front of the school where the elm trees reminded the masters of an English close. Unofficially, they threw baseballs about behind the school at recess.

Now it was a late afternoon in February, 1921, and Paul was playing hockey for his house in a junior inter-house league. The boys played in an open-air rink behind the school with the snow piled ten feet high back of the boards. The rink rang with skates and the knocking of sticks and the banging of the puck against the boards, sometimes with a loud shout from a boy or the shrill peep of the referee's whistle. Whenever the whistle blew there was an instant's silence while they faced off. Paul loved these moments when the game paused and he was able to get the whole feel of it: the full exhilaration of the air coldly still in the sunshine, the teams poised and the referee standing over the crouching centre-forwards, holding the puck above the crossed sticks, the sticks twitching nervously and the sweat warming on the face, the lungs charged with fresh cold air and the legs tired, yet the knowledge that you could go on like this forever if you had to.

Paul played centre-forward, and so he was in on every face-off. He had learned the trick of weaving so that his trunk swayed one way while his legs went the other. He had a quick change of pace and could keep his head up while he weaved and carried the puck, his eyes shooting left and right to see where the wings were as he went down the ice to make the openings. He was a natural play-maker and fed his wings generously, but he also had a quick low shot of his own which would have a snap in it when he got older and had more strength in his wrists. If he kept on improving he would be certain to make the senior team inside another few years. He was growing fast. Like all the Tallards, he was rangy, with long legs; but he had inherited a good chest and wide shoulders from Kathleen.

When the game was over, the boys took showers and changed in the locker room. Then, after a cold supper in the dining hall, they collected their books and went into prep. An elderly man with long front teeth and a grey moustache like an overgrown toothbrush presided on a small dais in front of the room while the boys sat at their desks and worked and squirmed and cribbed and passed notes through the two hours. Occasionally one of them jumped as the boy behind him stuck a pen-nib into his rear. When this happened the prep-master raised his eyes and tapped his pencil on the desk and the boys all looked innocent until he lowered them again. It was a usual prep in a rather unusual school.

Frobisher had been founded nearly a hundred years ago

by an Anglican canon in the days when Canada was a group of colonies run by a British governor who served the combined interests of the Crown and the compact of business families forming the upper classes. It was still an upper-class school, though not exactly aristocratic. Such snobbishness as it may have had was not conscious; it was simply an English-style school run for the sons of prosperous Canadians. The masters were all Englishmen, and most of them were young. They came out from England every fall and worked for a few years before drifting off into other jobs or other schools. The few who remained tended to become characters, each with his recognized set of mannerisms. But they all worked hard at Frobisher, and more or less enjoyed it. The school was a happy place while Paul was there, and the masters generally cheerful. Each master, no matter what his age, took the train for Montreal the day school closed in June and returned to the Old Country for the summer. They all came back on the same ship just before term re-opened in mid-September.

There was certainly no danger of standardization at Frobisher, for no two masters had ever been known to agree on anything except their opinion of the Americans. In spite of this, the place ran smoothly. It had some real colour of its own. The boys liked it, and the masters who stayed on grew so fond of the place they admitted they would never like to work in England. The boys believed that the staff had only two things in common. The younger ones were always upset to discover that Canadian boys mistook their exquisite English accents for a proof of softness, and consequently a major part of their work in their first teaching years was directed to prove this belief wrong. Some of them even froze their ears in winter walking around bareheaded to prove they could take it.

The other point on which the staff agreed was the calamitous proximity of Canada to the United States. The Americans were doubtless all right, but they would be far better if they were a thousand miles away. They did their best to offset this by teaching the boys British history and geography, and they even tried to teach them British manners as well. This never quite succeeded. The boys knew all the latest American slang, and used it. They played better base-ball than cricket. In October, when the World Series was played, a surreptitious betting pool generally operated in the basement.

But Paul got a thorough training at Frobisher. None of the masters went by a rule book, their teaching was careful, and if the boys did not do their arithmetic, English, French, Latin, algebra and geography, they were caned for it. All the masters were very cheerful as they bent the boys over and caned them, and Sergeant-Major Croucher liked to make a small ceremony of it, military style. When he gave them one crack, he said he was making them lance-corpor-als, when he gave them two they became corporals and so on up to the commissioned ranks. It was a matter of pride for all the boys to get a certain amount of caning, and if Croucher noticed that any of the shy ones were failing to qualify, he invented a minor crime and made them lance-corporals for the sake of their morale. When he caned shy boys he was so cheerful he made it impossible for them to be afraid. But once he bent them over he gave them a really good crack. Then they would run away with grins on their faces holding their backsides, knowing they could prove themselves men by taking down their pants and showing the red mark Croucher had given them.

Paul was at the top of his class in work and was good enough at games to be popular. He was no longer timid about little things as he once had been; he was frightened of nothing at all now. At first he had been homesick for Saint-Marc. In the evenings he had missed his mother talk-ing to him at his bedside, and on Saturday mornings he often had a moment's twang of loneliness when he thought of his walks with his father over the fields. He missed most of all never hearing French spoken around him. But the strange-ness soon wore off because there was so much to do, and when he went home to Montreal for the holidays his parents treated him as a special person. His father was pleased with his reports and his mother always took him to shows and gave him ice-cream afterwards. But when the holidays ended he was always glad to be back, looking forward to football in the autumn and hockey in the winter and boxing in the spring. He was a veteran at Frobisher now, and he counted for something.

The other boys never made an 'issue of his race. They never even thought about it, for he was one of themselves. They might have considered themselves superior to French-Canadians in a vague sort of way, but what few ideas they had on the subject were derived mainly from casual remarks they had heard at home. Frobisher was in the heart of the French-Canadian countryside, but the boys did not think this remarkable. When they went into the village to buy candy and ginger beer they accepted old Baptiste Doucette as a character and a part of the school. He had been running a tuck shop just out of bounds ever since anyone could remember, he knew all the boys by their names and he spoke a picturesque English they presumed had been invented for their own special benefit. The boys never worried themselves about national problems of any sort; indeed, they did not know they existed. Their home was the English section of Montreal; as a result of what everyone told them, their country was not Canada but the British Empire.

Under the yellow ceiling lights the boys sat at their desks and the long-toothed master continued with his corrections. Paul leaned back in his seat and looked across to the window panes. Through them a full moon was visible, rendered blue by the glass. His thighs and lungs felt pleasantly tired from the afternoon's hockey, but he thought it would be wonderful if he could skate when prep was over instead of going straight up to the dormitory. When he became a senior he would be allowed out on the rink after prep on a night like this. He thought of the crisp air and the snow squeaking under his heels, and then his skates biting the ice, running over it and lifting hard under the soles of his feet as he crossed the bumps where the water had bubbled as it froze, the rink like dark blue steel, the snowbanks around it dark with shadows in some places, ghostly white in others, with tiny sparkles flashing mysteriously here and there as the moon caught crystal and made it live.

He brought his mind back to his work, but after reading a little more he turned the book upside down and lifted his eyes to the ceiling. His lips moved and his teeth showed as he repeated to himself the Fifth Declension. The master looked up from his corrections. 'Not so much noise, Tallard!'

'But I'm working, sir!'

Paul made his voice sound bright on a reflex. The boys always looked their brightest whenever a master told them to stop doing something. The long-toothed master went back to his corrections, and Paul continued as though nothing had happened: *res, res, rem, rei, rei, re.* He knew this well enough to drop it; it was the easiest of all the declensions anyway, and the best, for once you finished it there were no more of them to learn. He thumbed through his Latin book until he came to the pictures of famous Greek and Roman buildings at the back. He looked at the Parthenon. One of the younger masters had been in Athens with the Navy during the war, and had told him about it so well he could imagine exactly what it was like, the white pillars with the strange copper stains near the top, the sun going down behind Salamis and Aegelos, throwing the purple shadow of the mountain ridges over the Athenian plain, the corona of violet light ringing the crests of Parnes, Pentelikon and Hymettus, and the Parthenon floating there like a miracle, resting apparently on the actual light that shot uninterrupted above the shadow that buried the plain.

Some day he would see it. He remembered stories from the *Odyssey:* the wine-dark sea, the rollers coming in over the beaches in the fog, the men rowing the small, narrow ships with beaks on their prows. He looked back at the Parthenon, and in the book it seemed plain and ugly, almost like a bank in Montreal. Why was a building beautiful in Europe when an exact copy of it was ugly here? But in Athens the Parthenon was framed by what lay around it, it was free in the air and sunshine, it was open. That was what the master had told him. Paul frowned, trying to figure out the differences.

The door of the prep room opened and the headmaster stuck his face in. The boys all stopped working to look around. The head smiled and nodded at the prep master and scanned the boys until his eyes fell on Paul. 'Come along, Tallard,' he said. 'I want to speak to you.'

233

Paul got up and left his desk, the boys watching curiously, wondering if it meant a caning. Paul tried to remember what he had done lately. The Sergeant-Major had made him a corporal that morning for being late for a line-up, but this was all he could recollect. He followed the head out into the hall.

'Come along to my study,' the head said.

Paul knew from the tone of his voice that he was not going to be caned. They reached the study and the head opened the door.

'Go in, Tallard,' he said. 'I'll be back presently.'

Paul saw a figure sitting in a chair by the head's desk and recognized Captain Yardley. Then the door closed quietly behind him.

'Hullo, there, Paul!'

'Hullo, sir!' Paul grinned with pleasure, showing his buck teeth.

Yardley got up and balanced himself, the old intimate kindness showing in his brown face. His hair was a little whiter now, but he kept it cropped short and his ears stuck out the same as ever. As Paul was trying to get over his surprise at seeing Yardley here, he noticed that the captain was not smiling.

'Is anything wrong, sir?'

Yardley put his hand on Paul's shoulders. 'I just came down to have a talk with you, Paul. The train was late. Man – you're growing so I can see it!'

Paul flexed his right arm. 'Feel my muscle, sir!'

Yardley felt the biceps, and then the muscles back of the shoulder. 'Biceps don't count for anything,' he said, 'only for show. Back there in the shoulder, now – when you hit a fella, thet's where it comes from – there and the calves. And what's the idea of calling me "sir" all the time? Haven't heard thet word since I left the sea. The Limeys teach you thet?'

Paul grinned and sat on the edge of the headmaster's desk, feeling bold as he did so. 'I don't know,' he said. Then, noticing that Yardley's face still showed no smile, his grin faded out.

The captain looked at the floor and traced out the pattern

234

of the rug with the point of his stick. 'Paul,' he said, 'you and me've got to go into town.'

'What's the matter?'

'I better tell you, Paul. Your father's pretty sick.'

Paul looked away, tight all over, not knowing what to do or say. Because of his embarrassment, tears were in his eyes. Then he felt Yardley's hand on his shoulder and turned back. 'Is P'pa dead?'

Yardley shook his head. 'He just wants to see you. I spoke to your headmaster about it, and he says the matron upstairs is fixing your things so we can ship right out. We got to change trains, but we can get to town by early morning. Got to sit up a good while in Sainte-Hyacinthe waiting for the train, I guess.' He limped to the door and opened it. 'Something new, Paul – you going places on a train at night.'

29

Athanase breathed, he existed, he lay in the sheets and heard as though from a great distance the mechanism which held the life in him running down. It was morning; the sunlight streamed in the window and sparkled on the snow-covered roof next door. It was afternoon, and the snow was purple with shadows. A shaded lamp showed it was night. But for him no real time had passed because he could not measure it. His mind was like water coloured by changing weather. His ears, like a doctor's instrument detached from his body, heard the rattle of his breathing. Some part of his brain, still living, recorded the fact that the rattle had grown louder. It would grow steadily, it would become a snore, it would become a thunder filling the house. He was alone with the rattle of his own breaking mechanism announcing his extinction.

'Try to take this, Mr. Tallard. Try to open your mouth.'

Something warm on his lips, a little moisture in his dry mouth, and again exhaustion. A cloth brushed his mouth and chin. He lay as before, motionless.

He felt a hand on his forehead and opened his eyes. Kathleen's face was bent over him, turned slightly away as if

235

to avoid his breath. She did not think he could see her. His jaw struggled to speak against the paralysis. 'Paul!' he whispered.

'He's coming!' Kathleen's voice was clear and normal. He could hear it perfectly. 'He'll be here by morning. John Yardley is bringing him.'

For many minutes Kathleen knelt by the bed stroking his forehead. Marius was at the foot of the bed, the nurse on a chair on the other side of it.

A faint tremor ran through the thin, motionless body. Something in him seemed trying to speak, a flicker passed over the face as though the mind were indignant because the mechanism would not serve it any more. 'It's dark. I've always hated the dark. I'm . . .' From somewhere out of the past floated a memory. 'Except when the candles are bright.'

Kathleen's voice was still and clear. 'The light's on, Athanase. It's not dark any more.'

His eyelids closed. Scattered recollections from his boyhood flickered through his mind, faded a second and then grew strong, not much motion or force in them but a smooth, silent process like shifting lights. He saw very clearly the prospect from the old house in Saint-Marc: the flat fields, the river like ink running through the snow-covered plain, then the river miraculously warm in the sun with the cloud-towers above it, Blanchard walking across a row of brown furrows smoking his pipe. His lips quivered, but Kathleen bending over them detected no clear sound. My father's house . . . our house . . . myself! Familiar faces he had almost forgotten swam into the light above the motionless lake of his mind, blurred and disappeared. A virgin's face, a nun's face with a blue snood over black hair. Marie-Adèle! A shiver of panic tried to communicate itself from his mind to his paralysed body. The jaw moved.

Kathleen bent to listen for his whisper. Nearly a minute passed before it came.

'Don't go!'

'I'm here, Athanase. I won't leave you.'

Nearly five minutes passed. The nurse in her chair on the other side of the bed had never taken her eyes from the face on the pillow. She rose with a rustle of starched linen and

236

wiped his forehead gently with a moist cloth. Marius remained at the foot of the bed, gripping the rail with both hands. Kathleen dropped quietly to her knees, her firm arms resting on the edge of the bed.

He whispered again. 'Marie! Marie-Adèle!'

Kathleen felt the colour draining out of her cheeks, and turning away she saw Marius' eyes burning into her. A wild look of triumph was on his face. She turned to the bed again and stared into her husband's eyes. They were opened half way, then they opened wide and looked into hers. His hair was as white as the pillow, the flesh on the cheekbones looked grey and worn out, but the lines about the mouth and nose were still dominant and dignified. His eyes still looked at her.

Drawing a deep breath, she forced herself to speak. 'Yes – I'm here. It's ... it's ...'

Again the jaw moved. 'Marie!' Then, after at least a minute, he said in French, 'Take my hand!'

Kathleen hesitated, but finally she took his hand and pressed it. It was limp and cold. She chafed the skin and laid it against her cheek. But remembering how he had always liked to stroke her cheek, telling her how smooth and flowerlike it was, she felt ashamed and lowered his hand again.

The nurse brought another spoonful of warm soup and held it to his mouth. The spoon rattled against the teeth, but most of the liquid spilled inside.

He spoke again, so low Marius could not hear. 'Pierre!' he whispered. 'Get ... get ...' His eyes opened very wide and his jaw seemed to be trying desperately to move, but no more sound came.

'What did he say?' Marius whispered.

Kathleen rose and passed the back of her hand across her eyes. Her face was very pale; in the dim light of the room it seemed to be floating under her hair. 'He doesn't know what he's saying. He doesn't know anyone called Pierre.'

Marius moved so quickly he seemed to dart from the end of the bed. 'He means Father Arnaud. Father Pierre Arnaud of the seminary. He was at school with him. They used to be old friends.' Marius seemed wildly excited. 'Thank God – there's still time!'

Kathleen stared at him blankly.

'Don't you see?' he said. 'He wants to come back!' Marius rushed to the door. 'Holy Mother of God, give me time!'

He ran downstairs to the telephone in the lower hall, and it was only after he had left that Kathleen realized what this meant. She dropped to her knees and whispered the Hail Mary, then tried to remember the Act of Faith. As her voice murmured into the room the red-haired Presbyterian nurse from Prince Edward Island looked at her in surprise. She had not realized this was a Catholic house. Kathleen's low murmur continued. 'I believe in God, I believe that in God there are Three Persons and that Jesus Christ the Second Person was made man for me and born of the Blessed Virgin, I believe in God, I believe . . .' Her voice continued for many minutes. Then her words changed and she murmured as she wept, 'Oh Athanase – forgive me if I ever did anything, forgive me, please!'

Marius returned quietly to the room. Taking the tray filled with bottles and instruments off the table by the bed, he set it on the floor. The nurse watched uneasily, but she continued to support Athanase's head and wiped his cheeks and forehead regularly with the cloth. This was a normal coronary case. There was nothing she could do except make the patient as comfortable as possible. There was no need yet to wake the doctor who was resting in the next room. She watched Marius wipe the table clean and set it up at the foot of the bed. He left the room again and returned with a vase of white carnations and another empty vase in his free hand. He separated the flowers, putting an equal number in each vase, and then he set them on the back corners of the table. He left the room again and returned with two candles in holders, which he set between the flowers. Then he placed a crucifix between the candles and went away again. This time he was gone more than half an hour, and Kathleen guessed he had left the house. When he returned his ears were red with cold, and he carried two basins of water. He placed them on the front corners of the table and stood off, looking at the whole arrangement. Then he raised his eyebrows and glanced at the nurse. She nodded quietly back. The patient's condition had not changed. She looked again at the table and noticed that a feather lay in the water in the basin on the right hand side. She supposed it was holy water, though she could not think how it had been consecrated.

Marius nodded to her to come to the door with him. She laid the cloth down and went quietly around the bed, then into the hall.

'How much longer?' he said.

She shook her head. 'I can tell better when the Cheyne-Stokes breathing starts.'

'What's that?'

'Well . . . ' She frowned.

'It hasn't started yet, this . . .?'

'It may any time. I doubt if he's conscious now.'

'Isn't he asleep?'

'I wouldn't call his present condition sleep.'

Marius turned away from her, the strain showing in the set of his shoulders. 'Father Arnaud should be here soon. He said he . . .'

The nurse, supposing the priest was coming to confess the patient, frowned again. 'He should have been here yesterday, Mr. Tallard. Your father won't be able to speak now.'

Marius smiled calmly. 'He'll speak.'

He left the room again, going downstairs. In the library he switched on the light and picked up a book, but he could not read it and within a few minutes was pacing the floor. A wild, excited exultation filled him. His father would speak. His father would come home. His father would be saved. He had been right all along, and now on the edge of darkness his father knew it. He would die in the Church, after purification he would rest in God. Marius could hear bells ringing in his mind and the voices of choirs, high soprano voices soaring into glorious golden light because his father was coming home. No matter what the nurse thought, his father would speak because he must.

Marius walked the floor for a half-hour until he realized that the reading light beside the armchair was pale. Outside, the snow was catching the first light. The light spread, doubly magnified by the sky and snow as it spread into the room. Marius went upstairs again, and found the doctor standing by the bedside counting Athanase's pulse. The doctor finished and withdrew his hand from the limp wrist, the nurse met his glance and they understood each other. There was nothing more to be done. This was perfectly normal, there was no disorder in nature, there never was.

When the doorbell rang, Marius jerked about and started down the stairs. But it was not the priest he saw arriving; Yardley and Paul were in the lower hall. Marius returned to the sickroom while they took off their coats.

Paul's eyes were large as Yardley ushered him into the room where his father lay. He stopped just inside the door in sudden fright. His father lay like a dead saint in a picture, and the candles on the table flickered in the draft made by the opening door. Kathleen put her arms about him and drew him toward the bed. He dropped on his knees beside her and stared at the flickering candles, not daring to look at his father. But all the time that he tried to pray, the noise of his father's breathing so filled his ears that he could think of nothing else. He felt a tap on his shoulder and looking up, saw it was Yardley. At a nod, he rose and followed him out the door.

In the hall, Yardley said, 'It happens to everyone, Paul. It's just as natural as living.'

'Is P'pa dying?'

'He can't see us. He can't feel any pain. He's just falling asleep.' Yardley's artificial foot slipped on the first step of the stairs and he had to clutch the bannister to regain his balance. 'You and me'd better go downstairs and get something to eat,' he said.

They sat in the dining room and the maid brought them breakfast. Paul ate, tasting nothing. His nostrils were constantly aware of a peculiar smell. It was close, a little acid, a little dank; he had never smelled it before. He wondered if it was the smell of death.

'Eat your porridge, Paul,' Yardley said quietly.

Paul ate a few spoonsful, but his mouth seemed filled with the strange odour. He wished it were all over and that his father were dead. Then death would take its presence out of the house. He wished things would not take such a long time to happen, then felt sinful for having had such a thought. He laid his spoon down again. The memory of the room upstairs wiped everything else out of his mind. The sound of his father's breathing was audible even here. It haunted him because it was so unnatural. Everything was strange. It was strangest of all that his father was helpless. Then he remembered the candles and the crucifix.

Looking at Yardley, he asked simply, 'Are we Catholics again?'

'I wouldn't know, Paul. Seems like somebody's got thet in mind, though.'

Tears filled Paul's eyes. 'Will P'pa go to hell now?'

'No, there's no chance of thet happening.'

'When he stopped – being a Catholic ...' Paul's words stumbled out, and he felt them like concrete objects slipping out over his tongue. 'He said there wasn't any hell. Now if he's a Catholic again it means there is ... doesn't it?'

Yardley tried to pretend he had not heard the question by buttering a piece of toast vigorously. But when he lifted it to his mouth he saw Paul's eyes on his face and he knew he had to answer. He laid the slice of toast down and blew his nose again. The noise he made, brazen as a bugle call, seemed to break the spell.

'I tell you how it is, Paul. Your father being a Catholic again – if thet's what it means, the candles and the things by the bed – well it means he got lonely and wanted to be what he'd been all his life, I guess. Or maybe it means something else so big I can't understand it.'

Paul said nothing to this, and Yardley ate his toast in silence. Then, after many minutes, Paul spoke again. 'Do you think there's a hell, Captain Yardley?'

'Well,' Yardley said reflectively, 'me being a Presbyterian, I wouldn't take any chances on there not being one. If there's no hell, I don't know where a lot of fellas can rightly be put.' Realizing that Paul might misunderstand him, he added quickly, 'Your father's not one of them, Paul.' He choked, and felt tears blinding his eyes. 'He's been as good a friend and I guess in his own way he's been as good a man as ever I knew.'

The doorbell rang and Yardley welcomed the opportunity

to drop the conversation. Telling Paul to stay where he was, he went out into the hall and closed the dining-room door behind him. Father Arnaud entered a small room off the hall and presently came out wearing a surplice and a violet stole. He was a great square man with a dominant nose and a head like a tree-stump whitened by light snow. He carried the Sacrament before him in a rosewood pyx, and the stairs creaked under his weight as he went upstairs after Marius, his surplice rustling in the silence. Yardley waited in the lower hall until he heard the door close upstairs. But it opened again almost immediately and Kathleen, Marius, the doctor and nurse came out, leaving Athanase alone with Father Arnaud and the Sacrament. Kathleen and Marius dropped on their knees in the upper hall, the nurse stood self-consciously by the door, the doctor took a quizzical glance around and cleared his throat heavily, then walked downstairs. He joined Yardley and the two men entered the dining room, closing the door behind them.

Paul could not tell how long it was he remained in the dining room with the two men. The doctor ate silently and the captain kept talking, appearing to speak to them both but really talking directly to Paul.

'One time I was shipwrecked. Not much older than you, Paul, I guess I was. We foundered off the ledges of Halifax County in a January gale and all the crew went down with the ship except me and the dog. He was a big Newfoundland, and he swam ashore with me hanging onto his hair. Me being a little fella then, it wasn't so hard to do. He dragged me up out of thet water across the ice clampers and the rocks into a sort of cave, and then he lay there in the mouth of it stopping the wind, and when fishermen who'd seen the masthead sticking above water came around in a dory a day later looking for us, he barked till they could hear him. Been kind of a religious man ever since thet day, Paul.'

Yardley passed from this story to another, and the time went by. Then the door of the room opened and the nurse appeared and nodded to them. The doctor preceded her upstairs, and by the time Yardley and Paul reached the upper room they could hear the voices of Kathleen and Marius praying. Paul slipped his hand into the captain's and both dropped to their knees, Yardley grunting heavily and having trouble with his wooden leg. Marius stood by the head of the bed. Paul watched the priest dip some raw cotton in oil and quickly anoint his father's eyes. His deep voice rose over the snoring breath of Athanase. 'Through this holy unction' – he made the sign of the cross – 'and of His most tender mercy, may the Lord pardon thee whatsoever sins thou hast committed by sight.'

Then, moving quickly and deftly, while Kathleen prayed with her eyes to the crucifix, the priest anointed the nostrils, the ears, the closed mouth, the palm of the hands, the insteps of Athanase's feet. The feet looked very pale and thin, they seemed strangely solitary, poked out into space below the raised blankets. Paul watched, each one of Father Arnaud's movements burning into his brain. He remained on his knees through the prayers that followed, his eyes blurred. Ultimately he heard the priest's voice resonant with confidence: 'Through the most sacred mysteries of man's redemption may God Almighty remit unto thee the pains of the present and future life, open to thee the gates of paradise, and bring thee to everlasting joys. May God Almighty bless thee; the Father, Son and Holy Ghost. Amen.'

Having made the final sign of the cross, Father Arnaud stood back from the bed. Marius with a quick motion came forward and seized one of his father's limp hands and kissed it. Then both hands were crossed and folded over the chest.

They went downstairs. The stillness within the house was broken only by the breathing of the dying man. Paul sat in a frozen stillness in the library. Yardley remained with him, and now made no attempt to talk. Then Marius came in and sat down with them. His voice was high with exultation.

'Paul . . . it was a miracle! Papa confessed. He was able to speak. Father Arnaud performed a miracle!' Marius got up and crossed to Paul. 'Now you'll never have to go back to that school again. You're not English any more. You're in the family again.'

Yardley tapped Marius' shoulder and shook his head. Marius accepted his glance, but his face was radiant as he returned to his chair. Outside the door they heard the heavy feet of Father Arnaud coming out from the small room off

243

the hall where he had changed. They heard his voice speaking to the doctor, and the doctor answering. 'I'm afraid he's got nothing. Too bad . . . they tell me he was cleaned out completely.' A pause. 'That's what did it, finally.'

Father Arnaud's reply was inaudible, but the two men continued talking.

It was quiet in the library. Snow had fallen in the night and now as the sun rose over it the new crystals flashed and glittered. Paul looked out the window and saw figures passing on the sidewalk, women in black Hudson seal coats with their hands in black muffs, men with fur caps and hands in their pockets, the hands occasionally jumping out to rub cold ears. A milk sleigh passed, the horse straining as it pulled up the hill, steam rising from its back and flanks. Three students from the university fraternity house at the upper corner came by with books clamped under their arms, their breath puffing in quick, disappearing clouds of vapour ahead of them. Then the stairs creaked once more and Kathleen entered the room. The skin was red about her eyes, but the rest of her face was white under the blackness of her hair. She came over to the sofa and sat down, putting her arms about Paul, her movements as indolent as ever.

'Poor boy – don't worry, don't fret! It's you and me now. Just the two of us!'

'Is P'pa . . .' Paul began, and stopped, biting his lip.

'He's asleep, Paul. He'll just slip away from us in his dreams.'

She turned from him with a swift movement and began to cry, silently letting the tears flow down her cheeks.

From the other side of the room Marius spoke in French. 'You'll come with me now, Paul.' He looked sharply at Kathleen. 'Yes . . . once I finish college you and I . . .'

Kathleen flashed around, her arm about Paul's shoulder. Her eyes seemed on fire. 'He's not yours!'

'He's my brother!'

Paul sat wretchedly with his head hanging. Yardley cleared his throat to say something. Then a loud voice broke the tension in the room.

'Stop this, both of you!'

They looked up and saw Father Arnaud standing in the

door, his great nose dominant in his heavy face, his hair very white against his dark skin.

'This is no way to go on!' he said. Then he crossed the room and laid his hand quietly on Paul's head. 'Don't be afraid, my son. Your father is in God's hands now.' He looked once more at Marius and left the room. Shortly afterwards they heard the outer door open and close. Paul sat frozen while Yardley in the armchair smoked quietly and Kathleen and Marius avoided each other's eyes. Upstairs the noise of Athanase Tallard's driving breath was loud, the house seemed to thunder with it, all that was left of him now for Paul. After another hour, it stopped. Kathleen's low cry was audible through the whole house, and then everything was silent.

30

Paul drew aside the curtains of the bay window in the living room and looked at his mother walking down the street to the shops. She was wearing a black silk dress and a light black coat trimmed with white. Her black hat with its white trimming was almost gay. She walked with a fresh expectant movement. Paul let the curtain drop and stepped back into the room. After the bright sunshine in the street, the apartment was very dark. The folding doors at the back of the living room were open. Dimly beyond them he could see the rumpled sheets of his mother's bed. Beyond that was the kitchen.

Paul sat down on the sofa, looking at the opposite wall. There was not much to see on it: just a stretch of wall on either side of the hearth. On one end of the mantle was a small photograph of his father, taken ten years ago. On the other end was a companion photo of his mother.

Paul and Kathleen had been living in this apartment for two months now, ever since moving out of the large town house Athanase had rented before his death. As he had died bankrupt, the mortgage on the house and land at Saint-Marc had been foreclosed. Nearly all the furniture of the town house had been sold to pay debts. What was left was crowded into these three rented rooms. Kathleen had

245

saved the red mahogany dining-room table and the eight chairs that matched it. She had kept a sofa on which Paul slept at night in the living room, and a double bed so large it almost filled her bedroom. The rooms were so crowded with furniture that even Paul had to squeeze between some of the pieces. One small shelf of books stood in a corner behind the armchair; these books and the chair itself were all that survived from the old library in Saint-Marc. The books were carefully selected. Yardley had picked out those he thought Paul would want to read during the next few years, and some he hoped he would want to keep all his life.

Looking for something to do, Paul took out his old Homeric picture book from the shelf and carried it over to the sofa by the window. As he read the book, he was able for the moment to forget where he was. He wondered what Achilles' face had really looked like when he had quarrelled with Agamemnon, whether his lip had lifted and he had talked out of the corner of his mouth, or whether his whole face had exploded with frank rage. It had always puzzled Paul why a second-rate man like Agamemnon had been in charge of the heroes anyway, why Homer took him so seriously. He must have had a dry kind of voice, and a smile that showed his teeth instead of his feelings. But apart from him, there seemed a sea-green freshness about all of Homer's people, a beauty you never found any more, the men like athletes in their white tunics and the women tall and queenly with blue-bordered robes trailing the ground. The air they breathed was so pure it sparkled, the days were sunny, and wherever you looked you saw the sea. He stopped at a picture of Troy by night, with Helen on the wall and the two Trojan elders sitting in the shadows out of her view. It must have been wonderful to live in a city like that where you could come up to the wall and see the whole of it at a single glance and know everyone inside it. You could look out over the plain and see the camp-fires of the enemy; but beyond them was the gleam of moonlight on the Aegean, and the danger made the moment even more beautiful than it was anyway.

He laid the book down, suddenly listless. He looked out the window to the houses across the street. It was no fun having nothing to do. There was nothing he could even think of doing.

Paul sometimes thought that being poor would not matter if only his father were alive. Then they would still count for something. Instinctively, he knew that they now counted for nothing, and that if they disappeared tomorrow nobody would care; at least, no one except Yardley and Marius. His mother had been sad when his father died, and sometimes she cried when she thought about how poor and helpless they were. But much of the time she seemed to Paul simply to be allowing time to pass over her while she did nothing. She seemed almost not to be able to care; and by not caring, she removed herself from him without even knowing it. Some nights while Paul did his homework she sat at the large table playing solitaire, concentrating on the game as though it were a great problem. Sometimes she talked to him, and tried to find games in the newspapers that would amuse them both. Sometimes after Paul was asleep she went out alone. She had made several new friends, but she preferred to go to their homes rather than have them come to her, so Paul seldom saw any of them. They all seemed to like dancing and bridge-playing, and he wondered if she went to dances so soon after his father's death. He did not think she did, but he knew she wanted to go. Lately she had begun to talk about their luck changing. Something would turn up and they would again live in a fine house with plenty of clothes and enough of everything. When Paul got older he would have a motor car of his own and be able to do whatever he pleased. But Paul was old enough already to know that luck had nothing to do with their being alone in three rooms in this side street of Montreal.

It had been a good street once. The grey, stuccoed Victorian houses had dignified lines, but the old families had long ago sold out to rooming-house proprietors. Beautiful old trees still grew out of holes in the concrete near the curbs and shaded the grey façades of the houses. When the light was soft, the street was like an exiled aristocrat trying to cover up his poor clothes and worthlessness with the fine manners he had never been able to forget. But during the day boys ran around on the asphalt and dodged traffic as they played catch, and trucks roared through constantly. At night the street was quiet enough. But three women, always the same three, wearing black fur-lined overshoes in winter and high heels in summer, patrolled the block regularly from eight to twelve. Occasionally a car with dimmed lights cruised past them and stopped. Then one of the women went over to the curb and talked in low tones to the driver. Sometimes the driver got out and went into a house with her, sometimes she got into his car and drove off, the car roaring fast in second and often grinding its gears loud in the silence as the driver hurried to get out of the neighbourhood. Most of the trade came to the women in cars, but occasionally a transient from the hotels wandered through the street on foot. Last night when Paul had been trying to sleep he had heard one of the women talking to a strange man just outside his window.

Restlessly, Paul replaced the book on its shelf. He decided to go out. It was Saturday, and a boy ought to make a special day out of a Saturday. He left the apartment and went out into the common hall of the house, being careful to snap the door behind him and test it to make sure it was properly locked. Then he felt in his pocket to see if he had his key, and walked out into the street.

He had no place to go, for he knew nobody. No games were provided at the public school he now attended. Five days in the week the boys sat fifty to a room that smelled of disinfectant when they arrived and of massed humanity an hour later. They were taught by a grim-faced spinster long in the tooth who knew that if she relaxed her face an instant the whole class would get out of hand. The school's functions ceased abruptly on Friday afternoon at half-past three. It taught its schedule, and that was all it tried to do or could do.

Walking with his hands in his pockets, Paul went up the slope toward the mountain. In the upper levels of town he felt some of the grey loneliness fade away from him. Here the streets were quiet as churches and canopied by stately trees: maples, and limes, and elms with fresh leaves, and horse-chestnuts spired with blossoms. Here he could smell the fresh earth of newly-turned flower-beds, look over hedges and see immaculate lawns and gardeners clipping them, the lawn-mowers singing high in the warm air. Some of the boys he had known at Frobisher lived on this street. Not many, for there were few houses on it; the houses were enormous brick-and-stone structures, some shaped like castles with gargoyles at the corners of the roofs, all with huge glass conservatories on their sides. But the boys he knew would not be here this morning. They would be playing cricket on the elm-lined field in front of the school, or breaking bounds by hiking across the river and trying to catch fish in the pool below the abandoned grist-mill near the road. He remembered that a small rod of his was concealed behind a rafter in that grist-mill. He remembered another rod he had forgotten in the scullery in the old house in Saint-Marc.

Loneliness returned to him with a fresh surge. He climbed a long flight of wooden steps that rose up the first ridge of the mountain, he crossed Pine Avenue and went up the winding dirt road toward the summit. Here it was almost like the country, for the city was behind and below him. In Saint-Marc, in the real country, the maples would be at their greenest this weekend and the first shoots would be visible in the ploughed fields. It was almost three years since he had lived in Saint-Marc. At school in the country he had almost forgotten it, but after his father's death the old life had come back to him vividly and he seemed to have left it only yesterday.

Thinking of Saint-Marc, he left the road and plunged into the dry bracken of the hillside until he reached a huge rock. It was dark grey, the colour of the house he lived in now, and a dust of lichen covered it. He sat behind the rock and picked up a stick he found there. Then, taking out his scout knife, he whittled it.

Marius said that as soon as he finished his law course – if he had enough money to finish it – he was going to sue some people to recover the old property in Saint-Marc, as well as the money his father had lost. Paul knew Marius was only talking to make himself feel important. You fell into debt and you paid your debts and then you were poor, and that was all there was to it. He wished Marius would not come around to the house so often, for whenever he did he quarrelled with his mother. Sometimes Marius would sit for minutes looking at her, his eyes shifting whenever she looked back. Then, for no reason at all, he would begin to quarrel, and Paul himself was generally the cause of it. Marius insisted that Paul ought to go to a French-language school, and this made Kathleen furious.

Lying behind the rock whittling away the stick, Paul felt the sun pour down on him through a gap in the trees. This would be a beautiful day on the river, the clouds white and interlaced with brilliant patches of blue. The last time he had been in Saint-Marc was the day his father was buried. The sky had been grey and cold.

Paul could not get that day out of his mind. The whole parish had attended the funeral, and important-looking men whom Paul had never seen had come from Ottawa and Montreal. But it was the old faces Paul's eyes had caught: Frenette, Polycarpe Drouin, Blanchard, even Ovide Bissonnette. Father Beaubien in his robes had stood at the head of the grave and the piled-up earth was like a brown wound against the snow. Then the coffin was lowered into the ground, the priest threw some frozen earth on top of it, and they went away, their ankles numb with cold and their ears nearly frozen. That evening Yardley drove Paul and Kathleen into Sainte-Justine in his sleigh. They took the train for the city and had not seen Saint-Marc since.

Restless again, Paul moved from behind the rock and continued up the road towards the top of the mountain. Occasionally horsemen came by, rising and falling on cavalry saddles. Near the top he came on a group of girls who were learning to ride. Their horses were knotted about an instructor who was explaining something to them. Paul drew near to listen to what the man said. Then one of the girls turned her head from the instructor and waved her riding crop.

'Paul!' she cried. 'Hi, Paul!'

He saw the up-turned nose and wide mouth and knew it was Heather. He longed to speak to her, but was ashamed without exactly knowing why. He made an elaborate pretence of looking over his shoulder to see whom she was calling, and when he glanced back again he saw that his

movement had puzzled her. 'I'm sure that was Paul Tallard,'
he heard her say as she turned to the girl on the horse beside
her. Paul stole a quick glance and recognized Daphne. She
looked tall and very slim on the horse, sure of herself, with
the sunlight on her hair. But the instructor was annoyed
at the interruption. He demanded attention, and before
Heather could get away from the group Paul slipped off the
road and disappeared in the shrubbery. There was no path
from here to the top, but a sheer wall of rock with large
cracks and hand-holes in its face. Concentrating on what he
was doing, pretending he was like the Swiss mountaineers
he had read about, he hauled himself up the rock face and
finally reached the top. He saw that he had cut a hole in the
shin part of one stocking and felt badly about it. His mother
had told him that his clothes would have to last him for years
now. He decided he must learn how to darn socks. His
mother hated darning, and he did not want to make trouble
for her.

He was breathless from his climb, but now he was on the
top of the mountain and could see the whole city spread out
beneath him. It looked magnificent in the sunshine merely
because it was large and he could see so much of it. The
upper part hugging the mountain was beautiful, soft lights
and shadows lying among trees and the roofs of various
houses quiet in the shade. But the central and eastern parts
were a raw waste of masonry with an occasional square
building jutting high above the flat roofs around it. In all
parts were the spires and domes of churches, more to the
acreage than any other commercial city in the world. About
the oval shore of the island the river curved in a great distant sweep out of the Lachine Rapids under the Victoria
Bridge, folded the slip of Nun's Island and the green bluff of
Saint Helen's. Factory smoke from Verdun drifted downstream on a light southwesterly breeze, but through it he
could see the plain spreading to the mountains across the
American border, sloping so gradually that at this height it
even seemed to be tilted downward.

Paul wandered about the summit, moving under the trees
and out again, for nearly half an hour. Then he went down
the slope again to the city, reached Sainte Catherine Street

and walked east to University his hands in his pockets. The traffic was thick at the noon-hour, the whole city beating about him: hundreds of acres of concrete, bricks, mortar, asphalt, street-cars, trucks, motors, advertising signs in flaring scarlet and white, crowds – everything hot under the sun. He saw by a clock in a store window that it was twelve-thirty. His mother would not likely be back for another two hours at least, she never knew what time it was. He walked down University Street to Beaver Hall Hill, down to Victoria Square to McGill Street, down McGill to the harbour.

He killed another hour by strolling along the waterfront watching stevedores loading and unloading ships. He saw vessels from England, France, Australia, India, Norway, Sweden, Holland, as well as the red-and-white lake boats that were always on their way past Saint-Marc in the old days. He felt a faint thrill of recognition, finding something here which fitted into the pattern of what he had read and of what he had been told by Yardley. The ships could still discover the Americas. But what was left for him to discover when he grew up? What could be new for him except old places like India and Greece? He walked along each pier to the sterns of the ships, and was fascinated by the names of their home ports: Liverpool, Glasgow, Saint Nazaire, Sydney, Bergen, Goteborg, Amsterdam, Bombay.

But finally he became so hungry he could watch the ships no longer. He had two miles to walk before reaching home, and no money in his pocket for a tram. He set out, going back up the successive slopes, with the hollow feeling of hunger growing inside him. The traffic became steadily thicker as he neared the centre of town, newsboys on every corner selling copies of the *Star*, magazines from the States, crowds speaking French and English around him, signs and billboards repeating second-hand the slogans they had learned from the Americans, beckoning with Players, Sweet Caps, British Consuls, Black Horse Ale, Mother's Bread, the signs screaming bi-lingually in red, white and yellow: BUVEZ COCA-COLA —— THE PAUSE THAT RE-FRESHES —— LA BIERE DE VOTRE GRANDPERE —— THE REMEDY YOUR UNCLE USED; street signs

252

telling him to keep to the right gardez votre droite no parking here ne stationnez pas ici, while in front of one movie house Theda Bara with hair flopping loose on her face was clasped by Lou Tellegen, and in front of another Mabel Normand smiled into the bleak and angular face of a huge American in a ten-gallon hat.

When Paul reached home the place was still empty and his mother's bed still unmade. He went into the kitchen and opened a can of beans, spilled the beans out into a saucepan and heated it on the stove. Then he cut a slice of bread and buttered it, and poured himself a glass of milk. The beans and the milk tasted good.

Towards mid-afternoon Kathleen returned. She found Paul reading on the sofa, the bed made and the dishes washed. She put her arms about him and held him, saying how wonderful he was to have done all these things by himself. He felt her warm softness and smelled the strange, fresh, remembered sweetness of her skin. He saw also the wonderful smile that had always made her seem lovely to him. But in spite of this the loneliness struck right through him. For now that his father was dead his mother seemed changed, a different sort of person; still herself yet somehow much less than she had been before. And he knew now that although her smile was as sincere as possible, it was still somehow automatic, a gesture as natural and unconscious as the sway of her hips when she walked, and that behind it her mind was a stranger.

Outside the street was hot in the afternoon sun, and the murmur of Montreal came in through the window.

Part Three   1934

31

Huntly McQueen was giving a dinner party. For the first time in many months, the huge house he had purchased twelve years before, on the mountainside opposite the Methuens, had guests in it. Daphne had just returned from England with her husband and the party was in their honour. It was the first time she had been home since her marriage two years previously to the Honourable Noel Fletcher. They had been living in London.

The guests sat around a thick-legged mahogany table in a dining room which had given McQueen special satisfaction ever since he had come to possess it. A better example of a style he considered correct could be found nowhere else in the city. It was a thoroughly solid kind of room and he felt it reflected his personality. The walls were panelled shoulder-high in dark mahogany; above the panels rough tan wallpaper reached to a lofty ceiling. The bay window at the end of the room was screened by draperies the colour of port wine with dust in it. From the ceiling hung a gigantic chandelier, at least two-hundredweight of metal and cut-glass prisms, almost enough potential energy to smash the table to pieces if it ever fell. On one wall was a line engraving, four feet by three, of Sir Walter Scott meeting Robert Burns at the Edinburgh Literary Society. On another wall was the painting of McQueen's mother which had formerly hung in his office. There were peonies under it now in a cut-glass vase.

When dinner ended they filed into the drawing room. This was another lofty chamber, furnished with oriental rugs, three ormolu clocks, walnut tables, chairs covered with rose brocade, imitation Constables surrounded by ponderous gilt frames, two bronze statuettes on marble bases and several Dresden figurines. The walls were covered with more tan paper. Heavy red draperies were drawn across all the windows, though this side of the house was overlooked by nothing but McQueen's own garden. He could never stand being in a lighted room with the windows unshaded.

Janet Methuen entered the drawing room first, wearing a severe black evening gown. Daphne followed in white with gold trimming, svelte about the hips and breasts. Heather was in lime green, which suited her cheerful youth. After a few moments they were joined by the men: Noel Fletcher, a head taller than the others; General Methuen who came along with a stiff, stalking movement, both hands in his waistcoat to ease it; then McQueen with a benign smile on his wide face and one hand on the general's shoulder.

McQueen's smile concealed a discomfort which during dinner had verged on irritation. Twenty years of increasing recognition by Montreal society had done more than mellow him. It had made him feel at one with his environment, which he was inclined to think was in many ways superior to any other in the world. It was an environment in which a man was not accustomed to being disturbed.

But during dinner Noel Fletcher had exasperated him. It was not so much what he had said as what he hadn't bothered to say. His arrogance was a new kind to McQueen. It went deeper than the arrogance one expected to find in certain Englishmen visiting what they considered a colony. Although only thirty-seven, Fletcher made everyone around him feel themselves to be his junior. He did it effortlessly, simply by existing in the same room with them.

Then there was Daphne. The change she had made in herself seemed to McQueen to be deplorable. She had acquired a flippant way of speaking about everything. She dressed like a Parisienne, and in her own way she had become as overbearing as her husband. McQueen wondered what her grandfather thought about her now. The general was really marvelous. At seventy-seven years of age he had eaten a full dinner and had not once complained about any of his vital organs.

255

'How about a rubber of bridge?' McQueen said.

Daphne turned in the middle of the drawing room, one long-fingered hand on her golden hair. 'But Huntly, aren't there six of us?'

The general stalked across the room to the screened fireplace, turned his back to it, his head on a level with the ormolu clock which centred the mantel. 'We'll take turns,' he said. To McQueen he added, 'Always like to play with you. Keep your mind on the game. Damned if I can see why no one in our house can do it too.'

The general's shoulders were still square, his back straight, his cheeks flushed. He looked like a much older brother of the major who advertises Army Club cigarettes in Piccadilly Circus. If he was a survival of a period his country would never see again, he clearly did not know it. Tonight he felt very comfortable. It was a fine June evening, the family was together, and he was pretty sure he was going to digest his dinner.

'Let Heather play,' Daphne said.

Janet's voice broke in. 'But Heather despises bridge!'

As she turned to look at her younger daughter the silk-shaded lamps cast heavy shadows over Janet's face. During the past years her features had become hawk-like. If she had not acquired an ease of manner, she had at least gained a self-confidence which took its place fairly well. Not a little of this self-confidence sprang from the knowledge that Daphne was in line for a title. She stood by the chesterfield, her eyes startlingly large with dark circles under them, skin stretched tightly over the bridge of her nose, tight also over the cheekbones. Her hair was neatly shingled, lay in precise waves over her head, all of it steel grey.

'Of course,' she said to Heather, 'you can play if you want to. I've always said you could learn if you'd only watch what other people do.'

McQueen cleared his throat. There was no particular reason why anyone should play bridge except that he had planned it. It disturbed him to hear his guests apparently talking at random, their words falling loose and going to waste. In front of the mantle General Methuen was saying to Noel Fletcher, 'Take Airedales, now. There's not a better dog in the world for catching bears. Down in New Brunswick . . .'

But Fletcher was paying not the slightest attention to the general. His head, with hair ash-blond and not too recently trimmed, was balanced evenly on a pair of wide shoulders as straight as a soldier's and as lithe as an athlete's. He had the tapering body of a middleweight fighter, and a sort of shining cleanness that set him apart from everyone else. His eyes were a brittle blue; boyish at first glance, disconcertingly mature on further acquaintance. He had been to Harrow and Sandhurst and had served in the Flying Corps in the last war. His words came out in a cultivated drawl. He was known as a ruthlessly competent man of business, owning a controlling interest in a large aircraft factory in England. McQueen, who instinctively judged people by gauging what they wanted in life, was completely baffled by Fletcher. So far as he could tell, Fletcher was disinterested in everything.

The general was still talking. 'After all, Hitler may be extreme, but he's not a fool.'

Fletcher looked into the cold hearth. 'He knows what he wants.'

'But how's he going to get it? The Boche has scuttled his own fleet. We'll blockade 'em to death if he tries any monkey business.'

'Oh, really?' Fletcher said. 'You think fleets still matter?'

'Damn it!' the general said, 'they always have.'

McQueen cleared his throat again, but nobody paid any attention to him. The three women were discussing Heather's dress. Fletcher was surveying the general's old face, which looked back at him with a certain dog-like anxiety.

'In the next war,' Fletcher said, 'the only thing a battleship will do is sink.'

'You talk as if you took another war for granted,' McQueen said shortly.

'Don't you?' Fletcher said.

Before McQueen could answer, the general began to snort. 'Too many sound people in Britain to let anything like that develop.' His old face carried the expression of a man who had never found it necessary to be intelligent but who knew right from wrong without thinking about it. His eyes seemed to be telling Fletcher that he knew his England as well as anyone. 'The British government,' he said emphatically, 'is the best in the world, and that's all there is to it. Over here we've always known that.'

Fletcher tapped a cigarette on his left thumb nail, put it between his lips and lit it, tossing the match on to the hearth. McQueen followed the flight of the match with disapproval and a touch of anxiety. Another inch and it would have fallen on his rug, an oriental that had cost him fifteen hundred dollars. 'Hitler knows the world's ripe for picking,' Fletcher said.

McQueen's heavy jaw lifted. 'What's your evidence for that statement?'

There was a moment of silence in the room before the Englishman answered. 'It's self-evident.'

Heather settled down on the chesterfield. 'You sound as if you were looking forward to a war,' she said.

In spite of his motionless face muscles, there was a sudden interest reflected in Fletcher's eyes as he looked down at Heather. 'You've missed the point. Thanks to Hitler, we're going to get a real airforce in England at last.'

'But who wants an airforce?' Heather said sharply. 'Or anything else in uniform, for that matter?'

'You mustn't mind Heather,' the general said. 'She's been a bit of a socialist ever since she went to college.' But as he spoke the old man looked at his granddaughter fondly.

McQueen decided the conversation must be ended by force. He cupped his short fingers below Daphne's elbow, touching as little of her skin as possible, and moved her toward the bridge table that had been set up in the far end of the room. 'Here,' he said, pulling out a straight-backed Victorian chair. 'We'll leave the armchair for your grandfather.'

Daphne slid away from his hand, moved to the other side of the table and sat down facing the room. 'It's so odd,' she said. 'Really it is. I don't suppose I'll ever quite get used to it again.'

'Get used to what?' Janet said.

'Coming home and finding everything – well, just as it

is, was and ever shall be.' She smiled at her husband as though her words were the key to a private knowledge they shared. 'You'll have to watch your step, Noel. No one over here gives the smallest damn whether you fly over Mount Everest or become an air marshal. Really they don't.'

The general marched over to the bridge table and sat in the armchair, and Janet followed him. Fletcher dropped on to the sofa beside Heather. After a look about the room, McQueen sat in the fourth place at the table with the cautious bend of a man who has never been convinced that a careless upholsterer might not have left a tack exposed on the seat of the chair. The general picked up a pack of cards and shuffled for the cut.

'Noel still hunt?' he said to Daphne as he spread the pack on the table.

Daphne appeared not to have heard the question. Her extended hand came over the table and she bent forward so that the barest outline of the division between her breasts was visible. Her face had assumed an expression of calculated innocence which annoyed McQueen intensely. He was not the fool these young people seemed to think. He knew perfectly well that Daphne was exposing herself deliberately to embarrass him, and he felt like spanking her.

'Daphne,' Janet said. 'Your grandfather has asked you a question.'

'Yes, grandfather.' Daphne's voice came out with exaggerated briskness. 'Noel hunts.'

McQueen cut the high card and began to deal with elaborate care.

'One thing I never could understand about the English,' the general said, as he patted each falling card into place. 'Otter hunting. Stand around in the mud of a river bank for hours and nothing happens.' He picked up his hand. 'True test of an Englishman if he hunts otters. Noel hunt otters?'

Daphne looked at him brightly, her eyes isolated from them all. 'He hunts everything with legs.'

Conversation stopped at the bridge table as the bid was opened. On the chesterfield Heather was trying to talk to her brother-in-law and receiving no help. He offered her a cigarette, lit it, and then appeared to forget her presence.

It made her feel acutely uncomfortable, as though she had just committed a blatant social error which Noel had decided to overlook but not forget. It was always like this when she was alone with him. At first she had thought it was her own shyness that made it difficult to know him, but tonight she was reaching the sharp conclusion that he simply found her a bore.

Daphne had met him three years ago when she had been presented at court. Two years ago Fletcher had come out to Montreal to marry her. There had been a quick round of parties, the wedding had taken place in the approved manner with herself a distracted and very busy maid of honour, and then they had departed. She had looked forward to their return, but now that they were back everything seemed different from what she had expected. Daphne had become a stranger, amused by her younger sister and satisfied with a knowledge Heather could not understand or guess.

Now Heather made a desperate effort to find a subject of conversation that would interest Noel. She asked him about recent plays in London, about his factory, about the flat they had taken in St. John's Wood, about the work which had brought him to North America. He answered each question with a monosyllable. Heather felt more gauche and awkward than she could remember having felt since her first formal party. She asked herself with inner desperation what was the matter with her. Noel talked easily enough to the men, even though he tended to use as few words as possible to express an idea. He must simply be wishing he were anywhere except having to sit beside her at McQueen's dinner party. There was no use going on pestering him with questions. For several minutes she sat in silence beside his self-sufficiency, listening to the flick of the cards as a hand was played out at the table.

When Noel did speak, Heather was startled. He made no movement, except to turn his head slowly and stare at her. His blue eyes took in her chestnut hair, the slightly tawny skin of her tanned arms, the full curves of her breasts under the lime-green chiffon. Then he said, 'If you'd get away from this mausoleum of a city you live in . . .' He left the sentence unfinished, lit himself another cigarette and tossed the match away toward the hearth. This time it landed on the edge of McQueen's rug.

Heather watched its flight and waited for Noel to continue, but it appeared that he had finished all he intended to say. At least he had indicated a subject which seemed to interest him, and she took advantage of it.

'I've often wondered what strangers think of Montreal,' she said. 'When one knows it so well, it's hard to think of it in comparison with famous cities one only visits.'

'It's priceless,' he said. 'Kensington – 1910.'

Heather tossed the wave of brown hair off her forehead. She was about to defend the city when Fletcher forestalled her. In the same tone of voice, he said, 'If you'd only give yourself a chance, you'd be damned good in bed.'

Their eyes met and held. The trace of a smile touched Fletcher's mouth and Heather's first impulse was to believe she had not heard correctly. But he went on. 'English women are hopeless. Now you Americans . . .'

Neither of them spoke or moved. Then Heather rose and left him, moving over to the table and pretending an interest in the game. Daphne was dealing. The general was feeling fine. 'Too bad your father isn't here, Janet,' he said. 'Wonderful, how he keeps up at his age.'

'I invited the captain, of course,' McQueen said hastily. 'He always refuses parties.'

Daphne divided the cards smoothly. 'The only time I've seen him since I came back he talked about his classes. It sounded too terribly weird for words. Whatever did he mean? I never got around to asking him.'

Janet pursed her lips. 'Your grandfather's incurable. He left the farm and moved to Montreal in order to relax and not work so hard. And now he's registered at the university for some course or other in the summer school!'

'Can't imagine myself doing a thing like that,' the general said. 'I tried to reread Sir Walter Scott the other day and I found him damned heavy weather.'

They began to bid and Heather leaned against her grandfather's chair. She thought she caught an expression of amused irony in Daphne's eyes, but she couldn't be sure.

261

Daphne had always been cool; now she was lacquered. It came over Heather in a wave that everyone she knew was sure of himself but her; they knew what to say and what to do and where they were going. She disagreed with nearly all their opinions, but it made no difference; she could never prove her disagreement. Growing up with Daphne she had always known herself to be less attractive, the plain sister of the most beautiful girl in town. Perhaps that was why she had been so grateful last week when Alan Farquhar had asked her to marry him. He had bristly red hair, round blue eyes, a raccoon coat and a blue Packard roadster with a fox-brush flying from the radiator. Her mother thoroughly approved of his family.

Without turning around she was aware that Noel had risen from the chesterfield and was standing behind and to one side of her. What had she done or said to make him talk to her like that? If he had been anyone else but Daphne's husband she could have laughed and teased him and forgotten it. After all, she wasn't a child. But he was so different from anyone else she knew, so sure of himself.

The hand was over and the general was intent upon talking about what might have happened if the cards had been played in a different manner. When the discussion had been settled to suit him, he began to deal. 'Your father finally got his price on that farm of his in Saint-Marc, didn't he, Janet?' he said.

Janet had answered the same question several times in the past few weeks, but her father-in-law always forgot. Now she repeated that the farm had been sold. She twisted the rings on her fingers. 'And a very good thing, too,' she added. 'At his age – out there among all those French-Canadians. It's always been embarrassing.'

'Might easily have been the death of him.' The general cocked an eye at the ceiling, still holding most of the cards in the pack. 'By the way McQueen – what happened to that factory you built out there?'

The factory had also been explained to the general several times. It was too bad, McQueen thought, how the old gentleman's memory was going. 'One of Rupert Irons' subsidiaries took it over,' he said. 'There are several factories in Saint-

Marc now. My original idea was sound, but I was always disappointed in the place. Irons will probably make something of it, with the help of the Ottawa Agreements.'

'It seems only yesterday,' the general said, 'since they weren't letting Rupert Irons into the clubs. Now he's into everything.'

'By the way, Huntly –' Daphne's clipped words cut through the conversation. 'Whatever happened to that Tallard family we used to know in Saint-Marc?'

Heather moved away from her grandfather's chair. She felt as if irrelevant objects were whizzing in all directions. McQueen seemed to have given up the bridge game for lost.

'*You* know,' Daphne went on. 'That funny old man who quarrelled with the priest and left the Catholics. He used to sit in the pew opposite us in St. David's after they came to Montreal. It seemed so funny having a Catholic there.'

'Athanase Tallard wasn't a funny man, Daphne,' McQueen said. 'His life was a tragedy.'

'Good name, Tallard,' the general said. Suddenly he began to deal. 'None better than those solid old French families. None better. I always insist on that when I hear Toronto people talking against them.' Then he stopped dealing with half the pack of cards still in his left hand.

McQueen paused to see if he would continue, but the general had forgotten what he was doing. 'That was a very sad affair,' McQueen said. 'How was I to know our factory would involve him in a quarrel? Athanase Tallard must have stood between two stools all his life – like so many people these days. But I understand he returned to the Romans before he died. Very loyal of your father, Janet, to stay with him.'

The general began to deal again, muttering between his teeth as he passed out cards to players who had lost all interest in them. 'Too much talk about the way they're leaving the Church. Don't believe a word of it. I've lived in this province all my life and I know 'em. They all die with candles in their hands.'

Heather went back to the chesterfield, hoping Fletcher wouldn't follow her. The name of the Tallard family had started a train of ideas in her mind. Only last week Alan

263

Farquhar had mentioned Paul Tallard. Alan had been on the university hockey team and had met him in the league. Paul had become a semi-professional during the winter, on a team made up of garage hands and factory workers who played hockey only at night for the money they could make. It was a tough outfit, Alan had said, and everyone talked about Paul because he was good. There was even talk of his making a club in one of the major leagues. Heather knew little about hockey, but it seemed poignant that a boy she had played with in childhood should now be living such a life. Every once in awhile her grandfather mentioned Paul, and she supposed he still saw him, but she seldom saw Yardley herself except during holidays and special family occasions.

The atmosphere of the room was stifling her. With a quick glance to be sure she was unobserved, she slipped out into the hall, then through the front door and across the street to the Methuen house. She smelled the loosened earth of flower beds and heard a sprayer tossing water onto McQueen's lawn. The gravel of the drive beside the Methuen house was excitingly white under the moon, and it crunched beneath her slippers as she walked to the garage at the back. She got into her car and started the motor, backed out and turned, and let the car coast down the hill.

On reaching the lower street she turned west, ran some blocks, and then took the long curving incline of Côte des Neiges. The tires whirred over the cobbles of the hill. She rushed into Westmount at sixty miles an hour, turned with a scream of tires and wound slowly up a terraced driveway to the crest of the mountain. At a terraced look-off she parked the car, shut off the lights and sat still. It was wonderful to be alone.

At twenty-three Heather felt she had reached a crisis in her life. Though she had not been reared to consider herself a rich girl, she had been fully aware that a great deal of money was behind her. That, together with the social position of her family, made her feel isolated from all but a few members of her own generation. Her mother had followed the Methuen pattern strictly: Methuens avoided all ostentation; they never prided themselves on their money, but their pride of position was overweening; they despised extravagance wherever it was found and Heather's allowances had always been kept fairly small. They lived within the tight cage of activities considered fitting for women in the Square Mile.

As Janet followed the Methuen pattern, Heather followed her mother's wishes. There had seemed no alternative. She had gone to school in Lausanne for two years, studying French as a social accomplishment rather than as a help to her in the province of Quebec. She had returned to make her debut, two years after Daphne, at a Saint Andrew's Day Ball. Then she had gone to college for four years, if not with Janet's enthusiasm behind the undertaking, at least without her disapproval. After that she had done nothing in particular, except attend dances with the sons of her mother's friends and sit on the executive board of the Junior League.

She knew that her friends were murmuring about her, considering her a failure. The majority of her school friends were already married, some of them in a fashion their elders termed brilliant. Two had married Englishmen with accents like Noel's, one was the wife of a French count, four had married bond salesmen serving time before becoming partners in their fathers' trust and mortgage houses. Since Daphne had been withdrawn from competition, Heather's status had become more noticeable. Her mother was definitely worried.

In public Janet was always considerate of her and tactful, but lately they had more than once come to the point of actually arguing at home. It always ended by a show of tears on Janet's part and Heather's contrite attempt at making amends. She could bear anything more easily than one of her mother's scenes. Janet never referred directly to the fact that Heather remained unattached, but it was hardly an accident that she had decided to spend their last vacation on the same beach in Maine where Alan Farquhar was staying with his family. It was certainly no accident that McQueen kept remarking, apropos of nothing, that Alan seemed a sound young fellow.

That was the whole trouble with Alan, Heather thought.

He was so completely sound that life with him would be a gigantic redundancy. His wife would have three children within the first six years, then no more. She would live in a house in Westmount until Alan's parents, by dying, enabled them to move into the gargoyled Farquhar mansion on the slope of the mountain above Sherbrooke Street. Their children would all go to prescribed schools where they would meet only the children of the same boys and girls she and Alan had been allowed to meet. Owing to the size of the house, they would have considerable servant trouble, and they would listen to a great deal of talk about rising taxes. They would play mild golf and tennis in the summers, ski a little in the winters and make an occasional trip to New York or London. Alan would spend the rest of his life in his father's trust company in Saint James Street. As he was a husky lad, he would show the first signs of corpulence in his late twenties. He would begin to wear black Homburgs in his early thirties and by his middle forties he would be lunching at the Mount Royal Club as regularly as McQueen. He would read little but the newspapers and popular magazines. He would be smilingly indulgent about her painting, provided it remained poor enough to be no more than a hobby. He would be kind, gentle, honourable and an excellent parent. But as he needed absolutely nothing to complete him, being set in the mould already, Heather felt that the girl who married him would not be marrying a man at all, but a way of life.

Since Daphne's return from England, Heather was more certain than ever that she must find something to do on her own or suffocate. Daphne had always overshadowed her in the past. She had found nothing of which to disapprove in her mother's way of life and she had constantly criticized Heather for not looking, thinking and acting like all their friends. But something had happened to Daphne in England. She no longer criticized Heather now; she merely scorned her. Whether or not she was satisfied with Noel Fletcher, Heather couldn't be sure; if she was, there was something drastic the matter with her.

However, it was one thing for Heather to say she wanted a career and a very different one to achieve it. She would certainly have to get out of Montreal. Since the depression some of her friends had found jobs of sorts, but they all pretended either to be working as a lark or to be doing it for charity. In Canada, a girl with background could seriously consider only one of three or four professions. She could nurse, teach school, work in a library, or be a dietician; she might even work in a hospital laboratory if she had the technical training. But whatever a girl chose to do in Canada, she was badly paid for it. All the careers American girls were making for themselves – advertising, designing, screen-writing, editing, decorating, selling, even executive posts in business organizations, law, medicine, architecture – were practically barred to women in Canada. Plenty of girls tried to make their way into some of them, but they were never able to get even halfway to the top.

Heather got out of the car and walked across to the parapet of the look-off, holding her chiffon skirt off the ground as she stepped carefully in her silver slippers. Her mother would consider it most improper for her to be here alone at night. Half a dozen necking couples sat in the darkness of parked cars and others strolled down through the shrubs along a winding path that fell below the terrace.

She leaned against the stone parapet and looked out over the city. 'Oh, lovely!' she murmured. Spread below, the city was moon-coloured, the great sweep of it starred by lights; it was almost like looking upside down at a patch of night sky. Because the summit of the mountain in Westmount is lower than the summit of Mount Royal to the left, only a portion of the city could be seen, but as far as the eye travelled to right and to left, the city was there, running down the slopes and spreading out over the plain to the river. Three miles to the east the chain of lights on Jacques Cartier Bridge flowed in parallel lines out of the city, leaped in geometric constellations at the towers in the middle of the river, swooped low over the dark mass of Saint Helen's Island, then flowed down into the plain on the other side. Over there the land spread luminous in the moonlight to the distant Green Mountains of Vermont.

Lines of poetry came into her mind, flashed out, returned and wove themselves into the mood of the evening. A low hum of noise came up from the city, very faint. The parked cars were as silent as stones. Just below the parapet, beyond the sloping park, large houses lay buried in the trees, and in most of them lived people she knew. She wondered how many of them were lying down there now with eyes closed in lightless rooms. How many of them were young, conscious of a warm, silent form beside them? It would be good to lie beside a man you loved, to wake at night and find him there.

32

As soon as his guests had gone down the walk and across the street, McQueen went up to the library at the top of his house. It was his habit to spend some time there every night before going to bed; among his books he felt it easier to catalogue the events of the day and put them in order. He also liked to read some part of a solid book for half an hour before he slept. The practice was useful to his spirit, and the information he gained increased his prestige in the literary club he had joined shortly after the war.

The club meant a great deal to McQueen. Tonight he expected to put in an hour's work thinking about a paper he was scheduled to read at the opening meeting in the autumn. Although the date was more than three months away, McQueen was leaving nothing to chance. The paper would be superior to anything the club had heard before, and the club had high standards. In style, he knew he could never match Masterman, the president of Minto Power and author of *Gentlemen, the King!* But McQueen saw no reason why he couldn't better Masterman in facts and analysis. The title of his paper would be *Canada: A Phenomenon of Stability in a Troubled World.*

McQueen smiled to himself as he thought of the impression he would make on the club. He was aware that the other members joked about him behind his back and called him a dry old stick, but it was the kind of joking he liked. There was respect and even affection in it. He had become something of a Character.

From his library windows McQueen could look over the tops of his elms to the city. The windows were open and the night air penetrated an atmosphere stuffy with the smell of old book-bindings and printer's ink. A soft glow from the street lights hung over the void to the south. He was sure he could detect an odour of roses from his garden four stories below. That was pretty good, to be able to smell them from this height. There were no roses to match them north of Sherbrooke Street. Then he heard the whisper of a sprayer saturating his lawn and he made a clucking noise with his tongue. He would have to speak to the gardener about it in the morning; the man was getting careless. This was the second time in a month he had forgotten to turn it off. He must be reminded that jobs were very scarce these days.

Faintly, like the snore of an enormous beast he had managed to control but still distrusted, the noise of the city stole up the hill, through the branches of the trees and into his windows. It was a minor sound at this hour of the night, intermittent and far away.

He turned his thoughts back to unemployment and the aspects of the subject which he must handle in the paper for the literary club. In the whole country there were now a million and a half souls on direct relief, one-seventh of the nation. Yet in spite of this total, the country remained quiet. There were no riots anywhere, and there had never been any nonsense like the New Deal. It gave McQueen a feeling of intense personal satisfaction.

His success had been so unbroken, his business judgment so sure, his nose for the market so acute, that he saw no reason to doubt his conclusions about anything. Take the working classes. One was supposed to feel sorry for them, but candidly McQueen believed that their troubles were of their own making. They never saved their money and their morality could be a great deal better than it was. They were also lazy; it was their laziness which prevented them from becoming a menace. They moiled about in the lower streets of Montreal, but they never thought of climbing the hill across the frontier of Sherbrooke Street to see for themselves the comfort in which their business leaders were able to live. Even though the socialists were throwing mud at men like himself, even at men like General Methuen, the working classes didn't seem to care. They probably knew it was not his fault they were out of work. If Wall Street hadn't been so reckless there never would have been a depression anywhere else.

McQueen's thoughts went off on a tack of their own without reference to the paper he must write. That had been very rude of Heather, running off from his party without a word. She was notably heedless, but he had never caught her doing a thing like that before. He wondered if Noel Fletcher might not have had something to do with it. He frowned and clucked his tongue. There was no doubt about it, Janet was going to have trouble with that fellow yet.

It was years since McQueen could remember having met a man who irritated him as Fletcher did by his mere existence. What was England coming to if she could produce a fellow like that? He was exactly the sort to be interested in aircraft. McQueen hated airplanes. He considered them the most diabolical invention Yankee ingenuity had so far managed to inflict upon mankind. They produced men like Fletcher; they turned settled people into nomads; they wasted money; heaven only knew how much property they would yet destroy.

Again the image of Fletcher appeared before his mind. He had ruined the dinner party. By Jove, he wouldn't trust a nice girl across the street with such a fellow! What was Janet thinking about, to be taken in by a man as unsound as that? See what he had done to Daphne! She had been a sweet girl a few years ago, and look at her now! He wouldn't be surprised if . . .

McQueen went back to the table and switched on a gooseneck lamp. He opened a card-index file and began to hunt through it. His mind relaxed into a more comfortable mood as he turned his thoughts once more to his paper. Last night, under *Politics*, he had inscribed a card for the file with what he considered a weighty thought lightly expressed. All during the day he had been remembering it with considerable pleasure. He found it and read it through again: *Every revolution is started by a crank, exploited by a politician, and terminated by a soldier.* That was a nice touch, about the crank. It would get a laugh when he read it at the club.

McQueen got up and padded around his library, pince-nez adjusted to his nose, its black ribbon flaring down to his breast pocket. He couldn't help admiring his shelves. Not many men in Saint James Street collected things; what money they spent on luxuries tended to go for golf, cars, clubs and whiskey. But McQueen collected books. No man in Saint James Street had a library as good as this. He picked out a volume of the collected speeches of Edmund Burke, hunting for a phrase he might be able to use. He took the volume to the table and sat down to read, wondering as he did so how many of his business friends had even heard of Burke.

Leaning over the table, McQueen looked thoroughly solid. His head rose like a domed globe out of his jowls as they rested firmly on the edges of his winged collar. His tufted eyebrows turned up and his heavy mouth turned down. His hair was grey and frizzy about the ears, the top of his head bald except for a single lock brushed carefully across its centre from one side to the other. His lips moved as he read and every now and then he scratched his right ear.

After awhile McQueen replaced the book on its shelf. There was no doubt about it, Burke was a great orator. The Prime Minister ought to study some of his speeches. There was no reason why stability should necessarily be dull. His mind skipped about over the subject of his paper and inevitably back to the dinner party. If Heather was a sample of the younger generation there was going to be trouble. McQueen wanted to be just, but he doubted if he was exaggerating. Where there was smoke there was generally fire. Heather had allowed some of the younger professors at the university to put ideas into her head. She had made some very unnecessary and annoying remarks at the table about the values of socialism. McQueen saw no necessity for it whatever. He was convinced that the last thing any socialist ever wanted was to be forced to accept power. Idealists were all the same. And yet they were mischievous. They opened up the masses to the real scroundrel who invariably followed them. Look what had happened to Germany! The socialists had preached idealism but the only result of their pernicious meddling was Hitler. McQueen clucked with his tongue. It served them right.

He wondered if he could possibly introduce into his paper

a paragraph on the influence of women like his mother. There had been no nonsense in the way she had brought him up, and his whole life had justified her. It was something for a boy from a small Ontario town, who had grown up in genteel poverty, to own a house at his age opposite the Methuens' on the slope of the mountain. It was something also for that boy to be on the board of governors of the university, on two hospital boards and a charity committee, to lunch twice a week at the Mount Royal Club, and to be a member of the Committee of Art. For the past ten years his picture had appeared in the newspapers as a pallbearer of millionaires, and he had been twice invited to dine at Rideau Hall by two different Governor-Generals. Finally, as a means of making a due return to the nation, he had drawn a will which completely satisfied him. On his death his entire fortune would be used to found and maintain a new Presbyterian theological college. It was to be located in the heart of the Ontario countryside, to have ample scholarships, and the chairs were to be so heavily endowed the trustees would be able to fill them with the ablest theologians they could import from Edinburgh and Aberdeen.

McQueen switched off the light and padded downstairs. In the last analysis, the soundness of a country was the soundness a man found in himself, in the city where he lived. It didn't take long for Montreal to brush the nonsense off a man's ideas and reduce him to scale. Look at himself. He was prepared to admit that when he was younger he had indulged his fancies more than was good for him. He had once hoped to organize the entire country. No man could have done it, not even Sir Rupert Irons, who had never even tried. It was the mark of a big man to be able to change his mind, as he had changed his. Even Irons consulted him now on occasion. Just imagine what the country would be like if it were led by the sort of men one met in Wall Street!

McQueen rubbed his hands together as he thought how he was going to prove that Canada was sounder than the United States. In the first place, so far as he could see, the Americans were as excitable as Italians. And look at the way they let their women hound them all over the place! If you let the women get that much hold, why not hand the

272

whole country over to them and let them run it? He wouldn't be surprised to see them do that very thing before long. He chuckled. The day they elected a female president it would serve them right.

In a state of dreamy contentment, padding slowly along the upper hall to his bedroom, McQueen thought how sharp a contrast he could make between the United States and Canada, if he went about it skilfully. In Canada, first of all, there were the two races: each could be employed to balance the other. Then there were the churches: they were filled every Sunday, and it was possible for the whole nation to excite itself over a theological dispute. But the real point was this: ten per cent of the college graduates, perhaps not the most brilliant men but certainly the most restless of the lot, found it so difficult to get what they wanted in Canada that you could always count on them drifting south to the States. That made enormously for stability above the border. Down there they could write their books and broadcast their ideas, and compared to the average American they were probably fairly stable citizens. Yes, McQueen thought with satisfaction, we have discovered a great social secret in Canada. We have contrived to solve problems which would ruin other countries merely by ignoring their existence.

By the time McQueen reached his bedroom he felt his mind had served him pretty well that evening. Without turning on the light he crossed to the window and looked out. The blinds in Janet's room, in the Methuen house across the street, were drawn, but the faint glow of lights came through them. Janet was getting ready for bed. He tried to think of her there, imagining her reflecting over his party, and again he told himself what a nice woman she was. She had done so well against so many difficulties, and now at last she was secure. He was thankful he had been able to do so much to help her. Ever since Harvey Methuen's death he had guarded her investments free of charge, and he had nursed them so carefully that her estate was now double what it had been when he had first accepted responsibility for it. He had nursed his friendship just as carefully. He could still remember the thrill it had given him, three years ago on Christmas Eve, to get the two girls to call him by his first name.

273

He felt something soft rub against his legs, and bent down to pick up his cat. It was a handsome tortoise-shell Persian. He laid the animal on the bed, turned on a light, and slowly began to undress. As he took off his tie he caught sight of himself in the mirror above the dressing table. Perhaps it was not too late after all? Janet was nearly fifty now. Something like excitement pervaded his blood, but the moment soon passed. It was ridiculous to think of marriage at his age, after rejecting the idea of it thirty years ago. It was even embarrassing. Besides, there was Heather. She was still unmarried, and it would be most unsettling to have someone like Heather as a step-daughter. He wouldn't be surprised but what Janet had her hands full with that girl before long.

He put on his pajamas and went into the bathroom, took a long time washing his hands and brushing his teeth and gargling carefully. Finally he shuffled back to the bedroom with his feet encased in a pair of stuffed slippers. He fell on his knees before the bed and murmured his prayers for more than five minutes. Then he rolled between the sheets and snapped off the light by a switch at the head of the bed. The cat leaped up and snuggled into the curve of his bent knees, purring loudly.

Slowly McQueen's thoughts grew more placid. It was just as he had said, no country had weathered the depression the way Canada had done. Difficult times had merely weeded out what was unsound and given the good plants room in which to grow. The country was sound through and through. In any kind of crisis there were always fifty ways of making a mistake and only one way of doing the right thing. Human affairs were so mysterious it was arrogant to lay down general rules for them. The deduction was obvious – it was the part of a prudent man to do nothing.

After reminding himself that he must note this last thought in his card-index first thing in the morning, McQueen fell asleep. The two round forms, his own and the cat's, lay tranquilly side by side, breathing evenly.

33

At the back of a small chapel in an old street near the centre
of town, Paul watched Kathleen getting married again. Beside him stood a sexton in overalls. He had hay-fever and
he sniffled constantly. He had been fixing a hinge on the
chapel door and was still at the job when the priest called
him to witness the ceremony. The door of the chapel remained ajar, and now the priest's words were dimmed by
the steady noise of traffic in the street. He was an old man
and he sounded very tired. Toward the end his words were
punctuated by repeated barks from the horn of a taxi caught
in a traffic jam at the corner.

Paul's fists and his jaw were clenched tight. It was an airless, humid day, hot even in the chapel. He felt the sweat
working out from the skin above his shoulder blades, making
wet patches on the back of his shirt. In the dim light of the
chapel his brown eyes were very large. Shadows lay under
his cheekbones. His whole body was lithe and controlled as
as he stood with shoulders bent slightly forward, watching.

He tried to fix his eyes on his mother's back, but the candles winking on the altar beyond held his gaze, as candlelight always did. Beside her kneeled Henry Clayton, in process of becoming his stepfather. Paul looked at the man's
rounded shoulders. They were inert and strangely humble.
And yet, for Clayton this moment was the end of a quest
which had occupied and taxed all his ingenuity and intelligence for at least nine years. From now on he would have
her, and could tell the world he had her. At fifty-two he
could take her home, to his small house in a suburb of Pittsburgh. At fifty-two, the only real purpose Henry Clayton
had ever known was accomplished.

If loneliness is a man's inability to share his feelings with
another, Paul had never been as lonely in his life as he was
now. The whole ceremony seemed shocking to him. The
food being blessed was stale; indeed it had already been
eaten. Alone at the back of the chapel, he tried to tell himself
that this marriage made no difference to him, but it was not
that simple. His mother was at the core of his life; she was

interwoven tight in the maze of feelings that threatened to choke him unless he could communicate them.

The priest raised his hand and made the sign of the cross. As his thin voice intoned the blessing another taxi horn barked outside. Clayton and Kathleen rose to their feet as man and wife. Clayton's bulk surged up jerkily, as though his knees hurt him, and Kathleen flowed from one position to another easily, with the same old languid motions. Paul and the sexton followed them to the vestry to sign the register and the priest's bony finger quivered as he held the page down for them. The sexton's signature spilled out in childish letters on to the page. Some ink splashed off the nib of the pen and made a smear on the paper, then it widened and spread when a worn blotter was applied to it. Paul's signature was small and neat, each letter spaced as though printed, yet containing evidence of a nervous tension no print could reproduce.

Then Paul followed his mother and stepfather out to the street, they all got into Clayton's car and drove back to his hotel. The wedding breakfast was eaten in the main restaurant of the Mount Royal. Next to them two men with obvious hangovers were eating tomato juice and oysters. Once Kathleen and Clayton touched hands across the table, then drew apart on a reflex when they saw that Paul had noticed the gesture.

Paul ate in silence. He was as austere as a priest, sitting there with them at the small square table. Clayton took out a cream-coloured silk handkerchief and wiped his forehead and the bald patch on his skull. His heavy face was dissolved in sweat, and every time he smiled the moisture ran down through a network of canals to his collar. Beside him Kathleen looked tranquilly comfortable. Her rich skin bloomed in the heat like a gardenia. There was a loosening in the flesh under her eyes which gave her a puzzled, wounded expression when her face was in repose. And when she lowered her head, her chin doubled itself. Yet she was still a handsome woman, still endowed with the accepting look that caught weak men, lonely men, disappointed men, warming them and making them feel better and stronger than they had ever felt in their lives.

276

'You'll come to Pittsburgh and see us soon, won't you? The familiar husky voice was pleading as she spoke to Paul. His lids dropped for a second, but lifted immediately. She loved him. She always had. She had never deserted him. He had been the one to desert her. Clayton was saving her from a barren old age, and it was senseless of him to feel as he did about it. In his own way Clayton was a good man; the kind of jolly man Kathleen should have married when she was a young girl. He had been born a poor boy in Texas and had made his own way. He had worked on ranches and on railroads, and finally had got some sort of education and worked his way into business. Big, hearty, solid-stout, he had a laugh that filled the whole dining room. And he loved Kathleen. Looking at his mother, Paul loved her, too. He had regretted her sometimes. He had fought against the helplessness she often induced in him. Her white hand, soft as though it had never done a day's housework in her life, touched Paul lightly on the wrist. She looked at her husband, pride in her eyes. 'Paul works awfully hard, Henry. He's always been such a good boy.'

Clayton tucked his handkerchief into his breast pocket. In spite of the heat he was wearing a double-breasted worsted suit with a pencil stripe. Already the creases had wilted over his knees.

'How did you make out in your exams, Paul? They're tough stuff – exams. I was too old for them when I wrote mine and . . .'

'All right, I think,' Paul said. 'Not that exams make any difference, these days.'

'Don't you believe it,' Clayton said heartily. 'What you young fellas need is confidence in the future.'

The waiter came with ham and eggs, whipped covers off plates, and disappeared.

'Henry is going to get you a good job in the States, Paul. We've talked it all over. A job with real money in it. Isn't that wonderful?'

Paul picked up his knife and fork and cut off a slice of ham.

'Why sure,' Clayton said. 'Down home – with the new government – business is picking right up so it'll be climbing flagpoles soon. Down in Pittsburgh not long ago they had an N.R.A. parade that took three hours to pass! When Americans feel that way about something there's no stopping them.' He laughed and patted Paul on the shoulder jovially. 'I know you people up here think we all shoot our mouths off, but just the same . . . You come down and see for yourself. I'll get you a good job in no time.'

'What kind of a job, Mr. Clayton?' Paul's voice was ironical.

Clayton grinned, and Paul would have felt sorry for him had there been any cause. The grin did not reach him, did not affect him, nor do the work it was supposed to do. But as Clayton didn't know this, it was all right.

'This is a swell country up here. It's been good to me and I've got nothing against it. So far as I can see there's no real difference between you and us. Only trouble is, things don't move fast enough up here. You people don't let yourselves get steamed up. Now down home, we're changing all the time. That's the American way, and' – the voice became confidential – 'I'm telling you, whether the rest of the world likes it or not, it's the way things have got to go from now on. When things with us begin to look up they don't stop till they hit the ceiling.'

Paul went on eating. He wondered how Clayton had managed to be successful in his business in Montreal. Perhaps just because he was so completely American, so much what Canadians fancied all Americans were, that people found it a welcome relief to deal with him? Five years ago Clayton had deliberately refused promotion because it would have removed him permanently to his home office. His wife was an strict Catholic and he had not even asked for a divorce. So, because Kathleen was in Montreal, Clayton had remained here most of the time while his wife stayed in Pittsburgh until her death six months ago.

'They talk about the depression like it was the end of the world,' Clayton said. 'Don't you believe it. Now take me – I've been through plenty that were just as bad as this. Take the one we had back in 1907. Take the one in . . .'

Clayton drifted off, safe on a wave of talk. Like so many men of the same age, he thought he could prove that the system by which he lived was good because it wallowed from one mess to another while he himself somehow managed to survive. Strained, worried, high blood pressure and stomach ulcers, but so what? And yet it was hard to imagine that Clayton had ever seriously worried about anything. Life to him was fun and business, and business consisted in making money and moving large objects from one place to another. Beyond production and profit he never thought an inch. He believed that the more mechanical equipment a man has at his disposal, the better and happier he is. No man could have too many gadgets, the world could never weary of working its life away producing labour-saving devices. As he talked, Kathleen admired him with her wonderful smile, the female's eternal smile for the man who loves her. And when Clayton's eyes rested on hers, Paul knew that her satisfaction was equally matched.

Suddenly Paul remembered the lean aristocracy of his father. He thought of the old house in Saint-Marc and his jaw set rigidly. And yet, there was no cause for anger, or even for surprise. The kind of beauty his mother possessed had never demanded an answering beauty in men. She wanted only affection and admiration, naturalness and the frank opportunity to be herself, and of course the kind of animal vitality which apparently Clayton also possessed.

The breakfast ended and they rose from the table in relief. Clayton picked up the check and examined it, then laid down a dollar bill as a tip for the waiter. They went out the screened, swinging doors, out of the dark warmth of the hotel into the humid heat of the street. Clayton's sedan was parked across Metcalfe Street, the back seat and trunk so filled with luggage that the springs sagged under its weight. They crossed the street and Paul held the door open while his mother arranged herself on the right half of the front seat. Clayton went around to the other door, and after sliding under the wheel, pulled at his trouser-legs and wriggled in his suit to make himself comfortable. He pulled a cigar from his breast pocket, eyed it, lit it, eyed the grey ash forming on the end, shook his head in approval, and replaced it between his teeth.

'Hell's bells, what a day!' he said. 'I met an Englishman

279

yesterday and he said it was hotter here than in Singapore. I can believe it.' He wiped his forehead. 'Well, we'll be in cool little Old Orchard tonight. I can't wait to wrap myself around one of those shore dinners.'

Kathleen patted Paul's hand as it gripped the door beside her. Clayton shot him a satisfied glance. 'Don't you worry, Paul,' he said. 'I'll look after your mother all right.'

Paul said nothing. He stood watching them, wishing they would go, yet longing for a crazy second that his mother would step out of the car and tell him this was all a mistake and that the last nine years had never been. Clayton started the motor. It throbbed as all eight pistons danced back and forth under the cylinder head. Clayton tapped the wheel, smiling. 'Give me one of these V-Eights any day of the week. Going out of Chicago last fall, along the dunes, I was making eighty-seven miles an hour, and what do you think? Another car passed me, and . . .'

Kathleen turned to Paul, her smile fading out. He felt a lump choke in his throat as he met her eyes. They were filled with tears. He leaned through the open window and kissed her on the cheek, her skin soft and fragrant under his lips. Then the car began to move.

'Forgive me, Paul!' He heard the choked whisper as he stood on the curb and watched the car move up to Sherbrooke Street, his mother's hand waving from the window like a fragment of trailing white silk. The car stopped at the red light at the upper corner, then turned and disappeared.

Forgive her! For nine years . . . for twenty-four years . . . for having conceived and borne him? He stood irresolute, running his hand through his hair. He had no place to go. It was not a new situation. The places he had to go were always temporary places: way-stations on the road through to somewhere else. He thought of some of them: school, hockey practices, games when the players' entrance to the rink was dark under arc lamps on cold winter nights, the spectators lining up under the bright lights in front, and then the hundreds of tight moments before the game started with the teams poised in the arena ringed by the crowd; stores where he had worked delivering parcels in his mid-teens in the summer; the train that had taken him north to the construction gang that summer when he was eighteen; that other train with the black leather seats in the colonists' car when he had gone west for the harvesting the year following, across Ontario and Manitoba to Saskatchewan. All those places to go, even the hockey, had been to get an education. They had provided the money for it. It was now, with exams over and a degree in his pocket, that he really had no place to go.

He walked up the gradual rise of the street to Sherbrooke, then along toward his room on Durocher Street. The hot air was tropically sensual under the tall elms of the McGill campus. The background of Mount Royal staggered in the heat. He felt empty. But it is not emptiness that fills a man so full he is likely to burst unless a valve is turned.

Paul's thoughts gathered themselves. He had things to do and a lifetime would not be long enough to do them properly. He had seen a second-hand portable typewriter in a store on Craig Street the other day. At the time he had counted his money to see if he could afford it and decided he would have to get a job first. The Corona would have to wait, like everything else he wanted these days. Again. like guilt in the conscience, the sequence of the last few years renewed itself: doors closing in his face, the regretful smiles of older, well-established men; the knowledge eating into himself and into millions of others month by month and year by year that nobody wanted them, nobody could find a use for them.

34

After the night of McQueen's dinner party, Fletcher left Heather alone. Sometimes he was sullen in her presence, more often he ignored her. He spent hours in his room poring over papers and blueprints. There were entire days when he also ignored Daphne, a mode of behaviour which flustered Janet more than either of her daughters.

About the middle of July he set out on a business trip to the American west coast which he announced would take about six weeks. On the day of his departure he was quite cheerful. Heather and Daphne both saw him off on the night train and when they returned, Janet was waiting for them with milk and biscuits. It was an old habit which she saw no reason to break. It was also a habit to talk about nothing that mattered to any of them as they ate.

Heather was almost undressed when Daphne came into her room, holding up an old middy blouse she had worn at Brock. 'Look,' she said. 'I found it in the back of the cupboard in my room. Why on earth it was left there I can't imagine. Isn't it a scream? What a beastly little prig I must have been when I wore it.'

Heather pulled a silk slip over her head. 'Sometimes,' she said, 'you were.'

'Well,' Daphne said brightly, 'I'm certainly not one now.' She tossed the middy blouse into a corner. 'Remember Miss Davenant? How she used to pitch into me when I played Cleopatra?' She mimicked the voice of a hearty English-woman and sat with her legs apart as she did so. ' "Cleopatra is a woman of the world, Daphne. You must remember that she is a queen, not a debutante." '

Heather put a dressing gown over her pajamas and curled up in a large armchair by the window. 'How exactly like Miss Davenant to select *Antony and Cleopatra* for a school play!'

'Poor lamb! She was frustrated and never knew it.' Daphne put her arms behind her head and her long fingers reached down to undo the buttons at the back of her dress. 'I wonder what she'd think if she happened to see me now.'

'Honest, Daffy – what's it like to come back here?'

Daphne smiled obliquely, her hands still behind her neck. 'How do you think I've been doing?'

'Depends on what you're trying to do.'

'Well, I feel about a million years old, of course. Funny, how we were all taught to believe in sin when we were young, wasn't it?'

Heather laughed, and the sound appeared to annoy Daphne. 'Look at me,' she said. 'Would you think a girl brought up by Mummy would ever be able to stand up to Noel and give him what he wants?'

The smile left Heather's face. 'I wouldn't know.'

'Well, I've done all right,' Daphne said. 'And believe me

282

– he knows what he wants. My God, when I remember those first few months . . .' She dropped her hands. 'Help me, will you? This damned button is caught.'

Heather got up and unbuttoned the dress. It made her think of the days when she had helped dress Daphne for parties, two years before she had been allowed to go to parties herself. Her hand touched the fine golden hair, lingered on it for a second, then dropped. She returned to her chair and Daphne pulled the dress over her head and gave her ruffled hair a toss. 'Noel was interested in you,' she said. 'Maybe you didn't guess, but I could see it.'

Heather felt herself flushing. 'But Daffy – '

'Never mind. He has an instinct with women, though. In spite of his manner. That's why he's such a shock. It's always a surprise when a man like that . . . you should see his father. Noel's not really a typical Englishman at all. He was always more at home on the continent, in spite of the English manner. His father's the reason. The old boy's as exciting as a play.'

Heather felt unable to feed Daphne the cues she seemed to expect. 'What kind of a play?'

Daphne's laugh was like running water. 'You *are* a sweet thing! It would be a shame if Noel – '

'I'm not a child,' Heather said impatiently. 'For heaven's sake, Daffy – when will you get over treating me as if I were a ten-year old? What's the matter with his father?'

'Really, I suppose he's an eighteen-carat beast, but he's such a terribly brilliant man one doesn't notice it.' She went on to tell Heather that he had been a major-general in the Indian Army. He was fanatically proud of his ancestry and had been reputed a competent officer. But his military career had ended with a court-martial when he was dismissed from the service for ordering his troops to fire on a crowd in Bombay. After that he spent a lot of time in Germany until the outbreak of war in 1914. Although he had served as an agent of the foreign office while in Berlin, it had not prevented him from acquiring a great admiration for the Prussians. He was living in Germany now.

Heather watched her sister take off the rest of her clothes until she was sitting naked on the bed. 'Do you mind if I ask you something?' she said quietly. 'Do you really love Noel?'

Daphne laughed. Her slim, lissom body, golden in the shaded light, moved gracefully as she threw her silk underclothes on to a chair. 'Give me a dressing-gown,' she said.

Heather went to her closet, pulled a garment from a hanger and handed it to her sister. When she had wrapped it tight about her body, Daphne stood for a moment watching Heather's face. 'Love is an old-fashioned word, darling. Why do you bother using it?'

'Do you know a better one?'

Instead of answering Daphne crossed to the dressing table and sat down before the mirror. 'It's not been exactly easy,' she said after a moment, 'going from Mummy's hands into Noel's.'

Again Heather was aware that she was irritating Daphne in a way she couldn't define.

'I like being at the top of the class,' Daphne went on. 'And you've got to be that to hold a man like Noel.' She scrutinized her face in the glass. 'I never really understood him until I went up in a plane with him. He's marvellous in the air. He's – he's new. A new species of human being.' In the mirror she caught a smile on Heather's lips and it seemed to anger her. 'My God – can't you understand what I'm trying to tell you? A man like Noel always tries to break his women down. He'd despise me if he could and he hates me because he can't.' She filled a dropper with yellow liquid from a small bottle, raised one eyelid and then the other, letting the lotion run beneath them. 'Brilliance has been bred and beaten into him.'

Heather watched as Daphne ran a finger over each eyebrow, pushed the hair off her temples and turned her head from side to side as she examined the line of her chin and neck. For the first time she saw that her sister's beauty was a weapon, a destiny, all she had.

'Never mind, darling,' Daphne went on. 'One has to grow up. Sex is much more devious than simply going to bed with a man. After all, even greengrocers do that.'

But Heather was no longer listening. Her whole attention was centred on the sudden new sense of freedom within her. All her life she had admired Daphne's beauty, had tried to adopt her opinions, had respected her because everyone else had admired her. And now it was gone, that dependence. She was free to judge Daphne and Noel with her own mind, to feel the cold European years that had grown like a shell around Noel Fletcher, to feel them through Daphne's words and the expression on her face. They had nothing whatever she wanted, for all they possessed was a cold surface beauty and his ability, motivated by a mechanical sensuality, to counterfeit the fire she knew was still alive in the world, somewhere, if she could find it.

35

The next morning Heather woke early, as though someone had called her. She lay still a moment, trying to remember what day it was and why it felt like a holiday. Then she recalled the conversation with Daphne. The rest of the house was still. She looked at the clock on her desk and saw how early it was, but she was wide awake and knew she could not return to sleep. She was filled with the clean excitement of going to new work on a clean morning in a clean place.

In a few minutes she got out of bed and ran a bath, and then she lay in the warm water and looked up through the window over the tub to the branch of a horse-chestnut tree that grew beside the house. Its triads of heavy, thick leaves were bright in the sun. It was going to be a fine day, after days and nights of the steamy heat that so often collects in the river valley in summer like liquid in a cup.

She lifted her arms and clasped them behind her head. The water stirred to the movement and she saw her legs shimmer and lengthen and shimmer back to normal again. She had always been self-conscious about her shortness; Daphne had called her chunky. Ever since she could remember she had longed for another four inches of height, and a slim waist descending through gentle curves at the hips into long lovely thighs. Like Daphne? Always like Daphne. But no longer. Now she seemed able for the first time to see herself as she was, not as she wanted to be. She supposed she was somewhat plain, but on the whole not too bad. Not the kind that men fell for easily, of course. A plain girl would have to be grateful for love all her life. It was too bad, in a way, because if she ever fell in love she would so much like to have something precious, something rare like Daphne's beauty, to give in return. Was that a romantic idea, she wondered? On the whole she thought not; it seemed only plain common sense.

She stirred in the water again. It was a fine day for something out of the ordinary. She decided to drive down the plain of the Eastern Townships to Lake Memphramagog to do some sketching. It would be good to get away from home even for a single day. The work would probably be poor, but for a little while she might be lucky and have the illusion that it was good.

Ever since leaving college Heather had missed regular work more than she had fancied it possible to miss anything. She had enjoyed every one of her four years at McGill, where she had taken honours in literature. Now she had a degree and nothing to do with it. Painting was something she had always done in one manner or another. She had always been able to draw well, and Janet had raised no objection to her taking lessons from anyone who could teach her anything in Montreal. But no one had ever taken her painting seriously except herself. She sometimes felt she might have been one of Jane Austen's girls, with her single accomplishment. But how could her mother, or her mother's friends, take her work seriously when they thought the pictures in McQueen's house the ultimate in good taste?

Heather was not bitter: she was not even unhappy. She had many friends, and it would be stupid to pretend they were not nice people. Yet none of them was able to keep her from feeling as though the realest part of her was beginning to fall asleep. Unless she did something drastic to wake up, the sleep would soon be sound. They tried to tell her in a roundabout way that it was her economic duty to be useless, but it made no sense. Who exacted such a duty? The capitalist class? Then capitalism was obviously all wrong.

She plunged her legs in the water and rose from the tub, dried herself and left the bathroom in her bare feet. She

286

dressed in her bedroom, putting on an old blue linen frock with large white buttons and tying up her chestnut hair with a white ribbon. Before leaving the room she glanced about; it was the only part of the house private to her. Four paintings hung on the walls, all in narrow, unpainted wooden frames. Three were her own: two simple landscapes of the Laurentian countryside, and the crayon head of a small boy. On the largest wall-space hung the nude torso of a Negro girl, done by a Czech painter she had met several years before. It was a bitter portrait, the breasts sagging and the ribs slatted like scantlings, one bony hand on a hip and a hopeless expression on the tired face.

Janet had been horrified by the Negro girl. Its presence in Heather's room led her to assume that her daughter was making some very unfortunate friends. She had asked McQueen to investigate the Czech and had been only partly relieved to discover that he was a quiet little man with a wife and three children and very little means. The Committee of Art had never heard of him, and Janet expostulated with Heather on the folly of buying a picture from a painter who was not only no good, but was impertinent as well. She hoped none of her friends would chance to see it hanging in the house.

Heather's books would have bothered Janet a great deal more than the Negro girl if she had ever read them. But books were generally safe things to leave around Janet. Heather paused now to select one to take along on the drive. If her sketching went stale she would want something to read. She glanced over the titles on the top shelf, her collection of post-war writers. All of D. H. Lawrence was there, all of Aldous Huxley and Dos Passos, some Hemingway and the social works of Bertrand Russell. She knew she was supposed to admire these writers for their realism, but actually she loved them for their style. She could not bear a book that lacked style.

Remembering her talk of the previous evening with Daphne, Heather was seized with a fit of pure amusement. She had been relying on novelists for information about the world outside her cocoon, taking their characters quite literally instead of thinking about them as symbols, as she sup-

287

posed she should have done. And now she had at last met a living character in Noel Fletcher, and he had turned out to be far more implausible than any of the people in the books on her shelves. Daphne could fit into the odd world of her favorite authors. Perhaps that was why Daphne and Noel managed to understand each other. Daphne could easily type for the wealthy nymphomaniac, and an amorous miner could get into bed with her and prove that she was no good in bed, and tell her so, and add bitterly that she was not female enough and not his woman anyway.

Heather twinkled. I *am* a bitch, she thought, and then her smile widened as she looked at the American books. Art was a strange phenomenon; true in one way, utterly false in another. And the Americans were so direct about everything. Her fingers touched the backs of a row of them. I never thought of it before, she said to herself. They're all men!

What did it add up to, that her favourite writers were all men? It was certainly a man's dream-world they all wrote about. Her mind played with it in parody. What a world! Everything was so lousy there was nothing you could do but take it; you could be a socialist and then the police proved their brutality by beating you up; you got some kind of venereal disease but you could take it; you seldom had a job and if you did you hated it, for everything was lousy, the men bitter, close-mouthed and inarticulate, with chips on their shoulders but sexually as potent as Hercules; to hell with everything because everything was so lousy you took a drink and kept on with it. But every girl you met rolled into bed with you if you were a man. Straight between the sheets. You were born with two strikes on you and the third was coming up. But if you were a girl in their man's world you were struck out before you reached the plate unless you were a bitch. If you were a bitch you got by. If you were a nice girl your only way of proving it was by being good in bed, smooth and lovely under the cool sheets with rain on the windows in the dark. And then afterwards they got you for it. You died in childbirth or you died from something else because that was the way it was. And always it was tough for the man, standing by your bed close-mouthed and too manly to say anything while you died, but before the lights faded out you at least knew he could take that too.

Heather pulled a copy of *Farewell to Arms* from the shelf and opened it. Immediately she lost herself in the splendour of the prose, and forgot her irony. She read the first ten pages without moving, and then she closed the book and kept it in her hand as she left the room. It was vibrant, it was beautiful, it was life! She would give anything to be able to create something as good as that.

She ate breakfast alone, and then she took her cabriolet out of the garage, drove down the hill and ran east along Sherbrooke to her studio in Labelle Street. It was a small room on the third floor of an old house. It cost her twenty dollars a month and many arguments with her mother. She took an easel, paints, brushes, pencils and a sketch-book to the car and set out through a network of narrow streets toward the river.

It was not yet eight o'clock. Stores and offices were not open, but a trickle of shabby men flowed down the sidewalks on either side of the street, hands in pockets, clothes looking as if they had been rained on, some without collars or ties. Many of them were her own age. She felt acutely uncomfortable as she drove past them. If she had earned the money that purchased her car she would have felt a little better, but she had never earned a cent in her life. She wished she could help people like these men, but there seemed no way of doing so. The idea of serving in a canteen supported by the Junior League had revolted her after a week of working in one. Girls who spent more money on their complexions than these men spent on food for their families, flattered their egos by passing out hand-outs to the unemployed in their spare time. The implicit insult had horrified Heather; she had seen the sardonic glances of some of the men she had served. Lots of the girls were completely sincere about it, but to Heather the whole notion of charity was repulsive. There seemed no excuse for girls like herself to exist so long as there was any need for charity. McQueen would say it was the men's own fault; he would add that they should have saved their money when they had it.

Crossing the Jacques Cartier Bridge she saw the river

blue against the white background of the grain elevators and the profile of the city stretching off to either side hazed by the heat. Too few factories were working to make much smoke. At the far end of the bridge the usual knot of hitch-hikers stood waiting for a lift. There were too many men of all ages for her to stop and single one out, so she drove by without looking. She followed the twisting road through Longueuil and then she was out in the open, running at sixty miles an hour across the flat plain with the sun in her eyes and on her lap. Maturing crops made the fields look painted green, and at the roadside white daisies and purple clover edged the asphalt. Her hair blew out beyond the white ribbon that held it away from her face, like a flag in the wind.

Soon the tall trees surrounding the church steeple in Chambly came over the horizon and grew steadily larger. She pressed the accelerator into the floor and the motor whined higher. The speedometer needle crept upwards and clung quivering to seventy-three. Blue water on Chambly Basin could be seen through trees, holding a million points of light from the sun. Her body was in alert and tense communion with the car, tuned to the high whine of the motor and the whirr of the trees, almost mindless with speed. She sang to herself:

> 'I sprang to the stirrup, and Joris, and he,
> I galloped, Dirck galloped, we galloped all three . . .

It was like Flanders: just as flat, but greener, more innocent, without the Flanders sadness. She raised her foot from the accelerator and the car slowed down into the village of Chambly Basin, past wooden houses hugging the street, under a garland of Papal banners strung across the road. In the further extension of Chambly Canton a priest crossed in front of her looking hot in his black soutane.

When she reached the tip of Memphramagog two hours later the lake looked cool and very blue in its pan of surrounding mountains. She turned south down the far shore of the lake toward Georgeville and finally stopped at a spit of land, found the location she wanted, and took her easel and kit from the car. She set the easel in the lee of a birch grove so the sun would be off her back and she could have a clear view of the lake. Her hands on her hips, her short legs apart, she stood analyzing the rhythm of the landscape.

Today's light made all the contours as soft as a Constable. It was the last thing she was interested in painting. She wanted the lines and colours hard and brillant, as they so often were in this part of the country. After a time she began sketching, but from the beginning she realized that nothing new was being created under her pencil. Mosquitoes buzzed about her ears and she had to stop work to slap them off. More mosquitoes arrived and began to bite her arms. She crushed them one by one and doggedly continued with her work, but more mosquitoes came in their place, and before an hour had passed she gave up. She went to the car and changed into a bathing suit, with a cow in a far pasture for audience.

Out in the water of the lake she felt wonderfully lazy and content, floating on her back, her breasts buoyantly independent under her suit, her thighs idly moving to keep her body balanced while she lay and looked up at the sky. The water caressed her nerves like a multitude of softly flowing fingers. It was good to be alone. At such a moment it was easy to see that she must get away from Montreal. She wished her painting were good enough to serve as an excuse for a year of study in New York, but she couldn't persuade even herself of that, much less her mother.

She stroked in to the shore, the water foaming in a steady swirl behind her fluttering calves and feet, then boiling up amber-coloured about her ankles as she waded into the beach over the stones. She rolled her suit down to her waist and lay on her back in the sun. This was what her painting had come to, lying in the sun doing nothing. But the sun was magnificent; hot and dominant it pressed her into the ground. She loved the feeling of well-being it gave her. A stream of thoughts passed through her mind, none of them very intense, and she wondered idly if she could have become a real artist if she had ever suffered. It was foolish to phrase her problem like that, foolish and romantic. She turned over to let the sun tan her back.

A mosquito tickled her thigh and she brushed it off.

Another came and another, and she stood up, beating them off, her body naked to the waist, her arms, legs and chest tawny brown, her ribs and stomach white. She heard a creak on the road about a hundred yards off where the birch grove ended. A farmer was standing in a moving wagon holding the reins while the horse dragged slowly in her direction. She thought she could see the man grinning at her, but the distance was too great to be sure. She ducked out of sight, and when the wagon was gone she dressed and drove back along the lake to Magog. The rest of the family had finished dinner when she returned that night, happy and silent with the memory of her day.

36

The heat wave continued to the end of the month. Every evening thunderheads bulged over Mount Royal, their sides purple and massive; shadows were dark as oil over lawns and streets, and through a few minutes of silence the birds called down the rain. The same thing happened every evening for a week. But each night, as soon as the sun had gone down, the thunderheads passed without breaking, stars came out in a hot sky, and the next morning the sun steamed the city again. Then, the last night in July, the storm broke. Lightning split a tree just above the head of the street where the Methuens lived, and McQueen sat in his library with his cat on his knees and brooded over the elements.

Heather felt exhilarated by the rain. It whipped the house in loud, colourless sheets and poured down the windows so fast the panes looked like opaque slabs of melting ice. She sat awhile trying to read, and then she went to her room, put on a raincoat, tied a scarf over her hair and ran out through the downpour to the garage. She put up the top of the cabriolet and secured the side-curtains, then drove out and held the car in second gear down the hill. The gutters were foaming with water and falling leaves spun down through the funnels cut by her headlights through the rain. She drove for nearly an hour to the eastern end of the island and back again, and finally she drew up before the old house on University Street where her grandfather lived.

The intensity of the rain had lessened. She ran through it up the steps, and then she opened the door into a small vestibule, passed through into the common hall of the house and pressed a doorbell beside the first door on the right.

'Child!' Yardley said when he opened the door. 'What a night for you to remember where I live!'

As she kissed him the rain on her skin wet his cheeks. He closed the door behind her and she took off her dripping coat, then dropped into a comfortable chair, her cheeks flushed with the weather, her wet hair curling near the ears and on her forehead. 'I'm saturated,' she said. She pulled off her rubbers and tossed them onto the cold hearth, one after the other, and they lay where they fell, limp and glistening. 'But it's a wonderful night out, just the same. I love rain.'

Yardley hung her coat on a hook behind the door of a closet. His hair was white now, it receded far above his forehead, but it still covered the top and sides of his head, and it still bristled. He looked very little older than he had done the year he first went to Saint-Marc. His ears stuck out as always and lines fanned out from the corners of his eyes when he smiled. But farming had left a mark on him; his shoulders were bowed with a permanent stoop and his hands were gnarled. In his city clothes he looked like a farmer dressed for Sunday.

As he limped to a chair near Heather she watched him, and after he was settled he returned her regard, his eyes twinkling behind his glasses. 'It's good to be here, Grampa,' she said. Her glance fell on the mantelpiece, above which hung a framed drawing of a full-rigged ship, and travelled to the windows. 'You do need some flowers to brighten it up, and something more cheerful in the way of curtains at your windows.'

Yardley grinned. 'I'm surprised at you, sounding like your mother. For some reason I don't know, she thinks I ought to move to a larger place.'

'Oh, well – you know Mummy.' But secretly Heather agreed with her mother. Yardley had only two rooms, neither of them with much light or space. The front room had a good hearth and high ceilings, but it was cluttered with tables, chairs and the bookshelves. Behind a pair of

293

folding doors, curtained with heavy draperies, was the bedroom, and beyond it was an alcove containing a sink, icebox and gas burners.

'Why don't you come down to Labelle Street with me?' Heather said. 'It's sort of far away from the campus, of course.'

'That's it. I'd rather – ' He left his preference unstated as the draperies over the bedroom door were parted and a young man appeared between them. Heather stared and the young man looked at her while Yardley chuckled. 'You two know each other,' he said. 'Don't need any introduction from me.'

Both smiled hesitantly, and then the young man turned his head to look at an old photograph of a woman and two small girls that stood on a table in one corner of the room. At that moment Heather remembered his father. He had the same high forehead.

'Hello, Paul,' she said shyly. She searched his face quickly, and immediately forgot about his father. His hair was dark and wiry, his forearms corded with muscles. His eyes, large and brown, looked straight at her. With a flash of recognition she saw that he was poor and objectively conscious of it, but that he had managed to make poverty contribute something instead of taking away what he had.

As he smiled, lines cut his lean face about the corners of his mouth, making it quick with vitality. 'I remember you now,' he said simply. 'We used to have fun in Saint-Marc.'

'It seems a life-time ago.'

'Sixteen years.'

'I'd have had to count up all sorts of things to know it was sixteen years.'

Paul came forward into the room, set the bottle of beer he was carrying on a table and went back through the draperies for another glass. While he was out of the room Yardley and Heather looked at each other, Yardley still grinning, but they said nothing. Paul came back and poured two glasses of foaming ale. Yardley shook his head when Paul held one toward him, but Heather accepted it. And then Paul drew a straight-backed chair toward the hearth and sat facing them, shyness catching hold of him as the

294

immediate need for action ceased.

Heather broke the silence by an irrelevant comment. 'What are you studying now, Grampa?'

Yardley looked from one to the other. 'Greek. Paul's helping me.'

'*Greek?* Whatever for?'

Yardley grinned at Paul. 'Well, mostly because I couldn't take astronomy. Thet's what I wanted. After all, I'm a navigator and I've been looking at the stars in kind of a personal way most of my life. The professor I talked to looked me over and thought I was crazy, and then he said they didn't have any astronomy courses in the summer school. So I asked him what was the hardest thing a beginner could take up, and he said Greek, still not taking me seriously. I remembered that Cato started learning Greek when he was eighty-eight, so I thought maybe I wasn't too old to start at seventy-six. A man's brain goes to seed if he don't use it.'

'Grampa, you're wonderful!'

'Well, thet's a better word than what your mother's been calling me all these years. Preposterous, she says I am, and she got it from your grandmother. The first time your grandmother called me thet I looked it up in the dictionary. It don't apply to me at all. "Contrary to nature," Webster calls it.'

The strained atmosphere of the room had eased. Paul and Heather both laughed with Yardley, but beyond the sound of his voice they were each trying to adjust memories of themselves as children to the persons they now were. Heather's face was openly eager and friendly, Paul's more withdrawn.

'Where's Daffy tonight?' Yardley said.

'She's home playing double solitaire with Mummy.'

'My grandson-in-law still around?'

'No. He went down to the States on business. He wants to see you when he comes back. I think he really meant it.'

'You remember Daphne, Paul?'

'Yes, of course.' Affection showed openly on his face as he looked at the old man. Heather glanced at his half-profile. She liked his mouth. The lips were generous, somewhat full, but firmly set and controlled. His face reminded her of someone she felt she knew well; not the boy she had known years ago in Saint-Marc, but someone else. The resemblance haunted her for a second, then vanished as he took out a package of cigarettes and offered her one. As he lit it she noticed that his hands were hard, the fingers powerful, and the thumb of the left hand was oversize, as though it had been injured.

'Daphne's married?' he said.

'To a Limey,' Yardley replied. 'With an accent you'd pay good money to hear.'

'Seriously, Grampa,' Heather interrupted, 'you're not really learning Greek?'

'Well, I don't know how much I'm learning, but I'm well past the alphabet. I've certainly got a good tutor.'

'He doesn't know yet what he's let himself in for,' Paul said.

She looked at him with interest and wonder in her face. 'Where did you learn Greek?'

'The usual place – at school.'

Heather flushed.

'Paul's a graduate of the University of Montreal,' Yardley said, looking from one to the other of his guests. 'Put himself through, too. Don't you ever read the papers, Heather? Paul's a big-time hockey player.'

'Not big-time,' Paul said. 'Just medium.'

'You could have been big-time,' Yardley said.

Heather met Paul's eyes and her shyness returned. They glanced away from each other, Paul to look at Yardley and Heather to study the beer in her glass. 'I'd heard you were a hockey player,' she added hesitantly. 'Do you know Alan Farquhar? He played for McGill.'

Paul thought a moment. 'There are quite a few players around.'

'He said you were awful good.'

'Well, I ought to be. I played sixty-four games a season for four years. Besides, I was paid to be good.' He made the statement quite simply, as though he were stating facts no longer important to him. 'But I'm through with hockey now.'

'Didn't you like it?'

'I guess I must have.'

Heather was becoming more accustomed to him now.

His voice was pitched low, but there was an underlying ruggedness in it. She noticed again the corded muscles of his forearms and thought what a fine study they would make for a crayon sketch.

'Better get some more beer,' Yardley said. 'We'll not do any more Greek tonight.'

Heather got to her feet. 'Grampa! I'm sorry. I'm spoiling your evening. I'll go now.'

'Sit down, child,' he said. 'I don't want to work tonight. You're doing me a lot of good.'

Paul came back from the ice-box with a dark green bottle in one hand and a glass in the other. Heather watched him take the cap off the bottle and fill three glasses, gauging the bead to the exact level of the top. She was acutely aware that she had been an intimate companion of this strange man in her childhood. When Paul held out the third glass to Yardley, he took it and Paul went back to the chair by the hearth.

For over an hour the talk went on, Yardley and Heather doing most of it. From time to time Paul glanced at her. Without knowing what she was doing, Heather was relaxing the tension inside him. He felt it and it disturbed him, along with the memories she called up in his mind. Her presence seemed to be saying, 'Tell me and I'll understand, and that will be enough because I like you.' He looked at his shoes and sat very still, an ability he had inherited from his mother. It fooled people into thinking he was calm, and all the time the tension grew inside.

For a long time now it had been growing, all through his teens, and getting steadily tighter. It woke him nearly every morning except when he was physically exhausted after a hard game. It was more than a physical state of nerves; it was a quality of mind, breeding a kind of solitude of its own. Soldiers' books written on their experiences in the war talked about the same thing: not so much the tightness produced by near danger as the way they had to lock a door inside themselves to prevent what mattered from spilling out. You had a choice: you could let it spill out, you could pretend it wasn't there, or you could guard and protect it and suffer with it. If you did either of the first two things you were finished. You became an empty pail if you let it spill out, or what counted inside you dry-rotted if you pretended it wasn't there. In the latter case, you knew it yourself even if others didn't see it, and then you were finished.

He noticed the glasses were empty and quietly rose to refill them. The other two went on talking. This was not one of his times to say much. He liked to talk, but he had also acquired the faculty of sitting in on a conversation, saying nothing and yet appearing a full part of it.

Heather said, 'Truly, if I hear Huntly McQueen tell me I mustn't be hasty once more, I'll do something to him. When you were young, Grampa, did all the older people tell you not to be hasty?'

Paul thought: so you feel that way too! Then maybe you know what it is?

Yardley grinned. 'Most often they told me to get a move on.'

Heather said, 'Some time I'm going to do a cartoon of Huntly McQueen sitting on top of a boiling kettle on the summit of Mount Royal telling the water it hasn't been boiling long enough to be sure the heat's going to last. It's too bad there aren't any really good cartoonists of human nature in Canada.'

Paul thought: is that knowledge of hers real? Does she know it comes down to people every time? Does she realize that the whole trouble now is that everyone is trying to make the facts fit their feelings instead of making their knowledge fit the facts? The sheep call themselves idealists, and the wolves call themselves realists. Does she know anyone like Marius? Would she understand that Marius finished himself the moment he began blaming everyone else for what he lacked himself? In Marius's mind, those who don't agree with him are traitors. What his theories add up to is as crude as voodoo. But if they shut you out everywhere, what do they expect to get but voodoo? For four years the depression has been screaming at people to surrender and go into the woods together and beat the tom-tom. What has happened in Germany is only what happens to any single man when he lets what matters spill out. So now there's a gigantic involuntary conspiracy to make everyone surrender in the name of everyone else, in the name of some abstract idea. You're young

298

and they tell you it's dangerous to be in a hurry to live. You work for an education and they tell you it's superfluous. Gradually you begin to think of the whole world as 'they', and then you feel madness rise, and you want to say to hell with them, and let what matters spill out, and go into the woods and beat the tom-tom with the rest.

He watched Heather from under his long, dark lashes. He was as suspicious of words as Marius was suspicious of people. She was too natural and easy in her nature to know in her bones what her words really meant. Besides, she was a rich girl with background. How could she know?

Yardley concealed a yawn with the back of his hand and Heather got to her feet once more. 'I've stayed too long, Grampa. Forgive me.'

Yardley shook his head, his eyes twinkled for a moment, and then became serious as he studied her. 'Come a little oftener, Heather. And a little sooner. I've got so used to getting up at dawn thet ten o'clock to me is like past midnight to you.'

'I've wanted to come oftener, Grampa. Honestly I have. Daffy and I tried twice last week, but you weren't in either time. And since you insist on not having a telephone . . .'

Both Yardley and Paul stood watching her, then Paul went into the bedroom and returned with his coat and necktie. 'Funny thing,' Yardley was saying, 'up in Cape Breton I once talked over what must have been the first telephone there ever was. Up in Bell's place there. Thet was years ago. We used to sit on the wharf and talk about all sorts of things. He was a wonderful man. But I got a prejudice against telephones all the same. Maybe my ears are too big for them. Besides, look what they do to a business man in an office. Specially if he's got a lot of them.'

Paul adjusted his tie and waited for Heather to make the first move to the door.

'Why don't you ever come to see us?' she said to her grandfather. 'I'll call for you with the car, any day you say.'

'Well, I've been thinking that maybe after this year I'll ship out of here for good and go back home.'

Paul moved to the door and paused with his hand on the knob.

'But I thought you'd sold the farm,' Heather said.

299

'I mean Nova Scotia,' Yardley said. 'I bet you've forgotten thet's where a good quarter of you comes from. When a man's been born down there it stays his home no matter where he goes to live afterwards.'

'But I thought you didn't know anyone down there any more?'

Yardley smiled reflectively. 'Nobody knows me anywhere now, I guess. Not even in Saint-Marc. It's been changing out there ever since your mother's friend McQueen put thet factory into it. It's pretty near a good-sized town now, all filled up with unemployed and every other damn thing a town needs to feel itself important. I was telling Paul just before you came in that Polycarpe Drouin died last week. Remember him – the man thet kept the store?'

Heather shook her head.

'So you see, it don't matter where I live now and I guess I might as well go home. Paul's shipping out of here too.' Seeing her troubled expression, he added, 'Don't get the notion I got anything to complain of. Man, if anyone's had a life like mine and don't know he's lucky, he's one of God's fools.'

Remembering how her grandfather always felt uncomfortable in the Methuen house and how seldom she had come to see him when there had been time, Heather felt a blur of tears in her eyes. 'Are you going soon?' she said.

'Not right off. But I guess pretty soon.'

'Where will you live? In Halifax?' She had a moment's poignant sensation that she was no longer necessary to him, and that it was her own fault. And yet, of all people in the world, he understood her best.

'I haven't decided yet,' he said. 'There's five thousand miles of coastline around thet province, taking in all the bays and inlets. There's plenty to choose from.'

'You've never really liked living here, have you, Grampa?'

'Well, it's nothing for you to worry about if I didn't. Trouble with me is I never could take fellas like McQueen seriously, and if you want to get along in this town you've got to take everything seriously.' He grinned at her. 'I never even tried.'

Heather reached up and kissed his cheek. 'I'll see you soon,' she said. Paul held the door open and when she had gone out he made an appointment for the broken Greek lesson on the next night, and followed her.

Yardley stood still in the middle of the room, listening to the doors close behind them. After a time he went to the shelf and picked out a book, adjusted his glasses and moved the light over the shoulder of the chair where Heather had been sitting. It was the Loeb translation of Xenophon's *Anabasis* which Paul had brought from the college library. For nearly half an hour he tried to puzzle out the Greek with the help of the English on the right-hand page, then put the book away. He decided he was too old to learn another language, and that perhaps after all there was something ostentatious in a man like himself studying Greek if he could not learn it properly. It was partly a sense of humour that had made him start it anyway.

He turned off the light and went into the bedroom and got undressed. Thinking of Heather and Paul, he reflected with wonder and some indignation that each was the victim of the two racial legends within the country. It was as though the two sides of organized society had ganged up on them both to prevent them from becoming themselves. Neither had much respect for their elders, but they were quiet about it. Shrewd, in a way. He wondered what Heather would have been like if she had been born without money. Or if her mother had let her alone? On both sides, French and English, the older generation was trying to freeze the country and make it static. He supposed all older generations tried to do that, but it seemed worse here than any place else. Yet the country was changing. In spite of them all it was drawing together; but in a personal, individual way, and slowly, French and English getting to know each other as individuals in spite of the rival legends. And these young people no longer seemed naive; older than he was himself, Yardley thought sometimes. Paul would never be as simple as his father had been. He would see to it that his battle to become himself remained a private one. And Paul was the new Canada. All he needed was a job to prove it.

As he got into bed, Yardley wondered if he would live long enough to see the country merged into a whole. He smiled ruefully. Paul might, but not he. Yet, there were so many things he still wanted to see and do, there was so much left to be learned. He might have three years more, perhaps five or six. His health was still astonishing, and no matter how much he tried to tell himself that he would be eighty in four years, it didn't make sense. He didn't feel much different from the way he had at sixty. After all, his own father had lived to be ninety-two. With the same expectancy, that would give him sixteen years more, and a man could do quite a bit in that amount of time.

37

When Paul and Heather reached the street they found that the rain had stopped, but the atmosphere was as dense with mist as though a cloud had moved into the town. Miles away thunder growled like a distant bombardment. On University Street the nearest arc-lamp cut a long cone of blue light on the pavement.

'Could I drive you anywhere?' Heather said.

'No thanks. I only live on Durocher.'

'But you haven't a raincoat.'

He looked down at her with the darkness between them. 'All right, Heather.' It felt strange to be using her name. 'Maybe I'd better go with you.'

He opened the car door, she got in and slid under the wheel, and he followed. When she turned over the motor it failed to spark. She pulled the choke all the way out and ground the starter for nearly half a minute and the result was the same. Then she snapped off the ignition lock. 'Now I've flooded it,' she said.

They sat for a time in silence and she tried again. The motor still did not spark.

'I'll take a look at it,' he said. He got out and lifted the hood, struck a match and looked inside, then put both hands in, touching something and said, 'Now try it.'

She pressed the starter and the motor roared alive. She caught and held it while he lowered the hood, then quieted it down. He got inside and closed the door.

'So you know all about cars, too,' she said.

'It wasn't flooded. Your choke wire was disconnected. That was all.'

'I wouldn't know a choke wire from – from a magneto.'

'Why should you? You'd only put garage hands out of work if you did.'

She sat for a moment in the dark, touching the accelerator rhythmically with her toe. Then she turned to look at him. 'There's something the matter with that remark, Paul.'

He made no reply as he wiped his hands on his handkerchief. Unreasonably, she had touched off the anger inside him. Unemployment could be nothing but an academic problem to her, if she ever thought about it at all.

'It shouldn't be economically necessary for people to be helpless,' she said. 'I'm ashamed not to know anything about the car I drive.'

His flash of anger died out; it made no sense. When he spoke again his voice was quiet. 'I don't know much about engines myself but rule of thumb. I worked in a garage for two summers.'

She set the car in motion and drove up the hill, turned off into Prince Arthur and along to Durocher. They reached the house where he indicated he lived within a few minutes. She kept the motor running, but he made no move to get out of the car. Neither of them spoke. They merely sat in the dark car and stared through the rain-splashed windshield.

Then she broke the silence. 'You know Greek, and you understand cars, and you're a hockey player. It's a fascinating combination. What else have you been doing since we all went fishing together in Saint-Marc?'

'Trying to get along, mainly. Why not tell me what you've been doing yourself?'

She tested the play in the wheel. 'What people like me always do, I suppose. Nothing of any importance whatever.

He opened the door of the car and she checked him with another question. 'Paul – am I very different from what I used to be?'

He closed the door, fished in his pocket for a package of cigarettes, and found them. 'I don't know, Heather.' He offered her one, from habit calculating how many he had left. 'It's a long time since we used to be.'

303

'You see Grampa often, don't you?'

'Since he's been in Montreal. Once or twice I went out to Saint-Marc to see him, but I didn't manage it very often.' He added that Yardley had written to him regularly once a month for years. He still had two shoe-boxes full of his letters.

'Do you think he's as wonderful as I do?' Heather said.

'I don't even know if he's wonderful at all. He's just a natural man, so far as I can tell.' He added, as if to himself, 'Men like him aren't being made any more. I wish I knew why.'

She tried to see his profile, but could discern nothing more than a blur of dark hair and eyes. 'After you left Saint-Marc, you went to Frobisher, didn't you?'

'Yes. How did you know?'

'I seem to remember someone telling me.'

'Frobisher, and a few other kinds of education, made a pretty good job of bastardizing me.' When she made no reply he added, 'At least, according to my brother.'

Swimming vaguely out of her memory, a lean, haunted-looking man came back to Heather. He was in a maple grove, slinking away from Daphne, Paul and herself. Then Daphne mentioning him to her mother, telling her mother what he had said to Paul. And after that she somehow knew that the man had been arrested because of something her mother had told someone, and they had left Saint-Marc with her grandfather looking sad, and never returned. It still made her uncomfortable and rather ashamed to remember.

Paul gave a sudden, short laugh. 'No wonder you don't know what I'm talking about. After all, you're English. It's a tribal custom in Canada to be either English or French. But I'm neither one nor the other.'

'I can't see what difference it makes.'

It was his turn to hunt for her face in the dark.

'Why did you learn Greek, Paul? Nobody I know takes it any more.'

He opened the door to throw out the stub of his cigarette, took hers when she handed it to him and threw it out too, then shut the door and turned back to look at her. He took his time to answer, and then he said without emotion, 'I

304

thought for awhile I was going to study for the Church. Marius tried to make me believe I had a vocation. If you're French and reasonably good in your school work, there's nearly always someone who thinks you ought to be a priest.'

'But *you're* not French!' she said. 'You haven't the slightest trace of a French accent.'

'I haven't the slightest trace of an English accent when I speak French, either,' he said with irony.

This time Heather's flush was lost in the darkness. Paul went on without bitterness, 'My father wanted me to get a scientific education. That's why he sent me to Frobisher. Not that Frobisher was much in science, but he thought I'd have a better chance there.'

'And science didn't take?' Heather never let her own confusions interfere with her intense interest in other people. 'What kind of science?'

'Any kind. Sometimes I'm sorry it didn't take. I did my best with it at the university. God knows it's the only thing that counts these days. After all, science is the new theology. I'd still like to be a first-class physicist. Then I could stick to my own job and tell everyone to go to hell. Maybe I could even discover some new process that would send them there. The only place where science isn't God now is in Quebec. We're pretty old-fashioned.' He laughed shortly. 'But I was no good in maths. I'm a B.Sc., but it doesn't fool me into thinking I'm a scientist.'

Again he opened the car door and this time he got out. 'Thanks, Heather. I'd better not keep you any longer.'

'Grampa said you were leaving Montreal soon. When are you going?'

'I don't know. It depends on whether I get a job. He's written to some people he used to know in a shipping company. I hope I can get aboard a freighter.'

'That's wicked!'

'You don't have to feel uncomfortable about it,' he said quietly.

'But it is wicked. And it's stupid. You – an ordinary seaman!'

'It will be a job. I've had a good many doors closed in my face lately, Heather.'

'Is that what you want? To be a sailor?'

He looked both ways up and down the street. 'I certainly want to see the world,' he said when he turned back. 'And I suppose that's one way of seeing it.'

A woman passed, walking under an umbrella with her head bent. She almost bumped into him, and he stopped talking until she had merged with the misty darkness again. 'Anyway, I've got to get out of here. It's choking me.'

A breath of wind rustled the elm tree overhead, and a small shower of rain came down with a whisper.

'Paul – let's see each other again!' When he hesitated, she went on quickly, 'I'm trying to learn how to paint. Will you come down to my studio some day and tell me why I'm no good?'

He laughed suddenly in the darkness. 'I don't know much about painting. Where's your studio?'

'It's just a little room on Labelle Street. Here.' She opened her bag and took out a pencil and a card and wrote a number on it. 'Not tomorrow. I've got to do something with Mummy. But the next afternoon?'

'I've no job to keep me away, God knows!'

'You'll really come then? About three?'

'All right, Heather. Yes, I'd like to.'

She drove away, leaving him on the sidewalk. He stood watching the tail-light of the car recede down the street, then disappear around the corner. In the distance, far beyond the immediate darkness that surrounded him, thunder growled again, and another puff of wind sent another shower of rain whispering down from the leaves to the pavement.

38

Paul stood in the window of Heather's studio and looked across the street. The brick walls of the buildings opposite were a dull red. They looked very old and European with their painted doors flush with the pavement. The storm which had lasted for nearly thirty-six hours had cleared the air. Now sunlight sparkled on the roofs, made the leaves bright green and dappled the pavement with mauve shadows.

He turned back into the room to take the cup of tea Heather was offering him. She had a single electric plate in one corner, a small table, a few chairs, a couch covered with gay chintz against one wall, and a work table covered with painting paraphernalia. He liked the smell of oil and turpentine, the look of paint stains on the floor, the composition of the canvases stacked against another wall.

Heather curled up on the couch, her feet tucked against her hips, and Paul sat rather stiffy on one of the chairs. She drew his attention to the canvas resting on an easel. 'Now tell me the truth about that one,' she said.

Paul looked at it again, as he had been doing off and on ever since he had arrived. He hardly knew what to say, for he knew nothing about the technique of painting. He did know there was a lack in it. He glanced from the picture to the girl on the sofa. There was no lack in her. He saw the curved outlines of her thighs and the mounds of her breasts rising and falling beneath the plain linen frock. Her small nose gave her face a frank openness, and the frown she wore at the moment made her seem very young. Perhaps she was too much like Yardley to be an artist? He could imagine Yardley building a ship, but never painting a picture.

He got up and set his tea-cup on the table. 'I'm not very good at this sort of thing,' he said. 'I know why I like it better than why I don't.'

It was a pleasant scene, an oil landscape of a Laurentian road, and it was well drawn. It showed a sweep of country beyond Piedmont, and it indicated that she had enjoyed being there. But she had missed the vastness of such a scene, the sense of the cold wind stretching so many hundreds of miles to the north of it, through ice and tundra and desolation.

'Maybe it would have been better if I'd finished it with a rougher surface,' she said, still frowning. 'I used composition board on purpose. I was afraid it would look like an imitation of A. Y. Jackson if I made it too rugged. That's the whole trouble. The Laurentians have been painted too much and too well already. It would take a really great person to say anything new about them, don't you think?'

'I wouldn't know,' he said. 'I've not seen many Canadian paintings. Or any other kind, for that matter.'

'But Paul, you ought to! There's some really wonderful Canadian painting. It's the best expression in the arts that we have.'

'I'm full of gaps,' he said.

She uncurled herself from the couch and removed the canvas, replacing it with another. In this one, figures climbed the flight of wooden steps that led up to Pine Avenue from the head of Drummond Street on the face of the mountain. It also had a mat surface, and the design showed a smooth rhythm of hips and shoulders as the figures mounted the steps. Paul stood away from it, trying to estimate how much originality it contained, but he lacked the frame of reference to judge properly. Because it responded to an idea of his own, he liked the picture, and still he felt there was something wrong with it. It was intended to be grim. The women were poorly dressed, almost in uniform like convicts, and their individual features were removed.

He swung around and looked at her. 'Did you believe it, when you did it?' he said.

She waited a moment before she answered, then she said, 'I think so. It's meant to be stylized. I wanted it to be a particular study.' She indicated certain parts of the composition. 'I wanted those lines to compensate for these. . . . It was the uniformity of their movement I was after.'

'You certainly got that.'

She was disappointed. 'But I've missed something else?'

He pointed to a splash of colour in one corner. 'That's the only part of yourself I see in it. That's joyful. It's good.'

She removed the canvas and went back to the couch. Suddenly her laughter bubbled. 'Huntly McQueen said something to me the other night that sounded just the same. He said I thought it was my duty to be miserable on account of the unemployed.'

Paul sat down on the chair again and looked at her intently. 'From what I've heard of McQueen, I'd hate to agree with him, but he's got something all the same. You haven't lived a rotten life. People haven't been rotten to you. Why feel guilty about it?'

'I don't. You don't understand at all. People have been altogether too nice to me.'

308

He laughed shortly and she tossed her head. 'Don't despise me, Paul. It's not my fault if I've never had to worry where my next meal was coming from.'

He picked up the two tea-cups and refilled them, handed her one and sat down again. 'You know as well as I do there's no meaning in that kind of niceness,' she went on. 'It doesn't cost anything.'

Paul gave his attention to the tea in his cup, though he didn't drink it, and Heather pushed the hair back from her temples. Silence grew between them and a sense of disappointment weighed on her. After awhile she said, 'Do you suppose anything ever comes off the way you really want it?'

'I'm stubborn. I think sometimes it can.'

'If you really believe that, it's wonderful.'

He felt the tension rising inside. 'But it takes time. That's the trouble. God, it takes time!' He was sitting quite still, and his stillness was giving more force to his words than he realized. 'An artist's brain is like a distillery. A distillery takes years to produce anything but hooch.'

'And I don't take the time?'

'Nobody does any more.'

Her eyes twinkled at his seriousness. 'In other words, I should go through hell and suffer first, and then try to paint?'

Paul paid no attention to her amusement. 'Forget the suffering,' he said. 'There's nothing romantic about it.' He leaned forward. 'You're a happy person. You've got joy inside you. For God's sake don't be ashamed of it. The world is dying for the lack of it.'

Heather was surprised by the turn of his mind. All the students she had liked in college had been socialists, and she had accepted their point of view easily. She had never known anyone who was poor or worked with his hands, but she had taken it for granted that Paul would be bitter and even resent her because she had money. She wondered if he had never read Marx because he had been brought up a Catholic. She watched him as he pulled more of her pictures from the stack against the wall and studied them one by one. Some he dismissed with a glance, others he set on the easel and looked at from a distance. When he had gone through the lot he put them back and began to talk again. Heather

309

listened quietly without interrupting him. If she wanted to paint, he said, she must look inside herself. If the mess of the world had crawled inside, paint it, because then it was hers. But never pretend it was there when she knew damn well it wasn't. Did Mozart look out his window at the slums of Vienna when he wrote the E-Flat Symphony? She had one source to draw from, herself. An artist had nothing worth offering the world, absolutely nothing, except distilled parts of himself. If what she had was joyful, offer it, and to hell with the class struggle. No politician could be moved by art; all they were interested in was power.

He looked down at her. 'But it takes time,' he added. 'It's got to grow inside first.'

Heather felt abashed. She also felt somewhat annoyed because he dismissed so easily the ideas she had worked hard to acquire. But her annoyance disappeared in the face of her natural good humour, and she turned her thoughts to the personal problems he represented, problems she had never considered before. 'Thank you, Paul,' she said, and her face broke into a smile again. 'I could believe you've thought that out long before this afternoon. What have you tried to do – and found it took time?'

This was touching his privacy. Instead of answering he looked at her curled up on the sofa and he thought how much he'd like to stop talking and sit beside her and relax. He looked at his shoes instead. 'I want to write,' he said. 'I hate admitting it. Everyone wants to get into print these days.'

Heather knew he had exposed his vulnerability, and suddenly she knew how he felt about many things. The simple statement had removed a subtle barrier between them. He no longer baffled her and she no longer felt that he was making her an outsider. A wave of gratitude warmed her. When she spoke again her voice had an intimate naturalness like the child he remembered in Saint-Marc. 'How long do you think it will take you, Paul?'

'They don't let a surgeon loose on the public until he's been trained seven years and certified. A writer's job is just as difficult, technically.'

He felt he could sit still no longer, but he forced himself

310

to do so. He knew hardly anyone with whom he could discuss written books, much less writing. Sometimes it seemed just as well. There was so much self-flattery in the idea of writing books; it made him superstitiously afraid of telling anyone that this was what he wanted to do. His own voice had surprised him as he made the admission to a girl who was almost a stranger.

'It's not just that I want to be a writer,' he said. 'I told you the other night I wanted to be a physicist. I'd like to be an architect, too. Every time I really look at a building in Montreal it makes me cringe. The only buildings in this whole country that suit it are the barns. On the whole, I'd rather be an architect than anything else.'

'Why don't you, then?'

'I told you – I'm no good in maths. My mind doesn't work that way.'

The tension rose to his throat and he got up and began pacing the room. It was impossible to sit still any longer and watch her. She made him want to talk about himself, for a few minutes to break the solitude. To change the subject, he told her that he'd been given a berth on a ship that was sailing in a week from Halifax. He stood looking down at her, and then it overwhelmed him like a bursting wave, the quality he had always found in Yardley, the quality that had permitted his nature to unfold without being struck back, without spilling. She met his glance and held it, and after an appreciable moment she said, 'It seems such a waste. With your degree you could teach.'

He shook his head. 'I've got to get out of here. I've got to see something else. Besides, there aren't even teaching jobs now.'

'Are you very bitter?'

He began pacing again. 'Sometimes,' he said from the other end of the room. 'But bitterness has stopped making sense.'

'It ought to be easy for everyone to have a job and plenty of everything, but people like Huntly McQueen just sit on their tails and do nothing.'

He gave a short, derisive laugh, and then he turned and grinned at her.

'You think I'm childish, don't you?' she said.

'No. Only optimistic.'

'But I'm not at all!'

He continued to laugh at her. 'You're probably a socialist,' he said. 'Or think you are.'

'But Paul!' She flushed with anger. 'Why should you be against socialism? Why should a man like you agree with McQueen?'

'I'm not against it. And so far as I know, I don't agree with McQueen, either.'

'But you said . . .'

'I'm sorry, Heather. I don't want to argue with you.'

She looked away, baffled and hurt. Then she picked up the tea-cups and carried them to the paint-splashed sink and let water run into them.

'You make me want to talk about myself,' he said, still from the other end of the room. 'Like your grandfather. It's simply that . . .' He hesitated. 'I don't seem able to look at politics as if it were a science. I look at people instead.'

She kept her back turned to him. 'But doesn't the system produce the people?'

'It would be pleasant to think so. At least you could change a system.'

'But you don't think so?'

When he made no answer she turned around to look at him. His face was in shadow, his back to the window, and his hands were clenched in his pockets. She returned to the sofa and curled up on one end again, and when she motioned him back he dropped down onto the other end, his knees spread and his hands clenched between them.

'Maybe it's just the way I've lived,' he said. 'Maybe I'm wrong.'

'I asked you the other night what you'd been doing. Will you tell me now?'

Their eyes met. He looked away and back again. For a time he said nothing, then keeping his eyes on the floor he began talking, almost as though to himself. Ever since the family had moved from Saint-Marc, he told her, he had had no real home. Everything seemed to come back to that. He'd no place to go. At Frobisher it was all right, but then his father died and they were very poor. Gradually he found out what had ruined his father, mainly the fact that even when he had his land and was a member of parliament, he'd never found out how to get out of the strait-jacket of his own nature. No one deliberately trapped him. Whatever it was, it was inside himself.

He paused and Heather felt a warmth spreading within her, entering softly like a visitor afraid of being noticed. Paul needed her, and the knowledge was new and rewarding. But she sensed a peculiar dominance in him, and an increased awareness of his strangeness, and she wanted to hold her breath, to say nothing that would cause him to withdraw again.

'I can barely remember your father,' she said quietly.

He seemed not to hear her. But he added that his father was a remarkable man. He would have been completely at home in nineteenth-century Europe, and that made him about fifty years ahead of his time in Canada. Paul had found some of his papers, and only then was he able to appreciate the quality of his father's mind. But the set-up had been too much for him.

'I must be stupid,' Heather said, 'but I don't understand. What do you mean?'

'You aren't French. You aren't in a minority. You English have always been on top of the world. You don't know the feeling of the strait-jacket.'

'Do *you* feel in a strait-jacket?'

'In a couple of them. If you have no money you're always in one. But a French-Canadian is born in one. We're three million people against a whole continent.' He looked around at her, smiling to take the drama from his words. 'I don't intend to stay this way.'

His voice became low and slow as he picked his words carefully. He had found one of her pencils on the couch beside him and he began to twist it in his fingers, end for end, end for end.

'When I was a kid, in the old library in Saint-Marc, I used to read stories from the *Odyssey* in a book of my father's. I realized a long while later that the *Odyssey* is a universal story. It applies on all sorts of levels. Science and

313

war – and God knows what else – have uprooted us and the whole world is roaming. Its mind is roaming, Heather. Its mind is going mad trying to find a new place to live.' He got up suddenly and went back to walking the floor. 'It sounds melodramatic. But it's true. I feel it – right here in myself. I've been living in the waiting room of a railway station.'

In the sunlit air outside the window a hawker was calling fish for sale. The man's voice, roaring an atrocious French, reverberated along the street from house to house. Paul returned to the sofa, and when he sat down he looked into her grey eyes. Had he intruded himself on her? Had he lost anything? Searching her face, he knew it was all right. When she asked if he wanted to go back to Saint-Marc he smiled and said that not even Marius thought he could go home by going back to Saint-Marc.

He told her a little about Marius, not because she asked but because he wanted to tell her. Marius was married, with more children than he could afford to support. When the Tallard land was lost he was old enough to understand what he was losing, but his idea of going home was to be a successful politician. He'd nursed his hatred of the English so carefully it was now a pretty fine flower. He could speak perfect English, but if anyone addressed him in English he affected not to understand a word of it. What he really wanted, of course, was vengeance. The only thing he really loved was a crowd. He always believed they were with him, and for a few minutes they generally were, but ninety per cent of them would go off and vote Liberal no matter what he said. 'If Marius were a European he might get somewhere,' Paul said. 'But not here. There are others like him. They're the safety valves for the minority. That's all they are, and God help them, they never know it. When one fizzles out another comes to take his place.'

Suddenly talk seemed stupid. He turned and took her in his arms and his lips found hers. Desire broke within him like an explosion. He felt the firmness of her back against the palms of his hands, her breasts yielding against his chest, her hips with an involuntary movement surging in to him, and for a second their thighs and shoulders were almost one. Then she pushed him away and swung back out of reach.

314

'Please, no,' she said. But her face was filled with wonder. 'Not now. It's . . . it's not . . .'

He looked about the room as though it were a cage, then he crossed once more to the window and Heather watched the line of his head and back as he leaned out. She wondered at the queer, sudden sense of fear he had given her. She felt as if she had never been touched before.

'Let's get out of here,' he said. 'There's still a fine lot of day left outside.'

As he turned he saw her sitting upright smoothing her frock. Then she looked up and smiled, her wide lips making her whole face generous and open, bringing back to it a young gaiety without a trace of smouldering emotion. He felt overcome with gratitude because that was how she was.

'All right,' she said. 'Let's. My car's downstairs. Let's drive. Let's even go for a swim, if you'd like.'

'Where?'

'Well, I know a place in Dorval. It's the house of a friend of mine. They're away for a month. It's got a beach.'

'All right. You'll have to stop at my place to pick up my suit.'

They went hand in hand down to the car. On the way to Dorval they decided to get sandwiches and beer at a roadside stand, and by the time they reached Lac Saint-Louis the sun was moving low, but it was still warm. Heather parked her car in the driveway of a large house on the lake front and led Paul through a garden to a private beach. At one end of the beach stood a boathouse. Beside the door Heather lifted a stone and found a key under it, unlocked a padlock and led the way in. She pointed to a pair of canoes upturned on the floor. 'You undress here,' she said. 'I'll go upstairs.'

'This is communism,' he said, 'the way you use your friends' property. Didn't they even leave a dog here?'

'No dog,' she said, her voice coming through the floor above.

Paul removed his clothes and laid them over one of the canoes. He was in his swimming trunks and on the beach before Heather came down. They swam for a bit, but the water was uninvitingly muddy and it smelled flatly of reeds,

315

so they went back to the beach and lay and watched the sun ruddy-gold over the lake. From where they were it was difficult to realize that Lac Saint-Louis was part of the Saint Lawrence. Relaxed by the swim and the sun, Paul lay with his eyes half-closed as he watched a red-and-white lake boat ploughing upstream. She was ugly like all of them; the propeller foamed as she passed slowly up the channel marked by red cone-buoys; soon she would be in the Soulanges, passing up through a narrow canal with fields flush with her decks. Half a mile away her upper works would seem to be sliding miraculously over the surface of farms.

One summer he had worked on a lake boat and he knew the route. It was strange recalling it now. He could remember only a few moments out of the general routine, but they were so vivid he would never forget them. One was his first trip to the lakehead. A sunset burned through Fort William and Port Arthur and hurled gigantic shadows of the grain elevators forward on to the trembling waters of Thunder Bay. After the grain had been hosed into the ship, they moved away, and as he looked back another grain-ship was caught in the flaming corona of the sunset like a black speck in a huge eye, the waters of the lake extending from the sun in a nervous, desolate plain, radiating into the darker east. As night closed over the ship the colour had died, and nothing was left but the sounds of millions of shallow waves turning over in the darkness, an astringent wind keening blindly out of the empty forest to the north, the quick spatterings of lifeless fresh water whipped by the wind over the waist of the ship and wetting the deck. It was only a few days later, away from this sense of desolation in the heart of a continent, that they were passing so close to shore in eastern Ontario he could look into the windows of houses when the lights were on after dark. He had seen men reading in armchairs and children going to bed, and once a naked woman had thoughtfully combed her hair before a window, her lips open as though she were singing to herself. The ship passed and left her there with a peculiar immortality in his mind, strangely transfigured.

Paul's thoughts came back to the present. Next week he would step aboard another ship in Halifax, quite different from the lake boats. He had no idea where she was bound. It might be Europe or South America, maybe only New-foundland or New York. All he knew for certain was the fact that she was a four-thousand ton freighter of British registry called *Liverpool Battalion*.

Yardley had said the Limeys were all right to ship with. He had added there would most likely be a Nova Scotian aboard, and if he turned out to be the cook, all Paul would have to do would be to show his appreciation of the old province and the cook would be with him, hair and shoulders against any son-of-a-bitch of a squarehead that shaped up to him.

Paul smiled to himself. It was eighteen years since Yardley had been at sea. He wondered if the pictures he gave of it would turn out to be true, or merely a part of Yardley himself. Only once, in all the countless stories Yardley had told him, had there been anything like tragedy or grimness. So apparently things were what a man's mind made them. You had to find out for yourself.

'What are you thinking about?' Heather's voice came to him softly, floating into the red mist the sun made on his closed lids, floating in among the moving nets of darkness that crossed and recrossed the redness.

'Your grandfather. I was wondering if he was a liar.'

She chuckled softly and Paul added, 'The kind of a liar I am myself.'

Leaning on her elbow beside him, Heather bent and looked close at his face. His eyes were closed and his lips slightly parted. She wanted to touch his hair and find out how it felt, particularly where it was a shade lighter and softer on the top of his head. Already faint lines showed at the corners of his eyes. It was strange to have him so quiet now, after all the talking he had done in her studio. She guessed it was more natural for him to be silent than other-wise. All his strength seemed to be held in leash. There was a scar on his left thigh, another on his chest; when he rolled over on to his stomach another appeared on the lower part of his back. She traced it with her finger.

'How did you get that?'

'Hockey.'

317

'All of them?'

'Yes.'

'It's a good thing you stopped playing.'

'That's not why I stopped.'

'Why did you?'

'It took too much out of me.' He rolled over onto his back again. 'After every game I was like a limp rag. And before every game I'd have to tighten myself up. You're useless unless you start nervous.'

'You love hockey, don't you, Paul?'

'I used to.' He shaded his eyes with his hands, his face wrinkling from the low-hanging sun. 'Some winters I felt as if I lived in the Forum. I knew every scratch on the paint along the boards. There was one long gash near the south penalty box I used to touch before every game, and remember how it was made.'

'How was it?'

'Eddie Shore kicked his skate into it once when he was sore.'

'Were you superstitious?'

He looked at her from under nearly closed eyelids. 'I was about hockey.'

She touched the scar on his chest and then took her finger away quickly. 'How did you happen to do it – play hockey like that, I mean?'

'Because I needed the money.'

'No – I mean, why hockey and not something else?'

He thought a moment. 'I guess it was the first professional game I ever saw. I was sixteen. Joliat, Morenz and Boucher were playing. After that I was willing to slave eight hours a day training just on the chance of being half as good as they were.' He reached up and stroked her hair. 'But now I'm an old man, and at the best I was never even a quarter as good.'

'Now you're very, very serious.'

'I know. Much too much so.'

She grinned down at him, liking the rhythm of his moving fingers on her head, warm with the sense of him. Some men who seemed gentle enough were clumsy with their hands, but Paul whose body looked hard, was tender even through his finger-tips.

318

'I wonder if you'd like Daffy now,' she said. 'She's a natural blonde.'

'What makes you think I like blondes?'

'She's tall and willowy, and she has skin like honey in the sun.' When he made no reply she added, 'And her figure is luscious. It looks as if it would melt in a man's arms.'

'It must be a full-time job, being Daffy.'

Heather laughed. 'And she has a perfectly dreadful husband. I'm rather sorry for him, but not very much. Daphne says he rapes her.'

'Is that possible?'

'Don't be horrid!'

'I meant, is it a physically possible thing to do? I've often wondered.'

He sat up and they crouched on the sand looking at each other, the moment poised between them like a bubble, and then he jumped up and ran into the water, charging it so hard he tripped and went down with a splash. Heather watched him stroking out to deep water. He dove once and came up blowing, cruised a little, then crawled back and ran up the beach and dropped down on the warm earth beside her. She sat and looked at the rise and fall of his chest.

'I wish I knew more about hockey,' she said. 'Mother's never thought it quite proper for me to go to the Forum. Alan used to take me sometimes. I've never seen anything more beautiful; not a single ugly movement on the ice.

'Morenz, Joliat, Gagnon, Jackson, Smith – the whole lot of them are about the best artists this country ever turned out.'

'Hooley Smith sent a man into the boards almost on top of me once. Without thinking what I was doing I booed him for it.'

'That shows you didn't appreciate him. He did it beautifully and you never noticed.'

She got up and walked to the car and he watched her as she returned with the sandwiches and beer. She put the bottles at the edge of the water, making them secure with small stones. Then she came back and stood over him. 'Did you get into fights and get penalties?'

'Not if I could help it.'

'I wish I'd seen you play.'

'Too late now. My hockey days are definitely over.'

They ate the sandwiches and drank the beer while the long daylight of a northern summer evening moved almost imperceptibly to dusk. Heather changed, and when she came back dressed Paul went to put on his clothes. 'The thing about Montreal I've always disliked most,' Heather said when he reappeared, 'is the way you have to drive for hours to get into real country. I'd like to walk through an orchard on a night like this. I'd like to go up to that ridge behind Saint-Marc and look at the river. I'd like to go down to a seashore and listen to the waves break in the dark. I'd like most of all to stand on top of a real mountain, and look at farmhouses lying scattered in the valley below.'

Paul put the empty bottles back in the car and then he followed her into the boathouse to make sure they had left it as they found it. 'Come up here,' she called from the upper floor. When he joined her on the small porch that ran across the front, she said, 'It isn't very high, but it's better than nothing.'

They stood looking out over the lake, silent as a dark steel mirror before them. It smelled flat and reedy, but the lawn that ran back to the house was full of mysterious shadows in the half-light, and the smells could almost be forgotten. Land heat brooded over the water's edge. In the west across the lake the coloured light still lingered and splashed a few tired clouds as the day forgot itself.

'Not bad at all,' he said. He dropped on to a canvas swing and pulled her down beside him. 'It's a funny thing. Three days ago I didn't think there was a thing in Canada I'd miss when I went to sea, except your grandfather. Now there's something else. I believe I'm going to miss you.'

She touched the hand that held her against his shoulder. 'I wouldn't be surprised but what I'd miss you, too.'

After a moment he said, 'Do you think we know anything about each other, really? I feel as though I'd known you a long time.'

'Well, you have. You know I'm not afraid to put a worm on a fish-hook, for instance.'

But he wouldn't be teased. 'When two people are alone, matter-of-fact things aren't important.' He thought about his words. 'That doesn't make much sense. If I went home

320

with you and met your family and your friends – all sorts of inconsequential things would matter then, and the important things about us would almost disappear.'

'Would they? I don't think so. But I do know what you mean.'

He ruffled her hair over one ear. 'Have you ever been in love?'

'I'm not sure. I've thought I was several times. First when I was fifteen, in Lausanne. But I always managed to get over it. So it probably wasn't what other people mean when they talk about love.'

He looked into the darkness that was gathering like a visible cloud over the lake. Frogs croaked in the distance, and the beat of crickets and katydids in the foliage around the house was rhythmical and persistent.

'Don't be in love with anyone, Heather.'

She stirred against him, but he held her still. 'Never?'

'They'll only spoil it for you. It makes you helpless, and then they get you every time.'

'Who's they?'

'Sorry. That's a habit. In my street we grew up talking about "they." '

She sat so still she seemed hardly to breathe, looking into the dark nothingness over the lake. Far out on Dorval Island a few lights winked through the trees. She was twenty-three and only one man she had ever met had been able to touch her, to reach through her mind to the person within herself. It took only a moment to happen; after that it was a fact; there it was, and nothing he could say now would change it.

A mosquito settled on the soft skin of her lower arm and she brushed it off. Paul felt one on his left ear. He loosened his arm from about her shoulder, took a package of cigarettes from the pocket of his jacket where it was thrown over a chair, and lit one for her, then one for himself. As the match flared in the darkness she saw his eyes large and brown; then it was dark again, with two small glowing points of light rising and falling on the ends of the cigarettes.

'Have you known a lot of girls, Paul?'

He waited before he spoke. 'I've known one woman,' he said quietly. 'Though she never really grew up at all. She

321

was so natural with all men she made it hard for me to be natural with any other woman.'

'Do you know her still?'

'She's my mother.'

As the cigarettes burned out, more mosquitoes came at them, attacking out of the darkness loud and sudden in their ears. Paul made batting motions with his hands, and Heather got to her feet. 'Perhaps we'd better go,' she said. 'They've got an army on their side.'

He followed her into the boathouse, closing and barring the door behind them, and then they stood still in profound darkness. 'Where are you?' he said. 'Wait until I light a match.'

'I'm right here.'

He stepped forward and came against her. Then she was in his arms, her face straining up to his, her lips soft under his own. Everything else was blotted out. He had never known this before, this sense of life in a girl, the essence of life stirring under him in a darkness so deep there was nothing else there, except her rich, generous self a part of him.

His mind groped out of the darkness like a diver struggling to the surface. She moved away and he began to hunt through his pockets for a packet of matches. When he found it he struck one, and her face leaped out of the darkness, blurred in the half light. She was leaning against the wall, her hands behind her, wonder in her eyes. The match burned his fingers and he dropped it, set his heel on the glowing coal and the place was black again.

'Heather – don't! I . . . it's the one thing I'm afraid of.'

'Why, Paul?'

'Why? My God – don't underrate yourself.'

Her voice seemed far away. 'I'm not afraid. Not now.'

He tore off another match, but he didn't light it. 'Next week I'm going away. We may never see each other again. Let's remember that.'

Silence filled the darkness, and then she said softly, 'You've known other girls, haven't you?'

'Not many.' He sounded absurdly annoyed. 'Not as many as you think, probably.'

322

'When you kissed me – I knew.'

'Did you mind?'

'No. No, of course not.'

He lit another match and held it high and she went ahead of him down the stairs. He lit another, and the dim outline of the canoes sprawled like mammal-fish in the damp, stuffy air. When they opened the door and stepped on to the lawn the night air seemed almost bright compared to the nothingness inside the boathouse. They stood still, side by side, looking up to a sky swimming with stars.

'I'll hate it when you go away,' she said.

He took her hand. It seemed small and soft in his own, but she pulled it loose and stepped away from him.

'You're the only person in the world who doesn't make me feel alone,' she said. Her senses seemed to bruise themselves against his silence. 'You don't have to be a French-Canadian to be born in a strait-jacket. Every girl's born in one, unless you're a girl like Daffy.'

She started walking over the turf toward the car. Though he made no sound, she knew he was close behind. 'I'm such a damned little fool!' she said.

His hand was on her waist and he drew her to him gently. 'We don't have to pretend with each other, Heather. I've worn out a lot of shoes looking for jobs in the past year. I don't have to remind you of that.'

'It's not fair. It's not fair!'

'Facts and fairness have nothing to do with each other. If it weren't for all the doors that have closed in my face, I'd be able to say a lot of things to you now . . . that I can't.'

Impatience dropped from her as she felt the strength and the support of his arms. The dark was a wall between them. What was love anyway, but a knowledge that you were not alone, with desire added? And there was no doubt about the desire. Paul knew he would wake up for months thinking about her, remembering her fresh resiliency.

They walked on to the car, gravel crunching under their feet as they turned into the drive.

'How long will you be at sea?' she said.

'A year. Perhaps two or three. I don't know.'

'Anything could happen in that time.'

'Anything – to both of us.' He looked up and saw the long arm of the Dipper overhead, reaching toward the city. There was a flaring haze on the sky in the direction it pointed, city lights shining into moist air.

On the road back to town she drove as fast as the curves would allow. Trees lurched past with long swishing sighs, and beyond them starlight was reflected feebly in the water. When they turned from the lakeshore into Montreal West the road was straighter, and when they passed through Westmount they could see a bowling green soft and glowing under spotlights, its lawn as smooth as a billiard cloth. The lights gleamed on the bald heads of elderly, flanneled men and the bowls rolled slumbrously forward over the grass. It was quaint and dignified and very English.

In a moment it was behind them and the gigantic Sulpician seminary was on their left, with hundreds of incipient priests locked behind its elm trees and stone walls. Then Guy Street, rich Protestant churches, McGill campus, and the great electric cross blazing on the butt of Mount Royal. Finally they reached the shabby, rundown street where he lived. On the entire run from Dorval they had spoken not a word.

Paul got out of the car when it stopped and closed the door. Then he walked around to stand at the door on her side. He took one small hand from the wheel and held it in both his own. 'Will you write to me sometimes? I'll want to know how you are, and what you're doing.'

'There won't be much to tell.'

'Don't say things like that. It's you – not the things you do.' He looked at her hand a moment, then he kissed it. 'You can always reach me through the shipping company in Halifax.'

She put her hand back on the wheel and released the clutch. 'Have fun, darling,' she said. 'And take care of yourself.'

As the car moved off she could see him in the rear-view mirror, standing there in the street looking after her. She turned the corner and lost sight of him. Her mind was suddenly blank with exhaustion, and she was conscious of nothing but her lips. They felt tired as her mind was tired, almost bruised from his, but exultantly alive.

When she had put the car in the garage and entered the house she saw Daphne reading under a lamp in the library. She stopped at the door and looked in.

'Well!' her sister said. 'Mummy's been worried to death. She's been calling everybody in town to find out where you were.' She stared at Heather and then she smiled broadly. 'Who was he?'

Heather looked at her sister as though she had never seen her before and went upstairs.

39

A week later Paul stood on the deck of the *Liverpool Battalion* and watched the docks of Halifax slip by as the vessel headed out to sea. With the ship under way, he had nothing to do. While they were waiting for the pilot to come aboard they had made the decks clean, battened the hatches and coiled every rope in its place.

The old town looked rich with a picturesque and individual shabbiness as they passed down the harbour. Each of the docks had its own smell; fishmeal from one, the dusty smell of feed from another, the stink of dried cod from a third, the mixed smell of brine and bilges and seaweed from all of them. The strong, raw odours were all new to him, different from any smells on inland water. As he looked up at the Citadel above the town he saw the Jack flutter on the signal mast and come slowly down on its halliard, waving gently in the evening breeze. He could hear the faint and random blasts of motor horns in the lower streets; Halifax going on with its routine independent of the coming and going of ships.

They passed between the terminal docks and the quiet bowl of George's Island, and then the outer harbour came into view, the plain of water spreading far away to the point where the sea and sky met in a soft shade of mauve, mysterious, cool, infinite. Behind the town the sun had set in flames half an hour ago, and now the sky was yellow as a daffodil and shining. A single shredded cloud ribbed with crimson sailed aloofly out of its yellow pool toward the sea.

A strange feeling of mingled excitement and resignation filled Paul as he watched the sunset, the sky, the harbour and the town. He let the sensations fall into his mind like rain. How long would it be? How many ships would he travel on before he came back again? The strangeness of everything made him feel numb.

A group of deckhands was standing forward in the waist of the ship. They all had the unconscious, reaction-soaked appearance of men who knew the rules so well they never thought about them. He knew they were sizing him up.

Tomorrow it would be all right, he would have no trouble with them, for he knew what they were like. He understood how to get along with men like that, to kill the difference between himself and them. He had been doing it all his life, and it was not so hard as it seemed.

The ship passed the breakwater, then slid past the park on the toe of the town, past the lighthouse on Meagher's Beach where the beam was already circling. The bluff of York Redoubt, shaggy with trees, loomed on the starboard beam, and then the shoreline dropped lower toward tawny rocks where groundswells broke perpetually with hoarse, intermittent surges. This was Yardley's home, Paul thought, Nova Scotia – where one-quarter of Heather had originated. It was as old as Quebec, but it seemed infinitely younger, without the Quebec sadness and the solemnity of the Catholic parishes. Nova Scotia was sea-washed and rain-washed, cooled by fog, thrust so far away from the continent into the ocean that it seemed a separate country.

Well, that was one way of looking at it. Glancing at the crewmen in the waist, Paul knew he could get another line from them. A hell of a place, they'd call it, cold enough to freeze your ass in winter and in summer nothing but rain and fog; no lights, no bars, the whores no good, and no place to take a girl you pick up but the bushes in the park. And just when you were all set, the rain generally came.

He wanted to go astern and lean over the taffrail, but he wasn't sure if it was permitted while the ship was at sea. The cook passed him on the way to the galley and Paul remembered what Yardley had said about finding a Nova Scotian on board. He'd been right; the cook was from Country

Harbour in Guysborough County, a square man with hairy arms like tree branches and a straight, silent mouth; the only Nova Scotian aboard.

Darkness fell as they cleared the harbour, and at the land's edge the sea doubled all the light that lingered in the sky, to hoard it along the surface long after the sun had passed into the interior of the land. Paul breathed deeply. For this one moment he could be himself, the man Heather had found and seen, for there was no one to watch his face and note the difference to use against him later.

He watched Thrum Cap slip by on the port side, a soundless fringe of foam white against its brown base. Some of the following gulls swooped away from the ship and went in to the shore in long glides. The ship lifted hard to the first groundswell, bit the sea, and with a rush of water under the bows gave a faint groan, and then a humming wind started in the shrouds. They passed beyond the farthest tip of McNab's Island, the air got suddenly colder, and looking up the coast of Nova Scotia, Paul saw a crescent of lights flaring out of continental darkness into the sea, steady beacons on every promontory. He leaned over the rail and felt the beat of the propellers under his feet, leaned far over and saw the wake boiling away from the stern, and then he stood upright again to watch the lights recede slowly over the horizon.

Part Four 1939

40

Athens was calm in the morning sun, the cone of Lykabettus
just visible over the low roofs of the Place de la Constitution,
the marble-topped tables at the sidewalk cafés mostly empty,
some men in dark suits buying newspapers from the corner
kiosk, soft-eyed Greek women passing, moving with liquid
ease in the warm morning, Levantine eyes calm with instinctive knowledge, like wells receiving light and retaining it.

Paul left the American Express office with two letters in
his pocket, one from Kathleen, the other from Heather. He
walked around the corner into the square, sat at a table and
ordered coffee. While he waited he brushed someone else's
crumbs from the table top and then sat still. He was so accustomed to being alone in crowded places that anonymous
people passing were a part of his mind, almost a frame in
which he himself became visible. In the five years since
leaving Canada he had changed considerably. His black
hair, once low on his temples, had receded, making his forehead seem broader. Although he was still a year under
thirty, his hair was foxed with grey barely visible against
its blackness. He seemed more solid through the chest and
shoulders, less quick in his movements. His hands on the
table were as strong as those of a labourer, but their skin
was cared for. He was wearing a Harris tweed jacket with
a white handkerchief in the breast pocket, grey flannel
trousers and brown brogue shoes. To a European he looked
English, but an Englishman would probably put him down
as an American.

He slit the envelope from Pittsburgh and pulled out his
mother's letter. Kathleen was keeping well. A smile touched
his mouth as he read her opening words; all her letters began

with the same statement. She went on to say that Henry had bought a new car with a good radio because last fall at the time of the Munich crisis they had been driving down to St. Louis in the old car and for several days they had missed hearing Kaltenborn so it was just about as easy to buy a new car with a radio as to buy a radio and have it installed in the old one. Next year Henry expected to make at least eight thousand dollars and then they were going to move again, to a better house. She wished Paul would be sensible and come home. There was no need for him to live in Europe and meet peculiar people. She was worried about him whenever she wondered where he was. She sent him all her love.

Paul raised his eyes and looked over the roofs to the cone of Lykabettus. It glowed in the sun against a deep azure sky. It was early May here in Athens but it was like June in Canada. Homesickness stirred in him like sexual desire, followed by a quick lift of excitement. After nearly five years, he was going home. Within a month or six weeks he'd be there. If he could work his way back he would; if not, there was enough money left to pay his passage on a slow boat.

The waiter came with the coffee and a glass of water. Paul put Kathleen's letter in one pocket as he reached in another for a few drachmas to pay the man. The waiter slipped away and he was alone again. A woman passed slowly: black hair and white skin, a soft body indolently alive at the hips. Two boys followed her, arguing vehemently.

Paul drank his coffee in three gulps. It was Turkish, brewed thick and syrupy, with heavy sediment in the bottom of the cup. He washed it down with the water that tasted flat with chlorine. Then he picked up Heather's letter and looked at it. There was an American stamp in the corner, a New York postmark, and the address was written in the tidy, imaginative handwriting he would know anywhere as Heather's. He broke it open and held the folded pages in his hand. For nearly five years he had been receiving her letters in strange cities and towns she had never seen, and because she was not afraid to talk to him on paper, he felt he knew her far better now than when he had left Canada. He could still desire her, but how much of the desire was the idea and how much memory he could seldom be sure, for the idea had been created by himself and it was pregnant with the same kind of life and reality he had put into the novel he had been writing for the past year.

The white sheets were unfolded in his hands and he began to read, but after seeing the words *Very dear Paul* he found himself looking over the roofs to Lykabettus again. How much had she changed in five years? It was a very long time at their age. They had both run away from Montreal for their own reasons, but in the simplest of terms it was to escape the strait-jacket of their backgrounds. Had she succeeded? Or did she feel as rootless in New York as he felt in Greece? Had she ever been as homesick as he was now? In spite of all the things he had done and the places he had seen, he was essentially unchanged: a Canadian, half French and half English, still trying to be himself and stand on his own feet. Through five years, that was what he had always been.

Between the summer of 1934 and the summer of 1937 Paul had been at sea almost continuously. For a year the *Liverpool Battalion* plied regularly along the American coastal route between Newfoundland and Trinidad. She carried salt cod, hardware, flour, salted beef and pork, along with various detailed supplies and consignments, from St. John's and Halifax down to the West Indies. She returned with sugar, molasses, rum for the government liquor stores, bananas, limes, lemons and pineapples. For awhile Paul worked as an ordinary seaman. He swabbed, chipped, painted, mended gear and occasionally worked with gangs under the bosun or the second mate making minor shifts in the stowing of cargoes in the hold. He passed through his first Bermuda hurricane just before Christmas in 1934. In February of the next year they ran into a gale in below-zero weather that followed all the way from Cape Race to Cape Sambro, and when they finally came into Halifax the *Liverpool Battalion* looked like a floating blanc-mange.

Toward the end of 1935 the ship was recalled to England. Paul went with her, and so missed Yardley when the old man returned to Halifax to live, in mid-autumn of that year.

In Liverpool the ship was laid up for nearly two months for a refit, and Paul rented a room in a cheap hotel and spent the time writing short stories. By the time the ship was ready to sail again he had half a dozen finished. They were all based on sea-life with accurate detail and great care in the descriptions, but the plots were largely formula. The day before they sailed he sent them off to an agent he had heard about in New York and several months later when they called at Liverpool again he discovered that four of them had been sold to American magazines.

Paul was a quartermaster now, and the holds of the *Liverpool Battalion* were always full. From the movements of the ship and the cargoes she carried it was not difficult to see that the postwar slump had developed into a prewar boom. From Stockholm she carried Bofors guns to Luebeck. From Bremen she took small arms to Spain. Once in Liverpool Paul saw a deckhand spit over the side when drums of high-octane gasoline were hoisted aboard on a consignment to Genoa. Later in Barcelona they were held up a week; the Spanish civil war had just broken out and there were no stevedores immediately available to discharge the cargo.

Paul remained with the ship into 1937, writing whenever he found time and saving his money. At first his work had seemed just a job and a job was something he had to have. Then he realized that he had attained a certain kind of freedom. And with the freedom he had found a way to understand the wounding soreness that his earlier life had left with him. As the artificial pulling of the two races within him ceased, the sediment settled in his mind.

By the summer of 1937 he had saved two thousand dollars, and then he left the ship for good. During the previous winter he had applied for a teaching job in a school in Canada, but he was informed that he must have a more advanced degree to qualify with the other available teachers on the market. It was then that he remembered his father's intention to send him one day to the Sorbonne, or even to Oxford or Cambridge.

Recalling the old house in Saint-Marc and his father's library, in a life separated from the present by what seemed a desert of years, Paul suddenly revolted against the sweaty

331

kind of ugliness that had surrounded him for so long. He wanted to relax, he longed to live again in decent surroundings. He told himself that he had a right to go to the Sorbonne or Oxford if he wished, and then he realized that he had enough money of his own for a year's fees if he wanted to use it that way. His degree from the University of Montreal would admit him to either university. After careful consideration he decided on Oxford because he felt that some formal study in English literature would help his writing. So in October, 1937, he was admitted to the university.

After sixteen years of being homeless, of working with harvest stiffs, hockey players and sailors, being in Oxford was like opening a door and finding himself in a room containing all the things he had tried to create out of his imagination from books. It was the first leisure he had known since his childhood; leisure to study and think without having to earn a living at the same time. Once a week he went to a tutor in Oriel, and because this was the only college in which he had any work, he came to think of it as his own.

He liked to look out his tutor's window across the front quad of Oriel to the tower of Merton which showed above the long dark roof. All through that winter he found himself waiting for the moment when the lights went on in the college hall and the coats-of-arms in the stained-glass windows began to glow like jewels in the dusk. On foggy nights he liked to stand by the porter's lodge to watch dons and undergraduates drift in their gowns across the quad and up the steps under the portico into the hall. And always he listened for the cadence of St. Mary's chime which preceded every hour with a full garland of sound. Nowhere else had he ever heard a bell note so pure, not even in Italy; it sang in over the tiles and chimney pots and through the windows, and the moment it ceased all the bells in Oxford began striking the hour in different keys.

During that year in Oxford Paul worked on a B.Litt., came to like his tutor better than any man he had ever known except Yardley, drank beer in the pubs, read dozens of books he had wanted to read for years, refused an invitation to play ice-hockey for the university, and laid the groundwork for the novel he felt had been stirring inside him since he could remember.

It was the novel which had brought him to Greece. Living was cheap there, and his tutor at Oriel had found a part-time job for him in Sparta with the Museum kept by the British Association. As a result of the past ten months, he had four hundred pages of completed manuscript to show for his divided labours. And now he was in Athens on his way home.

He might have stayed longer if he had seen his way to finishing the book, but suddenly it had stopped moving and he was haunted by a sense of failure. Homesickness had moved in on him and there was nothing to do but put the book aside and find a ship that would take him home. The title of his book held its meaning clear, *Young Man of 1933*. The year of Hitler's rise, a young man caught between the old war that was history and the new one whose coming was so certain it made the present look like the past even before it had been lived through. The idea had gripped him like iron at the outset. Why it had suddenly begun to grow foggy he didn't know.

He picked up Heather's letter and focused his eyes on her lines of writing again. 'You never knew my Grandfather Methuen, did you? He died today. He was eighty-two. I can't help feeling as though a good portion of Montreal had died with him. When I was little I was made to believe the whole city revolved around his whims. Now I know it will certainly go on without him, but something that made it stuffy and even rather funny will be gone. I'm going home on the night train and I can't suppose I'll come back. But don't you imagine that maybe it won't be so bad having to live there again after having once been able to get away? What do you think, Paul? Mummy and I will be all alone in that ark of a house on the side of the mountain. I can't very well leave her alone now. Poor Mummy, how she's worked to be at home in that house! Now it's all hers, gargoyles, conservatory and all!'

Paul stopped reading and looked again at the postmark

on the envelope, trying to think how many days it had been in transit. By now Heather would be living in Montreal again. And how much of New York would she have taken back with her? She had spent two years at Columbia taking an M.A. in the history of art. For a year she had taught in a preparatory school. During the past year she had been working in a museum. The coincidence of their most recent jobs had amused them both, in spite of the different nature of their occupations in their two museums as far apart as Sparta and New York.

He went on reading. 'Did you know Grampa Yardley was very ill last winter? I can't remember whether or not I've told you. I wanted awfully to see him, but New York can seem such a long distance from every place else once you're in it. Now I'm going down to Halifax after everything is settled in Montreal and I'll try to get Mummy to drive down with me. It should do her good. You probably know from Grampa's letters to you how many friends he's made down there, but he's very frail now and he lives all alone in one room. Suddenly I feel as though I can hardly wait to see him. So many old people, especially the decent ones, are slipping off one by one while there's still time. Who'll be left? Huntly McQueen, I suppose. What is it about men like him? Men his age? They seem anaesthetized against the world we're living in. In your novel, do you think you can really drive it through their heads how people like us feel? They hold on to the ball and won't pass it to one of us, and yet they don't seem to have the least idea what goal they're playing for! I don't suppose they think we do, either. Please come home soon, Paul. I wish you would. Now that I'm going back to Montreal I want you there, too. I can even wish you were here in New York right now. There's a quarter moon and the park is filled with young green things and in Rockefeller Center they've set out blue hyacinths and yellow forsythia. I keep wondering how you'd like that favourite spot of mine in all New York. If you said the R.C.A. Building couldn't equal the Parthenon I'd try to tell you how wrong you were. Whenever I get bogged down in despair about the States (isn't it funny how all Canadians do that, as if the Americans cared what we felt about them) I walk down Fifth Avenue and look up at that beautiful shaft and then I know that a country able to build such a structure can do anything....Look after yourself, my dear. And come home soon!'

Paul leaned back in his chair and the familiar presence of solitude was close. People sauntered past or sat at tables in the sun. A loudspeaker in the square was broadcasting Danube waltzes. An itinerant bootblack wanted to shine his shoes. Two girls with almond eyes passed, laughing vividly, and his eyes followed them. After a moment he got up and walked across to a kiosk on the square, bought a postcard and returned to his table. He wrote Heather a short note saying that he was leaving for Canada as soon as possible and she might write to him next at Halifax. He stamped the card and mailed it, then sat down once more in the sunshine.

Heather wished he were in New York. But that was many days ago. He wished she were here in Athens. He'd like to take her to dinner at the Grande-Bretagne, and afterwards they would sip wine until dark, and then before the moon was up they would drive to the Akropolis in an open carriage and he would lead her up through the Propylaea, then up the time-smoothed steps to the white floor of the Parthenon itself. The moon would rise enormous and round over Hymettus tonight. They would see Parnes, Pentelikon, Lykabettus, Aegelos and Salamis framed by successive pairs of columns; they would listen to the dog that howled at the moon somewhere among the broken stones and monuments behind the temple; and moonlight would touch the caryatids. Heather had a body like theirs; not the greyhound figure made popular by advertising models. Her lines were female and fruitful in the memory. They would stand touching each other while they looked across the dark plain where the Long Walls had run down to Piraeus. They would see the moonlight flickering along the coastal waters from Salamis down to Sunium, and he would tell her how in the old days, when the triremes rounded the cape on their way home, the quartermasters seeing the first glint of sunlight from the spear of Athene on the Akropolis had raised their arms to salute the goddess.

He got up and paid his bill, then strolled across the square toward the Grande-Bretagne. He had three days to

335

kill in Athens and there was nothing to do but walk around the city. Alone, and hungry for a girl he could love, there was no savour in it for him now. He went into the hotel and passed through to the bar.

The place had been invaded by passengers from a Strength-through-Joy ship which was anchored at Phaleron, and the corridors, lobby and bar thundered with their conversation. Paul found an empty stool at the corner of the bar, ordered a beer and observed the room. The young Germans lounged easily with their collars open, occasionally running their hands through their hair, and sunburn made their teeth seem brilliant when they smiled. They had a way of lifting their chins and laughing suddenly at each other. There were also a few Greeks at the bar, two French women who seemed to be residents of the hotel sitting at a side table, and an English couple in one corner. But the Germans dominated the room and their massed presence had already caused a mixture of fear, contempt and hostility in the others. With few exceptions, they were not particularly rugged. What Paul noted about them was their self-confidence. They knew they were hated here, that they had deliberately created the hatred, and they were enjoying it. He felt an unpleasant excitement grow along his nerves as he sat sipping his drink. If a fight started, he knew he was the only man in the room who could match any one of them.

Paul's attention was caught by a woman in her late thirties, evidently French, sitting near the bar smiling at a German who shared the table with her. Her face was soft-skinned and delicate, with large brown eyes and a small mouth. She was quite short, with flesh somewhat plump over very small bones, and her dress had been carefully designed by a couturier in the Place Vendôme to exaggerate the sensuous fragility of her body. Paul watched her. Hundreds of thousands of francs had been spent on her education and upkeep, and her accent as she spoke German was obviously Parisian. She wore a wedding-ring on her left hand, together with a square-cut diamond as large as her thumb-nail. She could not have known the German at her table more than three hours, but already her manner indicated an unspoken intimacy. He was the biggest and crudest man in the room, and many years her junior. His bulging body made him look like a cartoon of a Nazi; his head was shaved except for a stiff brush of hair in front and he had the hands of a prize-fighter. Once he turned to wink at a group of friends at another table and they raised their glasses to him. Then his right hand, thick, square and with broken nails, closed over the woman's fingers and pressed. An expression of masked pain touched her face, naked and erotic. Her eyes showed a peculiar mixture of gratitude, encouragement and fear, and the German seemed puzzled by it, his confusion at war with his eagerness to get her out of the bar and possess her as quickly as possible. He spoke to her again. She shook her head. He leaned back, baffled, and ran his hand over his shaved head, then remembered that he was thirsty.

'Bier?' he said to her.

Paul heard her answer. 'Was du willst.'

The German smashed his hand down so hard the table jumped. 'Bier!' he shouted.

Paul paid for his drink and left the bar. He was too restless to sit still any longer and had to keep moving. But now that he was on the street again, Athens seemed more nearly empty than ever. He walked up to the Akropolis, but the scene had nothing to give him. About four o'clock he returned to the lower streets and tried to dull the ache in his mind by reading week-old English and French papers bought at a corner kiosk. He sat in the same restaurant in the Place de la Constitution in which he had read his mail that morning. The afternoon wore on and the city surrounded him like a giant presence of loneliness. It was no new feeling; most of his life he had known it, and now it was recurring again like a periodic disease. This loneliness of all large cities, the solitary man reading his newsprint, the instinctive hope that there is new life just around the corner if you go to it, but around the corner always the same emptiness, the urgency which makes you want to prowl always a street further; and through everything, beating into the mind like a tom-tom, the shuffle of other people's shoe-leather counterfeiting the motion of life. He wondered if Heather had ever felt as he did now. Two

337

solitudes in the infinite waste of loneliness under the sun. People kept passing the sidewalk café, girls in light dresses, mature women surprisingly smart in Parisian fashion, with smooth, cultivated skins and quiet knowledge, a sense of sex accompanying them like a subtle perfume, instilling into his mind the belief that they were pregnant with a sexual learning he was too immature to understand. At the table next his own a woman sat smoking a long cigarette as she toyed with the stem of her wine-glass. He exchanged a glance and knew he could have her if he wished. Another time he might have let the routine take its course, but not now. He wasn't equal to that kind of loneliness today.

He left the café and wandered aimlessly a while longer, then stopped to eat supper in a small restaurant filled with workmen and smelling of cheap tobacco and goat's flesh frying in grease. He ordered what the menu offered, drank two glasses of vile-tasting resin wine and went out into the streets again.

His novel began to press forward in his mind. For awhile he tried to keep it back, not to think about it, but it was useless. He had lived with it too intensely for too long. It was like an obbligato to everything else he thought or did. He remembered the team of Germans at the Grande-Bretagne, the soft face of the Frenchwoman pleading silently with the German to degrade her. Drumbeats began to hammer in his head. The young man of 1933, the individual into which he had tried desperately to breathe life. 1933 – Hitler's year – when the *danse macabre* had burst out of the unconscious of so many millions, out of the alleys and side-streets into the open until it had become the world's way of life.

Young man of 1933 – the year when farmers had begun to plough under the cotton, to process the hogs, to burn the wheat, when stevedores under the spreading arms of Christ in Rio de Janeiro had dumped coffee into the sea, while in Russia the famine killed off three million people and in the west, in the lands of the Greek heritage, old men took water and washed their hands.

Without thinking how he had got there, Paul found himself back in his room at the hotel. He went to the window, opened it and leaned out. Young man of 1933 – the year the brazen cracking voice of Adolf Hitler invoked the new god while the sheep looked up. Eighty million sheep, remembering they were Goths. While in the west the old men lingered, piteous as doves in every parliament and stock exchange, naked to everyone's eyes and knowledge as they washed their hands.

And behind Hitler, what? The machine. The magic worthy of every worship, mankind reborn for the service of efficiency, the still small voice of God the Father no longer audible through the stroke of the connecting rod, the suave omnipotent gesture of the hydraulic press, the planetary rumble of the conveyor belt, the visions of things to come – whole cities abolished in single nights, populations uplifted according to plan, cloudy blueprints of engineers, millions calling for help and millions for war, millions for peace and millions for suicide, and the grandeur and the efficiency and the solitude.

Below Paul lay the city street. Athens could be London, Rome, New York, Paris, Berlin or any other great city. This was where it had started. In the city. Any city. The flop-houses of Vienna, the Babel of the Holy Roman Empire, emptiness dressed in baroque, the breaking of a dried-out heart sung through the nose in the Danube Waltz, the new city-hatred (contempt for all things but cleverness) of the slum man for the Jew, the owner for the worker, the worker for his fear of himself, the bourgeois for his own thoughts in the dark, the hatred of them all for the old men washing their hands.

In every city the same masses swarmed. Could any man write a novel about masses? The young man of 1933, together with all the individual characters Paul had tried to create, grew pallid and unreal in his imagination beside the sense of the swarming masses heard three stories below in the shuffling feet of the crowd. For long minutes he stood at the window. To make a novel out of this? How could he? How could anyone? A novel should concern people, not ideas, and yet people had become trivial.

After awhile he left the window and went to the table where he had tried to work. He laid a hand on his papers,

339

then tamped them together and put them into their box. He got undressed, snapped off the light and dropped into bed. Below in the Hodos Stadiou isolated figures still prowled with the furtive urgency of single men alone in a city after dark. In the far distance, somewhere in the streets beyond the Place de la Constitution, the horn of a taxi with a short circuit in its ignition system howled like a wolf in the darkness. Then it ceased as abruptly as it had begun.

41

John Yardley lived in a single room on the top floor of an old house in the south end of Halifax. It had once been a fine residence owned by one of the old importing families, but now it was a lodging house. Its change of status had not altered its appearance in any way. He had to climb three flights of stairs to reach his room and he knew climbing was bad for him, but he felt that the view from his windows was worth the risk he took to obtain it. He could look directly over the treetops to the harbour, and on foggy nights the harbour bells seemed to be sounding just below him. They reminded him constantly of other days when he had been free to move where he chose about the world.

During the past three weeks Yardley had been feeling very much better. The weather had been fine and clear, unusually good for a Nova Scotian June. Now it was early July and the lime trees were fragrant after sunset. He could almost persuade himself that his convalescence from the winter illness was real and that he was actually going to recover. No matter how tired or weak he felt, he got up every morning at eight and had breakfast at a table in his room, brought to him from downstairs. For his other meals he went to a nearby residential hotel. Most of the day he spent propped in an armchair by the window, but he refused to go to bed for the night until eight-thirty. Then he usually read a book for an hour or so and dropped quietly to sleep.

Of late he had not been lonely, for Janet and Heather had been in Halifax for a month. The only trouble was that Janet tried to rearrange his habits to something she considered more suitable for him. And she sat by his side hour after hour either from a sense of duty or because she could think of nothing else to do in a place where she had no friends.

As usual she was here today. She adjusted the pillow behind his head and for a moment her hand lingered on his. He smiled at her, comfortable in the armchair, but he resisted an impulse to lay his other hand over hers. He knew she would immediately withdraw her hand in fear of seeming sentimental. She withdrew it anyway.

'Life isn't easy for any of us, is it, Father?'

He continued to smile at her as he looked at her over his glasses. He wished that her face were less gaunt. It took a good deal of will power to keep the tears out of his eyes. Since his illness he had often been embarrassed by the way tears welled up in his eyes for no reason at all. Poor Janet! She had been worried about something or other ever since he could remember, and surely some of it was his own fault. If only he had been in command of a good education, or even if he had not appeared such a rough man, his daughter might have respected him enough to listen to his advice. He might have been able to teach her to find a little enjoyment in life. But her mother had made the child ashamed of him, and then her own conscience had made her ashamed of being ashamed, and after that there was no end to the impasse between them.

'What is it now?' he said, his voice full of affection.

She sat down in the only other chair in the room, beside the bookshelves which lined one of the walls. Yardley's armchair was by the window. A bed took up most of the space on the other wall, and beyond was a door leading to the common hall of the house. Except for his years in Saint-Marc, Yardley had never had any possessions except his clothes and his books.

'It's Heather,' Janet said. 'Of course, Father – if you're not feeling well this afternoon I don't want to bother you.'

'I guess I can stand anything you've got to say about Heather.'

She took a deep breath and let it out in a sigh. 'Well, when she came back for the general's funeral I thought she was home for good. I simply took it for granted she was through with all that nonsense in New York. If you only knew how I'd been looking forward to having her at home with me where she belongs! After all, she's twenty-eight, and it's time for her to settle down with some nice young man. She's had plenty of opportunities.' Janet pursed her lips. 'If only she wouldn't be so headstrong about everything!'

Yardley's eyes twinkled and he turned to look out the window. In repose his face looked shockingly old; all the colour was drained from it and the skin was like soft old leather. His head was completely bald on top and the fringe of hair over his eyes and around the back of his neck no longer bristled; it was as soft as down. But his ears still stuck out, the twinkle in his eyes had not diminished, and the twang in his voice remained.

'What's she being headstrong about now?' he asked.

'Of course, there may be nothing to it. There may be nothing whatever but my own imagination. But I don't think so.'

'Come on, Janet. Stop sounding like McQueen. I won't hold it against you if you make a mistake.'

She flushed. 'I'm not sounding like Huntly at all.' She fixed him with her dark eyes, and he admitted ruefully to himself that she had become almost hawk-like. 'Don't pretend you don't know what I'm talking about!'

'I haven't the slightest idea, Janet.'

'Well – since you insist on making me say it – it's that young man. I haven't seen him since he was a child, but I know about him. I've discovered that she's been writing to him for years. Imagine! She admitted it to me today.'

'Do you know who he is?'

'Of course I do.'

'Well, Janet, why shouldn't she write him? She and Paul were children together.'

'So you did know! You knew all the time!'

'Sure I knew,' Yardley said. 'He just arrived from Europe a week ago. His ship brought him right in to this port. Nice and convenient for both, I thought.'

'She insists on having him to dinner with us tonight. Of course, I'm very glad. I'd much, much rather know exactly what he's like than wonder.'

342

'Well' – Yardley's voice was tired – 'what are you worried about?'

'You know perfectly well what I'm worried about.'

He chuckled. 'Listen, Janet – if she's got any sense she'll marry him.'

'Oh, no! Father, that's a dreadful thought!' Janet's face showed violent indignation. This had always been her way; to bring into the open something she was worried about and then to show acute distress when what she already knew to be a fact was confirmed by another. The effect of this strained agitation on her father was worse than if she had exploded. Her tension charged the whole room, and he found it unpleasant and exhausting. Anything, these days, rather than tension!

'Try to be serious, Father. You know perfectly well it's unthinkable.'

'I can't say I do.' He looked at her hands. Not one of her mannerisms had changed in the past twenty years. She still clasped her hands so tightly together in her lap that the knuckles showed white. And what seemed to Yardley unfair about all this was that Janet reserved her tension and her scenes for members of her own family. She could be completely charming only to strangers.

'Harvey left the children to me as a trust,' she said. 'A sacred trust.'

'Any children are thet, Janet.' Glancing out of the window he added, 'You've never paid much attention to what I say about things. What does it matter what I think now?'

'Is that quite fair?'

'We mustn't quarrel, child.'

Her face softened. 'Do try to put yourself in my position. We're all alone now. Just Heather and I – and Daphne, of course.' Some private anxiety about Daphne must have crossed her mind, for her face clouded again. 'We're still the family. I had no sons, but I can't forget the family.'

'What family?' he said bluntly. 'The sisters and cousins and aunts of all the Methuens? Which is more important to you, Janet – Heather's happiness or what the Methuens mumble over their tea-cups?'

'What they say over their tea-cups happens to have a great deal to do with Heather's happiness. You've simply never even begun to understand what a family like that means.'

'All right, Janet. You started it, so now I'm going to tell you something about Paul you don't know. Why, his family was riding horses and living in castles and cutting throats for the king of France when the ancestors of the Methuens had only one pair of pants, digging ditches somewhere in England, running errands for country stores, or driving distillery Clydesdales around the Glasgow docks, or maybe not even doing thet much. Now take the other side – ' She tried to interrupt him with an indignant gesture, but he kept right on. 'This country's going to be mighty proud of thet boy one of these days. Heather's a lucky girl, and if you ask me, he's lucky himself, and he's had it coming to him. You asked my opinion. There it is.'

Janet looked down at her clasped hands and pursed her lips again. 'Really, Father – there's not the slightest necessity for being so violent. You'll only upset yourself.'

He passed his hand over his forehead. He was upset already.

'What you say about the Methuens,' she went on stiffly, 'is of course utterly ridiculous. General Methuen's grandfather was an officer at the seige of Badajos.'

'Maybe thet's where he got his start,' Yardley grunted.

Janet eyed him severely. 'Can you permit me to be serious for a moment, Father?'

'I guess I can.'

'Have you forgotten the facts of the situation? This young man may be perfectly all right. I have no doubt he is. But General Methuen always said it was most undesirable for mixed marriages to occur between French and English families. He had some fine French friends, too. Indeed, he was very fond of them. But he used to say that the French themselves objected to mixed marriages even more than he did.'

'Well?' Yardley said.

'That's only one part of it. He's not Heather's kind at all. He's worked in garages and he's been a professional hockey player. Just imagine! Why, he was even an ordinary seaman.'

'So was I, once.'

344

Janet flushed. 'It was entirely different in those days. This young man has never had a proper job in his entire life. He's twenty-nine or thirty or perhaps even more – I don't remember exactly. He's out of work now. I should very much like to hear what Huntly McQueen would have to say about a young man without a decent job at his age!'

Yardley's hand clenched on the arms of his chair. He hated anger in anyone; in himself most of all. It was even dangerous for him to be angry now. With a great effort he kept his voice quiet as he said, 'McQueen would have no more right to blame a young man for having no work today than a man thet stole the milk from a kitten would have any right blaming the cat for going hungry.'

'Please, Father – I can't stand it when you talk like Heather's socialist friends.'

'Then keep McQueen out of it. He never helped anyone in his life.'

Janet remained determined. 'Have you forgotten one thing that I can't – as Heather's mother – permit myself to forget?'

'What's thet?'

'He's undoubtedly a Roman Catholic.'

'Oh,' Yardley said. 'So thet's what's at the bottom of it!'

'It's one of the things that's at the bottom of it, but even you must admit it's decisive.'

'Well, I guess he might have been a Buddhist. Fella I knew out East, a real Methodist he was too, he married a Buddhist girl once, a real beauty, with a figure so nice she made all the English women in Shanghai hate her something terrible. Three years they lived in Shanghai, and he found himself a Methodist chapel, and I guess she went to the temple. Got along fine, till the time came for him to come home. Then he just left her there and I guess he had the marriage annulled, or maybe just forgot all about it, for when I last saw him he was settled in with a hatchet-faced old woman with little red eyes and a nose as mean as a ferret's, and she – '

'Father!' she said.

'All right, Janet.'

'Of course, the whole thing's unthinkable from any point

345

of view. But just suppose the worst did happen? How would Heather like to see her children brought up as Catholics? They insist on that, you know. You haven't a chance with them when it comes to the children.'

Yardley's eyes twinkled for a moment, but he sobered almost at once. 'Listen, Janet – one of the unfairest things we do in this country is to turn these religious denominations into flags. Why, thet boy's had all sorts of religion put onto him. He was a Catholic, and then he was a Protestant, and then he was a Catholic again, and between them they just about made a football out of him. What he is now I don't know because I've never asked him, but I do know he's got a personal religion of his own, and if Heather wants to find out where he goes to church all she's got to do is ask him. It's no more my business, or your business, than how a man makes love to his wife in his own bed after he's married to her.'

Janet winced. 'Do you really have to use expressions like that?' Then, quickly, 'They all die with candles in their hands. I remember General Methuen saying that ever so often.' She got up. 'Father, my daughter simply can't marry a person like that!'

Suddenly Yardley felt overwhelmingly tired. He struggled against the fatigue that pressed him down. This was no good; it was coming on with far too much power. In two hours he would have to walk down three flights of stairs and all the way over to the hotel for dinner. He must save his strength for that, for Paul would be there, too. The boy would be meeting Janet face to face, and he must be at his best to help him out. If he yielded to his weakness now he would be finished until the next day.

Janet seemed unaware of his fatigue as she continued along the train of her own thoughts. 'If only Heather were not so rebellious!'

Something seemed to snap in Yardley's brain. He leaned forward, flushing angrily. 'Thet's a terrible thing for you to say!'

She stared at him in astonishment.

'A human being tries to be herself and you condemn her because she does!'

346

'But Father – I'm her mother! Please remember the things I must consider.'

'Consider my eye! How do you expect people like Paul and Heather to feel toward people like us? Do you think we've deserved their respect? We've sat on them all our lives. We've managed our affairs so badly thet boys like Paul have had to spend their last eight years wandering like tramps from one end of the country to another looking for work. You talk to me about rebellion! I'm telling you something, Janet – the first word any child in the country hears said to it is "No," and the first sentence he hears is "Be careful." God only knows how it's happened thet way, for when I was a boy it was certainly different. You and your friends – you go crazy if a girl and a boy make love to each other before they're married. But another twenty million people can get killed because our generation can't manage its own affairs and thet's not even immoral! The way things've been going there's sure to be a bust-up thet'll surprise you. People get sick of hearing "no" all the time. Don't talk to me about rebellion, Janet, for I can't stand to hear it. If you'd done a little rebelling yourself you'd be a happier woman today!'

The anger faded and left nothing but fatigue. He had been trying to forget his illness, but his illness had not forgotten him. He was betraying his own organism by allowing himself the luxury of anger. 'Forget the last part of what I said, Janet.'

She sat very dignified, her long face severe, reproving and forgiving. 'It has always been your trouble, Father. You never think before you speak. As a matter of fact, that's precisely what Huntly says of Heather.'

'I bet he does,' Yardley grunted.

'And he's perfectly right!'

'I bet he is.'

'Well . . .' Janet got up from the chair. 'Let's say no more about it. I wanted your help because Heather has always been influenced by you. But since you refuse to be sensible . . .'

Yardley smiled wearily. 'You should have remembered, child. I've never been any good at being sensible.'

Janet forced a smile and he knew she was trying to break

the barrier between them. He also knew she had not the slightest chance of succeeding. She went over to his chair and adjusted his pillow, and he leaned back gratefully.

'Now, Father,' she said gently, 'you must take your nap before dinner. You shouldn't have excited yourself.'

'I'll be all right.' He grinned. 'Don't go adding me to the rest of your worries.'

But the moment Janet had left, Yardley sank back exhausted. It was as though the anger and excitement had wiped out all the patient months of convalescing. So Heather and Paul must be harrowed by the same kind of prejudices which had been too much for Paul's father! In the case of Athanase there had at least been a reason: the legend of a whole race had been against him, and Yardley had always taken it for granted that people prefer a legend to a reality. But for Janet to feel as she did about Paul was so depressing he could barely think about it.

With his head back on the pillow, he dozed for a while. The room and the air outside the open window were still. When he next looked up he noticed that the shadows had lengthened, and he had now forgotten all about Heather and Janet and Paul. He seemed to be floating in a cloud of his own thoughts alone in the armchair that was almost in touching reach of the top of the lime tree by his window. Looking over it to the harbour he was sure that George's Island was beginning to cast just the edge of a shadow over the water. Or was it his imagination that made him think so? He could not really see from here; in fact, he was on the wrong side of the harbour to see a shadow from the island at this hour of the evening.

But it must be getting quite late. It must be nearly time for dinner. On the grass below the window a robin was calling. Its nest was under the eaves very close to him, and in the mornings it often woke him feeding the chicks that had just been hatched. He ought to take out his watch and check the time, for surely it was near the dinner hour. Heather was going to wear a green dress he liked; she said for his own special benefit, but of course it was really for Paul. She was becoming a handsome woman. And she had learned to dress

348

in New York. He chuckled. Her mother was upset by her style.

It was comfortable in the chair. There was a time when lassitude was the most delightful thing in the world. Once in the East a Chinaman had tried to persuade him to smoke opium. He had not done so and was sorry now that he hadn't; from what the Chinaman had said of the drug, its effects must be similar to the lassitude he felt now. It was an informing quietness. Everything was so wonderfully clear and cool, like stones under still water in the early morning. The smells of old memories were rich in his nostrils: clover hot in the sun in the valley where he had been born, mingled with the salty odour of lobster shells from the wharf a half mile away. It had been a hard life in those days; nothing worth complaining about, for he and everyone else had always had their health, but it had been hard and narrow. The sea had been great: the feel of the ship living under you, the senses stretched taut as you fought her through a storm, the personal feeling you acquired for a ship, she hard to you and you hard to her. But also narrow. It was only in retrospect that you could pretend you had liked the life. The salted horse was so fat and rotten you had to be nearly starving to eat it. His first captains had all been fierce drivers, and he had seen more than one of them force a man over the side. They had been cruel enough, though cruelty was not a word you ever thought of applying in those days, for most of them were great church-goers when ashore. The first time he had gone to sea he had been only fifteen years old, but the mate had called him a son-of-a-bitch and sent him up the mast with his backside numb from his boot. It was part of the system, and better aloft than below, because the work was really less. And that mate could quote you Isaiah by the hour if he felt like it. After letting another mate drive one poor devil so crazy with fear he leaped from the top-gallant yard into a sea hammered hill-high by a whole gale, old Captain Hance had read the burial service the same day without a quiver of conscience in his voice. The first year he himself had been second mate he'd done things he found hard to remember now. He had cracked one man's skull with a wooden bucket and beaten another to the deck with his fists while the old man looked on. He would never ask a man to do a thing he wouldn't do himself, but that seemed a narrow way of looking at it when one got older. Some men just couldn't do what others did. But if he hadn't been hard the men would have broken him. It was the system. Maybe it was human life. He hated to admit it, but on the whole the ordinary man was just as likely to choose the worst instead of the best. Again old Hance's voice returned to his mind, that old hard-boiled son-of-a-bitch reading the service: 'The Lord giveth, the Lord taketh away, blessed be the name of the Lord!' He supposed it was people's ignorance; his own and the others. Always it came right back to what Jesus had said, they know not what they do. Jesus must have considered that message mighty important or he wouldn't have saved it to the end. It was funny he'd never thought of that before. Right at the end Jesus had given the plain warning not to expect too much of people. Yardley had always supposed that if people had been intended to know what they were doing, they would have been created with the faculties to make the knowledge possible.

It was strange how a man's life passed like a ship through different kinds of weather. Sentimental, he supposed, but a fact. Wonder in childhood; in the twenties physical violence and pride in muscles; in the thirties ambition; in the forties caution, and maybe a lot of dirty work; and then, if you were lucky, perhaps you could grow mellow. It seemed to Yardley that with the talent and the courage there was no limit to what a man could obtain out of life if he merely accepted what lay all around him. But knowledge was necessary; otherwise beauty was wasted. Beauty had come to him late in life, but now he couldn't have enough of it. It was something a man had to understand. Pictures and colours, for instance, and fine glass.

He had been allowed the use of the Dalhousie Library these past few years, and every day until lately he had spent some time in it. He had discovered much he had been too ignorant to enjoy in his active life. Only last winter, the week before his illness, he had found a book containing photographs of Swedish and Bohemian glass. In the lines of a single vase a man could find infinite pleasure if he were willing to let his imagination run. The old Chinaman who had tried to induce him to smoke opium had also attempted to interest him in rice-bowls and wash-drawings. He had been ashamed then of liking useless things which were merely beautiful, for he had been given a strict upbringing. And also – Yardley smiled as he remembered – he had somewhat despised them, and for no better reason than because he had possessed enough physical strength to beat up that Chinaman with one hand. It had seemed that a man grew soft if he let his mind run to those things, and that the next time a hardcase crewman shaped up to him he would be too slow with the right hook. So, after seeing the Chinaman's drawings, he had returned to the ship, and later that evening got drunk with the second mate, gone ashore and got into a fight with some men off a Boston vessel, and the next day put to sea again with a sore jaw and a hangover.

But the wonder was before him now, it was around him everywhere, it was within him, and he wished without any pain or regret that he could have just a little more time with it. On the whole, he saw no reason why he should not. If he were careful, this illness could be weathered. They had been very good to him at Dalhousie. He had become acquainted with one of the scientists at the university. The man had a passion for ships and had presumably thought him a character. Anyway, through this professor he had even been allowed the use of some of the laboratory equipment. He had examined stars through a telescope, and after seeing the rings around Saturn and the mountains and craters in the moon, he had turned the telescope up toward Orion and space had leaped gigantic before his eyes. But the greatest revelation had come through a microscope. It seemed appalling to Yardley that he had waited until this age before even seeing what most high-school children take for granted. He had spent hours studying, out of curiosity rather than any scientific purpose, the infinitesimal life-particles that swarmed beneath the glass, past thought and counting, life everywhere and in all things and in such infinite manifestations that the brain reeled unless the harmony of the whole entered the mind to reconcile you to your own ignorance and to beautify the pattern in which you yourself were a part. Considering such things as these, it seemed past credence how men had contrived such skill to make trouble for themselves, or why they considered politicians important. Unless . . . unless . . . he could not bring himself to conclude that men were just as helpless as the organisms they studied. No, he refused to believe that.

The robin, with a worm in its mouth, flew up to the nest beside the window. Yardley leaned forward to see what it would do, but the nest was near the corner and he could not quite get it within the focus of his eyes. He rose from the chair and gripped the raised sash with his hands. Then a sudden weakness took his knees, a sharp pain stabbed up from behind his eyes into his brain, he wavered and lapsed back into the chair and closed his eyes. A myriad of motes of light swarmed through a gathering darkness, the pain intensified until he tried to cry out, then faded away out of its own violence. He was conscious of opening his lips to speak, of his tongue feeling a sudden moisture on them, of wanting to tell someone that these motes of light were living organisms and that he was thankful he had been able to see them. His head fell back on the pillow and his breathing stopped.

An hour later, when Heather and Paul came to take him to dinner, they thought he was asleep.

42

A forthnight later Heather lay watching dawn enter the room. It came on a wind from the sea with the sound of gulls and gannets crying in the distance.

Moving carefully, she slipped out of bed and crossed on tip-toe to the open window. The scalloped cliffs known as the Three Sisters swept in knife-edged outline down to Percé bay where the great perpendicular sandstone rock stood offshore like a stranded ship. The dawn heightened, and Bonaventure Island became visible in a sea the colour of a dove's back. Northern dawn. Spuce forests and salt water. Field of saffron rising over the sea-rim.

Stealing back to bed she slipped in between the sheets, then rested on her elbow and looked at Paul's face. As the dawn heightened, its outline grew more distinct. Yet now his face seemed oddly bereft of light, not withdrawn but utterly defenceless, lips parted, even breath, steady beat of the heart, one arm over the blankets with fist loosely clenched. She looked at his hand. Strange hand. Those years when they were apart it was his hands she had remembered best. They were strong and powerful, yet so strangely delicate when they touched her skin that she felt she could know him by his touch always.

She laid her cheek against his shoulder and held it there, and he stirred quietly in his sleep, seemed to try to lift and turn, then relapsed again as she sat up. His sleeping silence seemed miraculous. With all the lines smoothed from his face he was so tranquil she felt she hardly knew him. Only the clenched hand and the rise and fall of the chest. And she thought that a whole life lay defenceless beside her in the dawn, one so different from her own that its presence was another miracle. For there was no loneliness now, not even when she was awake and he was asleep. Only fulfillment which after all these years had come to her with astonishing ease and generosity; and wonder at a kind of tenderness so fundamental she asked herself if only men with a touch of ruthlessness can ever possess it.

The whole room was bright now, and the crying of sea-birds louder. The gulls must be diving like mad down the line of the cliffs. She remembered them as she had seen them yesterday wheeling out over the water about the rock; beautiful, aloof, cruelly competent, and farther out were the gannets with wing-spread wider than a swan's and rusty eyes. When the gannets dipped their wings they plunged to the water like bombs.

Everything had helped them grow together during these last two weeks. She and Paul had driven slowly up from Halifax. Now at Percé they were nearly half way around the Gaspé Peninsula. It had been a beautiful drive through Nova Scotia, then up the long corridor cut by the road through the spruce forests of New Brunswick, then along the rim of the peninsula with the sea beside them, cliffs and breakers and an astonishing blueness in the sky, and more sea-birds than they had ever seen before.

Now as she watched him sleeping she knew that in spite of loving her he had never lost the sense of himself. She was not jealous of the part she could not touch. She could companion it, but she could not have it. What she did have was a hundred images of him engraved on her mind, all different. She remembered the concentration about his mouth and eyes as he had read beside her last night before they slept. She remembered the sudden, constantly renewed surprise when he smiled and his face became so much younger. Often his expression was reserved and ascetic, and he looked older than his age. That was why the moments were so marvellous when she touched him and his face softened; these, and the times when he looked at her naked beside him and his eyes showed that he loved the lines of her body, and she wondered incredulously if she were really beautiful.

Her past had drained away from her. Only these last few days with him counted now. Like being born again? For a girl it surely was. But for him? She couldn't know that. And then she thought about his novel and wished she had not begun to read it during these first days when they had been alone with each other. It had been her idea, not his, and they had agreed not to discuss it until she had finished the manuscript. The novel reminded her too much of his past, too much of the welter outside the time-shell into which she had crept with him.

He stirred beside her and she resisted a temptation to wake him. He was so very relaxed. She felt a second's mischievous pride. But soon he would wake and come back to her. He would wake and she would see the look in his eyes and then in a minute he would be loving her again.

Yesterday they had walked down to the shore together through an acre of gutted codfish drying on flakes. The air stank sharply of the cod and of the oakum a fisherman was using to caulk his boat. On the shore Paul had suddenly appeared to forget all about her. He had left her sitting on a rock while he crossed the beach to talk to the men at work. She heard him using colloquial French that was so rapid she could follow only a little of it, and she knew he loved the sensation of being back home in Quebec. Suddenly she felt frightened. Did all girls feel the same after they had committed themselves to a man and then realized how easily he could forget them? For nearly an hour he stood on the beach using his other language, sharing something with these men she could watch only from the outside. She was terribly conscious of their different races and languages then. But after a time he returned. Joy ran through her nerves like electricity as she saw him coming back over the stones to her. He took her hand, and the moment he touched her no differences existed. They began to climb the Pic de l'Aurore, moving up through a meadow foaming with the largest daisies she had ever seen, the cliff sheer on their right, and overhead huge clouds sailing in a high wind, gulls poised in the air-slip over the land's edge. When she tried to sing, the wind blew her voice down her throat.

The last two weeks flowed with calm finality through her mind as she watched him sleep beside her. There had been a complete finality about everything that had happened since Yardley's death. On hearing the news, McQueen had at once flown down from Montreal to help her mother, and had managed all the affairs of the funeral. Janet had been touched by this, for McQueen loathed airplanes. When the funeral was over he had returned to Montreal on the train with Janet, leaving Heather in Halifax to drive home alone. Janet was disturbed over the necessity of leaving Heather behind, but she didn't feel equal to driving back with her. She was tired out, and when tired she always got carsick.

Heather had read years ago that there are times when a person must speak or be dead for the rest of life, and this had been one of those times. Her grandfather was still very close to her, and she felt no grief remembering him. He had died as he would have wished to die. Her mother felt prostrate with grief, not knowing that grief is always for the self. One by one things were falling away from Janet, leaving her solitary in the way of life to which she had bound herself.

And then, alone in Halifax, as though on a signal from nature, Heather's own life had begun. Without premeditation or promises, she and Paul had suddenly decided to get married the day after Janet and Huntly left. She had seen the look in his eyes, known his consciousness that he had no job or money, and for once in her life she had spoken and made the words count. She had accepted the risk with her eyes open, knowing she could never go back. She loved him so utterly he had become her way of life. For a man it could never be the same. He had his work, he had the ruthless drive inside that would never let him alone.

Paul stirred beside her, and began to breathe heavily. She looked at him in surprise. And then a smile, half mischievous, partly delighted, touched her face. She laid the tips of her fingers against his lips and closed them, but an instant later they opened and he snored quietly again, and there was something so quaintly self-satisfied in the noise that everything seemed warm and a little funny, and she felt closer to him than ever. 'Oh darling', she whispered, 'to think you'd do a thing like that!'

He moved, his eyes opened and looked at her, and he was back again.

She grinned at him. 'You were snoring.'

'The hell I was!'

'You can't get out of it. You were snoring. You woke yourself up with the noise you made.'

'I woke myself up thinking about you.'

'You thought about me and then you snored!'

He looked at her gravely and she dropped her head close to his. She felt his body quicken with life as he turned to hold her, his hand on the small of her back. Wonderful hands, delicately rugged hands!

'Were you really thinking about me?' she whispered.

'Yes.'

'In your sleep?'

He seemed wide awake; she wondered if he would always wake so quickly.

'I woke up knowing something,' he said. 'I'd better tell you.'

'What?'

He paused a moment. 'I'm in love with you.'

It was strange how he said it. The statement was utterly factual, made in the tone he always saved for what came out of his bones. He had never said it before. She had known he was in love with her, but she had been left to wonder how much he realized it.

356

'Darling!' she whispered. She lay very still beside him, felt the musles of his arms stir slumbrously, then tauten as he folded her in against his body. She felt the hardness of his chest muscles, the hardness of his thighs, the quick flush of life through him, and she herself seemed small and protected, smoothly delicate beside him. He had said her skin was like silk and it was lovely to believe it, perhaps it really was, since he never said anything to flatter her. Perhaps he was loving the feeling of firm soft silkiness beside him now, the form not of just another girl, but of herself. She kept very still.

'For always,' he said slowly. 'That's what I woke up knowing. I'd never believed it possible but it is. I know I'm in love with you for always, no matter what happens, and that I'm not just myself but you too, and I thought I'd better tell you.'

After a long silence she whispered, 'Are you sorry?'

'Not about facts.'

Her lips felt the pulse in his throat. She kissed him long and slowly, and then the literal words he had said stood like separate objects in her mind and she raised her head and gave him a teasing smile. 'Darling – I so adore you when you say things like that!'

'It's true.'

'You love me because I'm a fact!'

'I love you because you're you. Because you're beautiful. Because – '

'But Daffy always said I was chunky. She said my mouth was too wide.'

'Daffy's a fool. I like it.'

'I should be at least four inches taller for you.'

'Then I'd have to be five inches taller than I am.'

'Darling, I suspect you want to overpower me. When you love me you want to overwhelm me entirely.'

'You underrate yourself.'

'Anyway, my eyes are too wide.'

'There is no excellent beauty but hath a strangeness in the proportions.'

'Where did you learn that? I like it.' Suddenly serious. 'I wish I were really beautiful for you, Paul.'

'You are. There are so many things about you I love, I

357

can't even begin to understand them all.'

'I'm so happy I can hardly stand it, but for heaven's sake don't love me because I'm a fact!'

'You're the most important one I know.'

'You're certainly the most serious one *I* know. Paul – I so want you to relax. I . . .'

'What do you think you've been doing to me lately?'

'I want you to have fun. I want you to be able to lie on your back and look at the sky for hours. I want you to be able to do all sorts of things without thinking all the time. Yes, I'm definitely going to do something about that awful seriousness!'

'Heather – remember yesterday on the beach?'

'What about it?'

'I turned around from talking to those fishermen and saw you sitting on the rock by yourself, waiting for me. Suddenly I felt as though I were home.'

The teasing smile left her lips. She met his eyes.

'It's a dangerous illusion,' he said quietly. 'I still have a long way to go.'

'Do you know, I rather like the smell of drying cod now,' she said. 'At first it seemed horrid, but now I like it. Don't you?'

He placed his hand over one of hers. 'You know I haven't any money or even a job. You've read enough of my manuscript to know by this time that there's not much point in expecting anything from it. I'd hoped . . .'

'No, Paul! No – it's wonderful!'

They were separated again, each feeling the separation and not wanting it to be there. He shook his head. 'I'm talking facts, Heather. They were there the day we got married, but I didn't talk about them then because I was sure you understood. I'll probably never be able to give you what you've always had with the Methuens. Do you know what that means? Sometime, though – '

'As if you had to give me anything – anything like that!'

She began to fold the edge of the sheet into pleats, watching her handiwork instead of his eyes.

'I can't ask you to share a single room with me,' he said. 'And I'm not going to take your money, either. You know that. It would break something inside me. For a long time I've been trying to convince myself that some day I'd have enough to give us both a decent life, but I wasn't going to talk about it until it was certain. Then suddenly in Halifax . . .' He stopped and watched her fingers at work. 'Do you realize what your family will say when they know we're married?'

'Yes,' she said quietly, dropping the sheet. 'I've thought about it. But it doesn't make any difference to me. It's . . . Paul, no matter what, you mustn't let them hurt you.'

Neither of them spoke for a few moments and she watched him run his hands through his hair and prepare to get out of bed. When he was on his feet he said, 'I'm not really worried about money. But I would like to have some sort of name for you. I never meant to ask you to marry me until I was a published novelist. Then you'd be justified in the eyes of your family, as well as in your own. Now we'll have to take the rap first and then I'll still have to prove to you, to myself, to everyone else, that I'm capable of a career on my own.'

'But you've proved it already.'

'No,' he said. 'I haven't. Writing isn't like any other job. All the work in the world can't replace a lack of talent. That's what I've still got to find out if I have.' He gripped the turned rail at the foot of the bed and looked her in the eyes. 'I'm bound to you, Heather. But you aren't to me. You're still free. Even though we're married, you're . . .'

She reached up and stopped his lips with her fingers. 'Darling,' she said, 'sometimes you talk like an awful fool.'

43

Next day the weather broke and they left Percé in a driving rain. By the time they reached Rivière au Renard the air was much colder and Paul noticed that the wind was hauling. At Mont Louis the rain had ceased and a straight norther was blowing hard across the gulf from Labrador. The sea was bursting on the shore over the road and the light on the water had the same hard, bleak colour he had often seen off Newfoundland. They followed the curve of the peninsula in toward the estuary of the river, but the norther kept following them and it grew steadily colder. The sun set in a watery sky as they drew in to Cap Chat. They decided to stay the night there and drove up to an old stone house with a sign by the road signifying that tourists were welcome.

When the woman who owned the place discovered that Paul had been at sea she couldn't do enough for them. She gave them her best room and sent one of the children up to lay a fire in it. Because the dining room was cold and there were no other guests, she allowed them to eat in the kitchen, and they sat at a large pine table while their supper was prepared. The kitchen was the largest room in the house. It had an enormous copper boiler beside the stove and the whole room was clean and shining. There was a picture of Christ in a small frame on one wall. Some exquisite wood-carvings of saints stood on the shelf of the dresser, and colourful milk bowls were arranged along its top.

Madame Rocheleau was a tall woman with black hair neatly done, and strong Norman features. When she moved she was grave and stately. She served them a wonderful dinner of vegetable soup and fresh boiled salmon, and talked with them while they ate. Afterwards she asked them to share a small carafe of wine with her. It was an excellent light claret. Her husband was a river pilot who was absent most of the time when the Saint Lawrence was open. She had eight children: the eldest a priest and the second a sailor working for his mate's ticket on one of the C.P.R. ships. It was this son who had brought her two cases of claret from his last voyage when the ship called at Le Havre, and she was very proud of him when she spoke of it. She was quiet-voiced, shrewd and very observant, and had a way of laughing cautiously, as though it were a luxury. After a time it appeared that she wanted to know if Paul expected a war. When he made a non-committal answer she looked at him gravely and shook her head. 'My son will join the Navy if there is war,' she said.

'Does your son expect it?'

'He has been in Europe.' She shrugged her shoulders. 'My son is well educated. He keeps his eyes open.'

'Do many from here go to sea?' Paul asked.

'There has always been a member of my husband's family at sea,' Madame Rocheleau said. 'His brother was lost at sea in the last war. You, Monsieur – will you also be in the Navy if there is war this time?'

Heather gave Paul a quick glance. The turn of the conversation surprised her.

'It will be easier to tell that when the time comes, Madame. But if it does – yes, it is probable.'

'My son says it will come.'

'They may prevent it.'

'When people do not believe in God they do not prevent such things.'

'Do others here believe there will be war?'

'They do not think about it. I am the only one with a son who has sailed to Europe, so for me it is different.'

She rose with the lamp in her hand and showed them upstairs to their room. 'You and Madame will be comfortable,' she said. 'When my husband is home this is our room.'

She wished them a grave good-night and went out, drawing the heavy door behind her.

When they were alone, Heather said, 'What a beautiful woman!'

Paul went over to the fire and crouched beside it. She saw the corners of his mouth move into a smile as he looked at the hot flames of the driftwood logs. 'She has a respect for facts,' he said.

'Like you.'

'Not like me at all. If this country were invaded and the Germans were ten miles away and it was time to pick the potatoes, she'd be out picking them.'

'What would you be doing?'

He made no answer.

'Are there many like Madame Rocheleau in Quebec?'

'So far there have been enough to guarantee that my brother remains an unsuccessful politician.'

She dropped onto the mat beside him, looking into the fire. She felt his hand close over hers. 'You're still French – aren't you, Paul?'

He laughed quietly. 'I certainly would be if I stayed long enough in a place like this.'

'Would you like to stay here?'

'You know perfectly well my likes and dislikes have nothing to do with it. But yes – here I get back the old feelings. It makes me remember when I was a boy in Saint-Marc. This is Quebec – small places like this. They may be simple. They may even be superstitious. But in places like this you meet Madame Rocheleau. What's in the cities is an industrial revolution, delayed by about fifty years. When the war starts . . .' He paused, but went on almost immediately. 'There may be quite a lot of dynamite lying around in the towns, and I don't look forward to the prospect of Marius lighting matches in the middle of it.'

'Paul – why doesn't Marius like you?'

He laughed again. 'Because I'm half-English. Because I'm not the pure thing. He knows I feel both races stirring inside me all the time. The pure race is everything to him. I suppose that's why he refuses to speak English. If you're completely at home in both languages you can't help thinking differently.'

'Does it feel funny belonging to both races?'

'Well, it makes it impossible to be enthusiastic about the prejudices of either of them, and that can be uncomfortable sometimes.'

'Does it still bother you – the way it used to?'

He shook his head. 'I've been away too long.' He stared into the fire. 'I suppose patriotism was originally nothing but the remembrance of childhood. Childhood is always magical. No wonder the politicians got hold of it and organized it.'

He was thoughtful for nearly a minute; the burning wood cracked loudly and a violent gust of wind made the windows rattle. He got up and looked out. Cap Chat was buried in darkness under the rushing wind and there was nothing to see. Coming back to the fire, he crouched again. 'Well, one thing is certain. The same brand of patriotism is never likely to exist all over Canada. Each race so violently disapproves of the tribal gods of the other I can't see how any single Canadian politician can ever imitate Hitler – at least, not over the whole country. But when the war comes . . .' He stopped and shrugged his shoulders.

Keeping her eyes on the fire and her voice quiet, she said,

'I suppose you meant what you said about the Navy?'

'I suppose so. Why not be frank? I've made up my mind.'

'My father was killed in 1918. I can't even remember him.' She turned. 'Oh Paul – do we really have to get into it again?'

'We'll be in it, all right.' He got up. 'Let's not talk about it. It just pulls the guts out of me. If you've grown up in a minority you can never feel simply about war. Quebec will enter it trying to save her legend. Many will go to it. Some like Marius will begin remembering each separate insult the English threw in their faces the last time. Some like me will have to feel for Quebec and feel for the whole country at the same time. No – let's not talk about it.'

'Paul?'

He looked down at her. She was curled on the edge of the hearth, staring into the fire. When he answered the changed inflection in her voice she still looked away from him.

'I've finished your manuscript,' she said.

He waited, but for a time she said no more. All day Heather had been brooding over what she would say to him about his book. Each knew how tightly their future was bound up with the quality of this manuscript. 'Well,' he said finally, 'do you think it can be published?'

'I don't see why not.' She was still watching the fire. 'Parts of it are wonderful. Your style is simply marvellous. I forget it's you when I'm reading.'

'But something is the matter with it. Something fundamental. You've spotted it. I can tell from your voice.'

His calm, factual tones made Heather's hopes sink. This book of his had completely baffled her. She was no professional critic, but her work with the museum in New York had involved a good deal of editing and she had helped write a small text book for art classes in schools. She had something of a professional approach to any form of written words. His theme was ambitious. Many sections had extraordinary power and descriptions were new and vivid. But the balance was not right and the whole was curiously unsatisfying.

They discussed the book for nearly half an hour, and he

took the manuscript and went over specific sections with her. At the end of that time she knew what had puzzled her.

The book was too ambitious for him. She herself had been dazzled by the scope of the design. The young man of 1933, intended to type a world in disintegration, had seemed so important that she had not questioned the validity of his plan. Now she saw that the trouble lay in the fact that Paul's emotions and mental analysis had not coalesced.

'Look,' she said suddenly, 'I read somewhere that the novelist's principal aim is to celebrate life.'

'I suppose it is.'

'That's what you do best of all. Every time. Your characters are all naturally vital people. But your main theme never gives them a chance. It keeps asserting that they're doomed.'

He frowned thoughtfully. Then he remembered a discussion he had had with his tutor in Oxford. 'Maybe I shouldn't have chosen a European scene. Of course, Europe is the focus . . .' He jumped up and began walking back and forth. 'My God!' he shouted, 'I've been a fool! A year's work! Heather – I've wasted a year's work!'

She looked at him in excitement. Her thoughts were on the same tack as his own. 'Paul, why didn't you set the scene in Canada?'

He stopped in the middle of the room. 'Because no world trends begin here. I thought of it, but – everything that makes the world what it is – fascism, communism, big business and depressions – they're all products of other people's philosophies and ways of doing things. A book about Canada – it would be like writing of the past century!' Having said this he wondered if it were really true. He sat down before the fire again, staring into it. Must he write out of his own background, even if that background were Canada? Canada was imitative in everything. Yes, but perhaps only on the surface. What about underneath? No one had dug underneath so far; that was the trouble. Proust wrote only of France, Dickens laid nearly all his scenes in London, Tolstoi was pure Russian. Hemingway let his heroes roam the world, but everything he wrote smelled of the United States. Hemingway could put an American into the Italian Army and get away with it because by now everyone in the English-speaking world knew what an American was. But Canada was a country that no one knew. It was a large red splash on the map. It produced Mounted Policemen, Quintuplets and raw materials. But because it used the English and French languages, a Canadian book would have to take its place in the English and French traditions. Both traditions were so mature they had become almost decadent, while Canada herself was still raw. Besides, there was the question of background. As Paul considered the matter, he realized that his readers' ignorance of the essential Canadian clashes and values presented him with a unique problem. The background would have to be created from scratch if his story was to become intelligible. He could afford to take nothing for granted. He would have to build the stage and props for his play, and then write the play itself.

Suddenly he began to talk. He got up and paced back and forth across the floor. He lit cigarettes and threw them into the fire half-finished and lit some more. Heather had never heard such a deluge of words from him. As she listened she felt sick from apprehension. He was telling her that his present book was a total failure, that he could do nothing to save it.

Then, as abruptly as he had begun to talk, he stopped and knelt beside the fire. It had burned down until the logs were glowing coals. After a time he took a deep breath and turned to her. His face seemed several years older than it had been an hour ago, but his eyes were bright. He laughed in sudden irony.

'And what have I discovered tonight?' he said. 'Something the whole world has known for centuries. An artist has to take life as he finds it. Life by itself is formless wherever it is. Art must give it a form.' He laughed again. 'So – after all these years – I learn tonight what my job is!'

Then casually, so casually she did not realize what he was doing, he picked up the manuscript and dropped in into the fire. With a cry she reached forward to save it, but the flames shot up and covered the papers. He took her by the arms and drew her back. 'Nc,' he said, 'that's finished. Burn the mistakes. Otherwise they'll haunt you permanently.'

She was frightened by the resignation in his voice, appalled by the fact that he was destroying what had taken him a year to create. She watched the mass of papers burning and her face became hot from the flames. Slowly they curled and shrivelled into quivering layers, blackening from the edges into the centre, and she knew she was watching more than an unfinished book going up in smoke. She felt she was watching the fire burn up the next two years of her own life.

44

It was early when they woke the next day and set out after a good breakfast. They drove fast along the river highway toward Quebec. At Rimouski they saw the wind sweeping up swathes of mist from the river like a broom brushing a floor. At Trois Pistôles the sun was shining. When they stopped for lunch at Rivière du Loup the day was hot and the mountains on the far side of the river looked mauve against a brilliant sky. Steadily the Saint Lawrence narrowed as they drove inland, and by late afternoon the Ile d'Orléans was on their right, its contours dark in the late afternoon sun. The land was richer here, the parishes older; they passed red-roofed barns and the lovely sloping roofs of old stone houses. In some fields farmers were already beginning to cut the hay; in others the smell of clover was as strong as an anaesthetic. Then, as they neared Levis, they saw Quebec across the river with the sunset flaring behind it, the Château and Citadel stark against the light and a pool of purple shadow lying like oil on the river underneath Cape Diamond. It was cool crossing on the ferry, but in the steep streets of Quebec the heat had lingered even past sundown. They found in a side street a small hotel Heather knew, left their bags and went out for dinner. Afterwards they leaned on the railing on the edge of Dufferin Terrace for nearly an hour watching the lights on the river, and then went back to bed.

At breakfast the next morning Paul saw the name Danzig on the front page of *Le Devoir*. After reading the headlines he threw the paper aside. War might be a certainty, but he was sure it would not begin before the harvest was in. Europeans always seemed predictable about things like that.

After checking out of the hotel, Paul drove the car back to the ferry for Levis. Heather made no comment. She remembered that on the usual highway to Montreal along the left bank of the river lay Saint-Marc, and wondered if he were deliberately avoiding it.

He drove slowly all that morning and Heather sat quietly beside him. Only a few hours before them lay Montreal, holding the tangled roots and residues of their separate lives. The city waited for them ominously, something that had tried to dominate them as long as they were in it, something neither had really escaped even now. Occasionally Heather glanced at his profile, wondering if his thoughts were the same as her own. Her husband. No, that word made no sense. It was for other people, a fence put up to keep others out. Just Paul. Heather and Paul against the rest of them.

She closed her eyes, clenching her hands in fury as she thought about the cage which had surrounded her all her life. They would humiliate him. Her mother and the rest would get at her through him. And inside her brain, behind her closed eyes, she saw what would happen if they knew she had married him. She saw how they would hurt him, slash at his pride as though they had whips in their hands. And now, just at the moment when she herself felt free of them, she knew they could hold her through what they could do to him.

Opening her eyes she looked again at his profile. His jaw was tight and his hands grasping the wheel seemed nervous. Was he thinking the same things? It seemed amazing that he had married her in Halifax, for he was really a careful man, aware of the odds and calculating them. Had he calculated them all now? She looked away. If only it were not for Montreal! If they could go away some place where nobody knew them! But he would have to get a job to be able to do that. And through working at the job, what would happen to his writing? She looked back at him again, drew close, laid her hand on his knee.

Shortly after lunch they saw the smoke of Montreal lying over the horizon, dulling the sunlight. The hot air held it like an umbrella. The river water began to look darker, they saw the giant cross on the top of Mount Royal, then the trestlework of the Jacques Cartier Bridge. A few moments more and they had reached its southern foot. Paul paid the toll and they moved onto the incline in a long row of cars. Then. as the bridge climbed over Saint Helen's Island which lay in mid-stream separating the channel from the shallows, he turned the car to the left and descended the ramp. 'Let's not go into town yet,' he said quietly.

They drove along the island and stopped on its farthest tip. There were few people about at this hour of the afternoon, so they sat on the grass side by side and looked across at the city. It sprawled there ponderously, miles of docks, warehouses, grain elevators, factories, slums, office buildings, homes; a huge encrustation of concrete. brick, mortar and asphalt spreading back over the flats to Mount Royal and beyond. an enormous property.

He said quietly 'Heather, do you think things have changed much since I went away in 1934?'

She forced herself to answer. 'Not much. My own part certainly hasn't. Huntly McQueen, Chislett, Rupert Irons – they're the same as ever, and so is everything else.' She looked fixedly across the river at the docks. 'I think I hate them.'

There was a long silence between them. He broke it finally. 'Have we both been thinking the same thing?'

She smiled ruefully.

'I don't think I've ever wanted property,' he said. 'But I've never been able to get the old house in Saint-Marc out of my mind. I suppose land is in the blood of all French-Canadians.'

She pulled a blade of grass apart as he went on.

'I'd like to have a place of our own sometime. I'm quite commonplace and banal, really. I'd like to see you cutting roses in the garden.' She turned away, and his voice continued. 'Somehow or other, we've got to get some graciousness back into human life. I seem to have seen so little of it. People may forget all about it, soon.'

Her hand found his and pressed it. 'We'll have all that, Paul. We will!'

'Not in a single room.'

She continued to gaze across the river. In her mind she saw one thing clearly. Janet would try to help them with money. It would be constitutionally impossible for her to stand aside if she believed that her daughter was living in poverty. And with her money she would humiliate him even if she restrained herself from hurting him in other ways. She would never understand how to respect Paul's way of doing things. She would never be able to leave him alone to arrange things his own way – slowly, tenaciously, by trial and error, as he seemed to do everything.

As if reading her mind, he said, 'Heather – when we were married, it was on our own terms.' He nodded across the river. 'Not on theirs. They aren't bad. It's an odd thing about this country – it has few outright villains. It's only their instincts that are wrong. People at the top now – their instincts betray them in everything they do. Look at Chamberlain.'

Her eyes remained on his. Keeping her voice steady, she said, 'Our own terms, Paul?'

He got up to watch the slow process of a ten-thousand-ton freighter being warped out of her dock by a pair of tugs. The stern came far out and he read her name: *Borkum, Hamburg.* The swastika was flying from her mainmast.

Still looking at the *Borkum*, he said, 'War's unavoidable now, you know. That's why I asked you to marry me before I had a job. Without waiting.'

She tried to hold his gaze, but she couldn't manage it. Looking away, she wondered how many millions of others were like them, waiting for war, all over the world waiting with different thoughts for it to come to them personally: to destroy the burden of their own identities, to give them jobs, to cut the umbilical cords that bound them to the past.

'All the way between Athens and Halifax,' he went on, 'I kept telling myself that the world you lived in wasn't my world, and that it was still in authority. I suppose its rules hold even now. No matter how you might feel about it – I told myself that it had no use for me and didn't want me. And all that counted in me didn't want it, either.'

The *Borkum* was casting off her tugs and getting under

way. A tiny ridge was pressed out from her cutwater, surface tension holding it from breaking.

'The day after war begins,' he said, 'you and I will be wanted.' With some bitterness, he added, 'Then we'll be respected.' His face suddenly broke into a smile and he bent down, helping her to her feet. 'But meanwhile the old rules still hold. I've got to get some kind of a job.'

A great wave of joy passed through her; joy at something which at first seemed quite vague, then almost tangible, then the most important thing in the world. Once more, each understood all that was in the other's mind. She knew that he was guarding his pride. He knew that she recognized it.

'If we weren't married,' he said, 'what would you do now?'

'I've promised Mummy to spend a month with her in Maine.'

He brushed a dried leaf from her dress. 'Go with your mother, Heather. I'll stay here and try to find a job. When I do . . .' The muscles of his face tightened. 'When I do, it will be time to tell them we're married. Do you mind?'

Watching him, she knew this was the only way it could be. Earning a living in any other way but writing meant wasting his talent. She knew he would have to stand on his own feet as he had always done. No matter what happened, she would never ask him to do anything else.

They walked back to the car, drove up the ramp to the bridge and on into Montreal. She left him with his suitcase in front of the old house where he had lived five years before. It still had the same sign by the door saying that it took roomers.

45

The day after they separated began one of the longest weeks Paul had ever spent. Heather's absence was like a physical pain. It produced a kind of homesickness sharper than anything he had known in Europe; being in Montreal made it all the worse. The old sense of failure, of marking time against a brick wall was heavy on him.

At the beginning of the week he went to the office of the

370

university to see if they had a list of jobs available to graduates. Nothing. Because he wanted only to write, he found it difficult to think of possible jobs, and still harder to knock on strange doors to ask for work. Judging by want ads in the papers, unemployment was still bad. No one wanted help. As usual. Always as usual.

During the next few days he walked the streets. He entered the offices of large corporations and made inquiries. He got the old smile and the old shake of the head. During one of his walks he passed the Forum. There it was, the length of half a city block, brown and forlorn in the grey summer weather; and years ago during cold winter nights he had played nearly two hundred games in it. It was hard to believe that he had ever been an athlete. He seemed suddenly old, with no sense of time.

There was a telephone in the common hall of the lodging house and it gave him a guilty feeling every time he passed it. He knew he ought to call Marius, but he dreaded raising the old ghosts that might surround him and put him back in the strait-jacket. Marius would be bitter because he had married an English girl, a daughter of the woman who had informed on him during the war. Old arguments would be thrown in his face, and again he would have to fight for his identity. Thinking of this, remembering in detail how far he had drifted since the family had been broken up, he was overpowered by a homesickness for Saint-Marc. He had not seen it for years; not since he was eighteen. Perhaps if he saw it again it would be easier to meet Marius without quarrelling. Perhaps he might even feel at home.

One morning in the middle of the week he went down the hill to the station and bought a ticket for Sainte-Justine. His mind filled with old memories: Polycarpe Drouin and Frenette in the general store, the look of the river from the maple grove on the ridge, Yardley limping along the road telling his stories, the cool feeling of dew on the thwarts of the boat when they went fishing between dawn and sunrise, swallows dipping silently out of the eaves of the disused stone mill. With the ticket in his pocket he wandered about the station waiting for the gates to open. But when the train

371

was called and the crowd began to pour through onto the platform, he turned and walked out of the station and back up the hill.

It would have been senseless to return to Saint-Marc. Polycarpe Drouin was dead. Yardley and his father were dead. Frenette was an old man now; after years of being his own master, he had been compelled to give up his forge and now was just another employee of the factory. Father Beaubien was in another parish. Saint-Marc was not a village any more; it was a small factory town, and some of his father's land had been turned into a golf course by the company. Instead of playing checkers in Drouin's store, coming into it informally whenever they felt like it, the villagers now played organized bingo games in a community hall on Saturday nights.

He knew that his home was irrevocably with Heather, in himself. His thoughts softened with recollections of her. You could be with a girl and never notice countless things about her. But afterwards, if you loved her, you remembered them. Now he recalled the expression of her face when they had loved each other: a sort of eager graciousness opening into ecstasy. Afterwards she always brushed the lobe of his right ear with her lips, held them there and breathed softly. Her life was in her breath and it entered his brain in sound.

When he reached his lodgings his neighbour's radio was on. It was always on these days, and because the man was deaf he tuned it so loudly it blasted through the walls. The man listened to every news release. He got the CBC at eight and nine in the morning, Super Suds at ten, the BBC and CBC at the lunch-hour, and in the evening more CBC and BBC backed up by American commentators. Every single war and peace rumour, every half-baked prophecy sold to the networks at a thousand dollars a guess blared through the lodging house.

Sunday came, and a return of the heat: humid streets bleakly empty, workers uncomfortable in dark suits going to church, business men also uncomfortable driving in cars to the rich Protestant churches on Sherbrooke Street. About one o'clock, when he knew Marius would be home from

High Mass, he finally forced himself to telephone. Emilie answered. He promised to have supper with them that night, and then he hung up the receiver with a faint sigh.

Marius was living in the same house in the same street into which he had moved just after he and Emilie were married. As more children came, they had taken the upper flat to get more room. Every house on the street looked as if it had been built from the same blueprint of the same contractor, of the same materials. Each was of two stories, yellow brick on the sides and back, grey stone in front All had identical outside staircases of cast-iron which darkened the windows of the ground floor as they rose in bulging spirals from the sidewalks to the second floor. All of them had mean little protuberant balconies overcrowded by large families on hot days. When Paul arrived at six-thirty the street was loud with the noise of playing children. He counted the stairs from the end of the block until he found the correct house, remembering that Marius was eleven from the corner. As he mounted the spiral, two nieces and three nephews darted inside from the balcony.

All that evening Paul felt a total stranger in his brother's house. It was so long since he had seen the children that he found it embarrassingly difficult to call them by their right names. He admired the way Emilie managed them. Although the clothes of the youngest had been handed down, they were all neat and clean. The supper passed pleasantly enough; even when Emilie inquired of Paul's mother, Marius made no comment. Then she went out to the back bedrooms to put the younger children to bed, while the middle one went down to the street to play, and the oldest boy left to visit a friend. Marius took Paul into the parlour. It was cluttered with furniture bought at auction years ago, a row of law books lay on a shelf along one wall and there· was a table where Marius managed to work in the evenings. Newspapers, periodicals, religious tracts, political pamphlets and notes for political speeches were stacked on the window-sill. It was easy to see that Marius had a poor law practice. But with him, it was just another cause for grievance and he seemed quite unable to understand the reason. He was confident that he understood French-Canada better than anyone else, without ever having accepted the fact that at least up to the present its basic characteristic had been common sense. Nowhere on earth was a bad lawyer spotted more quickly than in Quebec.

Marius refused to talk of anything but politics. His bitterness had retained some of its fire, but now there was a querulous note in his voice. His gestures were as automatically dramatic as ever. He claimed he was not a fascist; he was what he had always been, a straight-forward nationalist who hadn't changed a single opinion since the war. He criticized every other politician in Quebec: they had all betrayed the people, the whole lot of them had gone soft or been bought out. He kept repeating the same things over and over. Economics? What did economics matter? A pure race, a pure language, larger families, no more connection with the English, no interference from foreigners, a greater clerical control over everything – with these conditions Quebec would reach the millennium. Scientists could split the atom and circumnavigate the globe in a week, but Marius had no difficulty reducing everything to race, religion and politics. At one time or another he had belonged to four different political parties; after quarrelling with all his former associates, he was now trying to found a new one of his own.

For three hours Paul listened to a voice that now was sharp, now sinuous, now poignant, but always was consciously oratorical. Emilie sat in the corner quietly darning socks. Paul was obsessed by the pity of Marius, and what he stood for. With every sentence he uttered, Marius was binding the strait-jacket tighter and tighter around himself. Was this the same process he had witnessed in Europe? If so, Marius didn't know it. To try to handle science by nationalism! God, did they have to do that here as well? It seemed as though Marius had to bind others to make himself feel free.

Once Paul protested against one of his arguments, saying that it was absurd of Marius to claim that he spoke for more than three per cent of the population. Marius started in a spurt of personal anger. 'What right have you to talk? You de-raced yourself long ago!'

After that, Paul kept quiet. The frustration his brother produced in him was nothing new, but now he was more detached from it; now he could feel the pity of it. After twenty years of struggle Marius was a nerve-shot man with black hair splashed with grey. He had too little money. He had to talk all day long to retain his hope. And Emilie stayed with him, supporting his fading confidence with a wonderful mixture of matter-of-fact and inarticulate tenderness. He neglected her; not for other women but because he was chronically unable to think of anyone but himself. She never saw it. Emilie had the bearing of a happy woman. 'I hope you're still a good Catholic,' she said to Paul at the door. 'It makes it easy not to worry about little things.'

Some of the humidity had been blown away by a night wind, and as Paul walked home his mind cleared with the weather. Now he felt a terrific release and relief. In seeing Marius he had seen more than his brother; he had seen the symbol of much of his past frustration. Objectively, from the outside. Instead of going home he kept on walking till past midnight, when he stopped at a Murray's for coffee and a sandwich. He listened to the talk of night-workers around him. They were relaxed and easy with each other, French and English together, radio technicians, theatre operators, telegraphers, men who had walked up from the railroad stations. None of them seemed worried or strained. They were together because of the nature of their jobs, and because the rest of the city was asleep.

By the time Paul reached home he had forgotten how late it was. He drew a chair up to the table, found a stack of yellow paper and sharpened a pair of pencils. Now he wished he had seen his brother days ago. Out of Marius, out of his own life, out of the feeling he had in his bones for his own province and the others surrounding it, the theme of his new book began to emerge. Its outlines grew so clear that his pencil kept moving steadily until three in the morning. He was not formulating sentences; he was drafting the design of a full novel. He had never before been able to see so far into any work he had attempted. Its material and symbols lay ready in his subconscious: the dilemma that had nearly strangled him all his life and which at last he had

375

managed to escape. He could view it now as though it belonged to another person; with pity, with some tenderness, but clearly and at a distance. Outlines of scenes he would later create followed each other inevitably, one by one out of his subconscious. He picked up ten pages covered with scrawled notes, and as he reread them he found that each scene had retained in his mind the transparent clarity of still water.

He put the papers away and went to bed. For some minutes he lay awake staring at a patch of ceiling lit by the beam of a street light. He tried to calculate his project coolly, in relation to the future. If he had nothing else to do he might be able to complete it within six months. Carrying on another job, it would take at least a year. He had enough money to last until the end of September; that gave him two months clear in which to work. He thought of Heather and his promise to get a job as soon as possible. The imperious urgency of his project trod over it. She would understand how he felt. Until the end of September his job was here in this room, at the typewriter.

Then he laughed sardonically in the darkness. He was forgetting the war, the coming of which had given him the confidence to marry Heather Methuen. Even in Montreal, most people seemed to take it for granted that it would begin this autumn. No matter what they said, the instinctual part of the crowd, the incalculable part which is surer than the brain of a genius, knew that war was coming with the same certainty a flock of birds knows when it will rain. And it knew that Canada would be in it from the beginning. In some of the current magazines were predictions that England would stand aside a second time. Paul was sure she wouldn't. But until war came, nothing here would outwardly change. It was just possible – not likely but certainly not inconceivable – that he could beat a world deadline.

He turned over on his side and fell asleep.

When he awoke the next morning he was filled with a sense of urgency he had never known before. He began writing immediately after breakfast and kept it up until one o'clock. Then after lunch, he wrote until five. He slept until seven, ate a quick supper and walked for an hour. Then he worked until one in the morning. Day after day he kept up this pace, and by the end of the first week in August he had a hundred revised pages on his improvised desk and he had discharged about five hundred more into the wastebasket. The sense of sureness with which his outline had been made remained with him. The details of individual scenes cataracted constantly before his eyes, woke him up at night and kept him staring at the splash of light on his ceiling. He heard the voices of his characters talking to each other. The rhythm of the whole seemed to be pulsing in his blood.

Out of the society which had produced and frustrated him, which in his own way he had learned to accept, he knew that he was at last beating out a harmony. His fingers seemed to be feeling down through the surface of character and action to the roots of the country itself. In all his life, he had never seen an English-Canadian and a French-Canadian hostile to each other face to face. When they disliked, they disliked entirely in the group. And the result of these two group-legends was a Canada oddly naive, so far without any real villains, without overt cruelty or criminal memories, a country strangely innocent in its groping individual common sense, intent on doing the right thing in the way some children are, tongue-tied because it felt others would not be interested in what it had to say; loyal, skilled and proud, race-memories lonely in great spaces.

46

Heather lay on the packed sand of Kennebunkport Beach and watched the rollers coasting in. Through dark glasses she saw them arch up in the late afternoon sun, break and pause, swing in a long backward sluice into the next coming waves. The air sang like the inside of a sea shell. The sun held her firmly to the sand, it glowed on her skin, it increased and spread her happiness so that she wondered if it were visible. Tomorrow she would be going home to Paul. She wondered how he would like her now; her back and arms and legs rich with sun, the rest of her skin like milk. Tomorrow his eyes would have her again.

From his letters she knew he had no job, but that he was

writing and that the book was going well. She was glad. It seemed senseless for him to break off writing to look for a job now. Tomorrow she would return with her mother, would go back to living in the Methuen house on the side of the mountain. It wouldn't be good, but it could be done; at least until his book was finished.

She picked up her beach-robe and began walking along the sand to the hotel. It was already late afternoon. Eight people stopped to talk to her before she reached the veranda, all Montrealers. Back in her own room she took a fresh-water bath, then put on a light frock and joined her mother in the lounge. Janet felt rather disturbed because Heather refused to wear mourning for her grandfather, but Janet's black chiffon dress, black silk stockings and black accessories seemed to Heather enough mourning for one family.

Janet was exceptionally cheerful when Heather found her in the lounge. She had been playing bridge all afternoon with friends from Montreal. Over a cocktail she told Heather some of the details of the game, including the peculiarities of her partners, and then they went in to dinner.

'I've been thinking, dear,' she said, 'we might as well stay here until the first of September. As a matter of fact, I tried to find the manager this afternoon. I'd like to keep the rooms we have.'

'But Mummy –' Heather laid down her soup spoon. 'I thought we were leaving tomorrow!'

'It's been very good for us both,' Janet said. 'When you came back from Nova Scotia you were looking dreadfully thin and tired. I know I've needed the rest myself after this dreadful year.'

Heather picked up the spoon again. 'You're looking much better now, Mummy.'

A couple came into the dining room and left the door open behind them. The voice of a news commentator blared after them from the radio in the lounge. The situation in Europe had noticeably deteriorated in the past twenty-four hours, he said. It was rumoured that Hitler had summoned Count Ciano to Berchtesgaden.

'I do wish they'd turn that radio off!' Janet said. 'Really – the announcers down here have such dreadful voices!'

'Then let's go home,' Heather said gravely. 'So you can listen to the BBC.'

'One ought to be able to get it here as well. Florence was saying that very thing this afternoon. After all, there are so many quite nice Americans. Florence was saying she simply can't understand why they don't do something about it.' Janet finished her soup and glanced out the window. The light was fading off the beach and the incoming combers looked cold. A slight fog was drifting in from the sea. 'This is quite a pleasant place, you know. It seems foolish to go home when so many of one's friends are here. Florence and I were laughing about it this afternoon. Three past presidents of the club are here now.'

A waitress came to take their soup bowls. Heather took a deep breath. 'Sorry, Mummy. I've made my plans to leave tomorrow.'

Janet looked at her daughter with a flash of suspicion. 'But you can easily change them, dear.'

Heather looked out the window and made no reply as the next course was set before them.

'I don't understand you, Heather,' Janet said.

'Well, let's not talk about it until after dinner.'

'But, dear – you know I can't stay here alone.'

'I've enjoyed it,' Heather said. 'It's been lovely.' She concentrated on her plate. 'But you said we'd stay three weeks, and I have an appointment in Montreal.'

Janet toyed with her roast beef. 'It can't possibly be more important than staying with me. There's no one left in Montreal in August.'

Heather waited a moment, then she said, 'Tell me what Daphne said in the letter you got this afternoon.'

'Didn't you see it?' Janet relaxed and began to eat again. 'Of course, she simply never tells anything in a letter. I think she does it on purpose.'

But in relating what Daphne did tell, Janet consumed ten minutes, and by that time the plates of the meat course were cleared. Daphne had been in Paris in early June but had returned to London for the season. Noel was so busy she seldom saw him any more. His factory was working day and night and Janet asked Heather if she didn't think that was perfectly splendid. Noel himself was back in the R.A.F. 'Of course,' Janet said, 'if they'd taken Noel's advice there'd have been no need for anyone to worry now. But they didn't.'

'They could have taken the advice of other men besides Noel.'

'Oh, well – there's no real need to worry anyway. Florence Murdoch was saying she'd met Lady Norne just before she came down here – she was Pamela Smith, you remember. She says nobody in London is worried; it's only the Americans. That's what the general always said. Whenever the Americans are worrying about England's affairs, you can be perfectly sure England has everything under control.'

Janet continued to talk while they ate ice cream and cake. Heather lit a cigarette with her coffee but her mother refused to smoke. 'American cigarettes are so harsh on my throat,' she said.

They rose from the table and walked out through the long dining room to the lounge. It was filled with old ladies knitting, and groups of young children trying to put off the hour of bedtime. The knitting women all looked up to note the entrance of Janet and her daughter. In the middle of the lounge Janet stopped. 'Wait here a minute, will you, dear? I must speak to the manager now about holding our rooms.'

Heather touched her mother's elbow. 'Mummy,' she said quietly, 'I meant what I said. I can't stay any longer.'

Janet flashed her a sharp look. One hand smoothed the folds of the black chiffon over her flat abdomen as she glanced about the lounge and then back at her daughter. 'I do wish you wouldn't be so headstrong,' she said. 'There's no appointment you could possibly have at home that you can't perfectly well get out of.'

Heather held her mother's eyes. It was the same as it had always been; nothing she said ever made the slightest difference. She started to speak, and then she stopped. Finally she said, 'Paul Tallard is there.' Sudden fixity in Janet's eyes. 'We're – we're in love. We're – '

Janet's nervous movements ceased. She stood quite still, and then she said, 'Don't be absurd, Heather! You know that's quite impossible!'

The old ladies who watched them over their knitting saw no notable change in Janet's manner. Some colour must have drained from her cheeks, but her smile in response to nods from friends was as gracious as ever. From the corner of one eye she saw Florence Murdoch approaching, and easily, sweetly, she turned to her fellow-director on many club boards.

'We're all ready,' Florence Murdoch said. 'The table's set up in the sun-parlour tonight. And we've found a new fourth.' She laid chubby fingers on Janet's forearm and added in a stage-whisper, 'Mrs. Falconridge. We met her at tea yesterday. I do believe she'll turn out to be one of the nicer Americans.' She turned to Heather. 'Still not playing bridge?'

'Heather pretends to despise it,' Janet said brightly. She hunted for a white handkerchief in the black purse she always carried.

Florence Murdoch laughed. 'I was reading a book by Somerset Maugham the other day. You really ought to get it, Heather. Mr. Maugham says a good bridge game is better than an insurance policy. Or something like that.'

'Heather reads everything,' Janet said. 'Do you remember that passage, dear?'

Heather remembered it well. Maugham had said that to learn a good bridge game was the safest insurance against the tedium of old age.

'Of course! You were always so clever about books, weren't you, dear?' Florence Murdoch went on. She turned to Janet and began a long description of Mrs. Falconridge. Janet remarked that poor General Methuen had said only last winter that on the whole he felt the Americans were improving. Janet promised to join the bridge table in a few moments, and Florence Murdoch moved away. The old ladies continued to count stitches.

When Janet turned back to Heather she found that her

381

daughter had disappeared. Alone in the centre of the lounge she drew in her breath and lifted her chin. The purse was tucked firmly under one arm and the white handkerchief was clutched in her right hand. Again she took a deep breath and moved carefully, with measured steps and a consciousness of many eyes upon her, to the desk. When she spoke to the clerk her voice had never sounded more British.

'I want you to put through a long-distance call for me,' she said. 'Immediately. To Huntly McQueen in Montreal. I'll be in the sun-parlour when it comes through.'

47

Heather woke at seven the next morning after a broken sleep. The air was salt with fog and beyond the window was only a grey nothingness. For an hour she lay awake, her thoughts racing, and then gradually she quieted and fell asleep again. It was nine-thirty when she woke the second time. She felt rested, but fog still covered the beach and she could hear the voices of children below the window complaining about it. She dressed quickly and went downstairs for breakfast.

The dining room was almost empty as she entered. She walked through to their regular table before the windows, and stopped short when she saw Huntly McQueen sitting with her mother. There he was as solid and rotund as ever, nodding his head ponderously in response to whatever her mother was saying. His heavy face was a composition of curves and circles, tufted eyebrows turned up and the corners of his mouth turned down. The curve of his jaw was balanced firmly by the tire of flesh at the back of his neck. Although it was hot and sticky, McQueen was wearing a dark business suit and a polka-dot bow-tie in a soft white collar. His round head was balanced like a dome on his shoulders, his frizzy hair was a horseshoe around the skull. He caught sight of her and by an obvious effort of will smiled, his head moving slowly as he did so, like a turtle trying to be amiable.

Heather sat down, unfolded her napkin and smiled at the waitress who came to take her order. McQueen, who had jumped up at her approach, sat down also.

'Heather!' Janet said. 'After all – we have a guest!'

She studied the menu. 'So I notice.'

'Heather!'

McQueen cleared his throat. 'Come, Janet. Come now! It's all right. I quite understand.'

'I'm not hungry this morning, Marie,' Heather said. 'Orange juice and toast will be enough. And coffee.'

McQueen cleared his throat again. 'Well, well, my dear! Your mother and I have been talking.'

'Naturally,' Heather said.

Janet smiled at friends two tables away and her voice had never been sweeter as her glance came back to rest on her daughter. 'We are only thinking of your own good, you know. Huntly had a most uncomfortable trip down, too. You've always hated air-conditioned trains, haven't you, Huntly? Then he had to drive all the way here from Portland by car.'

Heather paid no attention to either of them, and for a third time McQueen cleared his throat. 'Now then, Heather. We might as well get to the point, eh?' He chuckled ponderously. 'Your mother tells me you've been getting ideas in your head.'

The waitress arrived with the toast, orange juice and coffee. Heather sat back in her chair until the food was placed before her and the waitress had departed. Then she said, 'Fancy my personal affairs being so important that Huntly had to come all the way down from Montreal!'

'I don't understand your attitude at all,' Janet said.

Heather drank the orange juice and laid the empty glass aside. 'Have you ever really tried to understand it?' she said. 'I told you last night I was in love with Paul. In view of the way you received the information, there seems nothing more to say.' She looked at McQueen. 'And I'm hardly prepared to address a public meeting.'

'What a thing to say!' Janet touched McQueen's wrist with her fingers. 'I'm awfully sorry, Huntly.'

Heather picked up her knife and began to butter a piece of toast. McQueen folded his hands on the table and hunched forward, as if gathering his forces.

'Let's be reasonable,' he said. 'I've known you all your life, Heather. Who else should your mother turn to in trouble but me?'

'Is Mummy in trouble?'

'Well, now...' McQueen pulled his waistcoat down. 'I don't need to remind you that your mother has been under a great strain these past few months. We must both have consideration for her.' His voice grew sonorous. 'Your attitude seems to be completely unreasonable. No one has said a word against your, ah – your plans. We just want to know the facts of the situation, that's all. There are many things to consider in a matter of this kind – particularly for a girl in your position.'

Heather looked at McQueen. 'I'm quite willing to discuss it with Mummy,' she said quietly.

McQueen looked from mother to daughter and chuckled. 'Tell me about your young man. What does he do?'

'He writes.'

'Oh! What else does he do?'

'At the moment, nothing.'

McQueen and Janet exchanged glances. 'That's what your mother and I both feared,' he said.

'You don't need to be afraid, Huntly. Writing is quite a good enough job for anyone.'

McQueen leaned back and his grey eyes seemed to be looking through the solid fog beyond the window. 'You know, I've lived in Canada all my life. I've been in every city in the country, and I think I can say I've met everyone of any importance in it. But apart from Ralph Connor and Stephen Leacock, I've never met a single writer who could live by books alone. Those are pretty important facts to consider, don't you think?'

Heather finished her coffee. 'I don't want to be rude, but I think it very probable that both Paul and I know a good deal more about the profession than you do.'

'Perhaps. Perhaps.' McQueen pulled his waistcoat down again. 'After all, I'm merely a practical man. From what I know of your young man's background, I should guess that he's far from a fool. After all, I knew his father well, you know.'

Heather gave him such a sharp look he quickly changed his tack. 'Anyway, my dear – I don't think I'm jumping to conclusions when I infer that under the present circumstances your young man is interested in a good job, if he can find one. I made a few inquiries in Montreal last night and I got the impression – correct me if I'm wrong – that he's never had any permanent kind of position. He's nearly thirty now, if my calculations are correct. And that's not a fact to overlook. When a man reaches that age it's high time for him to, ah – stop sowing his wild oats and get something solid under his feet.'

Heather lit a cigarette and made no reply. McQueen rubbed his chin. 'Of course I can't guarantee him anything in the writing line. As you say, I know nothing of things like that. But I can certainly get him an honest job.' He watched her face. Its expression changed and he felt a quiet satisfaction because the situation was obviously yielding to him, as all situations always did.

'What kind of a job?' Heather said.

McQueen and Janet exchanged glances again. 'Well, of course, I can't be explicit now. There's no need to be hasty. I'll have to wait until I get back to Montreal. But there's no doubt about it, Heather – if your young man is willing to work, I'll guarantee him a job.'

'What kind of a job?' Heather kept her eyes on his face.

'Now, now – please!' McQueen raised his index finger. 'That's something you'll have to leave to me. But I think, all things considered, I can safely say you have nothing to worry about. Give me his address and I'll call him as soon as I get back.'

With some hesitation Heather gave McQueen Paul's address and the telephone number of the house where he was living. McQueen put on his pince-nez and wrote the information in a pocket notebook. When pen and notebook were back in his pocket, he said, 'Now then, Heather. There's one more thing. Your mother is tired. She needs all our consideration. I want you to be a good girl and stay here with her for at least a week or ten days more. I don't have to remind you that we all have duties that can't be overlooked.'

'It's not just for myself, dear,' Janet interrupted. 'It's –

it's all sorts of things. I'm sure if I go back now in all the heat I won't be well. And now that your grandfather has gone – you must realize that I'm responsible for a great many things. We both are, now. Our family has its position to consider. And you and I are the only ones left in the big house.'

Heather rose from the table. 'I'm going out,' she said. 'For a walk.'

She left the dining room without glancing back, went upstairs, put on a raincoat and walked out to the sand. The fog surrounded her; cool, salt and wet on her cheeks and hair. She had always loved fog. Fog and rain. She loved it almost as much as she loved the sun. She walked rapidly down the deserted beach, with breakers beating steadily underneath the fog on her right.

Her thoughts beat in rhythm. She was twenty-eight, she had lived alone in New York for nearly four years, she loved a man and was his legal wife. In spite of this they still treated her as a child. Even if they knew of the marriage, it would still be no easier to make them understand what passed in her mind than it would be to converse with Eskimos. God in Heaven – why couldn't she be free of this! Love for Janet? Pity for her? Habit? She thought of McQueen with his Midas touch and his unaccountable ability to suck the work and energy out of everyone. He and Paul – both couldn't be right. The world of one or the other must yield. Had there ever been a time in human history like the present, when the older generation was blind to nearly every vital issue for which their children were prepared to fight and die?

She slowed her rapid walk, climbed over a rocky headland, and after awhile turned on her tracks and moved slowly back along the sand to the hotel, her hands in the pockets of her raincoat. She kept remembering Paul's matter-of-fact remark that men like McQueen could not help themselves, that the world had merely reached a point at which their instincts betrayed them in everything they did. Well, they could blunder into a war, but they couldn't wage it alone. She trembled and clenched her hands in her pockets. Day by day the size of the newspaper headlines had been increasing. It was coming. Inexorably, like the waves under the fog, it was coming upon them.

The indignity of her present position made her flush with shame. She realized now what she had tried to forget when she had been with Paul, that the instincts and training Janet had breathed into her were far from dead. She still dreaded a scene with her mother, dreaded the bitterness and hatred that might spring from it. All her life she had hedged and dissimulated in order not to upset Janet. Now she was burdened by a dread of what her mother might do to Paul's pride. Because his father happened to be French and his mother Irish – but most of all because he was poor – Janet's instinct would make her stab at his pride until she had inflicted a wound that might never heal.

When she reached the lawn before the hotel she saw her mother and McQueen sitting side by side on the veranda, huddled in raincoats like passengers aboard ship. Janet seemed excited, gesturing as she talked and McQueen was listening and nodding heavily. Ocassionally he raised his index finger and held it like a pointer to emphasize a remark.

Heather turned and walked back into the fog again. She walked for an hour, had something to eat in Kennebunkport village, returned again. By that time McQueen had left.

48

McQueen's taxi had a puncture on the way back to Portland and he sat in the back seat while the driver jacked it up and changed the tire. Inland on U.S. 1 there was no fog and the sun beat straight down through the moist air. When finally he reached Portland, McQueen had barely time to catch his train. He paused just long enough to pick up a newspaper, a copy of *Fortune*, and a left-wing weekly featuring an article on the British Empire.

When he reached his compartment he was sweating profusely and his hand stuck to the lining of his pocket as he fished for coins to tip the red-cap. He was tired, worried and overheated, and because the train was air-conditioned he was sure he was going to catch cold. If the Americans kept on with this mania for comfort, he thought, they would ruin the health of their whole nation inside another twenty-five years.

He mopped his forehead with a large silk handkerchief and stumbled through to the dining car. As soon as he had eaten, he returned to his compartment and locked himself in. He took off his jacket and waistcoat and put on a thick woolen dressing-gown made of the McQueen plaid. He removed his shoes and thrust his feet into a pair of felt-lined slippers, put the magazines on the seat beside him and tried to relax.

Last week a cabinet minister had telephoned from Ottawa to ask if he would consent to serve in his department if the worst happened. The thought of working for the government was revolting to McQueen, but if the worst came to the worst, he supposed he would have to do his duty. There was no doubt about it, they were worried sick in Ottawa, and so was he. Every time he read a newspaper he felt personally badgered by what was happening in Europe. He simply couldn't believe there would be a war. And yet . . .

On top of everything, it was worse than too bad of Heather to choose a time like the present to make trouble for her mother. She was showing no more sense of responsibility than a servant. McQueen's ponderous jaw hardened. He could not understand the lack of common decency and ordinary loyalty in young people these days. Everywhere he looked, he saw signs of decay. He wouldn't be surprised . . .

Well, McQueen decided, this nonsense was going to be stopped, for if Heather married someone like Paul Tallard anything might come of it. So he was a writer, was he? McQueen would very much like to see what he had ever written. Probably some modernistic nonsense about socialism and sex that no decent publisher would touch.

What Heather needed was a stable husband to make her toe the line. If she married this Paul Tallard, they would both sponge on her mother. It stood to reason the fellow was no good if he hadn't a decent job at his age. The moment they got their hands on the Methuen house they would sell it to some contractor and the contractor would demolish it. Then he would build a ten-story apartment house on the lot. Another house on the same level as his own, a thirty-room stone mansion with a conservatory and sixteen gargoyles, had been demolished last spring, and the mahogany panelling of its dining room had been sold to a funeral parlour. That was what happened nowadays if you let your standards down. He had worked hard all his life. And for what? To be able to associate on equal terms with people like the Methuens.

McQueen got up and wiped his forehead vigorously with a towel, then took a muffler from his bag and wrapped it around his neck. He felt much better now. He wouldn't be surprised if he escaped the cold after all.

He sat down and crossed his legs. There was nothing to worry about once you figured things out. He would stop this nonsense, all right. Paul Tallard might be a socialist, but he couldn't marry without money and he couldn't get it unless he had a job. Janet would see that Heather's allowance was stopped if she tried any nonsense. But then – McQueen chuckled at his own sagacity – Paul Tallard was going to have a job! McQueen intended to be perfectly fair. He would do the best he could for the boy. There was a job in British Columbia and he might consider himself very lucky to get it. If he worked hard enough, he might even think of getting married in ten years. But not to Heather! Oh, no! Once they were separated by three-quarters of a continent, Heather would soon come to her senses. Later on in life she would thank him for what he had done for her. He and Janet had been agreed on that.

McQueen picked up the newspaper and began to read. After five minutes he dropped it on the floor. Things were getting to be a nightmare. You gave a scoundrel like Hitler an inch and he tried to take everything. If a major war broke out it wouldn't matter where a man's money was. The government would get it somehow.

It particularly exasperated McQueen not to know what was going to happen, not to be positive. He had been positive enough a year ago. He had maintained after Munich that Mr. Chamberlain had shown Hitler the meaning of true statesmanship. But now? Last week Chislett had told him in confidence that if war broke out the government had no intention of making it attractive to business. Things were certainly bad if a man like Chislett forgot himself sufficiently to make a remark like that. It was the kind of phrase that could be given a nasty twist if the wrong people got hold of it. Well, if war did come, McQueen was prepared to thank God that the Prime Minister was an able man who knew how to keep his mouth shut.

Looking for something less disturbing to read, McQueen picked up the weekly. On the first two pages he was informed that the true cause of the world crisis was the selfish decadence of capitalists. They had made a mess out of their own affairs. They had sold Manchuria, Abyssinia and Czechoslovakia down the river, and now they were hoist with their own petard.

In a rage, McQueen hurled the magazine across the compartment. The Mounted Police ought to keep that sort of perjury out of Canada. So he was decadent was he? So he was supporting Hitler and Mussolini against the Bolsheviks? He'd like to see the socialist who would dare make a statement like that in a court of law. He had worked hard all his life, had saved his money, had never got drunk or gone with women. If anyone was to blame, blame the socialists. Hitler was a socialist himself. He had always said so, and he defied anyone to refute him.

His sense of outrage mounted. Let Hitler make another move! Just let him dare! Deep in his core, McQueen felt the reverberations of fighting ancestors.

49

On Monday morning McQueen reached his office before nine-thirty, and without taking time to glance at his letters, he ordered his secretary to get Paul Tallard on the telephone and tell him to present himself at his office at eleven forty-five.

Since the death of Miss Drew four years ago, McQueen had never been satisfied with the way his office functioned. He had hired three different secretaries and had fired them all. His present one was a silent-mannered, prematurely bald man who was understood to have had a bad time during the depression. He was better than the others, but McQueen did not think much of him.

He picked up the *Gazette,* glanced over the headlines and saw that the news had become even worse. He was about to drop the paper into the wastebasket when the secretary returned.

'Well, Hudson – what is it now?'

'I spoke to Mr. Tallard, sir. He – he told me he was busy and wouldn't come.'

McQueen gave Hudson a blank stare. 'Did you make yourself clear who it was wanted to see him?'

'I certainly did, Mr. McQueen. His manner was very brusque, if I may say so.'

McQueen grunted. 'Call him again. When you get him on the wire, connect me at once.'

Hudson departed noiselessly, sliding out the door on the balls of his feet. McQueen grunted again. He wouldn't even trust Hudson to mail a letter without specific orders. It was what he had always said, the people who had been unemployed in the depression had so little confidence left they were no good for anything.

The call came through and he picked up the telephone. He talked in his blandest voice for a full minute, then frowned as he received nothing but a monosyllable in reply. He became so irritated it required all his conscious force to keep his voice solicitous as he repeated his proposition. Another few minutes went by, and during that time Hudson entered on tip-toe with a memorandum in his hand. McQueen motioned him to lay it on the desk. 'A book on Canada? My dear boy . . . wouldn't it be well for you to see a little of the country first?'

As he listened to Paul's answer, McQueen's eyes picked out the words on the memo. Paul went on talking, but McQueen was no longer listening to him. The words on the memo stated that Sir Rupert Irons had died fifteen minutes ago.

McQueen heard his own voice saying, 'You're being very foolish, of course. I suppose you know what you're doing. You can be assured I'll report exactly what you've said to Mrs. Methuen tonight.'

He slammed the receiver down, picked up the memo in both hands and stared at it again, then snapped at Hudson, 'Get me Mr. Masterman at once. Get me Mr. Chislett. Get

391

me Mr. Buchanan. Oh yes – get me Sir Roderick Horson too. He's in Nassau in the Bahamas. Get him at once.'

McQueen lunched that day in the Mount Royal Club. Afterwards he sat in a deep chair and brooded over the obituary picture in the afternoon paper. In spite of the world crisis, the press had gone into mourning for Sir Rupert Irons. The square head, square jaw, square mouth, square shoulders and the small biting eyes had almost crowded Hitler off the front page. Much of the second page was occupied with the list of Irons' innumerable services to the nation, and the unbelievably large number of companies he had controlled.

It was hard for McQueen to credit it. For more than a quarter of a century Irons had stood in Saint James Street as four-square as the Duke of Wellington. Now his empire was passing without a tremor to the oligarchy which had served under his guidance during his life. By Jove, McQueen thought, there was a lesson here! A lesson in the meaning of soundness: Irons' affairs were in such perfect order that his death had not affected the market by so much as half a point.

Contemplating the picture, McQueen made clucking noises with his tongue. They were all going! MacIntosh had died last February, General Methuen had passed on in the spring. Masterman was beginning to look very seedy and Chislett had been on his last legs for years. But for Irons to go! Well, he would at least escape the war, if the war came. McQueen read all the paper had to say about the life and death of Sir Rupert Irons, and was forced to admit that when his own time came the spread given him would not be as large. There was no doubt about it, Irons had personified an era. He had been the great master in soundness. The country would never be the same without him.

As McQueen was to be a pall-bearer at the funeral, he was kept very busy during the next two days. He barely remembered to call Janet and inform her of his conversation with Paul. A funeral of this dimension seemed to McQueen something far greater than the mere burial of a friend. Each great city had some special way of demonstrating its communal spirit and showing its face to the world. London used the Lord Mayor's Show, New York the procession of a hero up Broadway, the French section of Montreal the parade on the day of Saint-Jean Baptiste. But in McQueen's opinion, his own Montreal reserved itself for an occasion more personal and significant. Only on the death of one of their own number did the real controllers of the nation, the businessmen who were as unobtrusive as a hierarchy, gather in force before the public eye.

McQueen could never remember a funeral which required so many arrangements as this one. Irons had no family or relations, and he had complicated matters by his last coherent wish. He had expressed the desire that the service be held not in his customary church, but in a small one in the factory district where he had lived as a boy. He had also required that a particular minister be summoned from Toronto to conduct the service. McQueen fussed considerably over these details, which seemed completely unnecessary to him. It was exactly like Irons to surprise everybody, right up to the last. The church he had selected was not only small and poor, it was so located that the mourners would have to walk nearly two miles before they could decently step out of the cortege. McQueen wouldn't be surprised but what Irons had thought of that. He wondered if Chislett would be up to it. Chislett had not walked a hundred yards since he had bought his first Rolls-Royce in 1912.

Hours before the service began, a crowd had gathered on the street opposite the church. As the mourners entered the vestry, each spoke his name to reporters stationed at the door, who wrote it hurriedly in notebooks for publication in the press the following day. English Montreal had turned out everyone from ten-thousand-a-year men up, and many had made the trip from Toronto, Hamilton, Ottawa and Winnipeg. The directors of four-fifths of the nation's major banks and corporations were there. They sat gravely together in reserved pews. The coffin was to be borne by men who between them controlled (now that Irons was dead) more than four billion dollars, paying the ultimate homage to the man who had made and controlled more money than any one of them.

393

The service began. The minister's voice, deeply over-toned with centuries of Presbyterianism, rolled over the heads of the directors, bankers, insurance presidents, rail-road heads, stockbrokers, brewers, distillers, justices, cor-poration lawyers, the board of governors of the university, the Committee of Art, headmasters, the boardmen of the charitable societies, executives, stock-holders, four poli-ticians, three aldermen, two cabinet ministers – and the others.

The Scriptures, the minister said resolutely, had left no doubt that it was easier for a camel to pass through a needle's eye than for a rich man to enter the kingdom of hea-ven. But the Lord, in His infinite wisdom and mercy, had never said it was impossible. Sir Rupert Irons had known this. No man who ever lived had been more fully aware than Sir Rupert of the spiritual dangers attendant on great wealth. It was for this reason that he had avoided all osten-tation in his life, that he had furnished his home with the barest of necessities, that he had never taken a holiday, in order to reserve his powers for the fuller service to mankind that his wealth had demanded. It was for this reason that he had always praised poverty as the best school of virtue. Few had known poverty more fully than Sir Rupert Irons in the days of his youth. Few had done so much by way of the thousands – nay, the hundreds of thousands – of positions created through his nation-wide enterprises, to alleviate the poverty of others. Recognizing that he lived in a commer-cial age, he had in all humility regarded himself as God's trustee, a faithful steward such as Joseph had been to the rich man of Egypt.

The minister asked the mourners how charities could exist without such men as Sir Rupert Irons. And how, with-out charities, could the nation thrive? He pointed out that Irons himself, remembering the Scriptures, had never failed to do his alms in secret. Legion though his benefactions had been, they were known only unto God and the recipients.

Everyone would recall Sir Rupert's favourite saying: 'A beggar may at least spend his last ten-cent piece on a cup of coffee, but a banker must render account of the utter-most farthing!" How well had their friend lived up to that homely motto! If the financial structure of Canada was still the soundest of all nations, if she was an oasis of stability in a troubled world, the people well knew whom they must thank.

When the organ struck up the Dead March, the coffin was wheeled noiselessly down the aisle to the vestibule, then borne to the hearse by eight directors of corporations, while press photographers snapped their pictures, and policemen saluted, and thousands watched. Then a tide of bankers, brokers, governors, justices, brewers, distillers, lawyers, executives, stock-holders and politicians, each with a silk hat on his head, flowed in solemn silence down the steps.

The street in that slum district was very narrow, and most of the mourners had not been within a mile of it in their lives. Now the sun gleamed sleekly on their silk hats, and the hats bobbed unevenly but with collective rhythm as they struggled up the hill after the hearse. Labourers, clerks, housewives, loafers, children and unemployed stood silently on the curb watching them. The street was utterly noiseless except for the shuffle of feet and the sigh of ponderous breathing, and as McQueen padded along and heard Chislett panting behind him, he was haunted by the thought that the man would never make Sherbrooke Street. There was no doubt about it, Chislett would be the next.

Finally they reached the boulevard. But not even in their own preserves would the outside world let them alone. In the near distance newsboys were bawling the afternoon's headlines. McQueen heard Hitler's name repeated over and over. The newsboys came nearer, running toward the crowd. HITLER SENDS ULTIMATUM . . . HITLER MOBILIZES . . . HITLER SAYS HE WILL FIGHT . . .

Why can't they leave a man alone, McQueen thought, why can't they leave us in peace?

50

In the hotels that line the Maine beaches from Portland to Kittery, the death of Sir Rupert Irons seemed, at least for a few hours, more important than the world crisis. Hardly a dozen of the thousands of Montrealers and Ontarians summering there had known Irons personally, but all of them had heard his name as long as they could remember.

The morning after the first Montreal papers arrived with news of the event, Heather met Mrs. Falconridge as she was leaving the dining room.

'Your Sir Rupert Irons must have been a very great man,' the American said.

'A great many people thought so,' Heather said gravely.

'It's the most amazing thing! You Canadians seem to know all about our affairs down here. I've met so many who agree with me on Mr. Roosevelt and John L. Lewis. But we simply don't know a thing about your country. You know, Heather, I'd never even heard of Sir Rupert Irons before this morning!'

'But Mrs. Falconridge – it's almost as though God had died!'

Heather caught a suggestion of understanding in Mrs. Falconridge's eyes as she left her. In the lounge the old ladies were still discussing Irons' affairs. They mentioned his devoutness. They wondered if some secret sorrow had prevented his getting married. They speculated on where his money would go, and how much the death-duties would be. One old lady remembered the time when he had defied the whole Dominion Government to do its worst. They all repeated to each other that the country would never be the same without him.

That morning Janet took her breakfast in bed. Some time after nine o'clock, Heather had poked her head in the door, seen her mother lying back on the pillow with her eyes closed, and shut the door again quietly. As soon as she had gone, Janet opened her eyes.

Never in her life had she felt more wretched. Ever since Huntly McQueen's telephone call the evening before, she had been so miserable that sleep was impossible. He had told her about Irons' death, and that he was very busy on account of the funeral. He had told her – she thought in a very off-hand manner – that as Paul Tallard had refused to take the job he had offered, there seemed nothing more he could do about the situation at present. Then he had gone on talking about Irons as if he had completely forgotten her problem. Who cared about Irons anyway, Janet thought. General Methuen had always called him a bounder. Why, General Methuen had said ever so many times that he could remember when Rupert Irons' father used to drive a wagon for one of the breweries!

Janet thought back on what a horrible night she had spent. Around two in the morning she had made up her mind that McQueen had let her down. At one of the most important moments in her life, Huntly had been so engrossed in his own selfish affairs that he had forgotten all about her! And after all the plans they had made together! Over the phone he had also wasted good time talking about the war news from Europe, as if she were incapable of reading the papers for herself. By three in the morning, Janet began to have serious doubts about McQueen's sincerity. He was a selfish old bachelor. If he hadn't been so engrossed in his own comfort he would have married long ago and had a family. What did he understand about what a woman – any woman – has to suffer?

When dawn came, Janet was so restless she took a warm bath. It did nothing to make her feel any better. Heather was her own daughter, she was all she had left, she had given that child her whole life and now Heather never gave the slightest thought for her happiness. It was nothing new. Heather was always criticizing her. She had sent her to college and after that the child had felt superior. As if she didn't understand her own daughter like an open book! Heather was always quoting outrageous opinions from things she read and expecting her to be impressed by them. It was a disgrace the sort of things they gave immature girls to study in college these days. Florence Murdoch had been saying that very thing only yesterday. They went to college and came out of it ungrateful, callous and selfish. They thought they knew more than their elders because some glib young professors without a penny to bless themselves with taught them a jargon nobody else could understand.

Now, at nine o'clock, after having nibbled at dry toast and sipped some tepid coffee, Janet got out of bed and went to the dressing table. On the way she put on a sheer black negligee and the black jet beads she wore at all times to hide

397

the scar on her neck where a goiter had been removed. Carefully she creamed her face, patted the skin with an expensive tonic, put on a layer of foundation cream, and then added a nearly-white powder. She refrained from using the merest touch of the rouge she generally wore.

As she studied her face in the glass she decided she looked ghastly. She wasn't well, and no wonder. She sat very still and listened intently to the beat of her heart. She sighed heavily, and slowly began to arrange her hair. As the brush swept back and forth fifty times, her mind examined every aspect of her immediate problem. She felt she was studying it with deliberate craft, softly entering into every corner of it, like a cat discovering a strange room.

She had taken too much for granted all her life, that was her trouble. Because she had sacrificed her entire life for her children, she had naturally expected a dutiful affection in return. And now she was faced with this! If Harvey were alive...

Tears stood in her eyes and she allowed them to rest there; they brimmed and overflowed and she sat quite still watching them erode the white powder on her cheeks. She was not well. She was all alone in the world and unwell, and at this particular moment Heather was deliberately taking advantage of her. All her life she had tried so hard; so hard she was really quite exhausted. She had always been ten times more careful to do the right thing than anyone else she knew. It was utterly heartless of Heather to disregard her at a time like this, only a few months after her two grandfathers had died.

Janet enlarged on the picture of her own desolation. One by one they had left her. First her mother, then Harvey. Then Daphne: she might as well have died as gone off to England. Then the general, her own father, and now Heather! Last of all Huntly McQueen had abandoned her.

A fury of rage shook her body as she thought about McQueen. After all these years – good heavens, after a quarter of a century! Who was Huntly McQueen, anyway? Where would he have been today if it hadn't been for her? He owed his entire social position to her and to the Methuens.

He thought he was very clever, but she knew, she could see through him. And now, just because Rupert Irons was being laid away in state . . .

She had learned her lesson, and she wouldn't be fool enough to believe what anyone told her after this. She was a sick woman, and she had to think of her health.

Janet gave a final pat to her well-combed hair and went back to bed. She arranged the sheet, the blanket and the counterpane neatly across her extended legs, smoothed the folds of the negligee across her flat chest, and then picked up the phone beside the bed. She asked the desk-clerk if her daughter could be found and sent to her at once. While waiting for Heather to arrive, she counted her pulse.

When the door opened, Janet's head was on the pillows and her hands were lying limply at her sides. 'Come in, dear,' she murmured. 'Shut the door and sit down. I – we must have a talk. It's too late to put it off any longer. I didn't sleep all night.'

Heather's voice was quick with sympathy. 'Mummy!'

'I don't want to frighten you, dear. Now sit down and don't worry.'

Heather's voice showed alarm. 'Mummy – is anything the matter?'

'No. No, I don't think . . . Please sit still and I'll be all right. I'm sure I will.'

Heather sat down. 'I didn't sleep much either, I'm afraid. It makes the morning after feel pretty rocky.'

Janet sighed heavily, and her escaping breath had a break in it. 'I'm glad you've been thinking things over too, dear.'

'Mummy – you're really all right, aren't you?'

Heather looked at her mother anxiously. Janet's face was like chalk and her eyes staring out of it were unnaturally large.

'Now dear, before . . . but I'd like you to tell me something first.'

'First?'

Janet made a movement with the fingers of one hand, as if she were too weak to do anything more. She forced the beginning of a smile. 'I'd like you to tell me that you didn't

399

really mean what you said to me the other night. I felt sure you'd think much better of it, once you realized how impossible it was.'

Heather pulled a package of cigarettes out of her purse, extracted one and lit it. Janet watched every movement closely. Heather exhaled the first breath of smoke and said quietly, 'I'd have been quite willing to tell you about Paul. But you didn't ask, and you showed as clearly as you could that you didn't want to discuss him. Instead you had to call Huntly down from Montreal and make some plans of your own behind my back. I don't want to be unpleasant, Mummy, but that's exactly what you did. I don't think you'd have appreciated it if your mother had done the same thing when you told her you intended marrying Father.'

Janet's right hand moved with a spasmodic jerk to her left breast. She clutched herself and an expression of sharp and sudden agony flashed across her face. 'How can you! How can you say such a thing to your own mother!'

'It seems quite a natural thing to say. Mummy – what's the matter?'

'I don't know.' Janet's voice seemed to be forcing itself out through an excruciating pain. 'I'm ... I'm ... in pain! It's ...' She whispered, 'It's my heart!'

Heather went to the bed and laid her hand under her mother's left breast. She felt the beat; it was distinct and regular. 'It's probably the lobster you ate last night,' she said. 'Would you like some soda?'

Janet began to moan.

'Please, Mummy! Please – don't go to pieces so easily. Tell me what it is and I'll do the best I can to help you.'

'How can anyone be so callous!' Janet cried at her. She sat straight up in bed. 'Such a tone of voice from my own daughter! I've done everything for you all my life. How can you!'

Heather frowned as she looked at her mother more closely. 'Mummy – please! I can't help how my voice sounds. I'm sorry. I thought you'd excited yourself. Where's the pain?' She placed her hand over her mother's stomach.

Janet shrank away. 'Don't! Don't touch me! Please sit down. It will pass in a moment. Sit down, Heather, and don't be so fidgety. I – I must talk to you – in spite of it.'

Heather still watched her. 'Would you like a doctor?'

Janet shook her head from side to side. 'No. I don't think so. Sit down. Don't stand like that.'

Heather sat down and her mother swallowed heavily, coughed slightly, and then lay back with her eyes closed. Presently she opened them and sighed. 'The pain is a little better now.'

'That's good.'

After another moment, Janet said, 'Huntly telephoned last night.' As Heather made no reply she continued, 'I'm afraid he's very upset. He has so much on his mind these days, and it was such a pity that – that rudeness and ingratitude should make it worse for him. Huntly's always been so sensitive – much more than people realize.'

'I've no doubt,' Heather said.

Janet's eyes were quite normal now, and so was her voice. 'He got in touch with the Tallard boy, exactly as he promised. Something exceptionally good turned up in British Columbia – a school. Huntly offered him a fine position there, teaching French.'

'At a thousand dollars a year?' Heather asked quietly.

'He didn't mention the salary to me. Your young man was so rude I very much doubt if Huntly even mentioned it to him. He practically told Huntly to mind his own business.' Seeing the trace of a smile on Heather's lips, Janet raised her voice. 'He actually refused to discuss terms with Huntly at all. Huntly is furious and I certainly don't blame him!'

'Did Paul give any reason for his refusal?'

'How can you expect me to remember everything Huntly said over the telephone? As if I didn't know anyway! That kind of a person – I've always said those French-Canadians were all the same. Oh, Heather . . .' Her voice trembled. 'As if I didn't know! You're well out of it. Very well out of it indeed!'

Heather's hands were clenched tightly on her purse, but her voice was quietly controlled. 'What reason did Paul give for refusing the job, Mummy?'

'What difference does it make? The point is, he's shown himself in his true colours. He's ungrateful, and he . . . Your grandfather always used to say that blood and breeding wii. tell every time. Let's both be thankful you found him out in time.'

Heather's face was expressionless. 'What else did Huntly say?'

Janet shook her head from side to side. 'Heather dear – can't you see this is all for your own good? It would have been such an awful mistake for you to have made – a mixed marriage like that. I'm quite sure he's quite a decent boy – among his own kind. You're . . .' Janet's hands were drumming on the spread. 'You must know this, Heather. I've devoted my whole life to your happiness. You'll make a really brilliant marriage one of these days. I'm sure of it!'

Heather rose to her feet, her eyes cool and sceptical. 'You needn't go on, Mother. I happen to know Paul better than any of you. Unless you can tell me what reason he gave Huntly you haven't told me a thing that matters.'

Janet shook her head and twisted away with an expression of acute distaste. 'Oh, he said something or other about writing a book. Of all the absurd excuses! Then he actually had the impertinence to tell Huntly we'd be at war before he could even get out to British Columbia. As if a French-Canadian would join the army anyway! And can you imagine the impertinence – a boy like that trying to tell Huntly McQueen about a thing like the war! Huntly's been confident all along there'll be no war. He did very well to wash his hands of the young man . . . and after all the trouble he had years ago with his father, too!' She sat up in bed and put her hands to her hair. 'Heather dear – I think perhaps I'll get up for a little while. Would you mind handing me my slippers?'

Heather appeared not to have heard her mother's last words. She stood very quietly in the middle of the room. 'So his work is going well at last! How wonderful!'

Janet stared at her.

Heather began to laugh quietly. 'I'm so glad you've told me all this, Mummy. It makes everything clearer than you know. I'm going home on tonight's train.'

'You're what?'

'If he refused Huntly, his work must be better than he

402

dreamed it could be. He has so little time left. Maybe I can help by looking after him, or copying his stuff, or –'

'Pull yourself together!' Janet said.

Heather looked at her calmly. Janet stared back.

'I forbid you to go.'

Heather held her mother's eyes for a long minute. Then, breathing deeply, she said in a low voice, 'I'm Paul's wife, Mummy.'

Through the window the slow surge of incoming waves made the only sound.

'I didn't want to tell you like this, but you've made me. Paul and I were married before I left Halifax – two days after Grampa's funeral.'

A low cry, half moan, issued from Janet's lips. Her eyes shut tight, and choking sobs began to pulse out of her throat. Tears flowed down her cheeks, staining the white powder. Her right hand clutched spasmodically at her left breast as if trying to reach through to her heart; then, like an independent claw, it jerked to her forehead, flattened out, passed back and forth through her hair. She made one single violent movement from side to side, then straightened out rigidly and lay utterly still. Her face was as white as flour, with long canals worn by tears through the powder that covered it.

Heather watched in horror. She bent over Janet, murmuring soothing phrases as she tried to push the hair back from the flushed forehead. She laid her head against her mother's lips trying to catch her breath, but detected nothing. She picked up one of her mother's wrists, tried to find the pulse but in her fright missed it entirely. When she dropped the arm it fell like a weighted pendulum, swung over the edge of the bed and hung dangling.

Afterwards, Heather had no recollection of reaching for the telephone and calling the doctor. An hour later she was sitting alone in her own room, still numb with fright. She had seen her mother upset before, but never like this. Dozens of times she had seen her mother break down and cry hysterically, but the fits had never lasted long. Janet's pride and will-power had always returned quickly.

There was a knock on the door and the doctor entered.

He was a white-haired old man with rather shaky hands, little eyes bright behind thick glasses and a furry voice. Heather knew little of doctors, for the Methuens had all been healthy. She did not realize that her mother was the first patient this guest of the hotel had seen in five months.

He shook his head. 'I'm afraid your mother's a very sick woman, Miss Methuen.'

'What's the trouble? What is it?' Heather's eyes fixed themselves on the old face.

'Well . . .' The doctor cleared his throat. 'Well . . . there's a certain condition of the heart. Nothing to worry about, perhaps . . . one of those things we all have to reckon with as we get older. One of those things. And at her age . . .' He patted her hand and she drew away. 'Your mother must have absolute rest and quiet for a week or two. Then we can have tests made. But she mustn't be disturbed in any way whatever.'

'It – it isn't a stroke, is it?'

'Well,' the doctor said, 'there are strokes and strokes. On the whole, I wouldn't say so. Not yet. But at the moment rest is the main thing. I've given her a sedative now, and I'll be calling regularly to watch her.'

'I see.' Heather hesitated. She looked at the man sharply but got nothing from his eyes. 'I'd planned to return to Montreal tonight. It's rather important that I be there tomorrow.'

The doctor shook his head as he conveyed a strong suggestion of moral disapproval. 'By no means! By no means whatever! I must absolutely forbid it.'

'Is it really that serious?' Heather scanned the grey face desperately. 'Are you sure there's anything I can do here?'

'She asked constantly about you, Miss Methuen. You must realize – a shock at a time like this might be extremely serious. Your mother's health to a large extent rests in your hands.'

'I see,' Heather said. Her voice was flat and lifeless. 'I'll do whatever you think best.'

The doctor nodded and went downstairs to join a bridge game. After awhile, Heather walked out onto the beach alone.

51

Just after midnight, in the early morning of September first, Paul was sitting at his desk when his neighbour's radio announced through the wall that German troops had crossed the Polish frontier. Beside his desk was a pile of manuscript two hundred pages high, almost half his book. At his feet the wastebasket was full. He sat very still for several minutes listening. The radio had fallen quiet, there were no noises in the lodging house, he could hear no street sounds through his open window. He picked up the manuscript, tapped its edges even, and put it carefully away in his drawer. Then he put the typewriter in its case, locked it and dropped the key in his pocket. Everything was silent.

52

Thirty-two hours later Paul was with Heather on the beach of Kennebunkport, Maine. They sat side by side on the sand while the sun glittered off the sea. They watched long waves roll slowly in and break, sluice back and roll up again, each one making a hissing sweep across the hard sand.

'Now tell me about your book, Paul.'

He shook his head, still staring seaward. 'There's nothing to tell about it. It's half finished. I may be able to complete it in spite of everything.' He shrugged his shoulders. 'Maybe not. I don't know.'

The waves continued to ride up the beach in endless monotone.

'Mummy's determined to hear Chamberlain when he speaks this morning,' she said at last. 'They're all sitting around the radio now, listening to anything that comes over. They say even the King is going to speak.'

Paul rose slowly, still staring out over the water; then he dropped his hand and helped her to her feet. 'Exactly what is the matter with your mother?'

She let her eyes rest on him as he continued to stare out to sea. His face looked tired and set, older than it had a few months ago. His eyes were narrowed against the glare, his hands hung at his sides.

'The doctor won't say anything definite.' Her voice was lifeless. Numbness in her nerve-ends, the skin of her face taut and dry, before her the sea, behind her the continent drugged with sun, in Europe the first bombers taking off. . . . 'Oh Paul – I feel so helpless. Smaller than I know I am. And ashamed.'

'Never mind,' he said. He continued to stare out over the water. Then his voice, calm, factual, 'Are you sorry you married me?'

She slipped her hand through his arm, her cheek brushed his sleeve, pressed against its harsh tweed. 'Don't!' she whispered. Then, more calmly, 'When I saw her lying there I couldn't leave her, Paul. I'd told myself my life was my own. That I was free. I'd sworn to myself I'd never let her hurt you. Then – ' She stopped; added simply, 'I was afraid she was dying.'

For a moment he did not answer. 'Has she done this often before?' he said at last.

'She's never been strong. Poor Mummy – she's had such a wretched life. Paul – why don't you curse me for being such a helpless little fool?'

'Has she honestly had a wretched life?'

Heather took his hand again. It closed strongly over her fingers. Her voice said, 'She always tried to be something she never was.'

'Like many others.' Suddenly he faced her. 'I want to speak to the doctor. Do you mind?'

'Of course not. He's usually playing bridge at this hour of the morning. Today I suppose he's listening to the radio with everyone else.'

He began walking. 'Come on,' he said. 'Let's find him.'

The moment they entered the lounge they heard the radio. A commentator was talking about the evacuation of children from London. Heather still held Paul's hand. 'He's that old man over there. I'll get him.'

Paul stood aloof by the door as she crossed the lounge to speak to the doctor. The gayness of her light gingham dress only heightened the grimness of the mood in the lounge. The

406

men and women sat listening with church faces to the radio, and when they spoke they used whispers. The few Americans present seemed ill at ease. Perhaps they felt what was happening in London as sharply as the Canadians did, they certainly hated Hitler as much, but it was not their war yet. Heather returned with the doctor. He came slowly forward with head bowed, bobbing slightly as he walked. His left hand clasped the lapel of his jacket and Paul saw a brown age-stain behind the knuckles, a tiny tuft of hair protruding from it. Heather introduced them.

'Would you mind if we talked on the veranda?' Paul said.

The doctor looked at him suspiciously, dropped his eyes. 'If you wish.'

They walked to the far end of the veranda where they could not hear the radio. The salt air blew up to them with noise from the sea. Heather stood slightly apart and looked at the two men: Paul intense, his face pale and tired but his eyes very bright, balanced easily on the balls of his feet like an athlete on guard. In front of him the doctor stood with a grey face, clipped white moustache and silver hair; as neat as a bird. Yet his eyes looked somehow lost and baffled. Heather thought: how many wars has he seen begin? What was the colour of his hair when the first airplane flew?

Paul was speaking. 'I want you to tell me frankly just what is the matter with Mrs. Methuen.'

The doctor's Adam's apple rose and fell. 'She's a pretty sick woman. She's been in bed a fortnight now. I've been seeing her every day.' An attempt at a smile. 'Miss Methuen's been very good to her.'

Paul kept his eyes on the old face. 'I understand she wants to get up to listen to the radio. Are you permitting her to come downstairs?'

It seemed to Heather that the doctor had become too old even to be tired. She sensed the suggestion of hostility; but vague, edgeless, like an object stirring behind fog. Old eyes on Paul's strained face, old face vaguely on guard against it knew not what.

'Miss Methuen – ' The doctor cleared his throat. 'I intended to tell your mother she could come down whenever she wished. I forgot. Will you go and tell her?'

Heather looked from one to the other, then turned and disappeared.

The doctor shifted away from Paul's steady gaze and began walking slowly back along the veranda, his eyes apparently counting the cracks in the boards. 'I'll tell you how it is, Mr. Tallard. These women like Mrs. Methuen – they excite very easily. There's nothing anyone can do about it when they start. Now take yesterday – when she heard the war'd started, she felt a lot better.'

The doctor reached the door and stepped inside.

'Are you telling me there's nothing the matter with her?' Paul said behind him.

The doctor turned slowly, his face weary and aloof, his remote eyes apparently looking over Paul's shoulder to the glittering sea, a bird-like dignity enfolding him. 'That's right,' he said, 'not a thing.' Without looking back he walked slowly into the lounge.

The radio was still describing the evacuation of the children, already disinfecting the reality of the war by concentrating on ordinary action and human interest in trivial details. Paul walked across to the desk and asked the number of Mrs. Methuen's room. Then he went upstairs to find it. When he knocked on her door it was Heather who opened it. He saw them there: mother and daughter. Janet's eyes black in a pale face, fierce, restless, old.

'You know Paul, Mummy?'

Janet's nod was barely perceptible. 'I'm on my way downstairs,' she said.

Heather faded back toward the window. She sat there frozen, her life in her eyes, watching her mother and Paul. She seemed to behold every action of their hands and flicker of their eye-lashes in slow motion. Janet was stiff and straight, her lips tightly pressed. She was wearing her black dress and stockings and her black beads. A wide-brimmed black hat was on her head. Her eyes were noting the details of Paul's clothes as though she were pricing them. And Heather sat frozen on the window-ledge, bitterly ashamed not only for her mother but also for herself. At that instant she knew that nothing was the matter with her mother and that nothing ever had been. She knew intuitively that if there had not been a secret part of herself which had welcomed the force of her mother's will she would have left her weeks ago, even when Janet was prone and apparently unconscious on her bed. She closed her eyes, remembered as if it were yesterday the touch of her mother's hand on her forehead when she had been a child. In her flesh her mother held her. Flesh of her flesh.

She felt ashamed of the unworthiness of this scene. The war had started, nations and perhaps civilizations had slid forward for suicide. She and Paul and her mother were part of it. Her mother's voice said, 'You'll excuse me, I trust. I must hear what Mr. Chamberlain has to say to us.'

Janet walked stiffly to the door, moving past Paul as if he were someone who had come to serve her. Heather opened her eyes, saw her mother's straight back, looked away. Then she heard Paul's voice. It was his usual voice, quiet the way it usually was. But because it was spoken in the presence of her mother it sounded different; shockingly unnatural, but wonderful. 'I can tell you what Chamberlain will say, Mrs. Methuen. There's no need to go downstairs to hear him. He's going to say he's sorry, and then he's going to declare war.'

Heather saw her mother's wide hat nod and wheel as she stared at Paul, her fingers tight on her black purse. The old posture, the old expression. Who said that truth will prevail, that mind conquer's all things? Force of the turtle, strength of the ostrich, sureness in the right!

'If you'll excuse me . . .' Janet's voice crisp and British. 'I wasn't aware that my wishes were anyone's business but my own.' She glanced around at Heather. 'Come along. We've no time to waste.'

'No,' he said quietly. 'Heather will stay here for the moment.' A pause. 'I think you will, too, Mrs. Methuen.'

Janet lifted her hand to her cheek as if Paul had slapped it. Her mouth opened and closed, and Heather watched her in ashamed fascination. She had seen Yardley crumble before her mother's nervousness, General Methuen break because of his pity for her, McQueen nod and smile at almost anything she said. Now she waited for her mother to strike, somehow out of her instinct to find where Paul was vulnerable.

But it was Paul who spoke. 'If you feel as you do because we were married without your knowledge, I understand.' He paused as he watched her. 'But I don't think that's why you feel as you do.'

Janet continued to stare at him, her fingers clasping and unclasping on her purse. Paul took a step backward, held out his hand to Heather and drew her beside him.

'Heather and I have been waiting all our lives. Now there's hardly any time left for us. Tomorrow I'm going to enlist.' Janet opened her mouth but his eyes held her silent. 'I don't want to do it. Everything that's in me cries out against the waste of the only talent I've ever had. But I've got to go. And when I'm gone, I'd like to know that you and Heather are together.'

Janet's tongue moistened her lips and once again she opened her mouth to speak, but no words came. Paul and Heather moved past her to the door. 'We're going down to the lounge now,' Paul said. 'Think over what I've said. Then I hope you'll join us.'

They went out the door, Heather not daring to look at her mother again. They reached the lounge and found empty chairs in a corner away from the radio. She felt Paul's hand close over her own. The crowd at the radio was bending forward, listening intently. Instead of Chamberlain, the slow, hesitant, sad voice of the King began to speak.

Before he had finished, Janet appeared and they saw her, coming carefully down to the foot of the stairs. She walked calmly toward their corner and joined them without a word. Paul rose and she took the place he had left. The King's voice went on, they listened in silence, and after awhile it ended. The lounge was so still they heard the laugh of a child a hundred yards away on the beach.

53

In that autumn of 1939 the countryside in Canada had never seemed more tranquil. There was golden weather. In

Nova Scotia and New Brunswick the moose came out of the forests on October nights and stood in silhouette against the moonpaths that crossed solitary lakes. In Ontario people looked across the water from their old river-towns, and seeing the lights of moving cars in the United States, remembered again that they lived on a frontier that was more a link than a division. On the prairies the combines rolled up the wheat, increasing the surplus in the granaries until it was hard to believe there were enough human mouths in the world to eat it all. In British Columbia the logs came down the rivers; people separated by mountains, plains and an ocean remembered English hamlets, pictured them under bombs, themselves islanded between snow-peaks and the Pacific. The Saint Lawrence, flowing past the old parishes, enfolding the Ile d'Orléans and broadening out in the sweep to Tadoussac, passed in sight of forests that flamed with the autumn of 1939: scarlet of rock maples, gold of beeches, heavy green of spruce and fir. Only in the far north on the tundra was the usual process of life abruptly fractured. Prospectors hearing on their portable radios that the world they had left was at war, could stand the solitude no longer; they broke camp, walked or paddled hundreds of miles southward, were flown out by bush-pilots, appeared before recruiting stations in Edmonton, Battleford, Brandon, in the nearest organized towns they could find, and faded into the army.

But quietly, without bands or parades, while advertisers warmed up the slogans of 1914, the country moved into history as into matter-of-fact. Engineers went out along the rivers and railroad tracks: shipyards for the Maritimes, biggest aluminum plant in the world for the Saguenay, factories for all the power they could breed out of the rivers, from Ontario tanks, trucks, Bren guns, shells and bullets, from the West food for the Empire, from Edmonton aircraft flying surveyors to the Alaska boundary, on the coast naval bases and more factories, from all the provinces men and airfields for the United Nations.

Then, even as the two race-legends woke again remembering ancient enmities, there woke with them also the felt knowledge that together they had fought and survived one

411

great war they had never made and that now they had entered another; that for nearly a hundred years the nation had been spread out on the top half of the continent over the powerhouse of the United States and still was there; that even if the legends were like oil and alcohol in the same bottle, the bottle had not been broken yet. And almost grudgingly, out of the instinct to do what was necessary, the country took the first irrevocable steps toward becoming herself, knowing against her will that she was not unique but like all the others, alone with history, with science, with the future.